PRAISE

MW00615259

"The compelling, poignant story of a family, with all its pain, joy, love, secrets and shared revelations. The colorful and engaging cast will draw you in, as they face their demons, deepen their connection to one another, and find the strength to move on. Peggy Lampman's characters will linger in your mind, and heart, long after the last page. Lively and rich, a gem of a novel."
—Alison Ragsdale, best-selling author of *The Art of Remembering*

"The waters are troubled in this emotional and suspenseful story that dives deep into the territory of family relationships and the nature of forgiveness. Even as a building hurricane off the coast of the Florida Keys tightens its coil in preparation to strike, a densely woven web of secrets kept out of love has begun to unravel between mothers and children, siblings and lovers. And either threat holds the power to shatter lives. The setting by itself is a feast for the senses, as evocative of place as it is of human nature. This novel is a true page turner!"
—Barbara Taylor Sissel, bestselling author of *Tell No One*

"*The Ruby of the Sea* is a powerful story about the meaning of home as a place of safety set against the fears that haunt every family. When three sisters reunite in the historic lighthouse where their parents live, they must confront secrets that include a painful truth they have avoided: the youngest sister suffers from bipolar disorder. Filled with evocative descriptions of the Key West landscape and mouth-watering Cuban food, this is a book to savor."

--Barbara Claypole White, bestselling author of *The Perfect Son* and *The Promise Between Us*

"In this beautifully woven tale of three sisters, Lampman explores the devastating impact of mental illness on family and creativity without ever losing sight of the glory of being alive and the transformative power of love. An important book, definitely one for the book clubs."

--Kerry Ann King, bestselling author of *Whisper Me This* and *Everything You Are*

"*The Ruby of the Sea* is a poignant and powerful story that unfolds quickly through Peggy Lampman's rich, lyrical writing. Strong, complex and colorful characters carry the heart wrenching drama, filled with secrets, that is the history of the troubled Chandler family. In the stunning setting of Key West, complicated relationships, the challenges of mental illness and the healing power of forgiveness are explored in a journey readers will long remember."

--Patricia Sands, bestselling author of *Drawing Lessons*

THE RUBY OF THE SEA

PEGGY LAMPMAN

ALLIANCE PRESS

For Rebecca, whose spiritual journey challenges my good reason in the place where the wine always flows.
Stay fierce, friend. I love you.

"If we have no peace, it is because we have forgotten that we belong to each other." —

— *SAINT TERESA OF CALCUTTASAINT TERESA OF CALCUTTA*

1. LINNEA

Through the small oval window, I glimpse the turquoise of the Atlantic. Heart racing, my spine stiffens. The plane pitches right, and I take a deep breath, forcing my mind to still. The red-stenciled sign affixed to the terminal looms beneath the tip of the wing:

WELCOME TO THE CONCH CAPITAL OF AMERICA.
CHECK YOUR BRAIN AT THE GATE.

OK. So, it doesn't include that last bit. But it should. Trust me, I know. Unlike my fellow passengers, I'm no tourist to Key West. But I wish I were. I, too, would like to shed my inhibitions in this wonderland of skimpily-clad, sunburned bodies while sipping a margarita and sauntering through town.

Eyeing the barf bag, reassuring myself it is within easy reach, the swoosh of the engine's roar vacuums up the last remnants of my spirit. I remember when flying was simply unpleasant. Now––between the stony-faced guards pawing through my personals, dehumanizing pat-downs, canceled flights and carry-on misery––it's unbearable. The wheels touch down, hitting the tarmac with a jolt, and my elbow and knee bump the woman at my side. Shifting away, her sharp, thin face twitches as the plane taxies down the runway.

"Oops. Pardon me," I murmur, pulling my arm into my side and crossing my legs, no mean feat for the long-limbed in the ever-diminishing economy section. Beneath fiercely tweezed brows, silvery eyes glare at me as if I'm covered in pox. What's up with this woman? After settling into our seats in Miami, she accepted my offer of gum, but her body language informed she wanted no additional communication. Eyes closed, the rapid drumfire of Deafheaven blasted from earbuds as her chipped black fingernails beat out a corresponding rhythm on the pull-down tray table.

Closing the *Delta Sky* magazine, I glance, once again, at her ensemble. She wears velveteen short shorts in a muddy shade of aubergine. A tatty Chromatics tank top peeks out beneath a denim jacket reeking of tobacco muddled with an antiseptic floral scent. She must fancy herself a rebel, a *stick it to the man* type of a woman. But who cares? She took the piece of gum. At least she could have done so with a smile and nod. A sequin on her jacket catches the overhead light, piercing the side of my vision.

My appearance must bother her. Perhaps I seem tragically bourgeois. My scrubbed face is several shades lighter than it was growing up under the rays of Florida sun. My near-black hair, silky from last night's wash, is pulled back into a tight ponytail. I straighten my cycling jersey over my tangerine speckled workout capris. What's considered clothing in Boise is referred to as gear down here.

I check the time on my Fitbit, which serves as a watch as well as fitness tracker: 3:16 PM. With the time change, it's 5:16 in Florida. I suppress a yawn, adjusting the time. I've been up since four AM and have been traveling over ten hours. At least it's happy hour. After this flight from hell, I could use a glass of wine. Some real food, too.

My aisle-mate unfastens her seatbelt as we taxi down the runway, even though we're not allowed. That confirms it—an insurgent. She appears to be around my age, somewhere in her early thirties, but it's hard to tell under the layers of mottled self-tanner and shimmery eye shadow.

She retrieves a folder stashed under the seat; papers and several bills slide out, landing on top of my feet. Bending, I pick up a couple of twenties, several documents and—pasting on a smile—hand them to her. She takes them without comment, not even meeting my eyes. Glancing at the top sheet, I note her originating flight was out of Fort Wayne, Indiana.

I'll bet she's here for the 2017 Festa-Palooza, the annual event staged in mid-May, a welcome injection into the economy as tourist season abates. It brings in more than three times the population of the island itself and is now in full swing. She doesn't want to taint her send-off conversing with me, a woman who appears as dull as dishwater.

But what I find as mind-numbing as a metal concert are the crowds swelling through my hometown. The event now rivals New Orleans's Mardi Gras for attracting tourists. The growing popularity is due, in part, to the fact outsiders can stoke eroticism in ways that are taboo on their own home turf. This annoys me. Key West is the destination to let loose, to be yourself. Festivals pepper the landscape throughout the year, but events like this are out of hand. Indulge your fetishes in your own backyard—don't pollute our quaint little town.

Organizers and the marketing team are quick to point out nudity is not allowed, but—determined to keep the cash spigot flowing—their definition of acceptable dress is as thin as a pole dancer's G-string. In fact, women may go topless as long as their breasts are painted, and they remain within the confines of a fenced-off area referred to as The Palooza Zone.

Growing up, my parents issued dire warnings to their three daughters, threatening grave consequences if we ventured into this land of titillating kink. Of course, their threats made the area all the more enticing. I've seen enough public body art and drunken nudity to choke Lady Godiva's horse. Other kids had the Internet to educate; I had Kitty Kat Kaul's triple D implants to inform. I'd prefer visiting my family when south Florida was hovering under the threat of a hurricane.

The parade is Saturday night, three days from now, which culminates the seven-day bacchanalia. Was I nuts to let Delphina talk me into helping her with a float? Her voice sounded strained, lacking its usual exuberance when she asked. That's understandable; she's a new mother. So, to hell with the festival and, I'll be the first to admit, my phobia of the sea. She's my identical twin. And however ironic her passions entwine with the ocean—my tormentor, stalker, my greatest of fears—Delphina's the only person I could never refuse.

Since infancy, I grew up watching every gradient of my face, elbow, feet, even the back of my earlobe, shining back at me. My breath catches at the thought of her.

We were preemies, born eight weeks early, and in the womb, Delphina saved our lives. During the first trimester of Mama's pregnancy, she was informed fluid was leaking from her placenta, and she would miscarry.

As if an embryo could sense the amount of love it took to carry us, Delphina felt the chromosomal nudge. She shifted around, plugging the tear in the amniotic sac we shared. I was fetal at the time, so can't be too sure of any of this, but the ultrasounds were certain. Her movement allowed Mama's pregnancy to continue to thirty-two weeks. Since I'm narrating my side of the story, it's obvious we survived. I owe my very existence to her.

My heart gives a sharp, painful lurch. My eyes well up and I pinch my cheeks so hard they burn—a tic I've had since childhood to stem the flow of tears. I miss her so much. I miss them all. Why now has my family come to mean so much?

It is safe to unfasten your seatbelt and retrieve your belongings.
Please use caution when opening the overhead bin.

I fumble with the silver hinge latched snug across my abdomen. It's kept flat as a washboard from a running addiction, which counterbalances my addiction to baking—pies are my specialty. Dipping my shoulders, I position myself into a gap in the center aisle, now packed with people. At five feet, ten inches, I'm wary of banging my head in tight enclosures.

In a flurry of knocking elbows and excuse me's, I reach into the overhead compartment and remove my pink and green floral tote. Monogrammed for Linnea Leigh Chandler, this is further evidence to my aisle mate I am totally uncool. A gift from my grandmother before I left home for college—almost fifteen years ago—it's not something I would have chosen either, but its plushness conforms well to overheads. One thing I do like about Key West, grunge, prep, glitter, gear—anything goes.

Her ripped and weathered backpack, intentionally worn I'm sure, remains in the compartment where I saw her put it earlier. Why assist a woman I find so rude? I sigh, pulling it from the cavity. Heavy as a wrecking ball, if swung in the right direction, this could do some serious damage. Mustering up another tired smile, I place it on the seat next to her, just vacated by me. The side of her lower lip pierced with a metal hoop tics up as if to say thanks. But then she frowns and rubs sanitizer over her hands with a vengeance, as if worried she will catch my affliction.

Wondering what it is about myself that offends, my smile fades, and I turn towards the front of the plane. Why would I let a stranger's bad manners hurt my feelings? With my current lack of funds and direction, I've better things to agonize.

The passengers shuffle forward, disembarking from the aircraft. I wish I were more like Delphina, who has moved forward in life never worried about what others may think of her or second-guessing her choices. And her decisions have served her well. I've even garnered a bit of fall-out from her happiness; I'm elated at becoming an aunt. My DNA has pushed its way into the universe despite myself.

I can also replenish my bank account. It's easier to make a quick buck in Key West's service industry than anywhere else I've traveled. It shouldn't take more than a couple of months to secure enough funds for a rental deposit in Idaho. I decided not to renew the lease on my apartment in Boise's North End. That place was all about families, Volvos and leashed labs awaiting a bit of granola muffin tossed to them by their master. When I return, I'll look for a loft downtown. More singles live in town, and I won't have to take the bus to work.

I thank the pilot, not taking it for granted the plane didn't nose dive into the sea and climb down the aluminum stairwell exiting the plane. Nike-clad feet on terra firma, I pause and lift my face to the brilliant blue sky. My torso dampens beneath the cloak of humidity; reacquainting myself with the thick, dense air will be another adjustment. A welcome gust of wind whips my ponytail around my neck.

Walking into the luggage claim area, small by most airport standards, a central bar peddles cocktails to get you in the *mañana* frame of mind. I retrieve my luggage from the carousel; all of my worldly possessions stuffed into two large suitcases. Maybe the fact nothing was lost is an omen this trip down won't be as unpleasant as the last.

The evening, sixteen months ago, still leaves a sour taste in my mouth. When we were heavy into the rum, my father called me out: Why wasn't I returning home for good? What does Boise have over Key West? I had no "real" career to keep me away from my people.

Mama called me a deserter, while Delphina and my little sister remained quiet. My sisters, not validating the fears driving me away, hurt me deeply. I interpreted the fact they mounted no defense on my behalf to mean they agreed I'd committed treason. Judged and sentenced without a hearing, I walked out of the Chandler family without even a trial.

I pull my Smartphone from my pack and call my father.

"I'll be there in a few," he says. "I hate making you wait, but I'm behind schedule. The festival traffic's hellacious and your mom got into a tangle."

"Oh, dear. The cats?"

"No, not this time..." His voice trails off. "Holy crap—a zombie wearing Nordic horns just passed. Almost crashed into my front fender." His volume amplifies, blasting in my ear. "There should be a law against driving in a costume. People assume the identity. I'll share details when I see you."

Poor dad. Every circus needs a ringmaster, and that distinction goes to him. I wheel my luggage outside next to the arrival entrance. Taking a seat on one of my suitcases, I watch the knots of families and couples catching cabs or herding themselves into hotel shuttles.

When outsiders ask me what it was like growing up in a town famous for its colorful eccentricities, I respond in hyperbole: *Key West is like living in a psych ward without walls.* This is one of several slogans, which are carved into coconuts or printed onto T-shirts lining the storefronts on Duval Street, the cash cow of the city. *We're here because we're not all here,* is another favorite.

I repeat the buzzwords because it's what people expect me to say, and I enjoy making people laugh. But aside from my eccentric mother and the old lighthouse where my sisters and I were raised, when you peel away the kitsch, my youth was spent like any other kid who grew up in a small town. Everyone knows everyone and looks out for fellow neighbors. We have no choice. Key West's population of twenty-five thousand crams itself into a four-mile radius. The southern-most city in America, its glory is it's the only town in this country where you are closer to Cuba than a Walmart.

Uneasy in this oceanic environment, my visits down here are rare. So, with my family tucked away in a sheltered place inside my heart, I've spent the past decade searching for a place where I feel safe. Bartending and catering gigs have been convenient for stockpiling cash to pay for my trips; ten months of work finances two months of travel. From Asheville to Albuquerque, Bennington to Boise, I've narrowed my options.

Planting stakes in the United States, for me, is a no-brainer —but only on the condition, my residence is landlocked. I grew up surrounded by the sea, so I've had a lifetime to contemplate her breadth.

Scientists have explored less than five percent of the world's oceans—we've better maps of Mars. That remaining ninety-five percent, however, has been well charted out in my nightmares, and I'll tell you this: it's an abyss, a freakin' hellhole. A twilight zone of aliens stalk the ocean floor with monsters so ugly they'd make a catfish look like Anne Hathaway's more beautiful sister. The puddle-jumper flight crossing the chain of islands to Key West is all I can handle. Even with an aisle seat, the inadvertent glimpses of the glistening sea beneath the plane make my stomach churn.

The one time I flew to Rome, knowing it would take five hours to cross the Atlantic—some 30,000 feet deep—I popped an Ambien. When that didn't work, I took the other, which was reserved for the trip home. Big mistake. At every altitude dip on the return flight, I envisioned the plane spiraling down into the sea, like a leftover sausage link circling the drain, soon sucked up by the disposal.

Understandably, I got trashed on Sangiovese. The stewardess stopped by my seat several times, eying me as if I might rampage. I haven't left the United States since. Delphina makes her living snorkeling ocean reefs with tourists, and it tortures me imagining her splashing about the waves, impervious as to what lies beneath.

Living in Idaho, I'd have to drive through British Columbia or Oregon to get to the Pacific Ocean. Rivers and lakes are comparably mother's milk. So, for this girl, nirvana starts with a BOY and ends with a Z: BOISE. Although I've yet to find that boy. Last month I broke up with a divorcé I'd dated since July. I knew he was emotionally unavailable—no worries there. Love is unreliable, and vulnerability rips the guts out of you. But it took me nine months to realize he wanted help with his two-year-old son more than he wanted a girlfriend.

Cradled into the Rocky Mountain foothills, I'm beginning to feel safe; like I'm under the right sky. Yet, a part of me flounders, uprooted, as if the Idaho soil's not solid beneath my feet.

My thoughts are interrupted as a woman waving her hand and shouting *"Stop!"* runs towards me, her suitcase wheeling behind her. Trying to catch the attention of a Sheraton Suites shuttle driver, she collides into me. I brace my feet to prevent myself from falling. She stops. Aghast. "Oh, pardon me." Her hand flies to her mouth, her eyes crinkling in concern. "I'm so sorry."

I smile. "No worries." Standing, I step off the curb and motion the shuttle to stop, pointing at the woman.

Strangers treating strangers with respect. It's called manners, the rules of civilized behavior; a concept I wish more tourists in this town would embrace. Over her shoulder, she thanks me profusely, and then clambers aboard the shuttle. I straighten my sunglasses, knocked from the bridge of my nose. Resuming my perch on the suitcase, I text Delphina I've arrived.

Many Key West residents, my family included, are navel-gazers. They're suspicious of folks who don't find the climate, with its tropical flora and fauna, to be the end-all and the be-all. Indeed, status is measured by how long people have lived in the town. It's a big world, folks. Exciting lives are being lived in places embracing the four seasons, even the ones with snow. I'm the only member of my family who doesn't love the Southernmost City with fury, abandon and without apology—a sentiment I reserve for my own flesh and blood.

That's not to say my family is without our issues. I mean, really. You tell me about a family without a certain amount of dysfunction, and I'll tell you that family is lying.

Take my little sister, Ivy. She lives at home and writes a blog about her life as a Key West artist. Some might describe her writing as exaggerated and intense. But, as in her paintings, her idiosyncratic view of life was silent during adolescence. Perhaps she'd been holding her breath so long, she's now exhaling in a roar. For instance, one day she wrote:

> "The brilliant bougainvillea beguiled and intoxicated, holding captive my paintbrush. Everything is gorgeous—breathtaking! You simply must come to visit."

The next: "Beware the mullet-sporting perfume peddler on North Duval. With his lavender lies, he squirted my neck with a mist stinking of decayed sassafras. I'm not writing to soften the danger zones. On the contrary. There's no room for gentle here. In Key West, explore at your own risk."

Her blogs are amusing, but between the lines, I sense something amiss. This visit, I'll spend more time with her; get a better handle on what makes her tick. And when I return to Idaho, I'll insist we regularly FaceTime. Ivy is a contradiction befuddling me more with every visit down.

As teens, Delphina and I found her preference for solitude and addiction to superhero comics odd. We tried tuning her out, but Ivy's not easy to ignore. She moved through youth with her head tipped down, her long copper curls falling over her face. She resembles our mother, especially in the eyes, which are green, streaked with gold and black. Almond-shaped, they catch the light like a cat's. A self-conscious beauty, she considered her eyes a curse, eliciting attention she didn't want.

Her petite body ripened her freshman year into soft curves. Carrying beauty, for Ivy, was bad enough. For such a sensitive young woman, sexy was an unbearable load. Refusing to take the bait prettiness requests, she insisted upon shopping in the boy's department and dressed in shapeless clothes as if afraid of her sexuality. To this day she continues to wear overalls, cut-offs and oversized shirts, splattered with paint.

Growing up in a crazy, gregarious, larger-than-life town, she was that rarest of birds: a loner. But we assumed that so engrossed in her cartoons, drawings, and writing, she was happy keeping to herself. The one thing which always seemed easy was Ivy—but my little sister turned out to be the most difficult of us all.

My former aisle mate startles me from my thoughts. Arms clutched around the torso of a beefy dude on a motorcycle, her bulbous pack is strapped to her back as she zooms away. Her jacket now removed, sleeves of tattoos are laid bare. Legs pressed into his as if intimate with his thighs, she waves at me, head held high, and the unexpected gesture catches me off-guard. I straighten and, by reflex, wave back, fitting on a smile. Why would she be so unfriendly on the plane and then act as if we're old friends now?

She whizzes off into the world—elated, exposed—as if not afraid to tackle life head-on. What would it feel like to be so confident, to feel so free?

I couldn't get any further away from my own skin if I tried.

2. DELPHINA

"Please, Sonny. Can you look again?" My grip tightens around the phone, pleading with my husband. "My name is CO'ed beneath the mailing address." I drop my voice to a lower level, emphasizing each word. "The return label should read Ribbons and Lace. The box would have come from New Jersey."

"I heard you the first time." His words are rushed, ringing with impatience. "I'm telling you the Parade Coordinator told me she'd received it yesterday. She put it with the rest of the packages, but now it's missing. I've searched every nook and cranny and have asked everyone here if they've seen it."

I sniff, pinching my nostrils. "Someone must have stolen it."

"Why would anyone steal a box filled with bows? Right now, I'm looking at a crate full of tools. An electric saw's sitting on top of it. There's way more valuable stuff to steal around here than bows."

"They're not bows. They're ribbons of silk." My voice breaks. "All this time you've been asking about bows?"

"Delphina, Delphy baby. Take it down a notch. I meant to say ribbon. But if someone were going to steal something, trust me, it would be this saw. And let's get real. Committee organizers are the last people who'd take stuff that didn't belong to them. More than likely, someone picked it up by mistake and will return it."

The missing bolts aren't run-of-the-mill polyester ribbon, the sort used for wrapping presents. I'd ordered extra-wide, one hundred percent silk in various shades of teal, which would reflect the different hues of the ocean. I'd planned to weave it around the fish and reefs on our float. Dusted with glitter, they would shine as if the sun were beating down on the water. My only extravagance, this would be the tipping point, helping us win *Most Creative* in the competition. To get the parade discount, I had to have it mailed to Committee Headquarters. Yesterday, I received a text that it had arrived.

I suck in my breath. "It's OK. Thanks for your reconnaissance, baby."

"Look," he says, his voice softening. "Call the company and have them overnight another case."

"I called them already. I already spent a fortune on the lost ribbon. Plus, it would cost an extra fifty bucks to expedite the shipping. Forget it. Mary's Crafts has an overstock of baby blue. It looks cheap but will have to do."

Money's been tight since we had to hire someone to cover for me on our tourist boat during my maternity leave. The craft shop has been happy to donate supplies in exchange for our putting their business logo on the float, but all they stock are the basics. The ocean has so much more going on than one shade of blue; a blue the color of liquid detergent. I choke back a sob. These days my hormones are crazy out-of-whack. Motherhood is supposed to be about joy and love. Why am I so miserable? I cry as much as my baby.

"Honey. You're upset. I wish I had time to cheer you up, but I've got to get back to the dock. The boat's packed to capacity. Not a cloud in the sky, so the sunset will be on fire. 'Course Melinda doesn't have your way with the customers."

"Tell her to smile more—crack a joke or two. Compliment their swimsuits. Conversation shouldn't only revolve around the procedure for sanitizing snorkeling masks."

"It wouldn't do any good." His drawn-out sigh is shaky, winded and exasperated—a sound he's never made until recently. "Melinda's competent with the boat, but she's not a people person. You'll be back to work soon, thank God. I'll be home around 9:30."

"See 'ya then. Linnea texted; her flight's arrived."

"It will be good to have her back."

"I love you, babe," I whisper into the phone, knowing he's relieved I'll have another ear into which to vent my frustrations.

"Love you back."

I'm taking time off from our business to take care of our firstborn. I'd imagined an artsy project would be a fun distraction. Participating in the Festa-Palooza Parade—expected to number over sixty-thousand this year—would also promote our snorkeling business. I can only imagine the publicity we'd receive if we win—even placing in the top three would be a godsend.

Last fall, during my third trimester with Ella, our float committee developed plans and began working on a Tropical Paradise theme in our garage. Sonny cleared away the bicycles and boat, and it's morphed into an art studio of sorts.

Most working stiffs, such as Sonny and me, live on the eastern side of the island in New Town. The guts of the city, it's a place to get your car fixed, shop in bulk, and watch your kids play baseball. For half the price, you get twice the amount of real estate than what you'd get in Old Town, the area where I was raised.

But Old Town gives Key West its charm, allure and distinction. Pastel-painted Victorian cottages tuck amidst tangled jungle landscaping and twinkling porch lights. Built by early shipbuilders in the 19th century, they comprise the largest wooden historic district in the United States. The houses line streets and alleyways, with whimsical names like "Love Lane," "Poorhouse Lane," and "Catholic Lane." I wish we could afford to live there. It's also closer to the docks where we run our business.

I kneel to affix the bottom fins of a paper-mâché Queen Angel into poultry netting. Majestic and graceful, the angels are popular with our snorkelers. Ivy painted a remarkable likeness of the fish onto the mold. Wide-eyed with navy lips, the body is bluish-green with lemon yellow scales.

My little sister, at last, has come into her own. Who would have guessed her paintings would command so much attention, even providing her a solid income? Prominently displayed in galleries across the state, they're reviewed as whimsical and bold.

But it's odd that at twenty-seven years old, she remains at home, her bedroom and studio tucked into the top of the tower. She and Mama are as thick as thieves, but Ivy's friends are few, most of them from art school and scattered across the country.

She's had boyfriends—her beauty attracts men in droves— but she casts them aside after a month or so. Ivy's on and off. For weeks she's Miss Congeniality, exhibiting a personality we never saw when she was growing up. And then she turns on a dime, secluding herself in the tower. Her behavior is odd, perhaps some loose screws upstairs? People need people; how could she not be lonely?

Linnea and I are boring in comparison. We thought of ourselves as a singular unit with joint identities, and in grade school, we never developed a sense of individuality. We answered to each other's names when growing up. It was simpler than making the correction. And the fact we wore the same uniform, as did all of the girls in our Catholic school, rendered us a double-blurred smear.

If we'd tried to differentiate ourselves from each other,

school made it difficult. Kids that go to a Catholic school give themselves over to the group, in dress, sport, song and prayer. Group projects and team spirit were encouraged. Originality was an affliction to be avoided, and conformity was fine with us.

But not so with Ivy, who stood out and apart from her classmates. Her knee socks were forever sliding, bunched up around her ankles. The white, squared-off collar on the back of her sailor shirt was unfailingly stained after recess, her bun, a messy ponytail by the end of the day. She was not a color, so easily blended.

She pestered Mama relentlessly to go to public school, and when Ivy was about to enter fifth grade, Mama agreed. My parents have always referred to her as *Our Girl*. The baby in the family, *Our Girl* always got her way. Still does. Forever a Mama's girl, maybe that's why she's odd.

Sonny's mother walks into the garage carrying my daughter, almost five months old today. My mother-in-law, Mariela, was raised in Cuba. We call her Lita, short for *Abuelita*, which is the Cuban endearment for Grandmother. Our daughter was christened Mariela, after her grandmother, and we nicknamed her Ella.

"*La pequeña princesa* was sucking on her toes when I came into the nursery." Lita coos, smiling into my child's face, rocking her in her arms. "She must be *hambrienta*." Although she's lived in Florida for forty-five years, her words ping-pong between English and Spanish. Referred to as Spanglish, it's a language unto its own.

I check my phone. "You're right. It's been over four hours. That's a record." She hands me my child clad in a pink cotton T-shirt and diapers. Her wee bit of dark hair is tied in a ribbon atop her head, Pebbles Flintstone style. Her tiny head knocks at my chest, rooting around, and I press my nose into the side of her neck, kissing her.

"It's also been hours since you've eaten, *chica*," Lita remarks. "I bring you something now." She brushes a dark piece of hair, streaked with strands of silver, away from her forehead. "There's plenty, too, for Linnea when she arrives." She hustles back towards the house, and I nuzzle my nose into Ella's belly; last week she began to smile.

On my first date with Sonny, he made it clear his mom was a part of the deal. It's said you should marry a man who loves his mother, and I was charmed. Moreover, I was swept away by his eyes. A dazzling shade of gold, they're much lighter than his skin tone, which is the color of apple cider. With his cropped black hair and sinewy frame, the man's a startling package. Not stingy with affection, the way he tilts his head and studies me before pulling me into his chest, demonstrates to the world he's in love with his woman. He's a different sort of man than my father who follows my mother's every directive while at the same time, keeps her at arms' length.

We added a mother-in-law apartment to our home soon after we were married. Sonny tells me that in Cuba, children are often as close to their grandparents as they are with their parents. Lita cooks, cleans and helps us with the baby.

But she's no pushover. Her short, squat body is designed precisely to block people's path. Her volume, indeed, her very presence, is amplified and exaggerated. Her opinions are spoken loudly and rapidly, punctuated with the swat of some random newspaper or kitchen utensil. Especially those regarding Fidel Castro and the communist tar pit he dug deep into a Caribbean island.

Her wardrobe consists of one black dress for somber occasions and seven billowing house dresses with matching headscarves. One outfit for each day of the week, they manage to be both flashy and functional. A collection of penguins and glass snow globes cover every square inch of available counter space in her apartment. To my eyes, they're dust-collecting clutter, and when a penguin or two manages to find its way out of her apartment, into the family space, I call her out. Immediately. If I give Lita an inch, she'll take a mile.

She's had a tumultuous life. The fourth daughter of a pipe fitter in Havana, when she was a girl, she was raped by her uncle. At eighteen years old, she paid a hundred dollars to be smuggled into Miami in a crate of grapefruit. She hasn't seen her parents, sisters, or eaten a grapefruit since. She's proud her only child married a gringo—*la clase alta*—enhancing her status amongst her friends.

Several years after her arrival into Florida, she married Sonny's father, of Italian descent, who died in prison when Sonny was a young boy. She speaks of these things—molestation, prison—as if they mean nothing to her. The woman is tougher than chromium, but her essence is a soft, sweet fruit. She tells us we are her blessing. I've friends who struggle with the demands of motherhood with only their partner for support, and I understand I'm fortunate. Lita brings levity to our lives and aside from the occasional spat when I want to wring her neck, I love her.

Her presence also lessens the sting felt by the indifference of my own mother. She's made it clear she and Daddy work around the clock, are all thumbs with babies, and could never be asked to babysit. Once, she was even so offensive as to voice suspicion of people who rhapsodize newborns, as if these doting, loving souls don't know how to get along with adults. Confused by her words—shouldn't all new grandparents be elated by the renewal of their DNA?—I keep my lips sealed, trying to understand.

My parents converted our family home, a historic lighthouse, into a Bed and Breakfast after Linnea and I left for college. They've a strict rule posted in all-capped bold writing on their site and promotional pamphlets: GUESTS MUST BE OVER TWENTY-ONE. Mama and Daddy insist upon setting an example, so we dare not bring the baby there. They manage to visit our place every week, but after five minutes of holding Ella, Mama returns her to me while rattling on about her latest *intrigue du jour.*

I settle into an armchair in the corner of the garage and bring Ella's face to my chest. Her tiny starfish hands light upon my breast as I guide her eager mouth onto my nipple. I feel the welcome latch, and my stress dissipates as tingling sensations shoot through me. Breathing a sigh of contentment, my mind wanders during this sacred time shared with my daughter.

Lita brings a plate of pork alongside the ever-present Arroz con Frijoles Negros, black beans and rice. It's a staple in our home, indeed in any household run by an Abuelita. She places it on the table at my side.

"You are too skinny. *La nena* needs your calories to make her strong. See." She points her forefinger at the meat, the lurid purple polish on her nail half chipped off. "I cut up the pork for you. Now you eat with baby. *A comer.*" She waves her hands in a flourish. "Eat."

I raise my brows at her, shaking my head. "I have, at the very least, eight pounds to lose."

I can barely squeeze into my shorts, and my breasts tumble out from the top of my bathing suit. Yesterday I noted a bit of puckering flesh around my armpits. I've never seen that before.

She wags her head and frowns. "No. *Jamás.* Look at you. You are perfect. So beautiful, like a Madonna. A bit of fat on your figure's good. Cuban men like *una mujerona total.* Not woman looking like a string of dry spaghetti."

Her grandiose, chauvinistic statements about what Sonny likes and doesn't are annoying, but it's not worth the effort disputing her. Slim or plump, hot-blooded Sonny loves me at any size.

"OK. Thanks, Lita. But I'm skipping dessert."

"I bring you flan when you are finished." With a flick of her wrist, she dismisses my words, unabashed in her insistence to feed. "This time I make coconut, *para celebrar la primavera.*"

Wiping her hands on her apron, she retreats to the house.

Thank God I'll be returning to work soon. Snorkeling keeps my body taut and firm, with the added benefit of clearing my head. Below the sparkling surface of the sea, the coral and fish inhabit a kaleidoscopic world unto their own. I'll begin weaning Ella in stages tomorrow; she's already had her first bite of puréed papaya. I switch her to my left breast to nurse so that I can eat the food with my right hand. The symbiosis of rice and beans, and how Lita serves it, pleases me.

First, she ladles a mound of steaming white rice upon a plate. Then, long-simmered beans and sauce are spooned over the top. The color of henna, a deep reddish-brown, they appear to be flowing down a mountain. She embellishes the dish with a garlicky, bell pepper sauce—a beautiful contrast of color, texture and flavor.

I dig my fork into this masterpiece and stir everything up until the rice, beans, pork and sweet peppers lose their individuality, morphing into a singular bliss. Bringing the fork to my mouth, I inhale the scent of cardamom and oranges, Lita's secret ingredients. My baby in my arms, comfort food at my side, why do I continue obsessing over that silk?

My appetite is enormous, and I finish the dish quickly. Linnea should be here any minute—our house is only a ten-minute drive from the airport. The thought of being united with my twinflower brightens my mood.

Born prematurely, we held hands in the incubator, according to Mama, and were inseparable growing up. At least until high school, when Linnea began distancing herself from our family. Especially me. After we turned sixteen, she pleaded with my parents for a private room. Although we didn't have the extra bedroom, they relented, clearing out an oversized closet so it could fit a bed. Compared to the spacious room we shared, her new cramped quarters felt like a prison to me.

My feelings were desperately hurt. Mama tried comforting me by explaining Linnea felt a lack of identity more keenly than myself. I suppose that's another one of her reasons for leaving home.

With twins, environmentally triggered changes accumulate over the years. My fondest wish is Linnea, at last, feels her own person, strong enough to shake away her fears and stick around for good.

And we need help with Ivy. Someone must do something; she's not right in the head. Mama's efforts are not enough, and she's a bit of a ding-a-ling herself. At this point in my life, every spare minute must be devoted to my daughter.

Linnea should, Linnea *must* help us sort out our little sister. What other obligations stand in her way?

3. LINNEA

Daddy's white van pulls to a halt beside the curb. It would be hard to miss since Ivy painted a hibiscus, the color of oxblood, on each of the passenger doors. The flower is part of the logo for their bed and breakfast, The Maiden Tower Inn, and the van is used primarily for shuttling passengers to and from the airport.

Emergency blinkers flashing, he jumps out, his grooming, as always, immaculate. As he strides toward me––tall, thin and agile––I'm reminded of a sommelier dashing off to procure a requested wine. The man never slows. I brush a kiss against his offered cheek. You'd think I'd at least get a hug; I haven't seen him in over a year. My father is reserved with his affections.

"Traffic's a mess with all this carnival nonsense." He takes my luggage and then hoists it into the back of the vehicle. "Wish we could have saved the Fog Horn House for you, but with this week's demand, even that's booked. We're getting twice the price for everything. Next week, when Season's over, bookings are down by half. Then, the place will be all yours."

Locals refer to the months between November and May as *Season*, when northerners invade our flip-flop mecca. The festival's end marks the official end of Season, when the Snowbirds return to their northern climes.

"No worries. Delphina's pullout will be fine for now. Besides, she needs help with that float she's been obsessing over."

Before Dad began monetizing the festival, he was one of the most vociferous of the citizenry insisting the increasingly lewd event disband. Now he keeps his mouth shut, defending the festival, saying that in a world filled with anger, rage and chaos, the silliness is refreshing. Just drunks enjoying life.

I climb into the passenger side and fasten my seatbelt. My father slides behind the wheel and then adjusts the rear-view mirror with the precision of a neurosurgeon. Cranking the ignition, he pulls out into the exiting traffic. Now seated, I note his waistline has thickened, a small bulge hangs over his belt. His hair, once black, has turned the color of fine-polished silver, but his glittering eyes haven't dimmed with age; they remain the color of the Atlantic. Beneath his prominent cheekbones, his face narrows into an elegant, cleft chin. There is no mistaking Delphina and I are his daughters.

"It's great seeing you, Linnea," he says, his eyes fixed steadily on the road ahead. "Will you be staying a while?"

"I'm not sure—I'll play it by ear. I can't wait to meet the baby. And I'm looking forward to spending time with you and Mama." I glance at him while shifting in my seat, tightening the seatbelt. "Ivy, too, of course. I also need to find employment—make some money before heading back to Idaho. They're forever looking for prep-cooks and bartenders down here. I'm thinking I'll be here two months. Three months, max."

Key West and Miami are the most vulnerable spots in the States for hurricanes. The early Fall stirs up the worst, so I'll definitely be gone by September.

Daddy's jaw is working, and his eyes shift from the road to glance at me. Next, I'll suffer through an interrogation about my choice of locale, which could get ugly. The future looms in front of me, shapeless, like an apparition. I change the subject before he has time to investigate further. After a decade of practice, I know how to deflect the inevitable.

"Is the inmate misbehaving?" I pull down the visor to block the blinding, late afternoon sun. "What's this talk about Mama getting into a tangle?"

He lets out a long, drawn-out whistle. "The Chicken Wars revved up. The waters have been tranquil for some time now, but yesterday she released a hen Bill captured."

For years Key West citizens have had divided opinions regarding the abundance of feral fowl roaming the streets of our town. Known as Gypsy Chickens, the mother hens and their baby chicks scratch around outdoor dining tables while the roosters weave in and out of traffic. One camp believes them to be one of the more charming aspects of Key West, another attraction to seduce the tourists. Others regard them as a noisy nuisance, indeed, a threat to public health. My mother's one of the more outspoken of the chicken huggers. Bill, our next-door neighbor, heads the opposition camp.

"Did you pay him off with rum?" The last time they banged heads over the chickens, a bottle of booze cleared the air.

"It didn't work this time. I even upped the ante with a Bermudez Don Armando. It's a Dominican. Aged ten years and is as good as it gets. He may as well have slammed the door in my face. Said he was going to file a complaint with the city—wants her arrested. Not sure how this will play out, but I guess we'll hear something soon."

"Arrested?" I scrunch my nose. "For springing a chicken? Unlikely. The police have enough on their plates with the festival. Have there been any incidents this year?"

"No incarceration for indecency, if that's what you mean. Typical this would be the week Nina calls in sick. I've had to make the guests' breakfast."

"Can't Ivy pitch in and help?"

"Our Girl can't even boil water, much less toast bread. Besides. Your mother insists we not distract her from her work."

What's this princess in a tower bullshit? There's no truth in his words. My most treasured moments with Ivy were back when she was a girl, and I taught her to make pie. It became our tradition, Ivy's and mine, to make one for every occasion. We'd use the scraps of dough as decoration, cutting the pieces into stars, sunbursts, whatever caught our fancy. How long has it been since the two of us shared the warmth of creation?

Daddy turns to look at me, his thumbs tapping against the steering wheel, bringing me back to the moment. Even his hands don't take a break.

"Today's the Tutu Parade," he continues. "This morning, before I'd even had my coffee, I knew the day was getting out of hand. It was like serving breakfast to the cast of the American Ballet Theatre on crack." He shakes his head. "This beer-bellied bearded guy was wearing a purple tutu. Had a matching sequined bra. His partner's tulle was done up in a lion's print with a long swishing tail attached. He cradled it in his hands, stroking it like it was a kitten."

I giggle. "You'd never witness that action back in Boise."

He glances at me, smiling, seeming pleased I'm amused. "Your mother made a grand entrance strutting down the stairs wearing that black feather number of hers. The guests egged her on until she pirouetted and almost fell onto her face. You should have heard their applause."

"Sorry I missed it," I say, my voice monotone. I turn to gaze out of the window, the palm trees whizzing by in a blur. Mama and her silly shenanigans. Her exuberance illuminates every room in our towering home, which lingers in varying states of disrepair waiting for Daddy's attention. He can fix everything except my mother's nonsensical behavior. Thank

God I'm staying with Delphina through all of this festival brouhaha.

"As usual, Our Girl stayed up in her studio, as she puts it, touching the clouds." His face hardens and lips thin, but an edge of pain laces his words. "In that tower, she couldn't get any further away if she moved to Fiji."

"Ivy's always been..." I pause, searching for the right word. "...unpredictable." Unpredictable is the only equivocal word that comes to mind.

"The guests are having the time of their lives," he continues, directing the course of conversation away from his youngest. "Whatever else you might hear, the festival's not going away. Too much money's to be made."

"Well, Daddy. I promise you this. The bottle you bought for Bill won't go to waste. I've sampled rums across the country, but, for my money, rum only tastes right in the Keys."

"As long as you hide it from your mama." He glances at me, raising his left brow.

I give him a conspiratorial wink. She doesn't have a drinking problem, but she's raucous enough sober. A shot of booze and you can't shut her up. My mother is an apt metaphor for a chicken. No. Make that a rooster. Flamboyant and color-ful, she struts about town as if she had the keys to the city. She has an abundance of friends who flock around her like baby chicks—my mother has a bitingly funny wit—but her behavior often embarrasses me. Delphina and I believe the excessive amount of hair product she uses to calm her curls have nuked her brain. She's a tough bird to decipher.

One thing you can say about Mama, she has the best of intentions. One day she's instructing the Garden Club on how to mount orchids in trees, the next she's enlisting the community into boycotting a shampoo tested on a rabbit. As kids, Delphina and I wished she'd spend some of her energy ensuring our school uniforms were pressed. We learned how to microwave frozen veggie burgers on paper towels at an early age.

"What were we talking about?" Daddy asks, interrupting my thoughts, his wedding ring tapping percussion on the steering wheel. "Oh, yes. Your mother, your mother. She knows bloody well Bill isn't eating them. Wild chickens are tough and stringy. They'll be relocated to Northern Florida and used as egg hens."

I search his face for annoyance, empathy or amusement. He's hard to read. There it is, his left eye is twitching. Daddy's irritated.

"I try to make her understand where Bill's coming from," he continues, his voice rising, hands now gripping the steering wheel so hard his knuckles are white. "They roost in one particular tree, which attracts bugs chickens like to eat. Well, that's the tree where his hammock is tied. They poop on his face when he's trying to relax."

"Well, Daddy. Surely you know by now those chickens have a perverted sense of humor." He glances at me, half-smiling.

I check my Fitbit. "Wow. It's getting late. Tonight, I'll catch up with Delphina and Sonny and introduce myself to the baby. First thing in the morning, I'll bike to the lighthouse and have a nice long visit with Mama and Ivy."

Stopping at the light, Dad swivels to face me and smacks the heel of his palm against the steering wheel. "Damn it, Linnea. I'm glad to have you back."

My cheeks warm. Wow. He's happy to see me. He misses me.

The signal turns green, and he accelerates suddenly causing us and the car to lurch forward. His attention snapping back towards the road, he turns right on Fogarty, the street where Delphina lives. "You can help keep your Mama in line."

There is an awkward pause as tension coils around my neck. Hasn't it always been like this? She's not my monkey, and this is not my circus. Unfastening the clasp on my seatbelt, I lean into him and peck his cheek.

"I can handle my luggage, Daddy." I eye the open door of the garage. "You go tend to Mama." I try smiling at him, but it feels heavy and wooden on my face.

"Oh, Delphina!" I drop my suitcase at the sight of my sister. I run to her, tears streaming down my face. Nestled in her arms is a cherub of a tot, splayed froggy legs kicking about all gurgles and coos.

Delphina stands and places her into my outstretched arms. As she tucks a pale green blanket around the baby, I feel unsure—have I held an infant since Ivy?

"Ella. Meet your Aunt Linnea. Linnea, meet your adorable niece, Ella."

I look from my sister's face, radiant with joy, into the face of this precious child who reminds me of a caterpillar wrapped in a leaf. The baby meets my gaze with a mouth-splitting gummy grin.

Delphina giggles. "Wow, Aunt Linnea. That's her biggest smile yet."

My voice, when I find it, is barely there. "Ella. You're so lovely."

I'm unable to take my eyes away from this miracle of a creature trying to kick off the blanket. Lowering my face, I kiss her forehead. How could this be? Only one minute and I've fallen in love.

Delphina folds the baby and me into her arms, and for the first time since I boarded the plane, I feel safe.

4. WWW.IVYCHANDLER.COM

Today I had lunch with a friend of mine who flew in from Brooklyn for Festa-Palooza. We attended art school together in Miami. She makes enough money at the event painting designs on human body parts to subsidize her not-so-lucrative career as a conceptual artist. Women's breasts and torsos are her specialties. Much in demand, she's overbooked, and I was lucky she could squeeze in some catch-up time.

How do I feel about her pimping her art? Pimping is too strong of a word. The human body is a work of art unto itself, so why not adorn it with butterflies and flowers? Why not turn buttocks into hearts and nipples into the eyes of cupid? The detail in her work is astonishing.

If modesty dictates, you can attend the festival without confronting these colorful displays. The Palooza Zone is the area that you'd want to avoid, which is Duval to Truman Avenue, trickling into their side streets. But honestly, folks. No one means any harm. It's all in good fun.

If you can't pay a visit, I've attached a slideshow of photographs to amuse. You might wonder how I approached these women to request a picture. It's perfectly acceptable to introduce yourself to a participant. Smile and ask if it's okay to photograph their bodies. Indeed. They want to have their picture taken as often as possible. Exhibitionists, you might surmise? Perhaps. But what a fantastic, flaming way of immortalizing yourself.

As for me? I'm in the middle of a canvas, splashed with images from this town, only abandoned when I'm compelled to eat or sleep. Or snap photos of innocent boobs, which I post to ensure my Google rank is strong (-:

As most of my work (exhibited through the summer at Conch House Art), it's whimsical and nostalgic, the colors infused and saturated with light. Logic and detail have no place in the image. It's a magical world where townsfolk and animals live side by side, jumbled together, the lines between them blurred.

For example, yesterday, I painted a woman and chicken. At the top of the canvas, they dangle upside down and side-by-side, eyes locked together.

C'est la vie in Key West!

Ivy. (aka—Blog Writer Girl)

I vy
I just uploaded my blog. Its URL is ivychandler.com, and I've thousands of subscribers. A photo journal of my day-to-day, most people find it in a Google search when searching for things to do when visiting Key West.

The blog is upbeat, promoting my art. It reflects the sunlight filling our town as its brilliance illuminates my paintings. That word: light. Fascinating to ponder, infiltrating layers of abstract significance. Light is the source of goodness, the spark of the spiritual, the divine.

Light is also the avenger of the other person who resides within me, the one no one knows, her code impossible to crack. Escaping the light, she hovers beneath tangled webs of binary data, hardware and transmission control protocol. She resides deep in the basement of the URL, uncensored, raw, and ugly.

With dispassionate curiosity, she watches me as I rhapsodize the light, dazzled. And when she beckons, after the curtain falls, I return to our hiding place. Into the dark.

5. LINNEA

Mama about knocks me over as she rushes into my outstretched arms. "Linnea, Linnea. My beautiful girl. You've been away from your family much, much too long."

I rest my head on her shoulder and lose myself in the flaming hair that fans across her back. Like a ripe peach sunset, it's as if the sun's always shining on it. With only a few streaks of smoldering ashes in the tumbling tresses of gold, her hair defies her age. Nuzzling into this miracle of a mane, relishing the feel of her arms clutched around me, I inhale her scent. Lavender. It's too hot in the Keys to grow the fragrant variety she prefers, so she orders oils, lotions and soap from a lavender farm in Michigan.

She pushes away from my embarrassingly sniveling embrace, and I touch my cheeks, surprised they're wet. Eyes dancing, she regards me up and down.

"Look at you. White as a ghost. The sun's fierce today. I hope you're wearing sunblock." Her sentences end in a lilt as if posed in a question, even if they're statements.

I take a step back from this woman––my mother––who I'll never understand but will always adore. I try to compose myself, swiping away the moisture on my face and gathering beneath my nostrils. "No worries, Mama. SPF 50."

"Good for you, honey. I wish I'd paid more attention to my skin when I was your age. Maybe I wouldn't look like an iguana today."

She arranges her hair into a knot behind the nape of her neck, her expression coy, a silent request my response be a compliment. Her skin, always tanned to a vibrant coppery glow, is crinkled about the corners of her eyes. But her complexion has fared remarkably well under a relentless southern sun. Most redheads have pigment that burns, but not Mama's and Ivy's.

"You look radiant, Mama. Not a day over 40."

She runs her finger down my arm, shaking her head to feign disagreement, yet smiling, pleased with my response.

"So, how's the baby? Precious, yes?" Her eyes dart towards the driveway, and she taps her foot preferring not to speak the expected platitudes about her grandchild. I get it. She hates clichés, loves sarcasm, and I spent my youth following her cues. I wrack my brain for a fitting response.

"Precious? Seriously? She's like a frat girl. Sleeps, eats, drinks, and pukes."

Mama smirks and slaps me playfully on the arm, encouraging my snarky banter. So...I continue.

"She's like Fox News and CNN. A running commentary of the same old crap."

Mama bends over, laughing so hard she begins to cough. I pat her on the back, and she straightens, smiling into my eyes.

"Goodness. I've missed you so much."

I return her smile but feel ill at ease, guilty having made a baby the brunt of my jokes. Although the reality of parenthood hit me like a freight train each time Ella woke me up wailing, this type of teasing should be off-limits.

Mama's not projecting normal grandmother behavior

either, egging me on. How could we poke fun of her only grandchild, my only niece? The intensity of love I feel for this heartstring-tugging bundle of preciousness startles me. Mama reads my thoughts, and the tips of her ears grow scarlet. Uncomfortable, we change the subject, both speaking at the same time.

"Sorry I..."

"You'll have to..."

"Pardon me, honey," Mama says, her words now solemn, the former edge of sarcasm diminished. "You go first."

"I was saying that I'm sorry I couldn't be here for your birthday. I know it was a big one." Mama turned sixty last month.

"But you look as fabulous as ever. Must be those wide-brimmed hats you wear. I hear they protect the skin as much as sunblock." Brushing her cheek with my fingertips, I do, however, spy an age spot, resembling a kidney bean. But her skin feels soft and warm.

"Darling, Linnea." She pronounces darling, dahlin', and her eyes soften, a smile playing about the sides of her mouth. "Just seeing your face, hearing your voice, has turned my day around."

With the flat of her palms, she smooths my hair, tucking it behind my ears. "Your daddy's finishing up breakfast. I haven't seen Our Girl, but I suppose she's painting. You must be worn out from your bike ride."

I check my Fitbit. "Hardly. This town's as flat as a pancake. It only took thirty minutes to get here." Placing palms on my knee, I push my right leg back, planting my heel to the earth, stretching my Achilles tendon.

"Daddy told me Nina's on hiatus." I glance up at her through the top of my lashes. "I promised Delphina I'd get back to help finish up the float. But I've time enough to wash dishes if you like."

"I won't hear of it. I've got all day to finish the chores. I'll let

Our Girl know you're here." She flings her arm towards the back garden. "Go, go. It's the end of orchid season. The Dendrobium Margaret Thatchers are exiting in a riot of hot pink."

Turning, she walks towards the front door. Barefoot, as she prefers--she has absurdly beautiful feet--the nails on her perfectly formed toes glimmer a brilliant shade of orange. Her long caftan, lime green with a splash of daisies, billows around her ankles, which are shapely and without fault. With her hand on the doorknob, she pauses, turns her head over her shoulder, and catches my eye.

"You hungry?"

I grin. "Starved. I'd love a bite. No coffee, though. I had two cups of Lita's cafe con leché. May as well have stirred amphetamines into Red Bull." I jiggle my hands in front of me and widen my eyes pantomiming a wired state, going for another laugh. Mama, however, frowns and tosses her head.

"I wouldn't know. Every time I set foot in that house, she hits the ground running. I have more interesting conversations with my orchids."

The return of her sarcasm has begun to wear thin, rubbing the shine off the day. First, the baby and now Lita? But pain is laced into the sound of her words. Something is amiss in her relationship with Delphina's family. The last time I was home, she was delighted with Lita and her amusing mannerisms.

Mama opens the handcrafted oak screen door, original to our home, and then walks into the house. The door snaps behind her with a jolting thwack.

I lock the bike to a rack positioned next to the Lightkeeper's Quarters; a three-room dwelling built several feet away from the lighthouse. It once housed the person who was responsible for maintaining the grounds and ensuring the glass in the tower was kept spotless. Growing up, we used it for storage. Since the conversion of our home to B&B, its been renovated and is the living quarters for my parents.

I turn, my eyes skimming up and down The Maiden Tower, the place I once called home. Everything and nothing has changed. A flood of memories moistens my eyes.

The lighthouse, Fog Horn House and Lightkeeper's Quarters have been designated a historical landmark, a bronze sign indicating such is positioned above the doorbell at the front entrance of our home. A flag, its horizontal stripes mimicking the hues of a rainbow, hangs above the door. Symbolizing Gay Pride, the flags are ubiquitous across town, another vivid complement to Key West's all-embracing vibe.

The bricks are painted white, and the shutters and door trim accented in the greenish-blue tint of aquamarine. My eyes journey up the teal band twirling snakelike around the cylindrical tower. It stops at the top beneath a circular glass room, the lantern room. Once it housed the light guiding ships to safe waters, now it's Ivy's studio.

Most painters, she says, prefer their ateliers lit with northern light, which is soft, subtle and without variation. She prefers *plein air* painting, which, in French, means to paint outdoors.

In the mid-nineteenth century, Expressionist painters—such as Monet, Pissarro and Renoir—preferred this environment for replicating the visual effects of sunlight. The dancing, dazzling light in the lantern room is the next best thing, says Ivy, and is captured in the brushstrokes enlivening her canvasses. Her bedroom is situated directly below, in what used to be known as the service room, where maintenance supplies were stored.

Despite my misgivings about it now being a B&B, I'm proud of our home. It's an iconic piece of property, rich with history. To the background of Mama's fingers lighting across the keyboard, every evening, the guests gather while Daddy recites the myth of The Maiden Tower. Mama's accompaniment is both melodic and haunting.

When we were six years old, Delphina and I overhead her describing rumors of the lighthouse's stormy history of lust, pillaging and mayhem to her girlfriends. Mama, basking in the rapt attention of her audience, forgot her impressionable daughters were playing hide and seek between the legs of the rattan chairs. Ivy, a toddler at the time, was too young to understand, but she did pick up on her big sisters' subsequent horror.

We twins, plagued with nightmares, awakened that evening screaming, which set off Ivy. Our terror resonated through the night, ricocheting off the lighthouse walls. It took my parents, bleary-eyed and horrified, several days to convince us it was simply a myth. Like the movies *Pet Cemetery* or *Gremlins*, they told their shaken daughters it was all untrue, made up in someone's head to entertain. These days, I dismiss rumors that the lighthouse carries secrets. I've enough neurosis on my plate.

I remove my pack from the bike basket and wander towards the garden. A picket fence, whitewashed and weathered, creates a sanctuary within the confines, separating the garden from Winston Lane, a side street to my left. Unlatching the gate, I sit at one of the wrought-iron café tables scattered about the terrace. The guests are enjoying the amusements of the streets, allowing me quiet communion with the landscape. Since the conversion, the garden and kitchen are the only parts of our home I enjoy. Removing my sunglasses, I chew on one end of the stems, my eyes drinking in the terrace's charms.

Paper lanterns are strung beneath the roofline of the house, and exuberant bougainvilleas drape the fence with a magenta so bright I squint. Bright yellow hibiscus adorns the outside wall beneath the kitchen window, giving it a cheerful appearance. Mama's collection of brilliantly colored orchids—some large and splashy, others small and delicate—are nestled into trees and planted in pots, hung onto a lattice wall. They include rare species friends have gifted her from their travels. A large oval mirror hooks into the trunk of a palm, which, in effect, doubles the size of this enchanted garden.

Soothed by the sound of water trickling from a fountain, I'm at once startled by an ear-piercing meow. Liberace! Our pet parrot, a Scarlet Macaw over two and one-half feet tall, bobs his head, teasing me from his perch in the aviary. A circular dome trimmed in brass, it was custom built to resemble the lantern room.

Growing up, Delphina and I would spend hours training Liberace to mimic animal sounds. Forever stamped into my memory was the day I asked him: What does a kitty say? He responded with a staccato meow. He could never mimic the sound of a mooing cow or a clucking chicken, but he has that yowl down to a science.

I stand and walk to the cage. Bending down, I crane my face forward to regard my old pal. "Liberace, what are you doing outside? Your job is to entertain the guests. Remember me? What's my name, pretty bird?"

He cocks his red-feathered head, and peers at me through yellow-ringed black eyes. "Cool your jets, Linnea. Cool your jets, Linnea."

I clap my hands, delighted, as Mama enters the garden from the back door, which leads from the kitchen. "Your daddy's fixing you a plate," she says, brushing crumbs off her dress.

"He remembers me, Mama," I say, pointing at Liberace, the smile on my mouth stretched so wide, it feels like it's splitting my face.

"Well, of course, he does, sugar," she says, taking a seat. "He's known you your entire life. He misses you as much as we do."

Liberace works his beak into the door's release, and I straighten, turning to Mama. "He hates that aviary. Poor guy. He's trying to get out. I'd be plotting an escape, too."

"Pshaw. Don't you be putting ideas into his head. Liberace's spoiled. His house is big enough for a fleet of parrots."

"He's a social dude. Why are you separating him from the guests?' I saunter back to the table, glancing back at Liberace, taking pity on the bird.

"He's been misbehaving, so now we keep him outside."

"What about his role in Evening Hour?"

Mama shakes her head and eyes Liberace, frowning. The bird squawks at her, furious at her disapproving look.

"We had to fire him. He's getting ornery in his old age and is less tolerant of strangers. Sometimes he acts downright crazy."

"For example?" I pull out a chair and take a seat.

"Last month, during Evening Hour when your Daddy was at the crux of the tale—you know, when the Maiden's lover..."

I slide my forefinger across my throat in a motion informing her to zip it.

"Oh, honey. Does that story still bother you?"

"You are surprised that deception, brutality and violence upset me?" I rest my chin in the cup of my hand, widening my eyes.

She sniffs, picking at a cuticle on her thumbnail, "Oh well. Anyway. Where was I?"

My parents are becoming forgetful as they age. I hope their energy doesn't wane, as well. Keeping up this place would tax a couple half their ages. I trace my forefinger around the edge of the table and glance up to catch her eye.

"You were telling me why Liberace's retired."

"Oh yes," she says, tapping her temple. "This woman, all decked out in costume jewelry, made this awful wheezing sound. I mean to tell you that rasp of hers was so loud it sounded like she was choking. Must have startled Liberace. Anyway, he flew off Daddy's shoulder, nose-dived to her ear and pecked at her earring. He used his giant beak like a set of pliers and pulled it right out. All the guests were screaming to hell and back, and it ruined our performance."

Noting her serious expression, I stifle a laugh. "What? He attacked a guest? That doesn't sound like him."

"He wasn't vicious. Just annoyed, like me, by her adenoids and tacky bling. Her earlobe was bleeding but thank God it wasn't torn."

She hugs herself and shivers. "We comped her two nights stay to avoid a lawsuit, and that, Linnea, put an end to Liberace's acting career. At the rate he was going, we'd have to make the guests sign a waiver and wear a toe tag."

The parrot begins to chatter, wanting to put in his two-cents worth. Then, he clicks his tongue against his beak, the way he does when he wants to get out of his cage.

Mama swivels to regard him, locking eyes with the bird. "Stop your bickering. You still have free rein in the Lightkeeper's Quarters." Then, she smiles at him indulgently. "Silly bird. Don't worry. You're a part of our family, and we love you. No matter how much you misbehave, we're not sending you away."

She studies her fingers, picking at a cuticle, mumbling beneath her breath. "I'm thinking of stuffing Bill into that cage. Let him know what it feels like when he's locked behind bars and can't move."

Here we go. Of course, our talk would segue back to what's really bothering Mama: our neighbor and the hen. Is it too soon to catch the next plane back to Idaho? I sigh. Might as well have the conversation. I heard Daddy's side, so now I'll listen to hers.

"Tell me what happened." I raise my eyebrows, forcing my expression to seem interested.

Regarding me, her eyes blinking rapidly, the corners of her mouth twitch before folding down into a frown. She grasps my forearms so hard it hurts, and then she speaks quickly, every word lit with passion.

"Chickens are supposed to roam free in this town. It's their birthright. But you could never say that to Bill. He trapped a hen and stuffed her into a cage, which could barely contain her. She was freaking out, trying to flap her wings, making all sorts of racket. Her baby chicks were outside of the cage, scratching the dirt and making these forlorn little peepin' sounds. Anyone with a heart would have let her go. Let the mama tend to her babies."

Mama's bulging eyes look like those of a runaway horse, but she wears the solemn expression of a saint. Nothing is ever in sync with her countenance. She's a paradox, a puzzle I'll never understand. She does, however, make a valid point about the hen.

"Maybe, Mama. Well, yes. That scene would upset me too. But what you should have done is knock on his door, speak directly to Bill and show him what was going on."

She releases her hands from my forearms, which are streaked red from the vise of her grip. "Would have done no good. The man's as cold-blooded as a snake. Furthermore, I'm beginning to believe he's baiting me. He left the cage in my direct line of vision." She points to an area beside his driveway, a grassy patch close to the garage.

"He's never been right since Alma passed," she continues, tears collecting around the edges of her eyes. "She'd never put up with such cruelty. The sight of those chicks about broke my heart."

"Now Mama. The birds can be a nuisance." My words are steady, trying to calm her. "He's within his rights to trap them, and I'm not sure your reasoning will stand up in City Hall. Now if I were you..."

She shakes her head and waves her hands in front of her face, her signal to inform she doesn't want to listen to my opinion. Closing her eyes, she mutters softly, as if speaking to herself.

"By now, Bill's probably told the entire town I'm a raging madwoman."

Pulling in a deep breath, her nostrils expand as she tries to clear her head. Opening her eyes, she straightens in her chair, tucking an errant curl behind her ear.

"I may be spirited, but I am not crazy. Anyone can see I'm fine. In fact, better than fine. Nothing wrong with me that time spent with my wayward daughter won't cure." She raises an eyebrow, giving me a sly little wink.

"Now, where was I?" Her eyes lift to the sky a moment, and she drums her fingertips on the table. "Oh, yes." She catches my gaze.

"If Bill doesn't like the chickens, he should pack his bags and go. They were here first."

Another point scored by Poppy. Brought over by early pioneers, the much-disputed birds have claimed the island their home for almost two hundred years.

When the Cubans descended in the 1950s, fleeing the Revolution and finding employment in the town's bustling cigar business, they brought their combative roosters with them. When cockfighting was deemed illegal, and meat and eggs became available in local markets, the need for families to keep chickens evaporated. The jailbirds were set free to roam the island and reproduce without predator. The wildlife center relocates them regularly, but it's challenging to turn a corner without running into a pack of free-range fowl.

"Agreed. The chickens were here before Bill." I sigh. "But this time it sounds like he means business."

Anchoring my elbows into the table, I place my head into my palms, speaking to her between outstretched fingers. "I'm too tired to think about it now. The baby woke me up every three hours crying."

Pushing back her chair, she rises, speaking between clenched teeth. "That's what babies do. I try to avoid 'em myself." Her eyes dart from mine and scan the garden. Walking to the wall of orchids, she begins pinching off blooms that have browned. "That's not to say I don't adore my sweet little grandbaby. Isn't she precious?"

Tired of talking about her grandchild and chickens, I don't answer and change the subject.

"So where's Ivy. I can't wait to see her."

Mama turns away from a specimen. A shriveled blossom dangles mid-air, pinched between her thumb and forefinger,

"The poor thing's in bed." Between her palms, she rolls the petal into a ball, walks towards Bill's house and then flicks it into his driveway. Then, she returns to the table and resumes her seat.

"Her room was pitch black," she continues. Bending down, she pulls out a weed making its way up through the gravel that covers the walkway. "She spoke to me from under the covers. Your sister has a headache. She gets them all the time."

Mama straightens, sighs, and brushes the dirt from her hands. Then, she rests a palm on my forearm, catching my eyes. "I'm sorry, sugar. I know she wants to see you. It'll pass."

Last night after the baby was asleep, Delphina expressed a gut feeling that our little sister was––for lack of a better word–– unhinged. She said it was critical I spend as much time as possible with her to help sort things out. Her words troubled me then, but now I'm pissed. I look up towards Ivy's bedroom. Pressing my lips between my teeth, I shake my head, a pain squeezing my heart.

"A headache? Are you kidding me? She published a blog yesterday indicating she's having the time of her life. I haven't seen her in over a year. Maybe she'll grant me a visit after feeding her pet unicorn." I roll my eyes, feelings hurt by my self-absorbed, princess of a sister.

"I've traveled across the country," I continue, my voice now shrill, "slept fitfully as Ella cried through the night, rode my bike across town to get here, and she can't even be bothered to descend from her tower?"

I stand, shield my eyes with the flat of my hand, and look up to the glass enclosure. "Rapunzel, Rapunzel, let down your hair. And take an Excedrin while you're at it." Frowning, I stick the toe of my shoe into the pebbles and shuffle them around. Then, I collapse into the chair.

"Aw, Honey. I misspoke," Mama says. A flash of pain crosses her eyes, hardening her features. "It's not any old headache. She's getting a migraine."

The lines between her eyes deepen. "They're awful. And stop making such a face. Y'all can visit when she's better. Show mercy towards your baby sister. You and Delphina didn't pay much attention to her growing up. She'd often get headachy when it was that time of the month. But lately migraines hit her regularly." Balling her hand into a fist, she smacks the other palm. "Bam. Kapow. They can level her for days at a time."

"I'm upset because I miss her, and planned to spend more time with her on this visit. I only know her through WordPress and Instagram. I want to know where her head's at these days."

Casting her eyes down, Mama speaks in a whisper, her words directed to the table.

"Migraines. That's where her head's at. I used to get them myself." She places a palm on her abdomen. "Maybe it's because of hormones, because of the change, but my headaches disappeared after I passed the age of bearing fruit."

She looks up, small lines radiating around her eyes like a bank of tributaries. She pulls her lips between her teeth, and I can see my words upset her. I need to shift gears; make her smile.

Crossing my arms over my midriff, I lean forward looking her squarely in the eyes. "Are you calling me an apple?"

"Oh, no. I'm calling you a mango, my darlin'. Remember where you come from."

Mama laughs, her face softening, and I resolve not to say another word about her youngest.

Daddy emerges from the back door carrying a plate topped with a toasted bagel. A couple of orange slices and strawberries linger beside it as an afterthought. With all of the luscious tropical fruits to inspire, all they're serving is strawberries? He places the plate in front of me.

I smile up at my father, thank him, and then nibble on the thin, bland bagel. At the very least, it should have a smear of cream cheese.

"Do you have a clue as to when Nina will return?" I ask, picking up a strawberry and popping it into my mouth. My parents hired the woman to cook breakfasts for the guests several weeks before they opened their doors for business. What I wouldn't give for one of Nina's killer breakfast burritos about now.

Daddy takes a seat at the table. "She says it's the stomach flu, but my guess is she's relapsed. Her voice was slurry when she called." A worried look deepens the lines in his face. "The street's especially tempting during the festival."

Nina's an alcoholic in recovery, who falls off of the barstool from time to time. Ever since the days of the pirates, the town's populace has had a predilection for strong drink. Staying sober, for many, is a struggle. I recall the vodka I once found stashed behind the toilet tank in the lobby's bathroom. We'd found Nina slumped over the butcher-block counter, sweet rolls crisping into cinder blocks in the oven.

"I imagine by now her liver smells like the water in Sloppy Joe's mop bucket." The bar, a notorious watering hole on Duval, was frequented by Ernest Hemingway back in the day.

"Ick. Linnea." Mama pinches her nostrils. "What an awful image. We cut Nina slack. She's had a hard life."

"I know, I know. I'll stop." I admonish myself for making yet another off-color comment that fans the flames. What is my freaking problem?

Grinding my molars together, I catch her eyes, pressing my palms together in a gesture of prayer. "Forgive me, Mama. Blame it on lack of sleep."

"No worries, dahlin'," she replies, smiling at me warmly. Then, she turns her attention to the bottom of her foot, picking out several pieces of embedded gravel.

My parents have never understood me and are still trying to figure out what I've become. I certainly don't want them to think I'm insensitive. I make a mental note to vanquish my snarky quips. When sober, which is about eighty percent of the time, Nina's indispensable in my parents' business. They've only two employees: Nina and her sister who tidies the guest's rooms and parlor. On Nina's days off, or when she's under the weather, her sister assumes kitchen responsibilities. She, unfortunately, left town to escape the crowds.

"How's the float coming?" Daddy asks, hoping to light upon a less stressful topic.

"I think it looks great. But you know Delphina. She's fretting. Says it's lackluster and is all freaked out about some missing ribbon. Sonny's down at Committee Headquarters now checking one last time for the missing bolts."

A swooping sound emanates from my pack, indicating I have a text. I remove my phone.

"Speak of the devil." I read the message. "No ribbon." I glance up at my parents. "She's been waiting until the last minute in hopes it would turn up."

Pushing away from the table, I stand and grab my pack. "Thanks for breakfast. I'd best hit the road. We've got an ocean to assemble before the parade tomorrow. I can only imagine how God felt that third day of creation, having to unleash every sea on the planet."

"We've barely had time to catch up," Mama exclaims, making a pouty face as Daddy blows me a kiss.

"We'll have all the time in the world once this parade is past tense." I brush crumbs off of my cycling shorts. "Y'all will be in the crowd, right?"

"We wouldn't miss it for the world." She stands and draws me into her arms. "It's so good to have you home, honey."

Over Mama's shoulder, I look, once again, up to Ivy's bedroom. A blind is pulled down, covering the window, and a cold hard pebble feels lodged in my throat.

6. DELPHINA

"Your ocean looks fine, Delphy." Sonny fingers the stiff ribbon arranged around the coral, which I fabricated with mesh, wire and spray foam.

"Whatever. Livin' the dream." I emit an exaggerated sigh. "And the dream's a freakin' nightmare."

Hunching my shoulders forward, I knead my aching neck. Ella woke me twice last night and at the crack of dawn to nurse. It's almost eleven, and I still haven't brushed my hair or teeth. I grasp the folds of a baggy t-shirt I slept in and ball it into my fists.

He checks his phone. "You've got to finish up. We need to be at the waterfront no later than two." He gives me the once over, a frown playing about his lips. "In costume and ready to go. Streets will be blocked off, and traffic's hellacious. We can wrap up details there."

Without thinking, I kick the wheel of the flatbed. I'm wearing flip-flops, and the force of the movement stubs my big toe. Jaw tightening, my eyes burn, and I plop onto the floor, cradling my foot.

Sonny squats down, cupping my chin into his hand. "You've got to push past it."

"Push past it? What is *it*? Where did you get that line? A Nike ad? We've worked on this float for four months, and *it* looks like crap." I squeeze my nose, which is beginning to run.

"Honey. Please. Take control of yourself."

I push away his hand, my voice high and indignant. "I am in control."

He stands and then pulls me to my feet. Why can't he be sympathetic? Bending over the float, I flick my forefinger at the offending poly-sheen with disdain.

"Not only is this slick, cheap material, but the wires aren't threaded into the edges. Linnea and I couldn't make it bend so it would look like waves rolling onto shore. Plus, the ribbon's only one-and-a-half inches wide. The bolts I'd ordered were four."

Tears mist my eyes, blurring the seascape we've spent months to create. "You can't buy the kind of promotion we'd receive if we placed in the top three. Besides. The ocean has given us so much. We should represent it as a thing of breathtaking beauty."

Placing my hands on his chest, I lean into him, look up into his eyes, and lower my voice. "Just acknowledge how much nicer it would have looked if I'd had the right ribbon. That's all. Just say the words."

Shaking his head, he brushes a strand of hair away from my eyes and tucks it behind my ear. "This conversation is ridiculous. Words can't sugarcoat reality. It looks fine the way it is. It's only ribbon, for heaven's sakes."

I'll never make him understand. And I must sound certifiable. Besides. Sonny feels bad because he couldn't find the shipment. He loves to be my hero. I rise on tiptoes and kiss him squarely on the mouth. "Sorry. I'll stop kvetching." I run my forefinger under my nostrils.

Turning to the float, Linnea tilts her head and scratches her chin. Then, she looks at us, her jaw set, determination on her face. "It's lovely. We made it work. The ocean on a calm day."

I try to muster a smile in her direction. Perhaps our family's feistiness is another reason why her visits are so rare. With her aimless wandering, she wears the hardened shell of a tortoise, carrying her home upon her back. But beneath that façade, she's reflective, hates conflict—especially amongst our family—and has a habit of arbitrating, trying to keep the peace.

But while she's out gallivanting across the country finding herself, she leaves me behind doing my best to keep our family patched together. I try shaking away these thoughts—God, my mood swings are crazy.

A wail from the house filters across the yard and into the garage. I feel my breasts tingling, milk letting down and leaking from the nipples. I pull out the neck of the T-shirt and stare at my breasts. They look like two beached whales.

"She sure has a set of pipes on her," Linnea remarks, rubbing her eyes.

I look out the door, towards the kitchen, shaking my head. "That baby may appear helpless, but she's a puppeteer, manipulating my every string."

Listening to Ella cry through the night is all the birth control my twin sister will ever need. After the last two days spent with my family, she'll likely remain childless for the rest of her life.

"Why don't you nurse her before we leave?" Sonny asks, concern mapping lines across his brow.

"Lita and I are trying to wean her. Before you know it, I'll be leaving her every day to go to work." I cross my arms in front of my chest, trying to stymie the sensations. "I'm only going to nurse her in the morning and evening from now on out."

"Seems to me you could make an exception. At least this morning when we're...."

The look I toss his way silences him.

"Got it." He bites his upper lip and turns towards the door. "Lemme check on Mom. See how she's handling this reign of terror."

I grab his hand before he leaves. "Make sure she uses the baby app. While I'm gone, she must record every time she feeds her and exactly how much formula Ella drinks."

"She'll never figure out how to use that thing. E-mail baffles her enough. It's one more chore and a pain in the ass."

"It will be very helpful to me," I say, giving him my most imploring look. "I also need to know when Ella pees and poops. At the very least, have your mother take notes. Spanish is fine. I can record the data later."

As Sonny leaves the garage, shaking his head, another death-defying shriek spills from the back-kitchen window. He hesitates at the door, turns around, and catches my eye. We haven't heard screams like this since she received her last bundle of vaccinations. This is torture for both of us, and my breasts seep at my daughter's every wail.

With a slight shake of my head, a flick of my fingers, I motion him to leave. Ella must get used to taking the bottle from Lita. Linnea's face colors as she looks at the front of my shirt, splotched with dark stains.

Growing up identical twins, people assumed my sister and I wanted the same things from life. Nothing could be further from the truth. As I can't relate to her choices now that we're adults, she'll never understand mine. Unlike myself, Linnea wants no part of motherhood. She doesn't have to say a word; it's written on her face every time the baby cries.

I also enjoy the simple pleasures. A perfect day for me is when the temperature hovers in the eighties, the skies are blue, and an eight-knot wind pushes through the sails carrying me to my favorite reef. Nothing is so intoxicating as the cool of the ocean against my flesh as I crawl through her waters.

Linnea, however, has some sort of phobia when it comes to

the ocean. It's even got a name: thalassophobia. It seems to be a mild case—she doesn't run screaming at the sight of the water —but she avoids the beach whenever possible. She loved the ocean as much as I did when we were girls. In high school, however, she began avoiding it as if the water was filled with contagions.

Linnea studies the float, intent upon the finishing touches, and then she folds the edges of ribbon over the sand exactly how I instructed. I walk to her and touch her back. Straightening, she turns to me. Her eyes, icy blue and wide, are the same shape and color of my own. As unlike as we may be, our spirits are connected.

"Linnea. I want you to know how...

"...thrilled I am to see you." We have a habit of finishing each other's sentence.

I grab her hands, weaving her fingers into mine. "I miss you so much. Isn't there anything you miss about home?"

"I miss you. Most certainly, I miss you." She squeezes my hands. "I miss Mama and Daddy. I miss Liberace. At least when he behaves." She giggles. "And of course, I miss Ivy. Speaking of whom, her migraine lingers, so Mama said they'll have to miss the parade."

I shake her hands out of mine and press my palms to my ears. "I refuse to listen to such bull. Our parents may as well live in Timbuktu for all the interest they take in my life." I fling my arms into the air and then gesture towards the float. "I've worked so hard on this project. The least they could do is join the crowd. I'm sorry Ivy's suffering, you know I'm worried to death about that kid, but there's always some excuse for them to bow out."

Linnea sighs, biting the knuckle on her forefinger. "It sounds like her episodes are intensifying."

"I never heard about her migraines until after the holidays."

I eye Linnea through my lashes. "Convenient for Mama, eh? Them arriving right after my baby was born."

"Oh, Delphina," she exclaims, grabbing my arm. "That's ridiculous. Don't think like that."

I am acting silly. Ivy should be our priority. I try smiling, but it feels brittle on my face. We both fall silent.

"At least the migraines haven't affected her work," Linnea ventures, at last. "Next week, I want to check out her exhibit at Conch House.""

"I don't know, Linnea." I take a deep breath, the nonsensical malice I was feeling moments before dissipating with the familiar haunting concern. "Her paintings are changing. They used to be so colorful and whimsical. Now they seem inspired by darkness, and not selling as well. Do you remember her birthday? When I gave her the necklace?"

Linnea nods, a shadow crossing her face.

When Ivy turned eighteen, I gave her a thin silver chain with a small dolphin charm affixed. Mama intended to name me after a flower, but the name Delphina also means dolphin, which suits me better. The pendant, always settled into the crook of my little sister's throat, symbolizes my love for her. It touches me it's the only bit of adornment she wears.

"One of the paintings is a rendition of that necklace," I continue. "But the chain is broken and hangs into the sea like a fishing line. The dolphin is affixed to the clasp, dangling under-water like bait."

I stare into her eyes. "Do you think this is some sort of metaphor, the way she sees herself? Vulnerable, helpless and being used by something or someone controlling her? Mama tells me that aside from her headaches, she's perfectly fine. But my instincts say she doesn't feel safe."

Linnea blinks rapidly, her brows knit together. "Did you tell her your reaction?"

"Of course. Two weeks ago, the day the show opened. The

gallery hosted a party for her, we went out for coffee afterward, and I explained my interpretation. She scoffed at my concerns. Artists are eccentric, I get that. It's the nature of the beast. Still––the painting creeps me out."

I bite my lip, uneasiness churning through my belly. "As I told you the other night. The kid worries me. Even her smiles look dark."

"I'm glad her Ferris wheel's not spinning in my brain," Linnea remarks, her lips twitching into a wry smile.

Her comment lends levity to our conversation, but her eyes search mine, looking for clues, which might help us make sense of our little sister.

"Maybe she painted it after suffering from a migraine." I continue, gathering up my hair, tying it into a back knot. "From what I've read, some folks are forced to hole up in bed for days. How depressing. I suppose Ivy's lucky to have Mama who would tend to her twenty-four-seven, if necessary."

Pasting on a smile, I shake away the sting felt about her comparable indifference to Ella. "When she feels better, we should take her out on the town."

Linnea grins, clapping softly, relieved to have a plan in place. "Oh, yes. Let's. Just the three of us."

Discussion of Ivy is draining me. I haven't been able to unclench since studying her dolphin painting. I feel like concrete blocks have been laid upon my shoulders, and these days, I can't carry any more weight.

"What else do you miss about this town?" I say, diverting us to the prior conversation. "Don't you miss the smells? I remember every morning when we were kids, you'd run outside and sniff the frangipani when the sun hit their blossoms."

Linnea's face softens, her eyes shining. "I still think it's the most wonderful fragrance in the world. Oh..." she says, her palm flying to her mouth. "Remember the time Danny Jack crushed those cockroaches into a powder, said it was cinnamon and told us to sprinkle it on our donuts? It smelled exactly like the spice."

My gut tightens at the sound of his name. "How could I forget? He said it would make our donuts taste like cinnamon rolls."

"I was wary," Linnea says, touching my arm, "but you covered your Krispy Kreme with the stuff. Gobbled it down in a couple of bites. You turned pea-green when he told you you'd eaten the equivalent of two Palmetto bugs. As I recall, you ran to the bathroom and puked your guts out."

"Don't remind me." Clutching my arms across my midriff, a sour taste crawls up my throat, and I swallow, drawing my eyebrows together.

"That incident followed me through elementary school. Remember them calling me Roach? Do you have any idea how miserable I felt when some of the boys told our classmates I was in love with a cockroach?"

Linnea's expression sobers. "Oh yeah. I totally forgot about that nickname. Sorry I brought it up."

My voice rises, words sputtering from my mouth. "But it was nothing compared to what he did to me when I was a teenager. It was like the guy was determined to ruin my life. You can't possibly have forgotten the hot minute we dated in high school?"

Grasping her shoulders, I pull her face into mine, our noses almost touching. I drop my voice to its lowest possible register, as if to insist she never forget my ordeal. "I was barely fifteen, and on our second date, he tried to feel me up. Then he spread those lies. Surely you remember."

"Yep," says Linnea, her mouth tightening, nodding at the memory. "How could I forget? Same guy. When you refused, he spread the nasty rumor about you being into threesomes. And he was like—what?—the only guy you'd ever kissed?"

I drop my hands and sigh, my arms dangling limply at my sides. "He was the second guy I'd kissed. But kissing was as far as it went."

"Whatever. I defended you to anyone who'd listen." Jaw clenching, Linnea shakes her head, adding, "I was beside myself. It was like he'd said it about me, the punk."

"But half the school believed him." My words emerge tiny, sounding more pitiful than I had intended.

I turn away from my sister, biting my bottom lip. The memory of the smirks, whispers and winks directed my way from knotted groups of teens insured my freshman year was unbearable. To this day, whenever I bump into a fellow Catholic school alum and note them gazing at me longer than necessary, my face burns. I'm ashamed of something I didn't even do.

Memories of my vulnerable younger self feeling so debased turn to rage. I swivel back to face my sister. "I've never forgiven him, Linnea. Can you even imagine me having sex at fifteen? Much less, with DJ and Ron Patten at the same time? Spreading those lies was about as low as a guy can go." Balling up my fists, my eyes drill into hers.

"And that Ron Patten character was such a delinquent," Linnea adds, opening my fingers gently like she was unfurling the petals on a bud. "I tried my best to make everyone shut their mouth. Whatever happened to Danny Jack? Did he complete his formal education at Florida State Prison?"

I laugh, wishing he was behind bars. "He runs a store, which sells fish for home and office aquariums. *DJ's Tropical Fish and Supplies.* He carries some of the more exotic species, which can only be caught in the wild. In keeping with his MO, I wouldn't be surprised if the methods he uses to catch the fish are illegal. He likes people to call him DJ now. I'm sure he thinks it makes him sound cool. I think DJ stands for dumb jerk, myself."

"He was only eight years old when he pulled the cockroach stunt," Linnea says, raising her right arm above her head and stretching her torso to the left. "I'll give him a pass."

"I got over the little boy prank, too. Although imagine eating roaches." I shiver. "He forever ruined me for cinnamon. Even today, the smell of it makes me nauseated."

"But the garbage he said about you in high school?" She pinches her nostrils as if a foul smell was seeping into the garage. "That's a different story."

"I know. Ruining my reputation? That, dear sister, I will never forgive."

"Who could blame you," Linnea responds. "You turned into Snow White after the incident." Clasping her hands together behind her head, she rolls her neck from side to side.

"Yep. I may as well have joined the sisterhood. High school was a battlefield." Bending, I pick up a box containing pamphlets that promote our business. "Several years back, we ran into each other, and he tried apologizing, the prick. Of course, I blew him off. So, then he wrote a letter. The son-of-a-bitch actually had the nerve to bring it to this house."

Emitting another pained little hiss, I shift the weight of the handouts so that the box rests atop my hip, "Can you imagine? Danny Jack Wilson came here. To my home. Holding some stupid letter while stammering out his apologies. Of course, I didn't let him past the front door. After he left, I ripped it up without even reading it. I was hoping he'd get his, but from what I hear, DJ's store doesn't lack for customers."

As I carry the pamphlets to the truck, Linnea trots to my side and then opens the back door. I place the box on the floor next to the fire extinguishers and crates of beaded necklaces, which we'll be tossing to the crowd. We ordered ten cases from Dollar Tree. No matter how spectacular your float, or how much your costumes dazzle, if you run out of beads, the spectators ignore you. I turn to face Linnea.

"His business also reserved a spot in the parade. If your paths cross, beware. DJ's quite the ladies' man. And as much as I resent his nastiness to me in high school, he's not bad looking. Although it makes me gag to admit it." I slam the car door with such force, Linnea jumps.

"I remember he had that girlfriend his senior year," Linnea says, a faraway look on her face. "You know, what's her face. Bleached hair to her waist?"

"Yeah. Serena. They broke up after graduation. I think she moved to Tampa, but I'm not sure." Linking our arms together, I shake away thoughts of that disgusting man as we saunter to the project.

"Linnea. Would you be a pet and follow the float? It will be jammed with dancers. You can pass out the pamphlets and serve as our spotter."

"Spotter?" She stops to look at me, a small frown tugging at the sides of her mouth.

"Spotters keep track of the space in the parade. You let the driver know when to speed up or slow down. The officials get ticked when a float causes a big gap in the line. We'll also need you to give us a heads up before we hit the Media Center."

"Fine by me. I'd feel like a fool up there, anyway. And while I'm on the subject of feeling foolish, that sailor outfit you want me to wear looks like our grade school uniform. Except for the skirt, which grazes a half-inch beneath my butt. I want to wear leggings and T-shirts like the dancers."

"Please? Indulge me." I brush her cheek with my fingertips. "The purpose of the parade is to entertain, and we are the entertainment. You won't be alone. I'm dressing up as a mermaid."

"Oh, right. I saw the getup hanging on your door. You'll look like Nicole Kidman at the Academy Awards. Meanwhile, I'll be playing *Daddy's little girl* in some pervert's X-rated fantasy. I want to wear the T."

Linnea steps away from me, lower lip protruding, and—fists on hips—refuses to budge on the matter. Stepping forward, I rest my hands on her shoulders.

"If Sonny can wear a King Neptune costume, complete with tights and a fur-trimmed cape, you can be a sailor."

All color drains from Linnea's face. Why would this costume bother her?

"I have this picture in my mind of how everything should look," I continue, steepling my hands in front of me, begging. "It's already half-ruined with the crappy ribbon. Please, Linnea. Please. You'll look so cute and the judges will love you. I'll owe you big time."

I give her my most pleading, wide-eyed look, all the while knowing she'll acquiesce. Falling back into our childhood roles, I usually have my way with my twinflower.

She sighs and rolls her eyes, color returning to her cheeks. "Well. OK. As long as I don't have to wear my hair in pigtails."

"Deal," I say, throwing my arms around her. "But the sailor cap is non-negotiable." I remove a piece of lint from her shoulder, place it into the palm of my hand, and blow it away.

"So, what's so intriguing about Boise?" I ask, changing the subject before she changes her mind. "Why does the place captivate you so?"

"Boise has its own smells."

"Like what?" I ask, wondering what could possibly compete with frangipani.

Linnea squints as if she's trying to peer through a haze. "Have you ever smelled snow?"

"You know I've never been further north than South Carolina. I always feel like some backwoods cretin when conceding I've been basically nowhere my entire life."

"The world can wait, Delphina. You've got a full plate at the moment."

I follow her gaze about the garage taking in the float and a stack of terra cotta pots waiting for the annuals I haven't had time to buy. I take in Ella's stroller littered with pacifiers. A beaded toy dangles lopsided from the security bar. Its clasp has broken, and I've meant to fix the damn thing for weeks.

"There is one place we plan to visit where you always see snow." I brighten at the thought.

"Where?" Linnea inquires, eyeing me curiously.

"Sonny and I want to take Lita on a trip to Antarctica. She's dying to see penguins marching through glaciers in the wild." I raise an eyebrow and wink. "Her favorite movie is *The March of the Penguins.*"

Linnea claps her hands. "That would be incredible. Can I tag along?"

Snickering, my shoulders relax. "Oh, no. We'll need you to babysit."

She quietens, chewing her lower lip.

"You're scared of a six-month-old." I flick my fingernails lightly at her shoulder.

"No doubt. But I almost forgot. Antarctica's surrounded by three different oceans. You weren't the only one traumatized in high school. But my drama messed me up for good."

Her face slackens, and she bows her head, pinching her cheeks, her technique to staunch the flow of tears. She's done this since we were in pigtails and the gesture melts my heart, making me want to cry as well. It's always been like this, even with her living across the country. Sometimes I feel something akin to phantom limb syndrome; although she's missing from my life, I know when she's upset.

"You remember, Delphy," she continues, wringing her hands. "When I was out there, stuck, floundering in the Atlantic."

Gritting my teeth, I raise my brow, struggling to fix a look of polite interest on my face. Here we go. If she's told the story once, she's told it a thousand times. I've never believed it a second, but she becomes agitated when I question her. I have to hand it to her. Rehashing the tale, her eye contact never wavers. She never looks away, but I can tell she wants to.

As she speaks, I study my twin, looking for some facial tic, a crack in her alibi. Seriously, Linnea? An empty tank of gas derailed your life? It was broad daylight, and help came quickly. I know you better than that. Something else traumatized you, triggering this fear, which is doing all of the talking. Whatever it is you're hiding, it's clear you've been desperately hurt. You've practiced fending off the truth for over a decade. Stick to your story, as ludicrous as it sounds.

"So back to snow," I say, when she's finished, sympathy for my twin inspiring a conversation shift. "How does it smell?"

She regards me, strawberry splotches staining her cheeks. "It's hard to articulate. I can describe the feelings I get when it snows—content, safe, cozy. But I can't explain the smell." She tilts her head to the side. "Snow is so beautiful, and yet when it falls from the sky, at least to me, it smells like nothing."

Chewing a cuticle on the side of her thumb, a puzzled look clouds her face. "Not everything beautiful in nature has a smell. Unless you'd consider nothingness a smell."

"Aha," I say, smirking. "You've combed the country searching for a place that suits, and all you're looking for is nothing? I suppose that's a healthy, Zen approach to life."

Linnea's eyes glaze over. When she speaks, it's in a hushed voice, like she's praying.

"When it snows, it's like a veil drops over the scenery. There's a stillness, a sanctity in the white space surrounding me." Wrapping her arms tightly around her torso, she shivers. "The landscape's a blank page. I snuggle deep inside myself and drift. It's a place where nothing can harm me."

Separated from her by inches, yet feeling worlds apart, I wish she felt this way about her hometown.

"It sounds like Boise makes you happy." I touch her hand.

Her left eye twitches, just like our father's when he's both-ered by something. Splotchy cheeks, twittering eye, her expres-sion contradicts her words: she's anything but happy and has been carrying around a suitcase full of misery for years.

"But you belong down here, Linnea." The inflection in my words is now pleading. "Your family loves you. We need you. This is your home."

She shakes her head so slightly that it's barely noticeable. I stare, transfixed at my sister as she looks at—well—nothing.

"What about you, Delphina?" she asks, at last, her eyelids fluttering as if awakening from a trance. "Are you happy?"

I sigh. "With all of my bitching, it sounds like my life's out of control. And you know what a control freak I am."

Linnea nods, a tiny smile crossing her lips.

"But the grass is green where you water it. Ella's thrown a wrench into our lifestyle, but I cherish her. A husband, a baby, a career I love—it's what I've always wanted. I love my messy life." Glancing at the float, I frown. "At least most of the time."

I check my phone. "Man. I'd best get moving."

Placing the tips of my nails and thumbs together, I create a perfect heart. She mirrors my gesture, and we press our love together.

7. LINNEA

"You've been a godsend, sweetie. We don't need you for anything else until the parade begins."

Delphina adjusts the webbed bodice, tugging it up to ensure her ample breasts—two sizes larger since Ella was born—are covered. It's a miracle the thing stays in place without the assistance of shoulder straps. I flinch as she removes two soaked pads from beneath her bra. And her baby is miles across town? Motherhood is too intimate for me.

"We've worked up a little dance to perform when we have our minute at the stands," she continues, dropping the pads into a paper cup. "Gotta practice the routine—smooth out any last-minute kinks."

She waves her hands towards the other floats. "Check out the competition, Linnea. Have fun. But make sure you're back before seven." She pops open a compact, leveling it in front of her face. Then, she slides a tube of magenta lipstick across her lips.

A group of eight men and women wearing tights, dance flats and "Reef Siren" T-shirts, take their place on the float. They also sport knit caps with fish snouts rising from the top.

Sonny turns on the sound system, and Madonna's voice begins to belt out the lyrics to *Swim*, an electronica tour de force and a favorite of Delphina's.

As the group sings the refrain, I turn, relishing the opportunity to escape. Everything in this town reminds me of the Atlantic. I was so busy with the float, I missed my morning run, which could have channeled my anxiety.

Steering my eyes away from the distant waterfront, I wander down the street. The floats, spectacular in their opulence, are in their assigned places in the line-up area. Glittering costumes and the spirit of this adult playground envelop me, brightening my mood. Everyone's laughing, cracking jokes, giddy with the elaborate silliness of it all. Like snakes shedding their skin after hibernation, people from all over the world have shucked their work-a-day realities to celebrate whimsy.

One of the floats is packed with a dozen or so women wearing green antenna and sparkling, minuscule bikinis. A woman points her ray gun in my direction and, in a distorted nasal voice, speaks to me through a megaphone.

"I am Linda Lightyear. Come with me."

I raise my hands in mock surrender, grinning ear-to-ear. Enjoying myself more than I would ever have guessed, I suddenly wish I were a pluckier, flashier woman. A woman who welcomed, even invited fun into her life. Perhaps I would have been if —

The last float, crafted to resemble a ship, stops me in my tracks. The deck and hull are painted red and, at three levels, it's larger than any of the others I've seen. Black skull and crossbones brand the starboard side, and the muzzle of a cannon protrudes from a small window. *DJ's Tropical Fish and Supplies* is embroidered onto the headsail, which flutters in an offshore breeze.

A large hand lands firmly on my shoulder. Startled, I turn.

"Well, well, well. Linnea Chandler." My name rolls around

the mouth of this gorgeous man like he is savoring a sip of rich Bordeaux.

I look up into eyes the color of milk chocolate, fringed with lush caramel-colored lashes. Who could forget those eyes? His hair is sun-bleached, the color of cedar driftwood, and it sweeps across his forehead, falling around his cheekbones and into the nape of his neck. Wearing a black T-shirt and faded jeans, his golden tanned, muscular body is a good four inches taller than mine.

"Danny Jack Wilson? Oh, sorry," I stammer, blushing under his gaze. "I hear you go by DJ now."

The man has morphed from a Dixie Cup filled with Kool-Aid into a tall flute of champagne. My neck dampens, and heart skips a beat.

"Yeah. It's like my mom wanted to name me after my dad, but she was confused as to who he was."

I'm not sure whether to smile or frown. She did have a slew of boyfriends, now that I recall. I keep my expression neutral.

"Seriously. What's it been?" He scrunches his brows together. "Thirteen years?"

"It's been fifteen years since I left for college." I twist a strand of hair, which falls beneath my shoulder around my forefinger.

"I'm surprised you didn't mistake me for my sister," I add, shrugging, trying to appear nonchalant. "Whenever I visit home, all the townies think I'm Delphina. Everyone's forgotten she has a twin."

"I never forgot. I hear you're living in Idaho."

I nod, perplexed he'd know where I live. Here I am, having a conversation with the boy who once fed Delphina cockroaches and later spread rumors that she was into threesomes. My mouth feels chalky, so I press my lips together, moistening them with the tip of my tongue.

"I could always tell the two of you apart," he continues,

smoothly. Smiling into my eyes, he slides his hands into the front pockets of his bleached denim jeans.

I raise my chin. "I'm an inch taller than my sister. Identical twins usually vary a bit. We're like two pies made from the same recipe."

I clasp my hands together, warming to my favorite subject. "Say, for instance, I made a Key Lime Pie, you made a Key Lime Pie, and we both used the same recipe."

"I know where this is going," he says, and then chuckles. A strand of hair falls into his eyes, and he brushes it back mindlessly. "You're referring to your DNA, right?"

"Smart man," I say, biting back my stupid grin. "Maybe our oven temperatures vary, which would cause my meringue to brown more than yours. Or perhaps you used Key limes while I used Persians. And don't get me started on the different brands of condensed milk. So even though our recipes—our genetic makeup—are identical, our pies would be different. Not by much, but they would still vary."

His eyes are wandering. I've bored him already. But so what? I shouldn't be talking to him in the first place. I force myself to quit babbling, I do that when nervous. Feeling my face grow hot, I bite my lower lip, glancing around. A man wearing a Martian suit with a headpiece resembling an oversized brain strolls by, and an older, heavyset woman with thick false eyelashes follows. She sports a Carmen Miranda headpiece, painted with the rich iridescent blues, greens and coppers of a peacock.

Now's the time to make my escape. Delphina painted this man as the root of evil, so why do I linger, my legs feeling like they're made of cement? I inhale his scent; a mix of spearmint on his breath, and musky aftershave around his neck. I'm aware of his physical presence in a way that rattles, even frightens me. It's a familiar feeling I get around a certain type of man. I take a step back, as if wary of stepping into a sharp-toothed trap.

"You obviously like to bake," he says, interrupting my thoughts. His eyes find mine and my fear dissipates as my thoughts latch onto cooking.

"I love to bake. Not only is it therapeutic, but it's also my currency. I preface small requests with brownies or cookies; larger ones with a torte or multi-layered cake."

I clear my throat, not liking the sound of my voice. How it quickens in time to the rapid acceleration of my pulse. He nods, his expression indicating he's interested in what I'm saying. So, I continue.

"For many, baking's a time-sucking hassle. But for me, it's soothing—an escape route. It's fun to get lost in the nuts and bolts of a recipe and be rewarded with something scrumptious and sweet. A kitchen, any kitchen, is my favorite place in the world."

Truer words were never spoken. Life is chaotic, and adding food prep to the mix can be daunting. But at least for me, when combining ingredients for a recipe, I can give shape to the mess. With life, it's not so easy. When depressing thoughts set in, the hum of the refrigerator and thwack of my knife stares my sadness down.

"Linnea. I have a favor to ask of you. I love sweets, so how about teaching me the basics? I've never so much as made a cookie in my entire life." He places the tip of his forefinger on my wrist and removes it quickly, shoving his hand into his pocket.

I steel myself to refuse his request, but the place where he touched me tingles. The volume of his voice is soft, and he seems curious about learning what interests me. There is something deeply seductive about this man. He tried to apologize to Delphina. Twice he tried, even hand-delivering a letter. There should be a statute of limitations when it comes to high school idiocy. And what could such a benign request hurt?

"Sure. I'll give you a lesson." I shrug, trying to appear indifferent, keeping my inflection neutral.

"So, it's a deal." His lips curve up into a smile as his eyes skim my body. Troubled, I tug at the back of my skirt, making sure it's covering my panties.

"I see you've retained the same fashion sensibilities. Your outfit reminds me of your school uniform."

I tuck my sailor shirt further into my waistband and then smooth my skirt. I despise this outfit and the way it makes me feel. Vulnerable. Easy. At least I refused the eyeliner Delphina tried making me wear. A complicated emotion––dangerous yet erotic––travels up my spine. I feel the heat rise in my face.

"Delphina owes me big time for this one," I say, a bit too loudly, searching for words to cover up my uneasiness. "I feel like a punk schoolgirl on her way to juvenile detention."

He smirks. "I should have dressed up as a cop. I could have handcuffed you and taken you to juvie, myself."

Beneath his wit, and the warmth of his soft brown eyes, my uneasiness fades. This man means me no harm. Flushing with pleasure, I turn to his float.

"You've got a nautical theme going. Ours too. It's a coral motif. My sister's passionate about the reefs."

"I know. Delphina's intense." He darts a side-glance at me. "Intense in a good way," he adds quickly.

You've got that right, I think, looking straight ahead. Why would she tear up his note of apology without even reading it?

"Your float's three-tiered." I shield my eyes with the palm of my hand. "Ours is only one level. I'm glad Delphina's not here. She'd freak at the competition."

"She has nothing to worry about," he replies. Removing a pair of dark Aviators from his pocket, he slides them over the bridge of his nose. "Let's be honest. This year's theme is *Space Gorillas,* and we're going with *Peter Pan.*" He points to the top level. "Captain Hook and Tinkerbell are adjusting the sail as we speak."

The afternoon sun hits his company's float at such an angle it's difficult to see their faces, only the silhouette of diaphanous fairy wings.

"I was hoping my staff could come up with something more original," he continues. "Something sexier." He fires a rapid glance at my skirt and my stomach summersaults. "Pirates are has-beens—it's a tired theme. Especially in the Keys. I've nothing against veteran Disney characters, but let's get real. Their careers aren't exactly smokin' these days. There have been more Peter Pan re-mixes than Disney can print money."

Removing his glasses, he wipes them on a fold of his shirt. "But I wasn't any help and had nothing to do with its execution. I'm all business. When God was handing out the creative genes, he passed me by."

I smile. A man who can poke fun at himself. Nice.

"Where's your pirate hat?" I ask, turning to face him. He's the only person, besides the organizers, not dressed in costume.

"I came to wish my staff bon voyage. I'm not one who enjoys playing dress-up."

"We have that in common." I adjust the clip securing my sailor cap. "What are your feelings about the fate of the Palooza?"

"I know many locals want it canceled. Not me. Quote Dr. Seuss: *Fantasy is a necessary ingredient in living. It's a way of looking at life through the wrong end of a telescope.*"

Something rises and flutters up from my chest. The man quotes Dr. Seuss. Charming. Delphina must be wrong about DJ. Everyone knows eight-year-old boys should be quarantined. And teenaged boys are worse––hormone puppets, best off in a military academy, a stack of porn hidden in their locker.

He glances at his phone. "I've scheduled a meeting and

need to get back to the store. In fact, I've got to dash. Hey." He slides his phone into the back pocket of his jeans. "I'd love to catch up. Hear more about what you're up to these days. Wanna' meet for a drink after the parade? I can finagle a table at the Bottlecap. Now there's some amazing people-watching."

My fingers dart to my mouth. Uneasiness hovers inside me. I don't doubt he's changed since high school, but would our meeting be worth upsetting my sister? Especially since my time down here is marked? Besides, my rules of the road include never allowing an adult beverage to pass through these lips until I'm sure. Absolutely sure it's safe to drop my guard. Alcohol muddles my fortitude—God only knows I've learned that lesson.

"I'm going to help Delphina and Sonny break the float down. Besides. I don't feel comfortable in these clothes." I tug at the loose end of a red scarf knotted around my neck. "Not my style."

Looking disappointed, he whistles softy. I feel his breath against my cheek. Gentle. Warm. When he regards me, it feels like we're in a separate space with no one else around, a world into our own. Looking up into his eyes, I soften.

"Maybe coffee sometime?"

I brush my twin sister from my mind. It's just coffee. And, if we click, if I'm sure he's a good guy, I'll figure out a way to help them mend the fence.

"Coffee it is," he laughs. "And then there's the cooking class you promised. Maybe at The Maiden Tower?"

So now this man—Delphina's mortal enemy—is planning two dates. I should make my excuses and bolt. But then again. There's his height, the breadth of his shoulders, the easy way our conversation flows. I feel a shiver of something—curiosity, desire? My resolve to exit falters.

He eyes me quizzically. "So, what's the real story?"

"The real story?" I repeat, my voice monotone, smile fading.

70

Does he want to delve into the nasty rumors he spread while we were in high school now? He said he has an appointment and the parade will be beginning soon.

"I mean, umm, is the hearsay true. About the lighthouse legend?" He speaks hesitantly, unsure, as if he knows what I'm thinking and wants to avoid the topic as much as myself. "It's been a source of local bar debate for years."

I emit a sigh of relief, accustomed to fielding this question. "To hear my father tell it, the Maiden's story is gospel. But I'm skeptical. Where's the evidence?" Smirking, I shrug. "Whatever. My folks have worked up an amusing schtick around the legend, which at least keeps the rooms booked."

"I know. Your famous Evening Hour." Eyes widening, he shakes his forefinger at me. "Some say the Maiden has unfinished business."

My laughter sounds hollow, bored. "Alcohol fuels nonsense. Don't the barflies have something better to buzz about than gossip from the mid-eighteen hundreds? I've heard the story so many times, it doesn't faze me." At least there's one fear I can wipe off the list.

He chuckles. "Well then, back to business. What's your number? I'll treat you to the best Key Lime Pie in town."

"Blue Heaven, right?"

"You read my mind."

I give him my number, which he taps into his cell. We gaze at each other, a beat longer than necessary, and I'm the first to look away, flustered.

"Gotta fly." He places his finger, again, on my wrist. His touch lingers a heartbeat longer than required and a thrill courses up my arm. Then, he turns, his long legs making swift strides towards town. Suddenly he stops, pauses a moment, and winks at me over his shoulder. I flash him a smile.

A glow sparks inside my sternum and then crackles into a flame sending sparks towards this man who has so clearly bewitched me. A siren goes off somewhere north of here, popping my bubble. I check the time: 6:55. I've only five minutes to get back to Delphina. Grinning, I break into a run.

No doubt I will spend the rest of the evening half oblivious to the parade, wondering if his touch was with intention.

8. DELPHINA

It's twilight, the sky's the crackling glow of the burning end of a cigar, and the first float in the procession just launched into the streets. We're sandwiched towards the front of this fifty-float extravaganza of fanciful characters, light shows and music. Linnea barely made it back in time to grab the pamphlets.

This is the longest time I've ever spent away from my daughter. Having changed my soaked breast pads three times, I've called Lita every hour to ensure all is well. She tells me Ella's taking the bottle, this time cooperating, and I'm saddened knowing we've traversed our first rite of separation.

Our float begins to inch forward, and I grab Sonny's hand to calm my nerves. Weaving his fingers into mine, he squeezes me back, and then we unleash our hands to wave at the crowd.

I force myself to smile and toss beads to the onlookers as our float ambles forward, secured to the back of the truck. The audience is thin, and the overall ambiance lacks the energy I was expecting. I feel self-conscious being the center of attention.

As the procession crawls down streets in the direction of the Gulf of Mexico, the hum in the sidewalks grows louder, the crowds increasingly dense. Our driver makes a sharp right-hand turn onto Duval, and I fall sideways into Sonny. A sudden explosion of discordant music, roars and cheers choke the air as we begin the one-mile stretch towards the Atlantic.

White flashes pop around me like a swarm of fireflies, and excitement courses through my veins. Any inhibitions I may have felt evaporate, and I join my committee members, shimmying and strutting across the float. Remembering our business intentions, I point to the sign, cup my hands over my mouth and shout: "Snorkel the reefs with The Coral Princess!"

My message is greeted with cheers and raised fists. Suddenly, I notice Ivy's head. How could anyone miss that golden festival of curls cresting the wave of the crowd? She's positioned on the shoulders of a dark-haired, bearded man, and a group of artists I recognize from the gallery surrounds her. She waves a cowboy hat into the air and shouts, "Hey Delphy. Throw me some beads."

I bend, grab a fistful of sparkling necklaces from a box, and fling them towards her. She tosses back her head, laughing uproariously as she catches them mid-air. That doesn't look like a headache to me. I search the crowd for my parents as Linnea breaks from the float and pushes through the mob. Ivy climbs down from her wobbly perch, and my sisters embrace. Whispering into each other's ears, they hug again, and then Linnea heads back towards the float.

Within the throng, an elderly man looks around. He appears dazed, confused and frightened. Grasping a flea-bitten mutt into his chest, his expression indicates he's mistaken the celebrants for an angry mob. I wave at him warmly and blow the man a kiss. Linnea walks to his side, speaks to him, and then pats him on the shoulder. She must have said something reassuring as his countenance relaxes. He smiles at her. Compassion is the way of Linnea. She has an innate sense of goodness and sensitivity, which most people don't seem to believe in these days.

Continuing our snail pace progression, a young woman on the street, weaving and obviously plastered, bends over and vomits. The folks around her scatter like mice. Two men, dressed in the attire of Parade Officials, scurry over. One man pulls the woman up and then links his arm under her armpits to steady her. She flops into his side and the crowd parts to let them through. The other man, a mop and bucket in hand, begins cleaning up the mess. Not a job for the faint-hearted.

Linnea trots up to the float and advises me the Media Center is coming up on our right. Photographers are swarming like flies, and I give a shout out to our group to assume their positions. Two dancers bend forward from their hips, each with an arm extending forward, and a leg stretching to the sky behind. The remaining troupe, myself included, pose in between the dancers. We squat—like a chorus of frogs—place our palms on thighs and cock our heads.

When we reach the Media Center, our truck pauses. Madonna's voice blasts from our float and, to spiked adrenaline and blinding lights, we break out into the choreography we've been rehearsing for weeks. Our one-minute time allotment passes in the blink of an eye, and we bow to the sound of screams, hoots and hollers from the crowd.

Captured in an adrenaline high, we continue down Duval. A little girl with chestnut-colored curls is waving her arms wildly in my direction. A man, whom I presume to be her father, holds her up so that she might capture a treasure. Leaning forward, and aiming a necklace directly towards her hands, I toss it gently. The unabashed, wide-eyed thrill on her face as she catches it mid-air, encourages me to scan the crowd for more children.

Excited shouts of *beads, beads, throw me some beads* rain down upon us. We've transcended our flesh and blood personas and are brilliant gods and goddesses showering our subjects with jewels. The feeling is epic; euphoric.

Linnea, again, is to the side of the float, pointing in the direction of a popular cabaret. "The Judge's Stand is up ahead on your left. Next to *La Te Da*." Once again, we repeat our performance, this time with an energy that's electrified.

Several minutes past the Judge's Stand, the truck comes to a stop. How could two and a half hours have flown by so rapidly? I feel like Cinderella after the ball. Closing my eyes, I hold onto this moment, clutching my glass slippers, keeping the magic alive. I want nothing to do with reality; I want to carry the momentum, excitement and glory forward.

Opening my eyes, I gaze around me, at the floor of the flatbed––the ribbon flattened and ragged from our dance––at the dancers, the makeup on their faces smeared in sweat.

A moment of silence passes between us, and then one of the committee members––unleashing a rebel yell––tosses his shark hat into the sky. We burst into laughter and then pull ourselves into a group hug. After untangling, we gaze at each other, panting, our eyes wide in wonder.

Pulling my dress up to my calves, I disembark the float, rubbing my jaw. My face hurts from smiling so much. Leaning against the front door of our pick-up, Sonny speaks to the driver, who lights up a smoke. I approach the men, and my husband envelops me into the wing of his cape. Looking up into his face, we kiss.

Linnea walks towards us, her face painted in rosy splotches of excitement.

"I gave out every one of your business pamphlets. The people seemed genuinely interested."

"Hopefully they're not swept from the street with the rest of tomorrow's garbage," I reply. Stepping away from the folds of my husband's cape, I smooth my hair and then adjust my bodice.

"But honestly, Linnea. Thank you." I give her a quick hug, consumed with the pride our mission was accomplished.

"So, what's with Ivy? Is that what you call a migraine?" I smile at Linnea as she fumbles with bobby pins trying to remove her sailor cap with seeming contempt.

"She said she was feeling much better so snuck out of the house," she replies. "She seemed perfectly fine. Exuberant, in fact. Just another fun-loving, beautiful woman in a fun-loving, beautiful town."

"She snuck out? Like a naughty teenager? Now I'm convinced. She's overprotected and out of touch with reality. That could be a big part of her problem."

"Maybe she'd come down to earth if she had her own place," Linnea adds, handing the cap to me with a shudder like it's contaminated.

"Will we see her later?" I ask.

With the hat, I fan away smoke wafting from the window of our truck, making a mental note to let everyone know that smoking is taboo in our vehicle. Doesn't the man see the baby seat?

"She had to return to the lighthouse," Linnea replies. "Apparently, Mama has her on a short leash. She'll freak if she noticed she escaped."

"That's ridiculous. Mama's way over-protective. Has been since she was a kid. But Ivy's a grown woman now."

"I agree, Delphina, but we haven't been asked to join that committee, have we?" Playfully, she bumps my shoulder with her fist.

"That was the first time I've seen her since I've been down," she continues. "We made plans to visit in a couple of days; when I'm situated at the Fog Horn House. But hey. The night is young. Let's go watch the rest of the floats come in." She claps her hands in excitement.

Turning to Sonny, in a teasing sing-song voice, I say, "Oh baby, float a twenty to me, 'cause I really need a drink, and I really need to pee."

His fingers tap a rhythm in the crook of my back, sparking a tingle in my neck. The man plays me like a million-dollar Stradivarius.

"I could use a high-octane brew myself, but it will have to wait." He turns away from me to pat his truck with the same affection he just showed my rear. "Someone must stay sober to get this monster home."

He opens the door of the truck and says something to the driver, who immediately stubs out his smoke. Then, he removes his wallet from the glove compartment. Bending over the seat into the back, he retracts my purse, which is hidden beneath a towel.

"I'll bring you back some street food," I say, taking my bag.

"You'll need more than a twenty." Sliding a hand down the slope of my hips, he hands me forty bucks. "And buy your sister a drink. She earned it."

"Bless you." I slip the money into my wallet, and, rising onto tiptoes, kiss his cheek. Linnea grabs my hand, and we maneuver our way through the throngs towards the street vendors.

After placing an order for Crispy Cajun Alligator, which tastes like a cross between spicy fried fish and chicken, I text Lita to inform we'll be home within a couple of hours. Then, I turn to my sister, grasping her shoulders.

"Wasn't that an absolute blast?"

"It was crazy." Linnea shakes her head, her eyes blinking furiously as if she were exiting the set of *The Last Jedi*.

"Such an amazing experience," she continues. "The ribbon made no difference in the end. It would have been flattened and trampled anyway."

"We'll know soon enough. The judges will announce the winner tomorrow." Linnea's words sound excited, and there is a wildness cast about her face that I haven't seen in years.

I pay for the snacks and grab a handful of napkins, stuffing them into the bag. We walk towards a tiki-styled hut, and I order a frozen mango margarita. Linnea orders a virgin one for herself, forever picky about when and where she imbibes. Drinks in hand, we worm ourselves into an opening on the street. At last, we can relax and enjoy the final few minutes of the parade.

Suddenly, the Parade Officials halt the floats, to shoo away teenagers who are collecting beads in the streets, dangerously close to the vehicles.

Linnea points to a woman wearing fairy wings, and a glittering lime green dress. Her arms are decorated with fish tattoos and––wearing stilettos––she twirls about on a three-tiered float. Eyes wide, my sister's fingertips light to her mouth. I look up, noticing the flag: *DJ's Tropical Fish and Supplies.* I scan the float, looking for DJ. Where's that perverted asshole hiding?

"You've got to be kidding me," Linnea murmurs, surprise in her voice.

"What?"

"It's her––aisle thirteen." My sister wears an expression of incredulity.

I take a deep swallow from my cup and then turn to her, regarding her blankly. "I have no idea what you're talking about."

"I told you about the pierced-up punkster sitting next to me on the plane." Her eyes cloud, confused. "You know. The one from Indiana. The woman who seemed so rude. She may be sportin' wings now, but I can guaran-damn-tee she ain't no angel. Crazy she's also in the parade."

I recall the conversation. Linnea wastes far too much energy fretting over perceived slights, especially from strangers.

"Small world." I take another slow lingering sip. Coming down from my adrenaline rush, I embark upon a different, less frenzied high and study the woman.

"Hunh. No surprise DJ's interpretation of sweet little

Tinkerbell would be a sex pistol. And it figures he'd have the biggest float. I'll bet he also drives a Corvette to compensate for his tiny..." I press my thumb and forefinger together and then open them an inch... "masculine organ. Although I certainly wouldn't know about that."

I smirk, giggling, leaning into my sister, glancing at her face, which is suddenly rigid and solemn. Linnea bites her lower lip, shifts away from me, and appears uncomfortable with my words.

"But her originating flight was Fort Wayne," she muses, shaking her head. "How can she live in Fort Wayne and work in Key West?"

"She could have been visiting relatives in Indiana. I've never seen her around, but she might live in town." I gaze at my sister, ready to end all discussion surrounding DJ's stupid float.

"Don't overthink it," I say louder, the sound of my voice sharper than I had intended.

Linnea points to the float, oblivious to my words. "Oh look, Delphina. She recognizes me. She's trying to get my attention."

Linnea reaches into the air and catches the beads, which the woman tosses her way. Beads dangling from her fingers and glittering like tiddlywinks, Linnea cups her hands around her mouth and yells, "Thank you." The woman, wearing a broad smile, waves at her with abandon.

Linnea studies the woman, scrunching her eyes together. Then, she nods her head and bites the side of her lip, as if forgiving Tinkerbell her previous perceived slight. She turns to me while looping the beads around her neck.

"I saw him."

"Who?"

"DJ. He introduced himself to me before the parade. Or rather, re-introduced himself."

"Don't make me barf." Sticking out my tongue, I point my

forefinger towards the back of my throat. "I hope he didn't douse you with his infamous charm."

Linnea's face colors and her eyes skim the crowd, avoiding my gaze and comment. "We should be getting back to the float."

"You go ahead." I hand her the bag of fried gator. "Could you give these to Sonny before they get cold? I'll hit a loo at one of the bars down the block." I lean over, grabbing my gut. "If I don't hurry, I'll burst a gasket."

Linnea squeezes my hand, turns, and then disappears into the crowd.

I fire one last glance at the float and catch my breath, stunned. My hands begin to tingle, and my feet feel like they're melting into the sidewalk. Sparkling sheaths of satiny ribbon in various shades of turquoise are woven together. Attached to the bottom sides of the vessel, they simulate the ocean, bending up, like waves lapping the hull of the boat. Dusted with glitter, they appear to be dancing in sunlight.

A burly man dressed up as Captain Hook walks towards Tinkerbell and swings a massive, brawny arm around her shoulder. He leers at me from the float as it begins to move away.

"That's my silk," I murmur to myself, my face burning. "DJ stole my damn ribbon," I say, much louder.

A woman glances at me and then looks away quickly, assuming I'm one more spectator who's had one too many.

Furious, I turn and plow forward blindly, into a knot of people trying to exit the parade at its conclusion. Cagey and irritated, most appear to be inebriated. Pressing into me, they're pushing and shoving, absorbing me into their mass. A man trips into me, and I spill my drink over the front of my dress.

"Hey. Watch it!" I yell, dropping the now empty cup onto the ground. His eyes dart around like a trapped animal, and he mouths *sorry*, as thick, sticky iciness streams down between my cleavage.

Disoriented and jostled, I'm forced to move with the wave of the crowd, praying for a side street to exit. Claustrophobia weighs heavy, and I'm having trouble catching my breath. Terrified, I wipe my eyes with my fists, blackening them with the stain of mascara.

Shoulders and knees bump into me and an elbow lodges into my bladder. I can't hold back, and warm urine escapes, trickling down my legs. There is no way out, and the mob holds me up, moving me forward. One guy swings a tight punch at another man's jaw, and then they begin to fight—grizzlies locked together within a heap of warm, pressing flesh. I cover my head with my arms, trading glances with a woman to my side. The fear radiating in her eyes is the same, I'm sure, in my own.

An ear-piercing whistle blasts behind me, as police officers elbow their way into our cluster. The group manages to unknot, disband, and scatter. My hem is soiled, ripped, and hangs about my feet like an umbrella destroyed in a storm.

Collapsing into the pavement, I roll to my side, pull my knees into my chest and cup my head into my arms. A metallic taste of copper and salt swims in my mouth. I must have bit my tongue when I fell, and now, I feel like I'm going to vomit.

"Delphina. Is that you?" asks one of the officers, stooping down, his face peering at me between my arms. "Honey. Are you OK?"

Sobbing, my body shaking, I lean into him. "Andy. Please. Take me to Sonny."

9. LINNEA

"These sandals are speaking to me," the salesman says, securing the buckle around my ankle. The man is sleek and attractive, impeccably coiffed from his combed-back hair to his crocodile driving shoes. He stands, steps back, and places his forefinger on his chin.

"What are they telling you?" I ask, rising from the banquette. Upholstered in luxurious crushed velvet, it's the shade of dense, rich Bordeaux. I lift my foot, admiring the thin black straps swaddling my ankle.

"They're saying that when you wear these shoes, you'll be admired as a beautiful woman who is carefree and"—he raises an eyebrow—"sexy."

Angling his head, he cups his palm to his ear.

"Wait. They're telling me more."

"What?"

"They tell me they're happy on your feet."

I giggle. "Is that right? Would you please tell the little darlings I'm delighted to be wearing them?"

"My dear. You two are now intimate with one another. You don't need me to serve as an interpreter."

Suddenly, I regret having been lured by these sirens in the window dressing of Sienna Leather, a store smelling of money and animal hides. This salesman is too good at his job.

I flex my toes and then bend to adjust the strap around the swell of my left heel. "What's the price for these flirty kittens?"

"Lucky you. We're trying to deplete last year's inventory before the season begins. So, they're"—he checks the price on the back of the box—"forty percent off." Squatting, he removes the shoes from my feet. Looking up, he bestows a conspiratorial wink, his voice a whisper. "A steal at one-hundred and thirty."

I glance at the box containing the shoes, which rests against my thigh as a companionable lover. I remove a sandal, fingering the soft leather. I've still got two or three hundred bucks on my Master Card before it's maxed out. I return the shoe to the box and smile at the salesman.

"Sounds good. I'll take 'em." I stand, and fumble for my wallet in the crevices of my shoulder bag. One of the straps is secured to the hemp-woven pouch with an extra-large safety pin. The salesman gives it a once-over, and a frown creeps across his face.

"We've got a collection of marvelous purses that would be stunning with your new shoes." He nods, his eyes drilling into mine. "All on sale."

"That's OK. I'm good." I smile at him brightly, as he returns my card. "Catch you later."

"Ta-ta for now," he says, as I exit the shop, turning to wave at him from around my shoulder.

What was I thinking? How did I get suckered into buying a pair of expensive shoes when I haven't yet secured a job? But I can't live my life in running gear. What worked as a wardrobe in Boise doesn't translate down here. Delphina gave me a couple of cute, swishy sun-dresses, which she claims to have outgrown. If she knew I was planning to wear the fuchsia number this afternoon with DJ, she might not have been so generous.

She was inconsolable after her upset at the parade last week. Sonny and I freaked when a cop—a tow-headed guy we grew up with—escorted her back to the float. With mascara-smeared eyes and the bottom of her dress ripped to shreds, it looked like she'd been in a fight. Seeing her in that state undid me, triggering long ago memories best left buried. We got her home and into a hot bath as soon as we could.

But more than being caught up in a street brawl and the humiliation she felt after peeing down her legs, she's furious about the ribbon, which decorated DJ's float. Delphina's convinced he stole the bolts from Parade Headquarters to torment her, just as he traumatized her when she was a child and teenager.

In our conversation, however, DJ said he had nothing to do with the float's construction. But I bloody well better keep today's meeting with him under wraps. I can only imagine her reaction, and it would be brutal. I'll speak with DJ about the incident. If it is, as Delphina swears, the ribbon she'd ordered, there must be an explanation, some sort of mix-up at headquarters.

I take a right, heading up side streets towards the lighthouse. Walking past the dense and tangled landscaping, I'm still surprised how a ten-inch houseplant in Idaho is a ten-foot tree down here. Last night was my first evening spent at the Fog Horn House, which, as The Maiden Tower Inn brochure states: *offers our guests a wonderful sense of privacy.* After a week spent sleeping on Delphina's pullout muffling Ella's wails with a pillow over my head, the plush double bed, soft lighting and quiet privacy is a God-send.

Arriving at the inn, and through the slats of the garden gate fence, I see Mama, Daddy and another man seated at a table. I've spoken to my parents of my recent cash flow issues, and they would think it madness I'd purchased shoes from a swanky store. The Fog Horn House is several feet away from the garden, so there is no way for me to avoid them. I'll slip into the front door of the inn, hide the bag in the kitchen pantry, and retrieve it later when the coast is clear. Then, if she compliments the sandals, I'll tell her I bought them in Boise.

Mama stands, her slender frame silhouetted against the late morning sun, and beckons me over with her arm.

"Linnea. Over here. We've a visitor."

My cheeks burn. But why should I feel like I'm ten years old and caught stealing candy? I'm thirty-three, will have a job soon enough, and have no reason to apologize. I walk to the garden gate and open the latch.

"Oh," Mama says, glancing at the burgundy and cream bag clutched in my fist. "Sienna Leather. I've heard it's a lovely store."

"You should check it out. The salesman looks like a matinee idol."

"They all do, honey," she says, smoothing her hair, which looks particularly wild in today's thick, moist air. She ties it into a knot at the nape of her neck.

"I bought some sandals. They're having a huge sale. All I have are running shoes, so I'm desperate."

She sticks her bare feet out from under her chair and wiggles her toes. "My favorite brand of footwear."

I laugh, relieved not to be reprimanded for my indulgence, and glance at our guest. Oh my. It's Bill, our neighbor. Aren't they enemies? An open bottle of rum is on the table—the *Bermudez Don Armando* Daddy mentioned—surrounded by three, half-emptied shot glasses. At eleven in the morning, no less. How are they supposed to run the inn after drinking? Mindless extravagance must run in our family.

Daddy notices my look of surprise and smiles, raising an eyebrow.

"You remember Bill?"

I place my bag on top of a vacant table and extend my hand

in his direction. "Oh. Bill," I stammer, casting a swift glance at Mama. "I never had an opportunity to express my condolences about Alma. She was such a lovely person. Always had cookies and kind words when we were kids."

He takes my hand, shakes it, and I pull out a chair. His face is sun-damaged, patched and peeling beneath the rim of his Panama hat. An avid fisherman, he often brought us snapper and grouper when we were growing up.

His chin trembles, and his eyes well with tears. "I miss her every day." He pulls a handkerchief from his back pocket, wipes his eyes and then blows his nose. "But at least I have wonderful neighbors to support me. You know Poppy brought supper over every evening for a couple of weeks after she passed." He turns to Mama, smiling. "She still does from time to time." Flushing, his gaze falls to his hands, appearing ashamed.

My eyes flit from Mama to Daddy, surprised at this turn of events with the alleged chicken abuser.

Daddy looks at me and laughs, noting my confusion. "This morning, after serving breakfast, I thought *enough is enough*. So, I went over to Bill's house, cajoled him into going to the garden, lingering by Liberace's cage and rattling the door. I wanted him to pretend he was going to set the old bird free."

He drums his fingers on the table, chuckling to himself. "I knew your Mama was washing dishes and could see him from the back window."

Mama regards my father, shaking her head, a solemn look on her face. But then she bursts into a peal of laughter.

"I ran from the kitchen hollering and screaming, *Liberace, Liberace*, about to tear Bill's head off. And then your father comes over and lets me in on their shenanigans."

She tops off their shot glasses. "Tit for tat, I reckon." Raising their jiggers, they toast. She takes a tiny sip and then swivels to face me.

"I didn't realize this, but Bill tells me that once the chickens are relocated, the new owners must sign an agreement stating the birds will only be used as pets." She cuts her eyes to Bill, shaking her forefinger at him. "Nevah' for Sunday dinner. The adopted chickens arrive with a signed letter from the Mayor, himself. Imagine, Linnea." She looks at me and smiles, wonder glistening in her eyes. "The Mayor. The letter certifies their authentic breeding as *Key West Gypsy Chickens*.

"Poppy," Bill says, shaking his head, his eyes cast down, looking like he's lost his best friend. "I'm so damn sorry. Sometimes I get so worked up by the insolence of those birds, I operate in a fury." He lays a thick, freckled forefinger on her wrist. "That said, I've been thinking. The cage was too small. And it was cruel of me to separate the hen from her chicks."

He turns to Daddy, his voice rising. "But those dang birds do whatever the hell they want. And their mating habits." He shudders. "They're so loud and barbaric in their passion, they could care less who's watching."

"It's like the world at large," Mama says, a dreaminess about her face. "A mess of unrestrained passion, ricocheting back and forth among all of God's creatures."

"The birds are descendants from the cock-fighting rings in Havana," Daddy says, admiration in his voice. "You can bet they know a thing or two about surviving."

"I wish Great Egrets ruled the island," I say, piping in, relieved the Battle of Bill has ended in a truce. "With their white-feathered carriage and those long delicate legs, they're like the descendants of royalty. I'd take them any day over brawling hens and roosters."

"Amen," Bill says, nodding his head, his eyes glimmering as if delighted to find a new ally.

"At least the chicken's appetite for cockroaches keeps those nasty bugs at bay," Daddy comments, taking a sip of the hallowed liquor.

An image of Delphina, with her plaited braids and rosy

cheeks eating the infested donut springs to mind. Then again, as a teenager, dampening her pillow with tears, certain everyone believed she was a tramp. I wince.

I stand, feeling guilty about meeting DJ, and tired of this rum-laced discussion about birds. "Oh well," I sigh. "I'm glad y'all mended the fence. I'm meeting a friend for coffee."

"Leah?" Mama asks, putting down her shot glass, giving me the once over. "Every time I run into her, she makes me promise to have you call her."

She turns to Bill. "They were close in high school."

"Those days are long gone, Mama. Remember? She sent me that birthday card with a talking horse telling me to put spurs on my boots and take the reins on my life. The horse kept neighing like it was about to gallop off of the card and trample me."

Mama tries to suppress a smile playing about her mouth as she studies her fingernails.

"Seriously, Mama. It hurt my feelings."

She looks up at me. "Aww. Forgive her, honey. Sometimes you take things too personally. You have such a great sense of humor. She thought you'd find it amusing."

I look down, muttering at my feet. "Like Leah's something special working the gift shop at Truman House." I scratch my nose, avoiding their eyes. "Maybe I'll call her next week. But today I'm meeting a woman you don't know. She knows a couple of places that may be hiring."

Mama told me white lies are acceptable if you're trying to protect someone's feelings. If my meeting with DJ got back to Delphina, she would be livid.

I look up and smile, changing the subject. "Any word from Nina? It's been almost two weeks."

Daddy glances at Mama before speaking. "Not a thing. Her sister's trying to get her to go to a sobriety clinic."

"She won't take my phone calls," Mama adds, worry lines fretting around her pursed lips as she takes a sip of rum.

"I'm posting the position on job sites today," Daddy says, suddenly serious.

Mama touches his arm. "No, you're not. We're gonna keep her job open a little bit longer."

"It's quite a dilemma." I glance about the garden, at a loss for what else to say. Bed and Breakfasts are demanding enough; they can't add breakfast prep and cleanup to their list.

"Well. Anyway." I sigh. "I'm gonna visit with Ivy before meeting my friend."

Mama's head jerks around, startled. "Ivy?"

"I haven't seen her since I got here," I reply, a whine hovering about my words. I don't dare tell her I saw my little sister at the parade. That would, no doubt, set off fireworks.

"Actually, this may be a perfect time," she says, her smile too bright and the snap of her fingers too forced. "I checked after breakfast, and her headache has vanished."

I shrug, *whatever,* and turn to Bill. "See ya' 'round."

Grabbing my shoes, I make a swift exit out the gate, towards the Fog Horn House. During renovation, my parents made it guest-friendly by portioning the sizeable circular space so that it would include a full bath and closet. It has a window with a view of the garden, and the room is decorated in a navy and red nautical theme. The weathered brass horn affixed to the roof is not in working order and serves as decor.

I slide out of my shorts and T, remove my running shoes, and then change into Delphina's sundress and my new sandals. With a critical eye, I study myself in the full-length mirror, recalling what the salesman said: *When you wear these shoes, you'll be admired as a beautiful woman who is carefree and sexy.*

Sexy? Not on my watch. Shuddering, I shimmy out of the dress, kick off the sandals, and slide back into the shorts, T-shirt and running shoes. Why not live my life in athletic apparel?

Leaving the house, I'm careful to lock the door behind me. When no one's in the garden, it would be easy for some vagrant to slip in unnoticed. I enter the inn through the front door and my nostrils flare. The house doesn't smell like my memories. It smells foreign; a muddled fragrance of unfamiliar cologne, hairspray and suntan oil.

I cross the parlor and then unbolt the door, which leads to the tower. Walking up the one hundred and forty-seven circular stairs to Ivy's studio, I ponder my little sister's erratic behavior. The familiar stairwell, at least, is reassuring; I know precisely which wooden step is going to creak.

Before electricity, the families who shared the home had one main job: to light a dozen whale oil lamps at sunset, and then extinguish them at sunrise. During an eight-hour night-time shift, they had to climb this cylinder of stairs three times a night, ensuring all of the flames were burning.

There is no door on which to knock. Back facing me, Ivy sits on a stool, her magnificent burnished gold curls—the most extraordinary color and identical to my mother's—tumbling down her back. She's barefoot and wears a yellow tank top and white, paint-splattered overalls, which have been cut off mid-thigh. Her being––haloed in light––gives off such a force, my sister appears to be spun from gold.

A graceful Chopin nocturne spills from her iPhone, which is outfitted with tiny speakers, and the piano composition ebbs and flows like the tide.

Her canvas rests on an easel in front of her, a drop cloth lies beneath. Several feet away, she's created an elaborate menagerie of props. Creatures half-human, half-bird, festooned with iridescent feathers and wings are spread across a cabinet top to inspire.

At first, her strokes are hesitant, creamy paint dripping from the end of her brush onto her palette. Then, moving in for the kill, she leans into her canvas and works with an urgency thrilling to watch. Trying to capture the dancing, fleeting effects of light playing about the room, she applies the paint in swift, tiny strokes. Bits of paper and foil are woven into the piece giving it a shimmery, multi-dimensional surface. She works quickly and doesn't notice I'm here.

In a soft sing-song voice, I say her name. Her hand freezes mid-air, and she turns.

"Heavens, Linnea. You should wear a bell around your neck. You startled me." She smiles and, with a flourish of hand, places her brush into the glass mouth of a jelly jar. Ivy's very feminine gestures often make her seem like a young girl.

"But I'm thrilled with the interruption and delighted to have you visit." She stands and hugs me. Like my father, she has the capability of seeming demonstrative with her affections, while at the same time remaining aloof. She drags a stool from the corner of the room and pats the seat cover, motioning me to sit.

"Give me one more minute," she says, returning to her painting.

A table is stationed beside her easel and is filled with the tools of a painter's trade. A cutlery tray crammed with half-used tubes of paint rests beside a pyramid of baby food jars containing a rainbow of color. Paintbrushes protrude from a wrought iron planter filled with glass beads. Standing at attention, their upright sable tips are a glossy brown, a faint whisper of color staining the bristles.

She peers at the painting, resumes her seat before the easel and adds a small dash of gold leaf. Leaning back, she regards the piece. Then, she selects a thin bristled brush and dips it into a greenish-blue color, cadmium, I believe it's called. She adds several small swipes and one long swish at the bottom of the canvas. The painting, at once, is transformed. She wipes the brush bristles in turpentine and then swishes them in water.

"A few small strokes can change the direction of everything," she says, passion underlining her words. "This painting is done mostly in oils, so even one wrong smidgen can blow the thing to bits."

Her shoulders heave forward, and she places the heel of her hand against her forehead. "Since the sun rose, I've been painting non-stop. The piece can rest for now."

She removes a butt from the center of a soot-stained saucer with delicate flowers painted on the rim. Lighting the joint, she places the dog-eared end between her lips and inhales. The skunky aroma of pot fills the room. Exhaling, her features relax, and she offers it to me.

"No, thanks," I say, crossing my arms over my chest. "Pot depletes me. All I want to do is eat pastry and watch *Dancing with the Stars.*"

She chuckles and smiles her crooked smile, the right side of her mouth dimpling. Holding the joint between her thumb and forefinger, she gazes at it thoughtfully.

"Maybe, Linnea, you haven't hit upon the right stuff." She fiddles with the dolphin charm huddled in the crook of her neck. "I prefer the Sativa strain—it's invigorating and pairs well with painting. I'm not good with the Indica. Not good at all." She regards me, catching my eye. "Maybe that's what you've had. That dope's a downer."

"I don't know. I'm more of a craft cocktail kind of a woman. Is pot legal down here?"

"It's been decriminalized if that's what you mean. But this is medicinal cannabis, legal in many parts of the country. It's not laced with anything funky and helps control my migraines. A friend brings it down from a dispensary in Miami."

Smoke curls from the burning embers, clouding her face. I feel like a stranger in her sanctuary, regarding her through a dirty window.

"She's bringing me another type to try next week. A hybrid." She takes another puff, exhaling rings of smoke.

"Something about the combination of triptans in pot, and how they communicate with serotonin in the brain. Whatever. But, for me, a few puffs a day decreases the attacks."

With the palm of her hand, she fans the smoke away from her face. "The challenge is smoking just the right amount of weed, so it doesn't interfere with my painting. Too much and it screws with my perspective. But as long as I manage the balance," she says, crushing out the joint in the saucer, "I can hum along at exactly the right pitch."

I stand, walk to the painting, and study her work. Flattened, cubist heads of men and women are splayed randomly about the piece. They all wear swim caps in colors of red, blue and yellow. The face of a clown in a jester hat is in the right corner, and a woman wearing a lace bandit mask is positioned behind him. Three fish are at the bottom of the frame. Caught in a wave, they're swimming upside down. Strange as the work would seem, like a painting by Chagall, the end result is whimsical, joyful, and engaging. What darkness was Delphina referring to?

"Wow, Ivy." I turn to my sister, in unabashed admiration. Like a white shirt that had been washed with red, her eyes have grown misty and pink. "This is fantastic. Where do you come up with these ideas?"

"Here, Linnea." She pats her heart. "It comes from here. For most people, words are the currency of their expression. Words are imperfect, but it's all they have." Her eyes blink rapidly, and then my little sister begins to circle her studio.

"Painting, Linnea, painting is my voice." She grabs a paintbrush and points the tip towards her canvas, and then to the cabinet top where her menagerie rests. "The canvas gives my soul an outlet to speak to the world. When painting, it's not like I'm listening to God or whoever's up there. Oh no, it's nothing so cosmic."

She stops, flattens her palm against her chest, and catches

my eye. "I'm listening to my heart. Perhaps it's how Chopin felt when composing his symphonies. The currency for his expression wasn't words, but musical notes and instruments. For me, it's my canvas and paint."

She draws a pattern in the air, and my eyes trail the tip of her undulating brush. For a brief moment, I see the outline of the image.

"Paintings and symphonies strike a chord with art lovers who have opened up their soul to experience it. And the experience is so much more than the sum of its parts." She stops and stares at me, and there is something untamed in her face. It's the same expression I often see on our mother.

"And it's about the experience. Yes, Linnea, yes. The experience of the audience and the artist becoming one with the medium. The experience is the emotional entity separating us from...." she points to the bottom of her canvas, "that fish. And even then, Linnea, I wonder. Perhaps the creatures have their own experiences with art."

I stare at the sliver of chain looped around her collarbone, mesmerized by the tiny dolphin bobbing to the rhythm of her words. Man, is she ever stoned. Ivy's been talking a mile a minute as if determined to transfer some of her genius to me. But she's wasting her time. I'm a mere mortal.

She places her hand on my shoulder. "It's the light, Linnea. I strive to create the light. It's a fight to the death, and sometimes I win. But lately..." She gestures towards a stack of half-finished canvasses muddled in splotches of khakis and brown, which lean against the wall. "Well, as you can see, lately I've been losing."

I chew my bottom lip. Staring at the deck of paintings, at the darkness Delphina was describing, a wave of inexplicable sadness washes over me.

"Whew, little sis. Powerful stuff." Fidgeting with my rings,

I'm at a loss for what else to say, except: "Will I see you at dinner?"

She glances at the painting and then closes her eyes. There is a long silence. "Perhaps. The work will decide."

Her face lightens like a bulb turned on, and she squeezes my shoulder. "Sorry. I'm intense when I talk about my art. At least I didn't start speaking Pig Latin."

I smile, remembering her secret language when she was a kid, back in the days when life was simple, back in the days when we used to make pie. Delphina was never interested in baking. It was Ivy and me, the two of us against the world. I'd instructed her to use butter—not shortening, as Mama recommended—for the best mouthfeel and flavor. I remember brushing back her gold tendrils of curls, which fell into her face as we'd roll out the dough over the cool marble top counter.

I giggle. "Iyay ovelay ouyeah."

"You deceitful woman. You always said you couldn't understand me." She tickles my arm with the bristles of her brush.

"We lied to you, Ivy. We knew what you were saying. It's how we got our most valuable information."

I pull her into my arms, giving her a tight hug, and feel her spine stiffen. "I'd love for us to slip into the old days," I say, my voice a whisper. "Maybe we can make a pie together. Follow our old recipe. Make something the two of us could share."

"I'd like that, Linnea," she replies, her back relaxing, words as soft as a sigh.

I step away, kiss my fingers, and place them on her cheek, which reddens beneath my touch. I notice a sketchbook flipped open to a line-drawing on her bedside table. I pick it up. The face is familiar, but I can't place it.

"Did you do this?"

"Of course I did, you goose."

"It's so realistic. Doesn't look like your style. That's all."

I scrutinize the intricate details that capture the depth in the woman's eyes and then regard my sister. "She looks old-fashioned. From another time. Who's your model?"

Her mouth gapes open, her expression incredulous. "How many years did you live in this house?"

I raise my brow. "Apparently not enough."

She smiles wistfully, angling her head to regard the pad, her cheeks dimpling.

"It's Rossalea." She says the name with reverence, and it floats from her lips as if she were reciting the first word in a sonnet.

"Oh yeah. How could I ever forget the Maiden."

Ivy's cheeks pale but then she shakes her head like she's trying to scare away a passing thought.

Rossalea was the daughter of the original lighthouse keeper; her portrait hangs in the parlor. This woman lived in our house almost one-hundred and sixty years ago. Indeed, that's how the lighthouse got its name: The Maiden Tower. Her passionate affair with one of the wreckers is rumored to have precipitated horrific events—the stuff of my parent's Evening Hour.

I flip through the pages of the pad, which is filled with charcoal and watercolor etchings of the woman. There's the back of her head, and on the following page, her profile. There's even a picture of her crying; the tears sliding down her cheeks resemble shards of broken glass. I return the sketchpad to the table. Our Girl has quite an imagination.

After we say our goodbyes, I begin descending the stairs to earth. She never asked me anything about myself or my life. But I'm okay with that. After thirty minutes in her studio, her passion has exhausted me. I'm colorless compared to my creative sister and offer nothing to embellish our world.

∾

DJ TAKES a sip from his glass and regards me, curiously. "Thirteen years is a long time to be away from home."

Home? I consider the word. Why does everyone assume that this is my home? Casting my eyes to the table, I trace swirls on the frosty glass before me, which sweats in the humidity.

"I did visit on holidays. At least the major ones. And it was fifteen years, not thirteen."

"Oh yeah. Sorry. You told me."

"No worries. Thirteen, fifteen...whatever." I lift my forearm, wiggling my fingers. "Time slips between my hands like sand."

It's two in the afternoon—between the lunch and dinner rush—and the perfect time to snag a table and enjoy the laid-back ambiance of Blue Heaven. Canopies of tropical foliage and a sail hanging between trees provide welcome shade from the late May sun. Chickens wander close to the table, scratching at the dirt floor searching for a wayward morsel, a scattered crumb.

"What's been occupying your time all those years?" With a toss of his head, he casts away hair that had fallen into his eyes. Raising an eyebrow, he winks. I recall a verse from Bible class--Proverbs?--saying if someone winks, they plot deceit. Can I trust a man who winks?

"Do you have a boyfriend pining for you back in Boise? A husband? Heck. In this amount of time, you could have—what—three kids back home missing their mommy."

I blush. His voice. That deep Southern drawl. I like the thick, rich honey in it, stirring up something I've done a good job quieting since the breakup with my last boyfriend. I gather my wits before trusting myself to speak.

"Kids? Hardly. After leaving college, all I've done is bartend, cook for catering gigs and travel."

"Nothing wrong with that. Where'd you go to school?"

"I went to a private liberal arts college--a leafy outlier

tucked away in the woods of Massachusetts. Hampshire College. Have you heard of it?"

"It doesn't ring a bell. I guess it doesn't have a football team."

"Ha. You got that right."

"College was never an option for me," he says. "My mother thought it was an accomplishment I'd even graduated from high school."

"I may as well have skipped it for all of the good it's done. My parents chose the school." I place a spoon into my iced tea and stir the sugar that's settled at the bottom. Like rum, sweet tea only tastes right to me in the Keys.

"Daddy even picked my major. History. Like father, like daughter." Plucking another packet of sugar from a dish, I tear off a bit at the corner and stir half of the pack into my beverage. "The school's alternative curriculum and liberal politics also appealed to Mama. She forgot I'd spent my formative years in Catholic school, learning the fine art of conformity."

Raising the tea, I take a long, cooling sip. Then, I place the glass on the table, catching his eyes. "At Hampshire, if you're not one of those brilliant people who debate with ferocity and manage to write insanely good essays while stoned off your gourd, you're better off somewhere else."

"Hey. You were valedictorian of our graduating class. Everyone assumed you'd turn the world upside down."

My lips twitch, and I lower my eyes. Academics were my refuge back in high school, and my four-point average was effortless. But in college, I began to lose focus and drift.

"I was planning to become a professor. Hampshire ranks first in the nation for the percentage of its history graduates who go on to attain a doctorate." Avoiding his gaze, I, again, stir the tea, mesmerized by the bottom layer of sugar that stubbornly refuses to dissolve.

"I liked the curriculum. but wasn't motivated. I dropped out my junior year and never graduated. Besides, my folks already wasted too much of their money on me." I look up to regard him, and again, I'm unhinged by his soft dark eyes. "It's not like they've extra to spare."

"Why did—ah, Delphina—stick around?"

He spoke her name with hesitation. Interesting he brought her up at all. I thought that would be my responsibility. My armpits dampen, and I shake the tea so that the ice cubes jangle against the glass.

"Since she was a kid, she knew she wanted to make her livelihood from the sea. She studied oceanography at Florida Tech. Unlike me, the ocean's in her blood. Her choices have worked out for her."

"No kidding. Their snorkeling business is the busiest in town."

"Rumor has it your business is bustling as well."

The waitress interrupts our conversation, placing a piece of pie in between each of our outstretched hands.

I run fork prongs across the five inches of frothy meringue, which crowns the pale-yellow custard and graham cracker crust. Tilting my head to the side, I lower my eyes to slits and regard him.

"Should I pay a waiter to taste this before I eat it? See if they start choking and collapse?"

He snorts. "Oh, God. Don't tell me you're still upset about that cockroach prank."

"Me? Hardly. It's Delphina who's scarred for life." I look at him, disparaging.

Placing the fork carefully beside the plate, I set my thumbnail between my teeth. After a few seconds of silence, I shake my head and frown. The memory of Delphina's young face swollen with tears and humiliation hits me like a fist in the gut. Enough cat and mouse.

"The donut episode is water under the bridge. What was

cataclysmic were those nasty rumors you spread about her...," I pause, searching for the words, practically spitting them out, "*sexual prowess*. You and Ron Patten at the same time? That greased up dude was a beast."

A reddish flush creeps onto his sun-varnished face. My heart is pounding at my outburst. The cards laid out, he bites his lip.

"I was an idiot. She's such a drop-dead beauty, both of you are. I guess I was trying to get street creds with my pals. Every time I think of her, I feel guilt. Shame." With his tongue, he wets his lips, his eyes dropping to his plate.

"I tried to tell her how sorry I was," he continues, his eyes returning to meet mine, pleading with me to believe him. Anxious to hear his side of the story, I lean into the table, scrutinizing his face for verbal clues allowing me to gauge his level of sincerity.

"A few years after we graduated," he continues, "our paths crossed. And it was just the two of us. We were in the hardware store, looking at nails. Since high school, I'd been agonizing over what I'd say when I had the opportunity. I finally had my chance."

He drums the table with his fingers, the flush now drained from his face. "I wanted your sister to know I'd been plagued with guilt for years. That I'd do anything to take it all back. When she looked up and saw me standing there, apologies started flying out of my mouth. I was blabbering like an idiot."

His voice cracks, and his eyes cloud with emotion. "She looked at me like I was a rabid beast and bolted out of the store. I felt more disgusted with myself than ever."

I feel a sudden impulse to touch and reassure him and then chase the thought away. As his fingers clench into a fist, I sit on my hands to quiet their shake.

"Then, I wrote her a letter," he continues, glancing around the courtyard and lowering his voice. "It took me days to get it right, and I wanted to make sure she received it. That she read it. So, I decided not to mail it and went to her house to deliver it myself. I swear, knocking on her front door was the hardest thing I've ever done in my life."

Beads of sweat dot his face and the muscles in his jaw flex. "I never did hear from her, but that's OK. I wasn't asking for forgiveness. I didn't deserve that. I only wanted her to know I've been plagued with guilt and was—I *am*—truly remorseful."

My chin quivers and eyes sting; I feel the sudden urge to cry. Delphina suffered horribly by his cruelty and teenage idiocy. But now I believe, to the gravel in my gut, that this man has paid the price.

His eyes, too, become glassy as sincerity and remorse map lines across his face. I'm silent a few moments, turning his words over in my mind. He was only fifteen. I haven't the heart to tell him she tore up his letter without even reading it. Oddly, I feel sorry for him. And he's going to freak when I bring up the ribbon.

"My apology—at least my attempt to apologize— came too late," he continues. "I should have cleared the air back then. In high school. Told everyone that I—Ron and I—were lying. But I was stupid, frozen." He mops his face with his napkin. "Missed opportunities. You can never go back."

No. You can't go back. But can remorse forgive the past? Or is it just a flimsy cover-up? For several seconds we are quiet, both of us trying to disentangle our twisted emotions.

"You were a kid," I say, at last. Again, I feel the urge to touch him, brush the hair away from his eyes, but refrain. "And it's clear you did your best to make amends with Delphina."

"I appreciate your saying that," he says, and closes his eyes a brief moment. "It helps."

Trying to add levity to our conversation, I raise the plate of pie to the side of my cheek, above my shoulder. "Look. It's as big as my face."

His shoulders relax at the conversation shift. "Didn't your mama tell you it's bad manners to play with food?"

"I'm simply trying to determine if this pie measures up to its fame."

Pushing Delphina to the back of my mind, I lower the pie to the table. I pick up my fork and push the side of it down through the monumental topping, and then it sinks into the custard and crust.

Cutting it into a manageable piece, I raise it into my open mouth. "Mmmm," I say, appreciating the perfect balance of sweet and tang. "It measures up nicely. You can tell the lime juice was freshly squeezed."

"Your wiggly white mustache is becoming." He reaches over and bats his napkin across my mouth. I smile and take another sip from the glass.

He catches my eye. "Running into you last week was the highlight of the parade for me. Too bad neither of our floats landed a prize."

"Yeah. Delphina was bummed. If their float had placed, she said the attention would have been invaluable for business."

At the sound of her name, his eyes dart towards the empty area where live music often plays. I fiddle with my napkin. Might as well air all the dirty laundry.

I clear my throat, and he jumps, startled. I wonder what he was thinking?

"You know, DJ. What I'm about to say might sound strange." I pull my hair, now damp around my neck, into a back knot.

"Delphina believes someone who was building your float took ribbon meant for her. Expensive bolts of silk worth several hundred dollars."

"Ribbon? Like ribbon for presents?" He searches my face to see if I'm serious or teasing.

I nod. "Elaborately-wrapped presents, perhaps. I imagine it's mostly used to decorate party props. Anyway, she said the ribbon your team used to create your ocean scene was identical to what she'd ordered. Apparently, it arrived at Parade Headquarters and disappeared." Squinting my eyes, I scrunch my nose. "Mysteriously."

He puts down his fork and resumes his rigid posture.

"Oh, geez. Your sister, of all people. Now she has another reason to hate me. She can't possibly believe that I, or any of my staff, was trying to sabotage her float." He winces. "Then again, why wouldn't she?" His face falls into his palms, and he shakes his head.

I shift, suddenly uncomfortable. There is no way this man took Delphina's damn ribbon. Feeling foolish, I bend to shoo away a chicken pecking at the lace of my shoe. But then again, it's more than ribbon to my sister.

He drops his hands and looks up to stare at me, wordless. I straighten and lean into him, pressing my elbows into the table, trying to make him understand.

"Granted, Delphina's been super-sensitive since having a baby. But compromising her rendition of the ocean's beauty was a big deal for her."

I speak slowly, taking pains to select the right words, leaning into him so close his features blur. "To Delphina, the silks she'd splurged on were a metaphor for the ocean's beauty. When they were misplaced––or, as she believed, stolen––it was a direct blow."

"Whew," he sighs. "And now this." He pushes his pie, barely touched, away from him. "But I get what you're saying."

"Maybe the receivers screwed up," I continue. "Or maybe it was a coincidence that both of you ordered the same ribbon. But I'd appreciate your looking into it."

Suddenly tongue-tied, I lift my hands, helpless, and he clasps them, mid-air.

"There's got to be an explanation. I'll speak to the people who built the float. Ask them where they got it. If they purchased it—which they should have—they'll have the saved the receipt."

The feeling of his hands in mine feels solid, warm and reassuring. Although relieved we've tackled the topics so heavy on my soul, I'm tired of talking about Delphina. I shake away my hands and smile into his eyes.

"Hey. Talk about coincidences. Flying down from Miami, I was seated on the plane next to your Tinkerbell."

His eyebrows knit together, and he shakes his head, confused.

"You know. Peter Pan's fairy—the one strutting her stuff on your float."

"Oh. Cassie. Stanson's girlfriend."

"I thought she was from Indiana."

"She was. Until she moved down here a few years back. Her grandmother lives up there. She'd been placed in hospice and Cassie flew up to help her get settled. She was pretty torn up by it all. Her mom had addiction issues, and her grandmother raised her."

I lower my eyes to my lap, swallowing hard and feeling a pang of guilt. So that's why she seemed such a callous she-devil on the plane coming down. Why would anyone want to make small talk with a stranger knowing a loved one was suffering?

I raise my eyes. "Does she live in town?"

"Close enough. Stanson and Cassie live on a boat anchored in Marina Village."

"The place on Stock Island?"

Stock Island's only five miles away from Key West, but their populace marches to a radically different drummer than ours. Put it this way, you won't see Gay Pride celebrated over the bridge.

"Yeah. Stanson's my most prolific tropical fish wholesaler, and his specimens are spectacular. He raises 'em in aquariums.

The babies, even their parents, are born in those tanks. Shares a warehouse with some dude on the island."

Our conversation now progressing into less rocky terrain, he slides the pie in front of him and takes a heaping forkful. After a moment, he swipes his napkin across those lovely full lips.

"You should come to the shop and see for yourself. Customers tell me that when they walk into my store, it's like snorkeling the reefs."

There it is; his unnerving wink.

"And while you're there, I'll introduce you to Tinkerbell, AKA Cassie. She does my books."

"Really? The winged wonder works with numbers? Who would guess?"

I blush, my hand flying to my mouth, embarrassed by my knee-jerk reaction to profile based on appearance. Her skill set trumps mine.

"You'd be surprised," he continues, seeming oblivious to my snarky remark. "She's also my liaison and will facilitate wholesaling product to an aquarium in Fort Wayne."

Appetite returned, he takes another bite, and I follow suit. Tensions fade when eating scratch-made pie. He returns his gaze to me and those eyes, like a gravitational pull, draw my face towards his.

"I'd like to take you out for dinner. There's a new place with an unusual take on conch."

This time his wink is subtle, barely discernible. I'm surprised he'd want a second date. Don't I remind him of a past he seems anxious to escape?

I hesitate, moistening my lips before answering. "Perhaps. But first, can you check into what happened with the ribbon?" I weave my fingers together as if to beg.

Color rises to his cheeks. "As soon as possible."

I smile, relieved, liking this man. A lot. A wave of annoyance clouds my chest. I would have agreed to a date had it not been for Delphina. The poor guy tried his best to make amends with her, and this ribbon situation is blown way out of proportion. You'd think someone sailed off with her catamaran.

And yet. Delphina. My heart blooms with love.

10. DELPHINA

Changing Ella's diapers in the nursery, I hear Linnea's greeting as she enters the house and her ensuing *happy birthday* and laughter. Tonight, it's Friday, June 2nd, and we're celebrating Lita's fifty-eighth. Our tiny, but raucous, Cuban family will use any excuse to party and birthdays tend to get out of control.

Sliding Ella into my front pack and adjusting her so that she faces away from me, her back pressed into my torso, we join the festivities in the kitchen. Every burner on the stove is occupied, and the room hums with excitement, filled with the smell of sofrito, a sautéed onion, bell pepper and garlic mixture. This is the hallowed base for much of Lita's savory cuisine.

Linnea hands me a cylindrical Tupperware container, which contains the cake she made to celebrate Lita's day. Then, she presents her with an orchid, the delicate white petals splotched with yellow and red patterns. Lita centers it on a windowsill and then draws Linnea into her embrace. I note, with disappointment, the plant is cello wrapped, the top bunched and tied with twine. Store-bought, obviously, and not from Mama's garden.

My parents were invited, yet declined. The demands of the

lighthouse, they told us, it's always the lighthouse. At least they could have sent her a card. I brush them from my mind. Their loss. Tonight's dinner will be over the top and inhibitions will be shed in time with the depletion of the rum. Sonny just brought out his guitar, and Lita, the bottle, which, after a few shots, is sure to incite crazy stories about her past.

"Linnea," she says, wasting no time. "Come. Join my amigo and me while we prepare the feast." She grasps the bottle by the neck, gazing at it with longing. "Meet my rich, intoxicating friend from the Dominican." She reads the label on the bottle, pointing at the name of the brand. "Señor Barcelo. The only man a woman needs to keep her happy."

Snatching a glass from the cupboard, she hands it to my sister. "Pour yourself *un poco de* rum, pull up a chair and join me and el Señor. I've been cooking all day. There's only a bit of this and that left to finish."

She glances at Ella and me. "Delphina. Would you and *el bebé* set the table for dinner?" Taking a spoon, she dips it into a sauce on the stove and brings it to her mouth. "Ahhh, *delicioso.*"

Linnea is a new audience for Lita, fair game to fan the flames of her memories. As I gather cutlery from the drawer—Ella trying to grab a fork from my hand—Lita's eyes dart to my sister. She wastes no time cutting to the chase.

"Speaking of the señores, have you met any *ardiente y magnífico hombre* since returning home?"

Linnea's cheeks flush, and she bites her lip, her head dropping to the floor. She appears uncomfortable with the question. Is she seeing someone? Impossible. I'd be the first to know. She glances my way before clearing her throat.

"No time for guys, Lita. I'm only here to visit family."

"Ah, girl. More's the pity. Life is to be lived. You still have the blossom of youth in your face."

After wiping her fingers on her apron, she bends to cup Linnea's chin in her palm and study her face. "But make no mistake. It will fade soon enough. Don't squander your beauty."

Straightening, she grabs her glass from the table and, tipping back her head, finishes the rum in a gulp. "But you must be careful who you choose," she continues, in a conspiratorial voice, her eyes narrowing. "Not all men are like my Sonny." She nods her head towards my husband sitting cross-legged on the sofa, picking out a melody on his guitar.

"I remember like yesterday when I first met his father."

She holds her empty glass mid-air towards Linnea, her silent request for a refill, and whispers, "*Mal hombre,*" under her breath.

Linnea pours some of the amber liquid into Lita's glass. Lita's words flow from her mouth anew, as if they happened yesterday.

"It was at a market in Miami. He slipped a bunch of sweet Cubanelle peppers into my shopping basket. "*¡Diablos!*", she mutters to herself.

Sliding out of her house shoes, she kicks them into a corner of the kitchen. Wiggling her bare toes against the cool floor tiles, her eyes darken. "He used black magic to gain my affection. Lying, worthless *esponja* of a father, *un bastardo.*"

Linnea—one to love a good story, particularly if circling the topic of fiendish men—stands to touch her shoulder, smiling, egging her on. Lita turns her head and beams into my sister's face, savoring every minute of this attention.

I've studied pictures of the slimmed-down, lipsticked version of Lita when she was young. I'm sure all it took was one quick appraisal of the feisty, young woman—with her snapping dark eyes, her market basket swinging beside an ass resembling two round guavas—for Alberto Pagano to desire her more than the flashiest Rolex on the avenue.

A good Catholic girl, Mariela was no fool and refused Alberto's advances until he could prove—a down payment on a house in a respectable neighborhood would suffice—that his intentions were honorable. Within months they were married, and ten months later found the young woman cradling Sonny in her arms.

Alberto told her the thick wad of bills he brought home most evenings had been earned in the construction industry. But with cautious eavesdropping and a prying, catlike curiosity, she came to understand the bricks that were building his empire were not made of clay, but of compressed kilos of pure uncut Columbian *cocaína*.

When confronted, Alberto defended his occupation. In such a lousy economy, how else could he keep a roof of pricey Italian slate over their heads? He said he never used—and to his credit, this was true. He insisted his instincts were sharp, focused, and he knew who he could trust.

And frankly, by then, Mariela had no further argument. She had acquiesced to a lifestyle light years away from the hustles of the street. She, unlike her friends from the old days, had no need to work service industry jobs (or worse), to scratch together funds to keep the lights burning and food on the table.

And being the mother of such a beautiful child, a boy that drew admiring clucks from passersby as she wheeled him down the boulevard, what more could she desire? And to think the stroller alone cost more than the car she'd been driving only two years before. I imagine the usually loquacious woman falling silent when gazing into the round, wide eyes of her boy, her *querido niño pequeño, su hermoso hijo*. Men had only caused her grief, and for the first time in her life, my mother-in-law— Mariela Pagano—was smitten.

Soon after he was born, she began taking birth control pills that she received from the corner clinic. She refused to bring another child into their house of cards. Alberto was none the wiser, ignoring his wife outside the bedchamber and attributing her barren womb to female issues.

Mariela barricaded herself into their home, busying herself with domestics, and—when the coast was clear—hiding wads of cash under the sixteenth kitchen floorboard before Alberto's evening count. When she'd bend to retrieve a bit of vegetable scrap that had tumbled to the floor from the chopping block, she'd smile knowing her, and her son's security lay beneath her fingertips.

And so, my mother-in-law's family stumbled along for the next four years—until one sweltering afternoon at a shipping port on the Miami River.

Alberto was conducting business as usual and was unloading a pallet of boxes, which had found their way across Caribbean waters into the trunk of his construction van. When federal agents blocked the truck and found 136 kilograms of coke with a street value of two million, the jig was up, the curtain had fallen, the house of cards had tumbled at last. The end, when you think about it, was reduced to cliché.

Mariela knew it was bound to happen. She just couldn't predict when. She also knew marriage has its privileges, at least under the law. And even though she was aware of his shadowy operations, she could stay out of the mess and not be forced to testify.

My mother-in-law feigned grief, but her relief was overwhelming. She had her son, she had their nest egg. And between that and the well-laundered proceeds from the sale of their Miami home, she was blessed with options.

For decades, Key West has been renowned as a haven for Cuban ex-pats. With a reputation for thick Cuban espressos and quirky, fun-loving Conchs who inhabit the island, who wouldn't want to live here? Mariela and Sonny—then, only a child—moved into a modest home a couple of blocks from where we live today.

Alberto was kept a dark secret between mother and child. For all the townsfolk knew, he had died, leaving her widowed.

Nine years passed without incident until Sonny's first day in high school: Alberto was murdered in prison, his throat slashed while taking a shower.

My mother-in-law never knew why and wasn't even curious to read the report. She was only filled, once again, with momentous relief. Now she'd have nothing to explain to the Catholic Daughters of the Americas when her prodigal spouse showed up on her front porch after his release.

Linnea turns to me after hearing Lita's story, her eyes stretched wide, shaking her head in disbelief. "I had no idea Lita led such a colorful life. I need to learn more about your family."

"What did I tell you? Lita teaches great lessons on the subject of men. You need to stop by the house more often." I point to the bottle of rum. "Particularly when el Señor pays a visit."

After situating Ella in her highchair, we take our places around the table. Bowing our heads, we give the blessing, which is another non-negotiable ritual in many of the Cuban households run by an Abuelita.

We pass a platter of mashed plantains topped with garlic-tomato shrimp, and a flank steak, which had been marinated in lime juice, seared and then topped with sautéed onions. To a chorus of *ohs* and *ahs*, we pass her infamous chicken, *Pollo Cubano*, the bird cut into large chunks and served over black beans and rice seasoned with coconut.

And so, my mother-in-law's stories continue through dinner, with us pausing to make faces at Ella, encouraging her bubbling little chirps and ringing peals of laughter. Sonny, mostly quiet, savors the food with unabashed relish. Then, pushing himself away from the table, he lets out a moan, rises, and walks to his mother's side.

"Oh, *Madrecita*. You outdid yourself again." He plants a kiss on the top of her head. "But you shouldn't be working so hard on your birthday."

"I made dessert," says Linnea, chiming in.

He turns to Linnea, tousling her hair. "You're a gem, and it's been way too long since I've sampled one of your treats."

He points his forefinger into her face. "You got an earful tonight, sister. But lemme set the record straight. Papa was an okay dude." He glances at his mother who presses her palms together, as if in prayer. She nods and then shakes her head, appearing to agree and disagree with his assessment.

"And we can't forget he was a wonderful tutor," Sonny adds, resuming his seat at the table. "In kindergarten, he taught me how to count and use a calculator. I gained proficiency with numbers while tallying up his dope money. Fifty-five singles plus one hundred and forty-eight tens, plus five hundred and forty-three twenties yields such-and-such. You'd better believe I had to count it twice."

Linnea's laughter bounces off the walls. I haven't seen her so animated since we were fourteen, listening to Britney Spears and The Spice Girls, talking about boys late into the night. I blow her a kiss.

"You're such a health nut, Linnea. You should stick around more. Family is good medicine. You need *chispa*––some Latin wit––in your life."

Wiping tears away from her eyes, she shakes her head in disbelief. "I've never heard such stories."

I've shared with her our skeletons in the closet, so she's not totally clueless. But I've never drilled down to the nickels and dimes of Sonny's life when he was a child.

I spoon a bit of chicken I'd puréed, *al estilo Cubano*, and coax a bite into Ella's mouth. Redolent with citrus, cumin and oregano, she pulls a cute little face and spits it back onto her plate.

Linnea regards Ella, and her giggles subside. Wincing, she

turns to Lita, putting her best efforts into ignoring the slobbery scene across the table.

"With the embargo lifted, don't you want to return to Cuba? Visit old friends and haunts?"

"Don't waste your breath, Linnea," Sonny says, eyes rolling to the ceiling. "Delphina and I would love to go—it's only a forty-minute plane ride from here. We've been working on her for months."

Lita's eyes flash, the black and gold of a tiger's gaze. "I want no part of that rotten enchilada," she exclaims, her preferred metaphor when referencing her homeland. "I hear from friends the food is now lousy and the accommodations, filthy. Señor Castro. He ruin everything. *Ese hijo de puta*—vicious, evil man. At long last he's dead! Cuba Libre!"

She waves her napkin into the air like it is a flag, and we follow suit, shouting, "Cuba Libre!" Now into our second bottle, Sonny taps his phone, and Gloria Estefan's exuberant voice spills out from his iTunes, singing the lyrics from *Cuba Libre*.

Lita leans into Ella and wipes her mouth with her napkin. Then, she turns to us, practically shouting, enabling us to hear her words over the music.

"Maybe things will improve over there in the future. But in the meantime, the only thing I keep from my homeland are her recipes. *Cuba está dentro del refrigerador de mi casa.*"

I turn to Linnea, who only understands the basics of Spanish.

"She's saying Cuba resides in the refrigerator of her house."

Lita smiles at Linnea, raising her brow. "And as far as travel? If I've said it once, I've said it a thousand times. I want to see snow and penguins in the wild."

"Come and visit me next winter in Idaho," Linnea says. "We may not have penguins, but we've got the white stuff in abundance."

"Thank you, sweetie, but no, no, no." The folds of flesh

beneath her chin and upper arm jiggle to the rhythm of her wagging head. "Plane tickets are costly. I save my money for Antarctica."

My husband and I exchange doubtful glances, imagining how expensive a trip like that would be.

Sonny coughs and then clears his throat. "This talk reminds me of an important piece of birthday business." Tapping his phone, the music halts. He stands and walks to the end table. Opening the drawer, he removes a small box wrapped in pale blue foil and tied with a silver satin bow. He walks to his mother's side, strokes his knuckles across her cheek and presents her with the present.

"For you, *Madrecita*."

Her face glows, basking in her family's attention. With the assistance of a dinner knife, she removes the wrapping and then runs the side of her palm over the foil to smooth it out. I'm sure we'll be seeing that paper again in celebrations to come. Opening the box, she pulls out a cloisonné penguin figurine. With brass detailing, its decorative blue, green and white enamel overlay will be a welcome addition to her collection.

"It's so beautiful." She presses her hand over her heart, her eyes welling with tears. "You are so good to me."

"And you are so good to us," I say, my heart brimming with affection for this woman brought to us in a crate of Cuban grapefruit. "You know we love you to pieces." I kiss my fingertips and reach out towards her, extending my hand to touch her cheek. As I lean in front of Ella, the little devil grabs at my dangling earring, almost ripping it out of my ear.

"Ouch, Ella." I draw back my hand and remove the earring, rubbing my earlobe. "That hurt." Looking at my frown, she squirms and begins to whimper.

"I've got something that will cheer her," Linnea says, standing. "Cuban chicken may not have been to my niece's liking, but she'll love my *Tres Leches* Cake. It's another classic made with three different types of milk." She stares fixedly at my breasts and winks. "It's the perfect cake for a child being weaned. Lemme get dessert." She walks into the kitchen, and I shake my head, chuckling.

In a few short moments, she returns to the table, her face glowing behind a towering white cake dotted with burning candles. She sets it in front of Lita. "Take a breath, make a wish, and blow."

Ella babbles, flailing her tiny hands towards the glowing candles. I wave my arms at her saying, "Light, Ella, Light."

She only comprehends three words, Mama, *agua*, and light, but we always understand one another. Communicating on love and instinct, there is nothing on earth I adore more than my daughter.

As Lita blows out the candles, I, too, make my own wish: to shed the blanket of sadness that my own mother is not at her granddaughter's side.

$\sim$

"We've been hit by an asteroid named Starbucks." I shake my head, biting my lower lip. "Dear God, please let this be the last of the chains invading Old Town."

"Sorry, babe. This will be quick. There's no easy way of hitting Coffee Queen today." Sonny glances at me from the corners of his eyes as he stops at the intersection of Front and Duval to grab a caffeinated fix. After last night's festivities, we didn't have time to make our usual pressed Cuban brew.

He pats my arm. "Take the wheel while I grab some lattes. Double skim espresso, right?"

"No. Not today." I massage my temples, pounding after last night partying. "I need something cold. Iced tea would be perfect. That black one—or whatever's the strongest." I reach into the back seat to grab our thermo-cups and hand them to my husband.

Putting on emergency blinkers, Sonny jumps out of the car, and I slide over to take the wheel in case we're forced to move; parking is illegal where he's positioned the truck.

He should be quick. The usual line out the door has vanished since most vacationers have left the island. I haven't visited my favorite reef since last July—eleven months ago. Then, well into my second trimester, the motion of the boat made me nauseated. Waves lapping against the sides of our sixty-five-foot catamaran speak a language I've missed.

Checking my phone, I smile at a picture I took of Ella last night. Her *café con leche* complexion is streaked with creamy goo; more frosting is on her hands and face than what went into her mouth. I'm delighted she's absorbed so much of the Latino genetics. It pleases my husband, and he deserves to feel proud. I admire Sonny's determination to be a wonderful father.

He was only six when his dad was locked up, and how much power he gives to the fact that he grew up without a father is his decision. I feel it was a blessing. He was spared the indoctrination of chauvinism, for which Alberto was renowned. Sonny regards me as his equal, but some of that latent machismo smolders. Fine by me, I like a bit of heat.

Sonny returns to the car, and we make our way to our dock, the sign to our parking area only a couple of minutes away.

Coral Princess Customer Parking Only.
Violators will get the bends.

He guides the truck into one of our reserved spaces. The majority of our customers walk from their hotels, but free parking for the occasional carful of snorkelers is a bonus our competitors don't offer. Smiling broadly, he unbuckles his seatbelt and leans over to peck my cheek. Handing me his coffee, he reaches into the back seat, retrieves a neon pink sunhat and places it on my head.

"I've missed having my partner on the sea," he says, adjusting the brim. The material is embroidered with our logo: the letters C and P embossed on the silhouette of a sail.

Opening the door, he slides from his seat, and steps into the parking lot. The flex of his bicep stirs me as he places his palm over the top edge of his polarized lens. Gazing at the sky, Sonny can set his watch to the angle of the sun. I check my phone: nine o'clock. Our first group will be heading out in an hour.

The ocean centers me. As a girl, it was my playground, but now it's our means of support. I adjust the shelf bra inside of my Speedo, still snug since my boobs remain a cup above their pre-pregnant size. I'm down to nursing Ella only once at night. Slipping into our element, I suspect this ritual nurtures me more than it does her.

Holding our beverages, I jump from the truck and kick the door shut. My eyes scan the kaleidoscope of blues and greens in the water, sparkling beneath the sunlight. I turn to Sonny.

"Nothing is so riveting as the beauty of the sea." I worm my way into his arms, looking up into his eyes. "Except for you."

His musky scent reminds me of last night's rum-soaked love making––the feel of his strong hands as they slid up my torso, the soft tickle of his hair as he pressed his head between my breasts.

"You breathe wind into my sails," I continue.

Pressing his keypad to lock the doors, his breath feels warm as he whispers into my ear. "And man-oh-man those sails. All of that tacking and jibing of the sheets. I love it when you come about."

I grab his butt, and then we burst into laughter. The silly sexy sailing lingo we use to tease never fails to amuse. Warmth creeps into my hips. Since Ella's arrival on the scene, I've had a hard time reigniting my humor, much less my passion. Last night was a much-needed exception.

He turns away from me to pull a cooler from the back of the truck. It's packed with beverages and sandwiches that Lita made this morning; a Cuban specialty of roasted pork, Swiss cheese and pickles. The guests love them.

"Time for business," he says, heading to the water. "I'll ready the Cat and meet you on board."

With pride, I watch my husband saunter towards the boat, our intimate banter having left a tingle that should last through the evening.

My father never encouraged me to express my feelings. In fact, when I told him I loved him, he appeared uncomfortable. I've never questioned his love for me, but it was never voiced. A hugging, kissing, gesticulating mama raised Sonny, and she was explosive with praise for her only child. He needs overt affection from me, as well.

But I'm wary. Tending my husband's self-esteem is like feeding an aquarium fish. If I don't give it enough food—or in Sonny's case, praise—it will die. But if I overfeed my fish, fawn ad nauseam over him, it might turn him into an egotist, which would be the death of me. Too much or too little praise—both are bad. Before the baby was born, it was easy to find the balance. These days, less and less.

My gaze returns to the water as I finish the last of my tea. We're booked for two jaunts today. Unlike some of our competition, we're not a cattle cart. Although the boat is rated for a maximum of 50 guests, only 36 passengers are allowed on our excursions to ensure everyone has plenty of room. Unless there's a storm, our boat is typically filled to capacity. Even in off-season.

My eyes light upon the first customers trickling towards the pier for the morning ride. Plastering on a grin, I saunter to the dock and collect their receipts. It's the usual cast of characters

—a smattering of couples and families anywhere from ages ten to eighty. Then, I escort them to The Coral Princess. As they climb on board, Sonny lends a hand to assist.

I pass out bottles of water and sunscreen, one of the few sunblocks available not toxic to coral. One young man rubs the lotion over his partner's back, paying particular attention to areas under the edge of her bikini, which won't be exposed to the sun. With eyes for one another only, I suspect they're honeymooners, and not interested in fraternizing.

Most guests take a seat in the cabin, while others lie on towels spread over the braided mesh netting that joins the two hulls. Referred to as the trampoline, it's like lying in a hammock strung out between trees. Sonny lets out the sails, harnessing the wind, and we begin our journey, southwest, to Rainbow Reef. It's further than the other more heavily trafficked areas, but our guests are rewarded with better ocean visibility and a more spectacular coral landscape.

Removing my hat, I shake out my hair and raise my face to the sky, imagining I'm a seagull. The buoyancy I feel above water, and the vast, unfettered landscape unleashes something wild in me, something held captive on the mainland. The impossible is possible, and the elusive is within reach. I inhale the briny air unleashing a grin of exultation. Three bottlenose dolphins ride the wake on the port side of The Coral Princess. The guests scurry over, cameras and phones aimed at the mammals, to get a better look. As their fins cut through the water to the cheers of our group, they seem to take delight in entertaining us, watching us as much as we watch them.

For a moment, I'm transfixed by Sonny as he lowers the sails. I love his hands. The best lovers have hands adept at feeling subtleties, hands that move with deliberation and grace. He touches me the way he feels the nuances of the wind when we're sailing. Raising his arms, his fingers strum through the breeze as they do over my body. The subtle cues of change—in moisture, how the air begins to stir—inform him when to come about and capture the wind, ensuring we have an exhilarating ride.

I'm not immune to the way women look at him when he's working The Coral Princess, the way their lips part as he hoists the sheets on the catamaran, light rippling over his body. When noticing the gold band encircling his wedding finger, sparkling in the sunlight, they glance my way. Noting my identical ring, they frown.

I dig into the utility container and distribute masks, snorkels, fins and buoyancy vests. A petite blond approaches me, shaking a wet suit. The form-fitting neoprene shimmies and shines as an oily seal in the sun. "Do you think I'll need this?"

"Nah," I reply. "The water is temping in the mid-eighties now. We only use those in the winter."

A tow-headed boy, a slip of a fellow, pushes his foot into a rubber fin. I bend to slide my fingers into the back gap and straighten. "Let me get you a smaller size. These will slide off your feet in the water."

A mother bends to whisper into her daughter's ear while smoothing her curls. I feel a kinship. "I love your cover-up," I say, smiling broadly. "Did you get it at the Lilly store?"

"I did. Their clothes are perfect for the tropics." She runs her palm down the side of the V-neck tunic patterned with a splash of teals and lavenders. "The store's across the street from my hotel. I don't snorkel, so I'll wear it as a sun protector."

"But I'm a snorkeler," says her daughter, jumping up and down as if she were on a pogo stick.

The woman is missing out on having an underwater adventure with her child. But I've learned from experience not to prod or encourage guests who tell me they don't want to join us. Linnea has warned me to respect their fears.

I inspect the guests, one-by-one, to ensure they're ready for the plunge. Removing my nylon shorts, I stuff them into my bag. I raise my hand towards the group to get their attention while delivering my spiel.

"It's up to us to ensure the survival of the coral and reef fish. Coral polyps resemble plants, but they're actually animals that have a symbiotic relationship with algae. Even the lightest touch can damage them." I point to the rope securing our boat. "I don't even touch the algae on our mooring line."

Sauntering to my side, Sonny throws an arm around my shoulder. "My wife, if you haven't noticed, is intense."

I brush away his arm and pretend to punch him in the gut. The guests titter as I walk away, giving him the stink eye over my shoulder. Our little dog and pony show never fails to amuse.

"Our stairway to heaven," I remark, squatting to affix a ladder on the side of the Cat. Straightening, I turn to the group. "The surface of the ocean is lovely to admire, but the treasure is what lies beneath. A secret life is on a reef, and you'll be swimming in a rainbow of wildlife."

I point to the gate at the stern of the boat. "If you'd prefer jumping, be our guest. When all of you are in the water, I'll join the group and lead you to the reef."

As the guests disembark, I watch a kayak gliding across the horizon in the distance, the oar dipping into the sea with glints and splashes of spray. I put on my fins, mask, and then secure the vest around my torso. The last snorkeler safely in the water, I jump, fins first, into the Atlantic.

With breaststrokes, I swim to front the group, beckoning them to follow me; at last, I've returned to my element. As we get closer to our destination, I point to a gargantuan fish swimming several feet away from our paddling fins. His skin is brown and appears mottled with age spots. Some of the snorkelers, alarmed, swim away.

"Don't be afraid. That's Ralph." Treading water, I speak

loudly so everyone can hear. "He's a Goliath Grouper and is protected by law. I don't know his age, but scientists say they can live up to fifty, maybe even one hundred years. He may look annoyed, but he's used to snorkelers and won't bother you."

A young man with long, shaggy hair plastered to his neck waves his hand, getting my attention.

"How much do you think he weighs?"

"Somewhere around six-hundred pounds. He reminds me of an elderly man patrolling the neighborhood he's lived in his entire life."

Beckoning the group to follow, I crawl beneath the surface of the sea, against the tug of current. Ten feet away from the reef, I rise to the surface.

"We're at our destination: Rainbow Reef. For the next thirty minutes, you're on your own to explore. Don't forget to stay several feet away from the coral heads. I've become intimate with most of them and consider these beauties my babies. If you like, you can follow me."

I adjust my mask and swim forward. Silvery light streams through the aqua waters and bathes the reef, which glows in a palette of blue, lavender and dusty pink. It's an enchanting backdrop for the kaleidoscopic creatures swimming around and beneath our paddling bodies.

I point to a large parrotfish in neon shades of lime and orange peering at us from a crevice at the coral's edge; tiny fairy basslets swim beneath the ledge. Rock Beauties, their bright yellows and blacks reminding me of a swarm of bees, dart beneath our swishing fins. My band of eager snorkelers are busy taking pictures with their underwater cameras.

Beneath my torso, next to gnarly fingers of sponge, a glittering object commands my attention. I pluck a triangular piece of red glass from the sandy floor and, filled with elation, swim to the water's surface. The sun peeks out from a bank of clouds, which moves across the horizon. I admire the vibrant ruby color. One side is smooth and frosty, the other has two horizontal ridges embedded into its thickness. Both sides are marked with tiny pores, which was caused by years of tumbling in the surf and sand.

Sea glass can take up to one-hundred years to acquire this patina. Further, the red colorant was rarely used due to the expense required to make the pigment. I'm holding a thing of value and slide it between my cleavage into my shelf bra. I'll save it for Ivy—we collected sea glass when we were kids.

Filling my lungs with oxygen, I dive back down, moving forward. Sea snails and Flamingo Tongues affixed to the reef, feed on soft coral tissues. Consumed with joy and a surge of well-being, my body feels like it's radiating energy. I am connected to the life surrounding me, which is sustained and nurtured by this reef.

And then I stop, paddling in place, surprised at what appears to be several oversized clumps of cauliflower on my right. Treading water, I shake my head—disbelieving—as the other swimmers catch up to me. The last time I was here, this coral was purple, the most vibrant color in the colony. It was a hangout for the anemones and gorgonians that anchored them-selves there. In the time I've been away, it appears to have been bleached. This once stunning coral is dying.

Several blue Tangs swim in front of me as I adjust my mask to see better, debating what could have caused this. I float to the water's surface and remove my mouthpiece. Heart hammering, I catch my breath.

Pushing my lens up, so that the mask rests atop my head, I spit water out of my mouth, dog-paddling in place. When the reefs die, so go the fish and every society depending on them for their sustenance and livelihood. I can't let my mind go there. Perhaps a temperature shift caused the change. If so, it should regain its health over winter. It's too soon to jump to conclusions.

The snorkelers emerge from the water, one-by-one, removing breathing tubes from their mouths. Talking amongst each other, they're laughing and smiling.

An uneasiness creeps into me. There's a slowness, a sluggishness to my arm as I lift it to the sky, waving at the guests, beckoning them to follow me. My movement causes the edges of the glass to dig into my breast, and suddenly, I feel adrift, done with the day, filled with sadness and longing for my child. The glare of the sun hurts my eyes. Sliding the mask down, I swim towards The Coral Princess.

11. LINNEA

"This is exceptional." I wipe away remnants of sauce from around my mouth. "Curried Conch Scallopini. At last. A restaurant realizing the potential of fresh conch, which is," I nod appreciably at the dish, "the most underrated fruit of the Caribbean."

"I agree," DJ says, smiling into my eyes. "I've had enough conch fritters and chowder to get me through the next three lives."

He takes a long sip of wine; a pricey Sémillon and Sauvignon Blanc blend the waiter suggested would go well with the complexity of the dish. I was tempted to have a glass but refrained. It would break my cardinal rule of not mixing alcohol and men. At least not on first dates. Second and third dates, for that matter. Not until I'm sure.

I place the fork prongs on the rim of the plate, my words directed more to the currant-dotted rice than to his face. "I'm sorry to have made such a stink about the ribbon. But that float was a big deal for Delphina." With my knife, I push the rice into the remains of the sauce, reluctant to mar the evening with unpleasantries.

"No worries. I totally understand. I was surprised by the

cost." Sighing, he shakes his head. "It was beautiful silk—so lovely, my staff saved it. Smoothed it out after the parade and put it in storage. Of course, we'll return it to Delphina, not that it will make her feel any better.

He blinks rapidly. "Hey. Remember my telling you about our bookkeeper, Cassie, the woman you sat next to in the plane?"

I look at him curiously. "Of course. Small world. Funny she reappeared in my life."

"Well, it was her, Tinkerbell. She solved the puzzle. When she couldn't find an invoice for the ribbon, she guessed what happened and called the company in Jersey. They told her the cost." He emits a soft drawn-out whistle through his teeth. "When your sister finds out, my number one spot on her black-list will be secured forever."

He delivers that annoying wink of his again, unleashing a fretwork of lines on the side of his temple. Perhaps it's a nervous tic.

I glance towards a couple sitting at a nearby table. The man—about DJ's age—has a soft double-chinned, dimply face and appears sincere as he smiles into his companion's eyes. Not the sort of man who'd wink at a woman, but a man you'd never doubt for an instant. A face to trust. I regard DJ, with his hand-some features and strong jaw, also wearing a smile. But is it a smile I can trust?

"I'll talk to her. Make her see reason," I hear myself say, not confident in my words or the assuredness of my composure. "It's good timing, anyway. She discovered a patch of dying coral on Rainbow Reef and has better things to worry about."

His eyes narrow. "For real?"

"Yeah. She's hoping that next winter when the water becomes cooler, it will return to good health."

"Let's hope she's right. If there's no coral, there's no fish, and every business related to fishing would shut down."

I sigh, shaking my head. "Worst case, it would be catastrophic. It's her favorite place to snorkel so she'll continue monitoring the area."

I glance at my bag, which contains a check made out to Delphina for $579.00. Apparently, her order arrived in the same shipment as DJ's. In his employees' haste to get their float completed, they weren't paying attention to label details and assumed the entire delivery was for them. I'll have to come up with some excuse for having this check.

I take a deep breath, dreading the conversation, which will have to be tomorrow as her family could use the cash. She'll inquire as to why I'd pursued the issue with him in the first place. Delphina will never trust him after that incident in high school.

Should I? When speaking with him at the parade, DJ told me he had nothing to do with the construction of the float. Anyone could understand how the mix-up occurred. After all, no harm was done. Delphina will be reimbursed, and she can use the ribbon, perhaps, in next year's festival. And how could I mistrust those eyes? Round and dark, they are as innocent and inviting as two chocolate M&M's.

"The saga of the missing ribbon is officially water under the bridge," I say, forcing enthusiasm into my voice. "So let's change the subject. I can't believe we went to the same school and I know so little about you." Except, I think, for the fact you tried to ruin my sister's reputation.

"Seriously, Linnea. Has any adolescent boy ever come clean about the truth of what's going on in their lives? Especially in their heads?"

"Funny. You were one of the cool kids. The strong, silent type."

"I was quiet. Yeah. You got that right. I learned to keep my mouth shut 'cause everything I said was bullshit. A bunch of garbage that hurt people."

His face colors and he glances towards the hostess station. I place my forefinger on his wrist, and he turns his head to face me. His Adam's apple bulges as he takes a sip of wine, swallowing with determination. Shifting in his seat, he appears miserable with the memory. Then—not saying a word—the black of his iris darkens his gaze, his nostrils flare, and he knocks his fist onto the tabletop. My slight shake of the head tells him that we don't need to revisit this topic tonight.

"Basketball was my refuge," he says, after a moment, changing the subject. "After school let out, I shot hoops for hours, avoiding all conversation that didn't circle around sports. It also kept me out of the house—I never felt comfortable around the guys Mom brought home. It was especially annoying when they tried to give me advice. Be my father or something."

DJ continues to talk to me about his mom, and how her parade of boyfriends embarrassed him when he was growing up. And as he speaks about his youth, how much he missed not having his father in his life, his features grow soft in the candlelight. The waiter removes our plates, and we order a dessert to share.

Turning the conversation to me, he asks why I left home. I describe Idaho and the sanctity of the seasonal changes; the brazen, burnt colors of autumn and the stark white blanket of winter snow. I describe how the virginal greens of spring speak to me in their dew-glazed elegance. His attention to my words is exciting, and something silenced deep within me begins to thrum. As we share a whipped papaya concoction swirled over a cloud of angel food cake, I float above the table, suspended in time.

"I don't know, Linnea. The Florida Keys for me—for most everyone I know—is paradise. Why do you think so many people save their whole lives to retire in Key West? And you're lucky your family lives here. Super cool people from what everyone says. What keeps you from coming home for good?"

Home. That word again. With his question, the mood is shattered, and I come crashing back to earth. Home is shared with the people you love. But home is also where you are supposed to feel safe. Love and safety are not interchangeable and should happily coexist. The thing I want most is to find my home.

"I am lucky," I respond, after finding my voice. "My family's here for me. They're a crazy cast of characters, but I love them." I fidget, avoiding his eyes. "I do enjoy a distinct change of seasons. But there's another reason, DJ, another reason why I can't move back."

Leaning back into the chair, he crosses his arms over his chest. "And what might that be?"

"I've got a fear. More apt, a phobia." I stretch my right arm out to my side, pointing towards the street, which is several blocks from the wharf. "A phobia of the great silvery sea."

His eyes narrow and his mouth drops open as if surprised by my words. I surprise myself, too. Why is this man so different from the others? Why would I reveal something so personal to someone I hardly know? But he's been so forthcoming with me, and I'm beginning to feel secure with him; comfortable revealing myself. At least the self I want him to believe.

Ever since childhood, I've been told buck up and be strong. Some things should never be talked out. Wipe the dirt from your knees and move forward. Drumming my fingers on the table, I feign indifference to the truth, the catalyst of my fears.

"Phobias are weird." I feel my ears grow hot. "They can seed themselves into a person when they least expect it. And all it took was one event when I was a teenager."

As an actress gearing up for performance, in my mind, I'm now stepping onto the stage. My pulse quickens as it's prone to do when sifting the agony away from my words. I take a sip of water, readying myself to deliver the lines I'd memorized so long ago.

"I often slept over at Tara's house. You remember her from high school, right? Sometimes we'd go fishing with her dad." Clearing my throat, I look down at my fingers, and fiddle with my rings. Glancing up at him, I watch his gaze travel to the ceiling, lost in thought.

"Oh yes. Tara Trent." Eyes snapping, he returns to the moment. "Pretty girl. Like you and your sister. Girls like you three scared me silly." His laugh sounds sharp and hollow.

"You've got to be kidding, DJ." Widening my eyes, I regard him with incredulity. "If you were so skittish, why on earth did you plant that horrible rumor about Delphina? I spent hours reeling with distress, knowing my other half was in agony."

I shock myself with my sudden outburst. We'd come to an unspoken agreement that this topic was off-limits, but I can't help myself. Trying to diminish the pain he caused us our freshman year is exhausting.

He shakes his head and sighs, his words, now whispered, directed at his plate. "I learned a lot about myself from the incident with your sister. And I hated what I saw. My attempts at apology were useless, and I don't know how to make things right. The only positive out of the mess was learning the power of truth."

I wring the napkin in my lap, clinching the fabric in my fists. Truth. An interesting concept. One that would never serve me well. Fabrication is my life-line, my salvation. I tilt my head to regard this man. Whatever else is going through that brain of his remains at bay. For several seconds he sits quietly, staring at his hands, which are balled up into fists on either side of his plate.

"I'm sorry for bringing it up again, DJ," I say, at last. "I promise I'm done. Later we can figure out something you can say to Delphina. Something that might pave the way for forgiveness."

His gaze drifts, a faraway look in his eyes.

"So...what were we talking about?" My emotions are scrambled. "Oh yeah. Tara Trent. After high school, we tried to keep in touch, but our lives had gone down such different paths. It's been a few years since we've spoken."

He clears his throat. "She married Robbie Cox, and they moved to Sarasota. I hear she has a couple of kids." Words tumble from his mouth, and the color returns to his face, apparently relieved at the subject change. "But her dad's still down here. He's quite the angler. Brings home an award from the fishing tournament every year. Once he reeled in a fifty-pound Amberjack."

His eyes drill into mine, narrowing. Leaning towards me, his elbows bear into the table as he weaves his fingers together, peering into my face. "So, back to your story. Did something happen to you on that boat?"

Fifteen years ago, I boxed and shelved the memories, began the work of forgetting it happened and came up with the lie to cover for my fears. I give myself a hall pass. The lies I tell others are nothing compared to the lies I tell myself.

Determined not to go off script, I'm as unwavering as a Catholic mass. I meet his gaze and lower my voice like I'm confessing to a priest.

"It was a Saturday afternoon. Tara and I were bored, so we decided to tag along with her dad while he fished. A few minutes after leaving the marina, the boat ran out of gas, and his radio malfunctioned. We couldn't call for help." I widen my eyes and wring my hands together, a well-practiced pantomime during this performance.

"And?" he asks, his jaw clenched, a warped frown crossing his face.

"I panicked and imagined the worst," I reply, my words

quickening. "Like we'd be swallowed up by some sea creature. On that boat, I realized us humans do *not* belong out there. We are a small, defenseless mammal in the ocean's food chain."

My shoulders have worked their way up to my ears, and I gaze, unflinchingly, into his eyes. "Eventually, her dad flagged down a cabin cruiser. But it seemed like we were floundering for an eternity. I was petrified. To this day I can't look at the ocean, much less be on a boat, without panicking."

I've recited the story so many times, I'm almost beginning to believe it. There is some truth in the telling; we ran out of gas, but a passing boat came to our aid in minutes.

My fears, however, are only too real; I smell them on my breath and taste them on my tongue. When I see the ocean—inhaling her salt, listening to her surf break on the shore—my throat clenches, my heart races, and my body breaks into a sweat. Even thinking about it puts me on edge. I place my hand on my thigh to quieten my tapping foot.

DJ studies me a moment before turning his gaze to the wall. He's really thinking about what I said. He takes a last, long sip of wine, finishing the glass and then catches my eye.

"That's awful, Linnea. I had no idea. I'm sorry that happened to you. How do you cope with the Atlantic being just a few blocks away?"

"As long as I don't have to come face to face with the water, I'm OK. But that's not so easy. It's like I'm a prisoner. In Old Town, my parameters—roughly drawn—are White, Thomas, Truman, and Caroline Streets."

"Good thing I didn't select a restaurant on the wharf."

"If you had, I would have come up with some excuse not to join you."

"Hey. No excuses, no lying to me, Linnea. Your fear doesn't freak me out. Even though the world's a watery place—and, man, that's glaringly obvious down here—we all have issues."

So far, he's not poking holes into my story or trying to play amateur psychologist. And that makes him all the more allur-ing. I would never have pegged him as the sort of man who really listened to a woman. Made love to them, no doubt. More than likely even used them. But never the type of man who truly paid attention, trying to understand them. Admiring the light cotton fabric of his shirt, which conforms so well to the slopes and valleys of his muscular arms, I feel like an explorer eager to map out a journey.

Taking a deep breath, I look around, admiring the mini-malist decor in shades of silvery blue, and the molding and trim painted in a bold tangerine.

"This place is lovely. Too bad they don't have any openings for a bartender. No one seems to be hiring until Season."

And I'll be gone by September, I think to myself, not daring to add my additional fear of turbulent weather patterns to the heap. He'd think I'm a grab-bag of neuroses. And he'd be right. My left eye twitches a couple of seconds and then stills.

"If you're looking for a job," he says, "I could use another salesperson."

I chuckle. "Working at your store would send Delphina spiraling over the edge. You obviously want my sister to come after me with a fishing spear, don't you?"

Through his thick fringe of sandy lashes, so wasted on a man, he eyes me sheepishly.

"You said you'd try to help fix things between us. Come up with a plan."

"Right," I murmur, racking my brains. My fingers dart to my lips. "Here's a thought. She knows I love experimenting in the kitchen. Maybe I'll invite her over to the inn, sweeten her up as we test drive dessert recipes. And you'll come breezing in—you know, unexpected."

"Just like that? For no reason, I show up at the lighthouse?" DJ shoots me a look of incredulity, and I feel my cheeks grow hot.

"I'm good at staging—I'll figure out something. You can impress upon her your business's dedication to reef conservation. We'll enjoy big slices of pie, you'll tell her you were an idiot, and all will be forgiven." I patter my fingertips together with glee. "Believe me, DJ. Peace treaties have been signed while eating my pies."

Patting his abs, he licks his lips, warming up to my suggestion. "A pie tasting? Great idea. Maybe we could stage a practice session. You did promise me a cooking lesson."

"Oh yeah. I made that promise before the parade. We discussed the science behind Key Lime Pie."

"How could I ever forget? You in that fetching little skirt. I was hoping you'd wear it tonight." He chuckles, shaking his head.

I tuck the folds of my sundress, which hits mid-calf, around and beneath my thighs. "You'll never see me in that number again, mister. Or anything like it."

He's lucky I even wore the dress Delphina gifted me. But this outfit is modest, even sweet. Wearing this, no man could ever think I was *asking for it*.

"Truth be told," I continue, "cooking is more of a refuge for me than it is a science. The kitchen is my escape. When creating a recipe from scratch, mistakes are okay, and messes are fine." Sighing, I shake my head. "Real life is not so accommodating."

I regard the ceiling, watching the blades of the fan whir above my head. "Those aren't the right words." I lean into the table, catching his eyes. "There's nothing to escape in the kitchen. For instance, when rolling out a crust and dusting it with fistfuls of flour, I feel grounded in my happy place."

His eyes burn into mine. Has a man ever looked at me this way? Impulsively, I throw caution to the wind.

"Those who know me well, know baking is my..." I lower my voice to a whisper, steadying my gaze into his, "passion."

At that word, he catches his breath. "Oh, Linnea. It's hard not to be mesmerized by you."

He reaches for my hands and cups them into his palms. I imagine how those hands would feel encircling my hips. Why am I leading him on?

My brain commands my emotions to silence. A feeling of danger slides into the water, swimming in my direction, and my heart hammers inside my sternum. This is going way too fast. Typical I'd fall for a hometown guy when hometown's the last place I want to be. If Delphina catches wind, she'll have me burned at the stake.

I wince and feel my face grow hot. He nods imperceptibly as if to sympathize with my confusion. Motioning the waiter to our table, he requests the bill.

"The night's young," he says, snapping his fingers. "And to quote our old boy Hemingway: *Don't bother with churches, government buildings or city squares, if you want to know about a culture, spend a night in its bars.* Shall we heed his sage advice? The Aut Lounge is a fifteen-minute walk away."

I raise my eyebrows.

"No worries. It's in Bahama Village. There's no scenic view; no opportunity to contemplate the vastness of the sea."

I shrug. "Never heard of the place."

"It opened last year and is the latest hangout. I'll wager their cocktail menu will coax you out of your abstinence. They craft drinks using juiced fruits, herbs and rum aged in oak barrels. But get this twist"—he says, shifting his shoulders towards mine—"the barrels were soaked in seawater."

"How interesting. Cocktails spiked with the Atlantic. But a local watering hole?" Gloomy, I stare ahead, giving him a thumb's down. "We're bound to see someone we know. Rumors would fly, and Delphina would freak. Key West is so small, it's lucky we haven't run into some townie yet."

For the first time in years, I'm meeting a man I'm attracted to. He's unattached, I'm unattached, but I feel the need to sneak around because of my sister. I feel as guilty as I would if I were hooking up with a married man. I take a deep breath and try exhaling away the irritation blooming in my chest.

DJ regards me, his features falling. And in the moments his eyes search my face, his silence speaks volumes. Then, he speaks rapidly, grabbing my hands, passion behind his words.

"I want to see you again, Linnea. As soon as possible."

His eyes drill into mine. I feel the same desire welling up inside of me, and I return his smoldering gaze.

"Let me talk to Delphina. I'll give her the check tomorrow and figure out something to say."

"Well, then." Pursing his mouth, a long soft sigh escapes his lips. "At least allow me to walk you partway home, towards the lighthouse."

Exiting the air-conditioned chill of the restaurant, the warm, inky night feels as inviting as a soft cashmere shawl draped across my shoulders. The evening sky is laced with stars––a sky full of promise, I think, relishing the feel of his long, sinewy fingers laced into mine. An eclectic array of music —blues, rock, electronic, and show tunes—spills out from bars and cabarets. Hand-in-hand, we walk down Duval, the early summer street far less crowded now that Season's over.

The grizzled woman who commands the corner of Petronia sits knitting, as usual, in her small, rickety chair. Her name is Sally, and she's an institution on this block. She's commandeered the same roost since I was a kid and I've watched the color of her hair transition from blond to oatmeal to steely gray. How old is she? Eighty-two? Eighty-six? Surely she's an octogenarian by now.

Tonight, she wears slinky purple pajama pants and the usual vest, which is knit in the colors of the rainbow. Her dog rests beside her on a stained, tiny pillow, outfitted in a matching vest bunched up around his midriff. This short-waisted mutt is some sort of terrier mix, and his stubby tail thumps to the bass rhythm from a nearby bar. Her last dog was a basset hound who, with his long torso, was much better suited for wearing vests.

DJ bends and places a five in the tin cup resting by her side. Stiffening on her perch, Sally salutes and then studies us, head-to-toe. I scratch around the dog's ears, but Sally gives no indication of recognizing me and points her cigarette at the dog speaking in a gravelly voice.

"I lost Prince Albert the Second last November. This here's Albert the Third—the latest mongrel who works for me. I might be too old to be getting a new dog—takes me weeks to recover after they pass—but there ain't much else for me to love in this world." The dog yawns, showing sharp yellow teeth, and I straighten. "He was a stray. Needed me as much as I needed him. Take a picture if you like. You two a couple?"

DJ looks at me and tilts his head, the brown in his eyes reflecting the purple flashing neon of a blinking sign. An embarrassed smile plays about my mouth. Dodging the question, I ask him to squat beside Sally and her dog. Pulling out my Smartphone, I take a pic, for my eyes only. As proud as I am to be with a handsome man like DJ, I would never post this on Instagram. What if Delphina saw? She can't learn about my feelings for this man. At least not now. Anyway, since my time down here is marked —maybe not forever.

Saying our goodbyes, he wraps his arms around me. An electric jolt zaps up my spine at the adrenaline-pumping thrill of being so close to someone so forbidden.

∾

WAVES THRASH about my thighs as I run into the ocean, the water cooler than the midnight air. Second-guessing my intent, I turn to face the shoreline, and on this moonless night through the blur of my tears, the beach is as black as the sea. The surf breaks in a thundering crash, leaving a creamy drizzle of foam in its wake. Sand shifts beneath me, and I stumble backward as the current tugs at my feet.

Having lost all will to fight, I turn to face the horizon, giving in to the demands, allowing my body to be pulled into the surf. Paddling forward, the ocean floor drops, and I dive downward, eyes shut to lessen the burn of the brine. Dress ballooning above my back, the wet volume sweeps between my fingers as I claw deeper into the sea.

A feeling of shattered glass rakes across my body. Stunned, I swim to the surface, heart beating wildly, gasping for air. Treading water, I've got the sensation that something—some things—are fluttering wildly around my torso. Like birds trapped inside of a cage, they knock against me, panicked.

Fighting the currents, my arms lash forward towards the shore, hands breaking the surface of the water like the cracking of whips. The creatures are following me. A wave swells above my head in a long, silent scream, followed by a crash of sorrow. I try clawing through the water towards the surface, but something has a hold of my feet, dragging me down. Everything goes dark.

I AWAKEN WITH A GASP, shedding the skin of this horrific dream, blinking with bleary-eyed confusion. Relief floods through me as I realize I'm safe in the Fog Horn House, the familiar pictures hanging on the wall. The sundress I wore last night with DJ—a pale-yellow number with nautical blue thread woven through eyelets—is spread across the back of a wicker chair. A rooster crows, and I put the pillow over my head to drown out the noise. The nightmares are returning.

Stumbling out of bed, I head for the coffee maker, the sensation of the dream—unsettling and sinister—beginning to fade. My neurotransmitters work best well-caffeinated, and coffee will coax away vestiges of my troubled sleep. Between sips, I slide into running shorts, a sleeveless T and lace up my Nikes, hoping they will persuade me into my morning run. Opening the door, the light splinters my vision. I grab my bag, digging through it for sunglasses, and then saunter into the yard.

Daddy emerges from the front door of the inn, a handful of guests trailing him like goslings following a gander. He walks to my side, takes my hand, and raises it to the sky.

"This is my daughter, Linnea. She grew up in this house. She's an ex-pat, now." Pausing, he turns to regard me, as if wondering what to feed an exotic pet. "Lives in Idaho, of all places."

The guests bob their heads, smiling.

"Let's get this show on the road," he says, releasing my hand. "Linnea can fill in the pieces. We welcome your questions."

I force a smile, wishing the earth would split open, and I could fall through the ground. My parents' life has turned into a performance, 24/7. I've been cast into their show against my wishes and without an audition.

"Construction of the lighthouse began in 1843," Daddy begins in his stage voice. "That's when transatlantic commerce began to boom. The far-reaching beams of light from the towers were essential. They warned of dangerous rocks and reefs, which helped the crew to guide their vessels into navigable waters."

His hand sweeps from the tip of the tower to the bottom of the foundation. "Alabama brick and Philadelphia iron were used to construct the tower and base. In testimony to its superior construction, it miraculously survived the hurricane of 1846, which leveled much of the town."

"That exact same hurricane was discussed on the other lighthouse tour," a woman remarks. "You know. The lighthouse three blocks west from here. You'd never find me traveling in the Keys during hurricane season."

The woman wears a T-shirt reading ROCKLAND HARBOR LIGHTS, which is a popular lighthouse in Maine. She must be a lighthouse groupie. There are thousands of people—pharologists—who take their vacations for one purpose: to see as many lighthouses as possible. My parents get them all of the time.

"I loathe redundancy." Daddy smiles at the woman, indulgently, and raises a brow like they were conspirators in some elitist pharological society. "But our lighthouses do share similar pasts."

He points to the top of the tower. "A catwalk surrounds the lantern room. After they'd double-checked the lights, the family took turns entering the walkway—pirate scope in hand—and scan the waters for shipwrecks. In the nineteenth century, over one-hundred ships sailed by Key West every day. Our waters were known as some of the most treacherous in the world. On average, at least one ship per week would collide into the reefs, giving the Florida Keys the dubious distinction of being the shipwreck capital of the world."

"When can we climb the tower and take in the view?" the groupie asks.

"That's off-limits. Liability issues and such."

"They let you do it at the other lighthouse," she says, a whine in her voice, her jaw jutting forward.

"Perhaps, but this is a private residence." My father's eyes shift, and he bites his lower lip. "The laws are different."

His answer is rubbish. The reason the area is cordoned from guests is that Ivy occupies the top. She would never consent to have her living space and studio made spectacles. Who could blame her?

My father continues. "Where was I?" He scratches his chin. I'm surprised at this lapse of memory; this is his favorite part of the story.

"The shipwrecks," I whisper.

"Of course," he continues. "The shipwrecks. When a wreck was sited, cries of Wreck Ashore would resonate across the island. In a practice referred to as wrecking, men would clamber to the docks, jumping aboard boats in their race to the reef. Many citizens built their fortunes taking valuables from shipwrecks foundered close to shore. Sold at auction, the courts awarded anywhere from twenty-five to fifty percent of the booty's profit to the wreckers."

A bumblebee darts around the group and the guests jump around, waving their hands, trying to swat it away.

"Ignore it," I say. "Bees usually vanish as quickly as they arrive." The group settles down, and the bee zips into the sky. I look at Daddy, nodding and encouraging him to continue, anxious to escape the group and begin my run.

"During that time, our Fog Horn House—which we now use as a guest house—was constructed." He points to the small circular structure, the place where I'm staying, which stands adjacent to the garden. "In inclement weather, when the lights were more difficult to see, the horn was sounded. Its lingering, resonating wail also alerted the townsfolk of a vessel's misfortune."

The groupie cracks her gum. "I heard this same spiel at the Shipwreck Museum on Mallory Square. Only the guy giving the tour was wearing a pirate costume."

Another guest, a coiffed middle-aged woman wearing a pink golf shirt and Kelly-green skirt, speaks up, glaring at the woman. "Well, I haven't heard it. Please, let Thomas finish the story. I'm interested."

The groupie's nostrils flare, and she takes two steps backward, distancing herself from the woman. My father continues unfazed. He's used to dealing with annoying guests.

"Tower lights were automated in 1955, and—as befell all lighthouses dotting coastlines across the country—lightkeepers were no longer needed. These days ships and boats have navigational electronics, but many lighthouses remain in use as a backup plan."

A thoughtful look passes my father's face as he slides his hands into the pockets of his pressed navy shorts. "Another local attraction—The Key West Lighthouse—stands ten feet taller than ours. It was built in the same era and is situated across the street from the Ernest Hemingway Home. It's a prime spot for attracting tourists, so that lighthouse was leased to the Arts and Historical Society."

He points to the groupie, addressing her. "That's the lighthouse you must have toured. The one where you climbed to the top of the tower."

"Yeppers. That's the one." Beaming, her eyes dart around the group, happy to be vindicated by his attention.

"Our lighthouse, however," my father continues, "was deemed too expensive to maintain, and was closed in 1969. After almost a decade of neglect, it was put on the public auction block. And the rest is history." He places his hand on my shoulder. "Poppy and I purchased it and raised our three daughters here. When they were grown, we converted it into what stands in front of you today: The Maiden Tower Inn."

He folds his arms across his chest. "And that, my friends, recaps the days of yore."

As the group applauds, he takes a slight bow and then straightens. "Are there any questions?"

I glance at the groupie, willing her silence. Surprisingly, she obliges.

"Don't forget to check out the Pet Parade down the street at 5:30," Daddy says, as the group begins chattering amongst themselves. If you're interested in learning the legend surrounding The Maiden Tower, we'll regroup in the parlor at eight for our Evening Hour."

I elbow his arm, shooting him a warning side-glance. He

clears his throat. "If you're easily spooked, may I, instead, suggest The Rum Bar on Upper Duval. Their collection of rums is extraordinary, and the seats on the front porch are great for people watching."

The guests disband, some returning to the house, others walking towards the street. Entering the inn for pre-run hydration, I stop to admire the painting hanging on the wall behind the piano; the life-sized portrait of Rossalea.

The painting's a startling contrast to the contemporary works painted by Ivy, which are also hung throughout the inn. Ivy must have a fascination with the woman; her sketchpad is testimony. I, too, admire the Maiden's elegance; her soulful dark eyes, the arch of her brow. Gold, maroon and blue-green ribbons are woven into her dark thick hair, which is tied, twisted and piled up about her head.

I have a sudden desire to study her portrait more closely and flick a light switch, which doesn't work. I forgot. This socket's been dead for years. Renovating and maintaining this lighthouse turned out to be more than my parents had bargained for, but Mama maintains the work is her calling. She told her wide-eyed, trusting young daughters that she was a lighthouse keeper in a previous life. Comments such as this frightened us when we were kids.

The second floor, formerly the lighthouse keepers' living space, houses four bedrooms. Growing up, there were five rooms, but my folks knocked out a room and a couple of closets to ensure each bedroom had an adjoining bathroom. All guest rooms should be *en suite*, so guests don't have to share a bath. The ground floor, where boats were once stored, now hosts the reception area, parlor, dining room and kitchen.

Entering the dining room back in the inn, I help Mama clear the table. Nina's still out, but her sister has returned, and is now upstairs, cleaning the rooms. I hear the whir of the vacuum from above. The leftovers look mundane; squares of pre-cut fruit, thawed frozen quiche and coffee cake from Publix.

I pinch off a piece of cake and pop it into my mouth. Ick. Fake sugar. "Don't you think the guests are sick of aspartame-spiked coffeecake?" I ask as we walk into the kitchen, each of us holding a tray filled with dishes.

"I know, I know. I grabbed the fat-frees by mistake." Exhausted, Mama places the tray on a table and topples into a chair. Her face is drained of color.

"We need to replace Nina." She speaks each word slowly, in a monotone, her voice void of its usual expressiveness. A ruddy color travels up her neck as she shakes her head. "There's nothing else we can do."

The kitchen is dirtier than I've ever seen it. Vegetable shavings litter the floor, the sink is filled with a clutter of pots and pans, and the stovetop is streaked with grease. I shudder at the thought of the health department paying a visit today. I grab a cup, pour a glass of juice and down it in three large gulps.

A misty pink sheen wells in her eyes as she stares, vacantly, at a crumbled dishcloth. "And I'm beside myself at the thought of it. What if she recovers only to find out she's lost her job? She'd think her family abandoned her. What then?"

An idea springs into my head. We could have a win-win in this scenario. I walk to Mama and place my hand upon her shoulder.

"Why not hire me? I've cooked for catered gigs since my exit from college. That way you can let things ride a while and pay me what you paid Nina. I'll make breakfasts—delicious and made-from-scratch—for the guests. I'll hold the position open for her until she gets her act together. It shouldn't be much longer."

Mama wipes her eyes with the edge of her shirt collar. Looking up at me, her smile trembling, she grasps my right hand and squeezes it so hard it hurts. I wince, and she releases it. Opening my palm, she begins to trace each line with the tip of her forefinger.

"Linnea, the twinflower, firstborn of my daughters." The slow, gentle touch of her fingertip tracing the lines on my flesh tickles, but I remain silent.

"A Pisces to the core, you are compassionate, hard-working, dedicated and reliable. Born under the twelfth sign, your element is water, and your symbol is the fish. Why have you journeyed for so long," her gaze rises to search my eyes, "and moved so far away?"

I shake my head, imperceptibly, and her gaze returns to my hand. Her forefinger trails along my palm and then stops, her fingernail pressing into my flesh.

"You will cross troubled waters."

At these words, nausea rolls over me as I remember my dream. I snatch away my hand, placing it behind my back. Mama's hands return to her lap and then she clasps them together, looking at me, a sad smile playing about her lips.

"You will always be a part of our family, my darlin'. And, try as you may, you can never escape us." Again, she reaches for my arm, unfurls my fist, and kisses my palm.

12. WWW.IVYCHANDLER.COM

With trepidation and sadness, I bear witness to the vast gentrification underway in Key West. A new generation of money is displacing the funky counterculture that has, up until now, defined our town.

Yesterday I bade farewell to a couple—Sidney and Adam— who made hammered silver and sea glass jewelry for Conch House. They also earned additional income contributing to Key West's evening vibe; Sidney's sprite-like soprano accompanied Adam's ukulele at the Green Parrot and other bars around town.

If no venue was available, the pair took to the street, staging their quirky brand of musical pop-up long into the night. But their bright, bubbly sounds are moving upstate. In the past couple of years, the town's become unaffordable. The rent of their cottage, for example, has doubled, so they've secured new digs in the Panhandle. Our loss, Grayton Beach's gain.

The monied who can afford to buy up houses are also importing their own vernacular, which I find particularly annoying. They call Key West, for example, The Island. Recently overheard:

"You must try the conch ceviche on The Island." Or, "Does anyone on The Island make a decent espresso?"

My favorite to date:

"We spent most of last Season catching up with the Weitings on The Island. You remember them—they have the darling loft in Soho? You know the one—next to Raoul's—the place with such divine tartare?"

The Island. Ha. It makes Key West sound remote, detached, and, therefore, covetously desirable. Ahem. Begging pardon. We're not, as our poor cousin ninety miles south, some floundering archipelago trying to recover from a communist dictatorship. And surprise, surprise—English is our native tongue.

Aside from the local color being rapidly hosed away, there's nothing exotic or adventurous about our destination. There's no need to have your Deet-sprayed body airlifted into our jungly landscape when the Overseas Highway is so lovely to drive. No need to enlist a guide to navigate the terrain when the on-the-hour Conch Train Tour will show you the sights. Your only strategy will be to study the cruise ship's docking calendars to determine when to avoid Duval and its arteries. That's when the voracious party animals debark and come roaring into town for on-shore libations.

The most exotic thing about Key West, frankly, are the chickens.

But today we're bringing fresh culture into our parks, museums and storefronts, which will capture our unique and whimsical flavor. I, and a group of other local misfits—a stainless steel sculptor, fused glassmaker, and photographer—have been commissioned to create a series of art projects and installations to be placed about the city.

The possibilities I'm considering for my next paintings are thrilling. Unchartered waters, landscapes—perhaps, I'll paint an electrified cityscape—something to bring fresh funk back to town.

So here you'll find me—ivychandler.com—paintbrush in hand, part of the resistance and airborn with possibilities!

Ivy (aka, Blog Writer Girl)

I vy
Part of the resistance? Hogwash. By now you know that we misfits, as unhinged as we are, are terrible narrators of our own stories. We can't be trusted.

This summer we've been commissioned to execute artscapes to serve as a zoo of endangered species, roped off for the public to admire. Misfits can undoubtedly use the cash. But are we, too, imposters, part of the cultural malaise? Gentrification spawns a bourgeoisie; will the future judge our art as poster children for conformity?

Not on my watch. Multitudes of worlds exist between this planet and me. I've crawled into yawning black caves where none have dared journey; slept on beds of needles painful to the flesh; bitten into pestilent fruits while listening to yowling sounds of an excruciating timbre.

So, in the spirit of not being afraid of the dark, I'm retreating from the light and luminosity that usually graces my work. To the point, it's exhausting living in a town flooded with sunshine. I've begun to paint a landscape of tangled flora, vines the size of a muscled arm, and leaves so dense the light can't penetrate.

Tropical, most certainly. But if you look closely and have a botanical knowledge of native plants, you will see this flora is not common to our area. It's invasive and threatens our landscape. These species have thrived and adapted so well, they're displacing our native plant and wildlife communities. These exotics are taking over, crawling up buildings, ceilings caving beneath their weight, their roots breaking through sidewalks. They are endangering us to the point of extinction.

It's too late to stop them.

≈

I STARE at my computer screen, chewing a cuticle on my pinkie. Did I write those words only yesterday? What was up with that frightening rant about endangered species, yowling sounds and darkness? What happened to the charming fun-loving lady airborne with possibilities? Thank God I didn't post that last little doozie. What would my readers think?

They wouldn't like me. They'd unsubscribe from my blog. They'd find me certifiable; a nonsensical blustering idiot divorced from reality. That's what they'd think. But they'd be wrong. Totally off target. For today I am perfectly sane and—not meaning to boast—really quite fabulous. Viscerally attuned, I'm invincible.

Tonight, The Conch House Gallery is hosting a party, by invitation only, for patrons and artists. Freaky Ivy, all wrung out and so frightfully fearful, shuns events such as this. But not Blog Writer Girl. I'm back on track, bursting with energy and better than ever!

Last month on a day like today, when the air smelled of honeysuckle and life was aglow in twinkling lights, I purchased new clothes and makeup to better reflect the me I want to be. And here she is! I gaze at my reflection in the mirror, delighted with the woman who smiles back. I'm wearing skin-tight faded jeans, strategically shorn at the thighs, and a turquoise sparkle shirt with plunging neckline revealing a fierce décolletage. Where did I learn that word? Adjusting my breasts up higher into my bra, I giggle to myself saying the word slowly, adding a French accent for show: dey-co-la-tege!

My face is transformed by a slash of red lipstick and a triple coat of mascara. Green eyeliner slanting up at the far edges of my eyes is so artfully applied I resemble Cat Woman. "Meeeaow," I say to this vision in the mirror. Leaning over, I shake out my ponytail and let my hair fall in golden rivulets in front of my face. I straighten, flinging my head back, and run my fingers through my hair. Pursing my lips, I cock my head. "Purrrrrfect," I whisper, trilling my "r's."

I check my phone: 6:30. Linnea and my parents should be in the kitchen, preparing the goodies for Evening Hour, which begins at eight. Just last week, Linnea began making breakfasts for the guests and pies for the nightly show. I should have enough time to sneak out the door without detection—Cat Woman on the prowl.

With five-inch heels dangling from their straps between my fingers and a small clutch secured under my armpit, I grasp the railing of the stairwell. I tiptoe down the circular stairway, stepping over the stairs that creak. Fifteen steps up from the parlor, I press my back against the wall and scan the room. Daddy's arranged the seating for tonight's performance, and the coast is clear of stray guests. Pressing my hand across my mouth to suppress a giddy laugh, I scamper through the parlor without a side-glance at Rossalea. Undetected, I scurry out the front door and onto the street.

I step into my heels and begin a wobbly, feline mince down the sidewalk towards the gallery. Tourists don't know me, and shopkeepers and townies don't seem to recognize me but, judging by the heads turning my way and their face-splintering grins, everyone loves me. I love them back! Before I know it, I'm standing in the threshold of Conch House Art Gallery, towering over Whitney—the gallery owner's assistant. She glances up at me, her eyes vacant.

"I'm sorry. This is a private event. We open to the public tomorrow morning at ten."

My laughter rings out like wind chimes, sounding exactly like Mamas. I place my palm on her shoulder. "Whitney. My work is splattered all through the gallery, and you won't let me in?"

She straightens her glasses, which rest across the bridge of her nose.

"Ms. Chandler?" Her eyes squint as they travel up and down my body. Her gaping mouth forms an "O" of incredulity.

"I didn't recognize you in all that..." Her hands flit about, as she seems to be at a loss for words. She gives a funny half-smile, smoothing her tidy black A-line. "I must say, Ms. Chandler. You look, well, different."

"I'm not Ms. Chandler. Please. Call me, Ivy."

"Well, sure, I...vy." She draws out the *I*, her favorite word.

Whitney thinks everything revolves around her, especially her opinions about what constitutes art. Her adamant disdain for my recent work might have stung yesterday, but today I'm made of Teflon—nothing sticks to the surface. She pastes on her *general public sales smile* and then swivels around and grabs champagne from a café table. Turning to face me, the glasses wobble on a tray beneath my gaze.

"Care for some bubbly?"

I regard the flutes and shudder at their frothing mouths, but paint on a face to mirror hers; one associated with parties and companionable small talk.

"No thanks, Whitney." I peer over her head, surveying the crowd. I want nothing messing with this glorious mood, fitted on with this wonderfully normal personality.

I walk into the room, thrilled the show is having such an excellent turnout. Oh, there's Jonah, the stainless-steel artist commissioned to create a sculpture for the city. I wave at him, wiggling my fingertips, admiring how my fresh coat of fuchsia polish sparks shimmers across the gallery. Regarding me curiously, he untangles himself from a knot of patrons and walks to my side.

"Ivy?"

With five inches added to my stature, I'm his height. The plaid shirt he wears mirrors the colors of his eyes—brown, flecked with yellows and greens. There's even a bit of russet in there. Gorgeous! I've never seen so many colors in a pair of eyes. How could I have ever considered us misfits? Side by side, we tower above everyone, the Queen and King, reigning over our subjects.

"Jonah!" I place my clutch onto a table and fling my arms around him. His champagne sloshes, and he backs away. Placing his glass beside my handbag, he wipes his palms on the back of his jeans.

"Eek, sorry sweetie." I grab a random, crumpled cocktail napkin and batt it against his butt.

"No worries, Ivy." His cheeks, peeking out above his beard, redden and he takes a deep breath, seeming at a loss for words.

Pursing his lips, he exhales, emitting a long, shallow whistling noise. "It's good to see you. At the meeting, you said you couldn't make it."

"Ah well, you know me. Plans change." I make a sweeping gesture to a small tubular steel structure in the corner. Three tiny lights are strategically placed to illuminate the brilliance of the creation.

"Is that yours?"

"Yes," he says, his eyes wandering to the piece. "It's my mock-up for the installation. I plan to get going on it next week." His gaze returns to me, his bottom teeth scraping against his upper lip. "But I'd like your opinion first. I'm concerned about how the angles on the right side balance with the left."

I grab his hand, weave my fingers through his, and smile into his eyes. "Oh, yes! How fun! Let's trade notes."

Lucy, the gallery owner, saunters towards us, nodding at and weaving through through the crowd. Earrings made of conch shells dangle from low-hanging lobes, and she wears a hot pink sheath patterned with lime green ferns. I'll bet it's a Lilly Pulitzer. I love the bright, vibrant colors in that clothing line, reminding me of the colors in my happy paintings. I need more of that palette in my wardrobe to inspire.

Arms akimbo, she stands in front of me gaping, as if I were a circus monkey. "Ivy Chandler. Is that you?"

"Of course, it's me." My elation slides down a notch. Why does everyone keep saying that?

Judging by the rapid-fire blinking of her eyes, Lucy must note my discomfort and quickly adds, "I'm just so used to seeing you in your signature paint-splattered overalls. But this new Ivy is a vision of, well, *fun*."

She nods at Jonah, untangles my fingers from his and links her arm into mine. Jonah backs away, wordlessly, and shoves his hands into his pockets.

"I must introduce you around. Many of our buyers are here because of your work." Leaning into me, she lifts her chin, cups her hand against her mouth and whispers in my ear. "These days I've spun you as the reclusive artist who creates masterpieces in a tower. You know—add a bit of intrigue and romance. This rare appearance is sure to make a splash." Her eyes flicker to my cleavage, and I detect the shadow of a frown.

"First, there's a couple who seem quite interested in your dolphin piece. They're down from Palm Beach and didn't flinch at the cost. I was surprised it didn't sell at the last show. Perhaps it's a bit, umm, depressing?" A sharp crease burrows between her eyebrows, as if she's lit upon an idea. "Maybe if we milk that angle a bit—spin the dark side of your work?"

She opens her mouth as if to say more, and then shakes her head as if deciding against it. Her lips seal, almost disappearing into her face.

Not the dolphin piece. Anything but the dolphin piece. My hand flutters to the silver charm at my throat. Delphina's interpretation was right—I'd painted it when out of control, being used as bait by the beast, dragged across the ocean floor with a hook affixed into my mouth.

She guides me through the knots of patrons and fellow artists. Some do a double-take when they see me but recover quickly, touching my arm, telling me how great I look. Lucy pats my arm as she stops to stand in front of the painting, and I find myself face-to-face with the last person I want to see—my dark side, which has taken on a vivid, saturated look. As if witnessing a fatal car accident, I can't help but stare at the horror.

Lucy smiles brightly at the potential buyers, who regard the painting curiously from under silver coifs, their arms crossed over their midriffs. He wears baby blue pants, small whales patterned around ironed pleats, and she, a lemon-yellow wrap dress. A diamond, the size of a macadamia nut, sparkles on her ring finger, the skin as wrinkled as fine yellowed parchment.

"Mr. and Mrs. Johnson, may I present Ivy Chandler, the artist behind the work."

"Oh, my dear, this piece is fascinating. We'd be so interested in your interpretation." I jump, startled. The woman's gravelly, drawling accent sounds like that of my late grandmother, Grandma Rose.

I glance again at the dolphin—skin mottled, body bloated—trapped underwater. My heart clutches, twisting in a vise, and I turn away, swallowing hard. Lucy nudges me, her large, square teeth glistening with such brightness I wince. My eyes cloud with tears. Lowering my head. I press my face into my palm, trying to steady the shake.

"There. You see?" Lucy says, patting me on the small of my back. "As I was telling you. This painting is obviously heartfelt, it means a great deal to Ms. Chandler."

They think I'm a nut job. A lunatic. That I'm losing my mind. Is that why they find this piece so fascinating? Of course, after all, they're right. I'm as crazy as the bat that bullies me, circling me, nipping at my neck wherever and whenever it has a hankering. Through my fingers, I regard the man's brown leather loafer, tap tap tapping. Coming here was a terrible mistake. What can I say, what can I do to let them think I'm fine? Right as rain. Nothing wrong with me that a Zyprexa can't cure. Someone touches my shoulder, and I look up. Thank God. Jonah.

"I'm sorry, Lucy. Can I borrow Ivy? There's a group about to leave, and they've been waiting patiently to meet her."

I turn to the couple, who are furrowing their eyebrows, regarding me curiously. I speak between clenched teeth. "Lovely meeting you, ah." I struggle to remember their names. "Yes. Mr. and Mrs. Johnson. Yes. Lucy's right. This painting is... it...." My words won't cooperate.

Jonah rushes me away before Lucy has time to protest. As he pulls my hand forward, Mr. Johnson hands Lucy a credit card, glancing sideways at me. Which is he purchasing? My painting or my madness?

I look at Jonah, vastly relieved. "This party is bringing me down."

"I was watching. You seemed upset, so I made up the excuse."

"I owe you." Feeling a lurch in my chest, my festive mood's resurfacing. "But I'm fine now. Better than fine. I'm absolutely fabulous. Do you mind if we leave?"

He grins, grabs my bag from the table, and hands it to me. We exit the gallery with a flurry of heads turning in our direction. I'm sure tongues will fly at our departure.

"Where to?" he asks, stopping beside a building to catch his breath. Pulling a pair of Aviators from his back pocket and adjusting them over his eyes, he looks up at the sky, his back against the window of a storefront.

"What time is it?" I ask. At our abrupt escape, my heart pounds inside my chest.

He checks his phone. "About 7:30."

I clap my hands. "Perfect. We've enough time to make it back to the inn for Evening Hour."

"Great idea. I've heard about your parents' performance. It's got quite the reputation––everyone loves it. I thought it was for guests only."

"It is. But you will be *my* guest tonight. Plus, attendance is down in summer." I shoot him a glance. "But can I be honest? Tell you my preference?"

"Sure," he says, the edges of his mouth lifting into a slow smile.

"I detest listening to the legend of the lighthouse. It totally undoes me. If you don't mind, I'd rather introduce you to Linnea, one of my sisters."

His face falls, and I press my forefingers into his chest.

"Don't look so glum. She's famous for her pies, which she's pulling out of the oven as we speak. We'll give you the biggest piece. She hangs out in the kitchen during the show. I don't spend as much time with her as I'd like."

"Sounds like a plan," he says, his smile returning.

Walking towards the inn, hand-in-hand with Jonah, that glorious feeling of being airborne returns. We climb the stairs to the front porch, and I pull open the door, ushering him into the parlor. Guests are sitting in chairs and on the ottoman, absorbed in slices of pie with lemony fillings, which rest on side tables or atop their laps. I sigh, grinning broadly, immensely proud of this picture of whimsy and old-fashioned charm. Mama sits on a bench at the piano, laughing with the guests.

I step in front of Jonah and, without a misstep, perform a pirouette finishing my twirl in a bow. Quite a feat in heels. Mama's eyes widen. She stands hurriedly and rushes over to me. The guests––mouths full, forks dangling mid-air––follow her with their eyes.

"Mama. I wanna introduce you and Daddy to Jonah." As I gesture towards him, Mama catches my hand mid-air. She pulls it towards her, linking her forefinger into one of the bangles on my wrist and lowers her forehead so that it touches the bracelet.

"He's a metal artist," I continue. "We were at a party at the gallery and became hungry for a piece of Linnea's pie."

"It's a pleasure meeting you, Mr. and Mrs. Chandler. I've always wanted to take a peek inside The Maiden Tower Inn. It's quite the legend in town."

Daddy's eye twitches as he looks away, muttering something under his breath. Mama releases my wrist, bites her lower lip, and shakes her head. My parents have lost their manners.

"We don't want to disrupt Evening Hour," I continue, my voice high-pitched and shaky, taken aback and confused by their reaction to my bringing home a nice man. Isn't that what they want for me? "We'll just mosey on into the kitchen. Go visit with Linnea."

I swivel, nod at Jonah, and take a couple of steps forward. Mama grabs my shoulders, trying to block my path, and her eyes fade to darkness. "I had no idea you'd left your studio. Where on earth did you find that get up? Oh, honey. Look at you."

Why is she embarrassed about me when her antics are a legend in town? Like mother, like daughter, right? She's doing it again. Being nasty to me for no reason.

"What, Mama. You don't like my dancing, my clothes?" I tug at my top. "I want to see Linnea. Introduce her to Jonah."

I stare at her twisted face, her eyes filling with tears. My spirits plummet, sliding down my torso, my shimmering world crumbling beneath my feet. The chorus of voices returns to repeat their taunting chant: She's ruining it again. She's ruining it again.

"No, honey, no." Her eyes dart wildly about, gripping my biceps so hard they burn. "We need to close the windows in your studio. Heavens to Betsy, Ivy. You left them wide open, and I believe the humidity has damaged that piece you're working on." Her words sound off-kilter, foreign, their thick-as-honey drawl vanished.

The room begins twirling around me, all of the guests morphing into an ugly blur, crumbs spilling from their mouths as they devour the pastries in front of them. Rossalea points and laughs at me from her stance in the portrait like I'm a fool, a disgrace. Why would *she*, who understands my suffering, *she*, who is my closest of allies––turn against me? The incessant chatter in my head won't stop, and I kick off my shoes, pressing my palms to my ears. Daddy rushes over to Jonah.

"Hey, son. Let's go outside. I'd like to show you the foghorn we had restored. You might find it of interest."

I watch them retreat, tears spilling from my eyes, as Mama leads me to the stairwell. The guests have abandoned their pie. Now, they're perched like eagles, rigid in their chairs. Their heads rotate around, scouting me as if I were their next prey.

"All we wanted was pie, Mama." My words feel thick, stuck in my throat, and emerge from my mouth, sounding disembodied, like they belong to an old woman. "Why won't you let me see my sister?"

She grips her hands around my hips, pushing me forward, up the stairs, following close behind.

Arriving in the service room, she takes my hand, leading me to my bed, to the canisters of pills at my bedside. My senses on fire, her touch feels like a third degree burn. The windows are shut to retain the air-conditioned chill. There's no humidity in this room. She lied. Another one of her ruses, her tiny bits of trickery to make me obey.

Flinging off her hand, I begin pacing the room, hands on hips, regarding my mother, this puppeteer. One yank and my body turns right, another pull, my arm flings left. She beckons me towards the bed, and, like an obedient child, I sit. She unscrews the tops, one by one, shakes the medication into her hand and then puts it into a small plastic cup.

"You can't force me to take them, Mama." I shake my head, furiously.

My diaphragm lifts with a heaving force; a levitation at the base of my spine. Heart thundering in my chest, I am thrilled at what lies beneath me.

"I'm riding the tips of the waves, Mama. They are fantastic." I fan my hands towards the floor, agog at the infinity of silvers in the mercurial waters roiling beneath me spewing sea foam onto the beach.

"Oh, my God. Look how they shine." My hands begin trembling, out of control, and I claw at the air, searching for a paintbrush. "I need to paint them, Mama. I need to get up into my studio."

"I know, sugar. I know." She speaks softly. Taking my chin, she edges a pill towards my mouth.

Am I a feverish infant? I yank my head away. Her fingertips are bruising me. Again, she turns my face towards her, and with practiced hands, opens my mouth, placing the pill on my tongue. Then, she presses a glass of water against my lips. Without moving my mouth, I maneuver the tablet under the back flap of my tongue and take the sip of water. When she turns to get another pill, I spit it out, sliding it under my butt.

The performance is repeated, and then she pulls me into her breast, stroking my hair. Under the spell of her fingers, for a few blessed moments, I feel calm and at peace. Then, a pulsing pain at my temples begins throbbing, a mile a minute. I lurch away from her touch, the wind knocked out of me, and tumble––headfirst––into the ocean.

Gasping for air, soul-bashing hopelessness reclaims its estate.

13. DELPHINA

I lie in bed, knees scrunched up towards my chest to form a surface for my computer screen. Sonny's hand, stroking my forearm, wanders over to fondle my breast. His groping fingers cause my arm to jiggle, and I screw up the spreadsheet. I grab his hand, place it on his chest, and adjust the pillows behind my back, so I can face him.

"Please, Sonny. Can you give me some space, a moment of peace? This is the first minute I've had all month to reconcile accounts receivable."

His nostrils flare. "What about sparing a minute in your busy life to work on our relationship?"

My mouth falls open, and I shake my head, incredulous. "You've got to be kidding me. This is our livelihood. Someone's got to pay attention to the business end." I point furiously at my computer screen.

With an exaggerated sigh, he turns over. His back now facing me, he speaks to the wall. "I love you, baby, but you don't give me the time of day. You're prioritizing everything but our relationship."

I clench my fists. What a beast. He puts his physical needs above us being able to pay our mortgage.

"Allow me to translate," I sputter. "What you mean is, you haven't been laid in a couple of days and are pissed. You need to find a way to be a less needy partner while I ensure we have a roof over our heads."

His silence infuriates me, and I continue working, grinding my teeth.

∾

LAST NIGHT I SLEPT FITFULLY, as did Sonny, but there's no rest, I suppose, for the weary. Or is that no rest for the wicked? I don't know. We're too exhausted and angry with each other for wickedness.

This morning finds me rushing about the family room, harried, as usual. Dismantling Ella's baby gym, I return it to the box and shove it under the sofa. Straightening, I fluff up pillows on the couch—the ones I'd chosen to add splashes of color to the pale lavender-gray palette of my decor. I swipe away crumbs from the cushions into the palm of my hand. Last night, before coming to bed and annoying me, Sonny must have devoured an entire box of pita crisps while watching TV.

Trotting to the trashcan, I knock into Ella's stacking nest toy. Red, green and blue lights flash as the blocks topple down. Startled, I trip over her musical ball, which sets off a Mozart allegro and drop the crumbs on the floor. Heading towards the kitchen to get the Dustbuster, I step on Esteban, a knitted pink mouse toy, who squeals. Placing my face into my hands, I shake my head. Even when the baby's out of the house, this place is like walking through a circus tent.

Why do I feel such compulsion to lend an impression of normalcy to our home when it's obvious it's anything but normal? It seems we've converted this place into a Gymboree. Sonny wants three kids, but even with the help from my mother-in-law, I'm not sure I could manage two. Not to mention being able to afford them.

Lita's at St. Mary's, and Ella's settled in their church nursery. As Lita says, she's never too young for *Madre María's Iglesia*. The three-hour respite each Sunday morning is sacred time for me, as well. We reserve Sundays for charters or boat maintenance, and today Sonny is replacing the mast on The Coral Princess. Cha-ching, cha-ching. I was up and down with Ella through the night, am fried, but no matter. My sleep is broken anyway by matrimonial angst and an overdue mortgage.

Jarring me from my thoughts, a voice outside shouts, "Delphina, I'm here. It's me."

I glance at the clock: 10:25. Already?

I circle the room, surveying the wreckage. I was hoping to have this mess straightened up before Linnea arrived. I glance at the crumbs, scattered about the tiles and shake my head.

"Give me a minute." I scoop up Estaben and the music ball, now resonating with a sonata, and return them to the toy box. The shrill of a train whistle—*woot-woot*—is launched. Geez. That thing goes off at the slightest movement.

I unlatch the front door and watch as she removes items from the basket attached to the handlebars on her bike. She climbs up the entry stairs and onto the porch. Stepping into the house, she holds a small grass-woven basket half-filled with shells and a covered Pyrex dish. My sister never walks across a threshold empty-handed.

She scrunches her nose. "Heavens, Delphina. What's that racket? You said Sunday mornings were your quiet time. It sounds like I've fallen into a Pixar film set."

A cacophony of muffled noise emerges from the purple and pink striped crate, and I flick my fingers towards the box. "I lined up some entertainment for your arrival."

She laughs, her eyes darting about the wreckage, and then hands me the container.

"I whipped up some carob, carrot and granola muffins for the guests this morning. I made extra for us."

"You stole food from The Maiden Tower? I hope Mama didn't see you leave. You'd get fired your first day."

"Silly. She knows I'm coming to see you, and said to give you a kiss." Linnea tilts her head and pecks my cheek.

"Ha. She's happy there's a proxy. Now she and Dad won't have to visit this afternoon."

Linnea's eyes dart from mine and then she crosses the floor, taking care to walk around the crumbs. Centering the basket on the coffee table, she glances over her shoulder.

"Don't be a whiney cat, Delphina. You know she loves you."

Deflection from unfortunate family topics is her favorite refrain. Placing the dish on the dining table, I cross my forearms over my midriff, turn to face my sister and stomp my foot. Biting my lower lip, I try to contain myself, but explode.

"Damn it. Mama cares more about those freakin' chickens than she does her only granddaughter." I fling my arms into the air. "Lita treats Ella as if she's the center of the universe and my own flesh-and-blood can barely be bothered."

"Don't let it ruffle your feathers, Delphina. Mama means well."

"It's hard not to take it personally." I take a deep breath, trying to calm down.

"They're overwhelmed with guest duties, now that Nina's gone. But I'm back for a while and can take some of the load off their backs."

"Are you making time for Ivy?" I ask, my voice surprisingly shrill. "She needs space from Mama. That could be part of her problem. You'd think our mother was her press secretary, the way she manages her schedule. She even does her laundry."

Turning to face me, Linnea's voice sounds annoyed.. "I'd love hanging out with Ivy, but she's rarely available. Like you said, Delphina. It's hard getting past her secretary."

She winks at me, but I see a flicker of worry—or is that pain?—darting about her eyes. My heart twists thinking about these dysfunctions in our relationships. Are all family dynamics so splintered and complex?

"Let's make a date," I say. "Me, you and Ivy. Like old times. We're way overdue."

Linnea waves her fist, victorious, over her head. "I love it," she exclaims, her enthusiasm returned. "Sometime this week, perhaps?"

Placing my fingertips against my temples, my words are directed at the floor. "I'm working the Cat tomorrow through Thursday and need to spend those evenings with Ella. Lita's volunteered at the food pantry on Friday, and if I don't schedule some alone time with my husband ..." I falter, not wanting our conversation to wiggle into that can of worms. I look up, raising my brow. "How about the week after? I'll talk to Sonny. Then, we can carve something in stone."

"I'd love that, Delphina. Let's dress up, go into town, and have a ladies' night. Adult beverages, music, the whole bit." She speaks rapidly, her eyes dancing at the thought. "I'll have to pass it by Mama, though. Ivy, too. Seems her work takes precedence over people."

Deflated, I shake my head. "Ridiculous. It's just an evening out, for heaven sakes."

Linnea's smile fades. She bends to remove a small conch from the basket and runs her forefinger across the pearlescent open lip.

"Ivy used the shells as a still life for her painting. She gathered them from the beach but says she has no use for them now." She brings the shell up into the light, studying it. "Now that she's changed direction in her work. Now that she's done painting beachscapes."

I stoop to pick up a pacifier that found its way under the sofa. "I know. Her uploaded paintings are more *tortured artist* every time she posts. I subscribe to her blog. It's the only time we visit. A rather one-sided conversation, wouldn't you say?"

Linnea doesn't respond and returns the shell to the basket. Taking several steps away from the table, she places a forefinger on her chin and sighs.

"If you don't want the basket here, I'll bet they'd look nice in your bathroom." She glances at me, a question in her eye, steering the course of conversation away from Ivy. "I know counter space is limited, but you can place them on top of the commode or something. They'd look pretty there."

I walk towards the table and select a rectangular shaped shell with rounded edges.

"Pretty? I don't know. This shell looks like a coffin." I look up at Linnea. "That's what shells are, after all." I return it to the basket. "Empty coffins. Empty because the animal died and then rotted away."

Her face falls. "That's depressing."

I bite my lower lip, cupping my palm on her shoulder. "Sorry. Lack of sleep makes me morose. Of course, they're beautiful, Linnea, and thank you. I'll find a place of honor for them."

I motion to the couch. "Hey. Take a seat. I'll get coffee. And I can't wait to dive into those muffins."

Linnea's face brightens, and she plops onto the sofa, trying to get comfortable amongst the throw pillows and stuffed animals. I retreat to the kitchen and arrange the muffins alongside pats of butter on pottery teal plates reserved for company. Not that my friends come to visit these days. I'm the only one of my old group plunged into mommy-mode and idle time is nonexistent. I bring the tray to the family room and place it next to the shells.

Sitting next to her, I swing my arm around her shoulder, and she jumps. What's up with that? The girl is wound tighter than I am.

"Oh. Delphina," she says, her voice breathless. "It's you."

"Who else would it be?"

She exhales sharply and then blinks several times, regaining her composure.

"Sorry. Thinking about the pies I'm making for tonight's performance at the inn. The Lemon-Chiffons have been a hit of late." She smiles, avoiding my gaze. "Hey. By the way, I brought over something else." She hands me a sealed blank envelope. I look at her, glimpsing Dad in the twitch of her eye. "It might come in handy."

She sniffs. "Come on. Open it. It contains the answer to a puzzle. Use the tip of the knife, so you don't rip the contents."

"You and your games," I say, as she hands me the butter knife. I slide the blade along the edge. Opening the envelope, I see a check, which I remove: five-hundred and seventy-nine dollars made out to me from DJ's Tropical Fish and Supplies.

"What?" I stare at Linnea, my jaw agape.

"It's reimbursement for cost of the misplaced ribbon."

I feel the heat rising onto my cheeks. "You mean the *silk* that was *stolen*," I say, spitting out the words. "I knew that cockroach-serving, reputation-bashing son-of-a-bitch sabotaged my float." My palms close around the check, crumpling it.

"That's not nice of you," she says, her words almost a whisper, touching my balled-up fist. "It's your money, Delphina." I allow her to pry open my palm, and she removes the check from my hand. "Let me explain what happened. Don't do this."

"There's an explanation? Why are you even involved?" I search her face, and her left eye begins twitching uncontrollably as if a fly tunneled into her iris.

"Last week I bumped into Danny Jack Wilson on Duval," she says, rubbing a knuckle into her recalcitrant eye. "I asked him if he'd double-check and make sure all of the materials used on the float were his. I mentioned your missing ribbon."

She lowers her head and leans into the coffee table,

smoothing out the check with her fingertips. "He said he'd look into it and give me a call."

"How did you know it was DJ?" Sour bile crawls up my throat just saying his name.

Her eyes flicker up to catch mine, the left one now steady. "I told you I ran into him the night of the parade. It was he who recognized me. And why wouldn't he, anyway?"

I vaguely recall her telling me she'd met him before I was nearly trampled in the crowd. It's an evening I've tried to forget.

"The next thing I know, he calls me at the inn," she continues, folding the check and sliding it into the pocket on my shirt. "Said your shipment got mixed into theirs."

I remove the check and study it. "I don't believe his story for a minute—the guy's a con. And I'm sure we would have placed in the competition if we'd used the silk." I sigh, my shoulders heaving. "But we could sure use the cash."

"His staff saved the ribbon. He'll return it. You can use it for next year's float. There's no need for me to be the middle man, so he'll bring it to you." Her face colors.

"Honestly, Linnea. No thanks. Even if he wrote a book of apologies, that ribbon now stinks of DJ juju. Not only did he sabotage our chances of placing in the competition, he ruined a whole year of high school. *That*, I can never reclaim." I place the check under the basket of shells. "I don't trust the man; his intentions or his shady operations. I want nothing to do with him."

I squeeze her hand, which lies limp in her lap; it feels clammy and cold. The venom in my voice is upsetting her, so I bite back further comment. "But thanks, sweetie. I appreciate your efforts. Last week we bought a new mast. With that and everything else, expenses are crazy this month."

Linnea nods, her smile weak. She dots my cheek with a tiny kiss and rises, making haste to leave. The muffins and coffee remain untouched.

14. LINNEA

"I think, DJ, everything's cool. At least no blood was spilled. Although it may take a while for her to warm to you." I push the buds that are attached to a cord on my cell phone tighter into my ears, so I can hear him better.

It took some heavy peddling to release the stress I felt after leaving Delphina's. A better sister would have spit out the truth; told her I've got something going on with DJ besides missing silk. But I couldn't. It would be akin to me telling her I was importing elephant tusks from Africa.

I'll work DJ into our conversations with caution. Besides. If I'm thrifty, I'll have enough money to move back to Boise within the next couple of months. If Nina returns to work, maybe sooner. Although his store's closed on Sunday, DJ's at work doing inventory. It's hard to make out his words under the noise of the streets.

"I just mailed some bills for my parents," I say, veering my bike away from a clucking hen and her chicks. "I'm heading towards Fleming now to pick up a bag of lemons."

He reminds me his store is around the corner and asks if I could swing by. I hear the yearning in his voice. It's the same desire I feel, which—since our last date—has settled like a mango pit inside my belly.

"That would work," I say. "I'll see you in a few."

There are plenty of lemons back at the inn for my pies, but I need an excuse to be in his neighborhood. I don't want to seem eager. Pedaling past the post office, I admire the clusters of orange blossoms in the Royal Poinciana. Known to natives as Flame Trees, in June they ignite the town. Their blooms in the trees provide a lovely contrast to the white wooden homes, and the blossoms litter the streets. Tiny purple orchids and exuberant red bougainvillea drape picket fences.

Whizzing past all of this loveliness on a bright summer day, I revel in the scent of flora encircling my face. The smell of such macerating sweetness still has the power to stop me in my tracks, peeling away the decades. I'm a young girl again, pedaling along-side Delphina. Euphoric, fearless, we imagine ourselves tumbling off the edge of the world. Heading towards DJ's store, my feet move slower now, in time to the beat of my thumping heart.

DJ said that owning a tropical fish store had been a fantasy of his since childhood. It took a large amount of start-up capital, which he borrowed from a certain big fish his mother had been courting. Apparently, the man had been married. DJ was privy to their affair, so it was understood—without words—the loan was hush money. DJ was proud to pay back the man within the first five years of business and maintained his silence. After all, the cuckquean—the woman married to the adulterer—turned out to be a favorite customer. Only a serious prick, as DJ explained to me, would ever want to hurt her.

The fact that there are no big-box pet franchises allowed in town is a huge boon to his business. His store is a big fish in a small pond and is, from what Delphina told me, thriving.

DJ waits for me, leaning into the open doorframe of his store. His smile is broad, and those perfect white teeth glisten like a pack of Chicklets in the sun. My eyes zoom in for a closer look at his lips.

"Where are the lemons?" he asks, looking at the empty basket on my bike.

I bite my lower lip, my eyes darting to the street. Why didn't I grab a bag at Faustos to give my story credibility?

"Oh, yeah. The lemons. I decided to pick them up on the way back."

He secures my bike and then gazes at me, assessing and questioning, as if trying to decide something. I remember our conversation that first date: *No lying, Linnea.* I deliver to him my most innocent Catholic girl smile. White lies, black lies, grey— they're woven into the fabric of my life. Hey. Who do they hurt? He presses his fingers against the base of my spine, steering me into his store.

Bluish lights cast a warm, oceanic glow within the showroom, and I gasp, my palm darting across my mouth. "It's beautiful. You're right. All of these iridescent fish swimming around me. I do feel like I'm snorkeling a reef."

I'm also feeling seasick at the thought of it. I remove a pack of gum from the pocket of my shorts; chewing eases my anxiety. I offer him a stick, which he takes, his fingertips pausing when they come in contact with mine.

Crossing his forearms in front of those finely-honed abs I'm so tempted to stroke, he begins walking the length of the room.

"The number one headache is keeping all of these tanks spotlessly clean. The labor costs involved in maintaining healthy landscapes is much more than I ever imagined." I trot behind him like a well-trained terrier. He glances at me over his shoulder. "Nothing turns off a customer more than a dingy tank. And, of course, clean aquariums make for vigorous fish."

I stop to peer into one of the aquariums. A neon yellow specimen darts around a rock, in pursuit of some teal and orange fish, their tails swishing merrily.

A woman emerges from a side door, and I recognize her in an instant. Today she wears jeans and a golf shirt, the store's logo stitched above the shirt pocket. Her makeup is not as garish, but the point of her chin and those silvery eyes still remind me of a shark. I glance at the hoop earring piercing her lower lip—a shark caught on a line. She extends her hand, greeting me with a smile.

"Hi. I'm Cassie. Crazy coincidence, right? Us sitting next to each other on the plane; both of us participating in the parade. And now you're here. Standing right in front of me." She shakes her head in wonder, arms folded across her chest, making cracking sounds with her gum. "Small town."

I chuckle. "I know, right? Thanks for tossing me beads. I recognized you, even in that Tinkerbell costume. I'm surprised you remembered me."

"Ladies like you stand out in this town. The picture of innocence, even wearing that crazy short skirt."

I feel DJ's eyes on my profile. Embarrassed by her words, I feel my face grow hot. "I was flying out of Boise. How about you?" I don't want her to know I'd spied her documents.

"Fort Wayne, Indiana. That's where I'm from. I was helping out my grandmother. I also met with a tropical fish retailer interested in doing business with us." She rakes fingers through her hair, which is colored in a shade of orange that would only be natural if it were growing on a tree. "My boyfriend, Stanson, harvests more fish than DJ can sell."

"That word you use: harvest," I ask. "What does it mean in that context?"

"Tank-harvested to be precise. A large percentage of the fish we sell are born and raised in aquariums." She tips her head towards the row of bubbling glass enclosures.

"We've decided to expand operations by wholesaling to other retailers," DJ adds, raising an eyebrow. "The store in Fort Wayne will be our first account. Cassie will be my liaison." He glances her way and smiles. "It will also allow her the opportunity to see more of her grandmother."

"Wow," I say, impressed with his kindness and business acumen. Maybe I can be his liaison with a fish retailer in Boise. Silly I'm thinking these thoughts when we haven't even kissed.

I turn to Cassie. "Your partner must have one hell of a hatchery. But what about the other fish? The ones you don't"—I pause a second, searching for the words—"tank harvest?"

DJ clears his throat, answering the question I'd directed to her. "There are several species we sell, which can only be collected in the wild."

I swallow hard, at once drained. The electric sensation I'd felt upon seeing him is now replaced with mistrust. Delphina said this practice of harvesting fish was illegal. My eyes cut his way. Observing him through a different lens, that breezy surfer boy manner I found so alluring, is beginning to take on the sleaze of a snake oil salesman. Queasiness churns through my belly, and my attraction to him dims. I shudder, relieved we didn't take this *whatever it is* to the next level. I seem to have a knack for attracting the losers.

He touches my wrist, worry crossing his face and speaks earnestly like he's reading my mind. "Everything we do is environmentally friendly and monitored by the Fish and Wildlife Service. We follow all protocols, have the proper permits and only purchase fish caught with nets."

"I don't know," I squat down to tighten the laces of my shoes, removing myself from the touch of his hand. "Why not stick to tank-harvested?"

"Consumer demand," Cassie replies, hastily, noting my wariness. "The wilds are the most desirable. Demand for clownfish went through the roof after the release of *Finding Nemo*." Her sandal-clad feet shift from side to side. "Fortunately, Stanson figured out a way to breed Clownfish in tanks.

He hasn't had luck with the Blue Tangs. Too bad. *Finding Dory* caused another buying frenzy."

I look up and catch her eye. She raises her shoulders and shrugs. "If they don't get them from us, they'll shop elsewhere."

"Unlike our competition, we keep it local and don't import fish from outside the Keys." DJ's voice sounds anxious, pleading, trying to make me see his point. "Some unaware therapist in Los Angeles hasn't got a clue his office aquarium is filled with species shot with cyanide for easy capture." I feel his palm on my shoulder. "That practice is illegal in the States. If consumers buy fish from us, they can rest assured knowing their fish were harvested without harm to the habitat."

My fingers, gripping the laces of my shoes, begin to relax. I stand, mollified, but unsure about my feelings towards these two.

"I'll introduce you around," Cassie says, linking her arm into mine. "Our finned friends have personalities and feelings just like us. They need attention, love to play, and I see to it they're happy. Each aquarium has a separate theme—sorta like Disney World."

She leads me to a tank. A castle replica is centered over a sandy floor, multi-colored rocks scattered about the landscape. "This one's my favorite. Look at those tetras swimming through the castle gate. Oh. Here's a beauty for ya—an angelfish. I named her Angelina because her lips remind me of the actress."

She shakes her finger at the fish. "But I may have to separate you if you don't learn to chill."

Cassie straightens, her face aglow. "Even after clocking out, I don't want to leave. Watching these guys play is so relaxing. I could lose myself for hours."

I gaze, mesmerized, at the fish. Suddenly, a door opens and is slammed shut. A booming voice draws near.

"What the fuck, man. Have you read the news?"

It sounds like he's been running and he wheezes between sentences; his rasps make a screeching noise like a hinge that needs oiling. A strong smell permeates the air, and I turn to meet a pair of heavy-lidded eyes, amber and glistening, what might be referred to as whiskey-stained.

"There was a bust at some warehouse in Thailand." He pronounces Thailand as *Thighland*, but if anyone ever thought of correcting a guy like this, they'd be ignorant about the art of survival.

"Place was jammed with tanks of exotics waiting to be shipped out," he continues. "I saw pics. Some of them parrot-fish would take your breath away."

Hands on hips, panting, he glances around seeming to notice me for the first time. "And you are..."

DJ places his palm on my shoulder. "Stanson. This is a friend of mine. Linnea Chandler. I've known her since we were kids."

He extends an open palm to greet me. His flexing biceps must be at least twenty-four inches wide. Stubbly whiskers protrude from acne scars denting his face, and curly thatches of black hair cover the tops of his hand. I'm loathe to touch it. Tentatively, I extend my arm. For such a hard-bit man, his grip is gentle, but my flesh recoils at the damp feel of his clammy palm.

"You look like someone I know," he says, his eyes scrunched together. I remove my hand from his as discreetly as possible. This is the guy who picked up Cassie at the airport, but he wouldn't know me; he never glanced my way.

"I've got a twin sister who lives down here. She has a snorkeling business with her husband."

"Oh yeah. I've seen her and hubby at the wharfs. That's a nice boat they got. Musta cost a fortune. You're a paler version of your sister." I smile, and he snorts, shaking his head. "So, what brings you to our fish farm today?"

Cassie pipes up. "She moved back to town."

I raise my brow. "Just for a few months. I'm helping my parents at their bed & breakfast. You may have heard of it—The Maiden Tower Inn?"

His jaw drops. "The place that's haunted?"

DJ's grin is broad. "With unfinished business."

I smirk, rolling my eyes.

"That don't bother me," Stanson continues. "Ghosts—witches, anything beats tying up cruise ships and serving conch fritters to tourists." He proceeds to crack the knuckles on his hands, making a sound that makes my flesh crawl. "That's what I was doing before I got into the fish business."

He turns to DJ. "Wanted to let you know everything is good to go. The Queens and octopus are packed and ready for shipping."

Flinging his arm around Cassie, he nuzzles his face into her neck. "You're gonna love this, baby. That seahorse you've been watching gave birth a couple of hours ago. I recorded it on my phone."

"I'm sorry I missed that." She turns to me. "He may act like a tough guy, but he loves his babies as much as I do."

DJ nudges my elbow. "Did you know that male seahorses incubate the babies and go through childbirth? Some think it's creepy watching dudes regurgitate hundreds of babies from their gut."

I shiver. "The thought of everything in that inside-out world freaks me out." I tighten and straighten my ponytail. "But maybe males having to go through pregnancy and childbirth isn't such a bad idea." Everyone titters.

"Hey, jokester," Stanson says, head bobbing my way. "I got another one for ya." Shuffling his feet, he crams his hands into his pockets and gazes at the ceiling. "They say there's plenty of fish in the sea." He catches our eyes, and I brace myself for the punch line. "But until I catch one, I'm stuck here holding my rod." He grabs the crotch of his pants and then bends over, snorting with laughter.

Cassie's face flushes. "He's impossible to train." But she joins in, laughing along with DJ, who winks in my direction. Noting Stanson's thick neck, a chest that's fifty-eight inches wide if it's an inch, and perspiration that reeks of garlic, tobacco and testosterone, I force myself to join their mirth.

Stanson's laughter turns into a coughing fit, and he puts his hands on his knees, catching his breath. We all remain still, barely breathing, waiting for his next cue. In a flash, he rights himself and slaps Cassie on her butt.

"Time to hit the road, babe. Grab your helmet. It's back to the factory."

Cassie scurries off into a side room, I presume her office, and emerges with her backpack. I recognize it from the plane. After our goodbyes, the pair exits, but the sour odor remains. DJ and I fall quiet, and I feel uncomfortable. Chewing the inside of my thumbnail, I'm not sure where to look.

"All day, he pops garlic cloves like candy," DJ says, trying to apologize for his offensive employee. "Says it's good for digestion." DJ pinches his nostrils together. "I wish he'd switch to Tums."

"If he ate a bunch of tomatoes, he'd smell like marinara."

DJ laughs, his shoulders dropping, relieved at my attempt of humor. "He's not a bad guy. Treats the specimens like they were his kids. He had a rough time growing up. No one knows what happened to his mom. His dad raised him on a boat. Folks tell me what an asshole his father was. Screaming and hollering at his son all the time, the old man was drunk more than sober."

With Cassie gone, the room seems to grow dark, the aquariums bubbling and sinister. I return to her favorite tank. Angelina, teeth now bared and looking fierce, is chasing a baby Tang that now hides—quivering—behind a castle wall.

Closing my eyes, vibrant colors flash across my mind: The

orange face of a digital watch. A royal blue towel. The silvery
glow of ocean foam. The blackness of fear. I grimace and turn
away from the tank, beads of sweat moistening the back of my
neck. I've got to get out of this place.

DJ walks to me and takes my hand, a question in his eyes.

I force a smile, speaking brightly. "Best get back to the
kitchen."

Vexed, his shoulders slump, and he shakes his head. He
squeezes my hand with such pressure it hurts. "Ouch," I say,
pulling my hand away and shaking it.

"Oops. Sorry, Linnea. I guess I'm upset." His eyebrows draw
together. "You just got here. I was hoping we could hang out.
Grab lunch or something."

I walk quickly to the cash register. Feeling off-kilter, a
feeling akin to being seasick, I grasp the counter to steady
myself.

"Another time," I say, catching his eyes in a quick glance.
"I've got to pick up those lemons and get back to work. I'm
making Lemon Chiffon Pies for Evening Hour." I give a little
wave and bolt through the door.

15. LINNEA

The timer dings and I remove the pans from the oven. I'm making four pies today to accommodate the guests and my sisters. I added toasted coconut to this batch to give my usual graham cracker crust a tropical flair.

Dessert has become a welcome addition to my parents' Evening Hour and patrons have been raving about my creations on TripAdvisor. Pressing my fingers into the small of my back, I thrust my hips forward and raise my face to the ceiling, easing the tension in my shoulders.

Settled into the Fog Horn House and a comforting kitchen routine, I've been having second thoughts about moving back to Idaho. My family is giving me something that, until recently, I'd never known I'd lost. I'm coming to appreciate what a gift a family is. And—I think, flushing—there's DJ, who's never far from my mind.

That same nightmare, however, has been assaulting my sleep. The more I try dismissing my fears by day, at night, the stronger they become. Of late, Delphina has joined me in the dream, and we swim parallel to one another. She reaches for my hand, trying to help me escape the apparitions, but my fingers slip away.

I wake up choking, fists flying, battling the bedsheets twisted about my arms. The ocean may not be in my face or lapping at my toes, but I know she's there—only a few blocks away—biding her time.

I once saw a cognitive behavior therapist who tried helping me separate reality from the fictional monsters I've imagined in the deep. Her counseling got me nowhere. I don't even know what's going on inside of me, so how could I explain it to someone else? The therapies of cooking, however, provide blessed relief, an escape from my angst. I locate the zester, which found a hiding spot amongst the cutlery.

Mama enters the kitchen, carrying an empty pitcher and glasses, lipstick staining the rims. "Guests are raving about the strata you made for breakfast."

In the bowl of an electric mixer, I zest a lime over egg yolks "I'll make them more often. They were a cinch to whip up and allowed me to use stale bread and veggie scraps."

"Seems it doesn't have to be served hot to be appreciated." She walks to the sink, placing the dishes into the soapy water. Wiping her hands on a dishcloth, she approaches me at the prep table, chuckling.

"This week's guests are a raggle-taggle crew." She pulls out a chair and sits, her eyes on my hands as they dart about the island, assembling ingredients.

"At breakfast, a Baptist preacher from Mississippi insisted that he deliver a prayer thanking Jesus before eating. After that, a gentleman from Dearborn, Michigan asked that his devotion to Allah be heard, which was followed by a young woman chanting Zen incantations."

I chuckle. "Throw in a Wiccan prayer and every gate on the eternal highway would be open."

"No doubt. But by the time everyone was finished beseeching their Almightys, breakfast was cold."

Relaxing into our banter, I turn on the mixer. She picks up a rectangular pan containing fillets coated in an orangey powder. "So what 'cha gonna do with these?" Her voice is amplified over the whir of the blades against metal. Turning off the appliance, I pour a can of sweetened condensed milk into the bowl.

"Since you and Ivy vetoed our lady's night out, I'm making dinner for my sisters instead. The grouper Bill brought over yesterday inspired me." I point at the fillets, covered with Adobo seasoning. "After they're grilled, these beauties will be transformed into fish tacos. There's a Chipotle Cream Sauce and Salsa Fresca that can't wait to join the party."

I touch my left shoulder and right, and then cross my thumb over my index finger, making the sign of the cross. "Et Spiritus Sancti—a meal fit for the Goddesses."

Mama's mouth twitches in an attempt to suppress the obvious delight that my presence is now a part of her daily routine. "July is by far the best month down here for catching fish. And now that we've a chef in the house," she says, her eyes dancing, "we can start experimenting with the bounty. Maybe start serving dinner to the guests."

I give her a three-finger salute, which she bats away, laughing.

"You and dad are welcome to join us before the show begins." I pour lime juice into the mixture.

"You don't need us around. And I'll also have to make sure Ivy's up for a get-together."

For heaven's sake, I think, gathering the dirty dishes onto a tray. She's got to stop. I sigh, looking down at her, and then take a seat by her side.

"Please don't interfere with the evening we've planned, Mama. Chill. What Ivy needs most is camaraderie; to be with her sisters. Delphina and I never get a chance to spend time with her."

Mama's face flushes, and her eyes dart from mine.

"No, no. I'm not trying to interfere. It's just that sometimes, well, sometimes with those headaches she's not herself. I want you two to see her at her best." Her gaze meets mine. "But this morning she did seem better."

There is a slight tremble in her voice, and her posture stiffens, her eyes narrowed. Her usual jocular manner now seems forced as if she's trying to steel herself against unpleasant thoughts.

"Maybe she should lay off the pot. It makes a lot of folks antisocial."

"Don't say that, Linnea," she says, her voice strained. "Weed's a blessing. In on-line chat rooms, folks say it helps control..." she pauses, the sentence dangling as she bites her lower lip. "Well, that it does wonders for migraines."

"Could be. At least it's a natural substance. From what I hear, medical marijuana's come a long way in helping folks cope with pain. Sure beats prescription drugs."

A flicker of worry crosses Mama's face. I've had this feeling before. That she's hiding something from me about my little sister. Of late, Ivy's looking so pale, thin and drawn. Her once elegant bone structure now looks bony and sharp, smudges of darkness reside beneath her eyes. Mama shifts in her seat and looks out the kitchen window into the shadows of the late afternoon. Her lips are pressed together as if to stop the next sentence. The silence turns awkward.

With resolution, she presses the heels of her hands into the table and stands, clearing her throat like she's made up her mind about something.

"All in all, I'm thrilled the three of you are spending some alone time together. Why not join the guests for the show after dinner?"

"Only if Liberace's invited." I raise my brows. "And released from prison for good behavior. He's been a gentleman of late and adds such color to Evening Hour."

"Ha. He's no gentleman. He's an old trickster, that's what he is. That bird can hold a grudge, and he's mad as hell at me for keeping him in his cage."

She twists ropes of her hair into a messy bun. "I'm sure the old bird has some fantastic plot of revenge up his sleeve."

Clearing my throat, I level her with the most unflinching gaze I can muster. "But tonight, his sisters will be in the audience. I'm sure he'll be on his best behavior."

Mama emits a long, drawn-out sigh. "Well, all right, then." Pinching her chin, her eyes thin. "As long as he remains calm. But if he leaves your father's shoulder even for a second, it's back to his cage. At least I gave him a pedicure last week. Those weapons of his have lost much of their sting."

She turns to exit the kitchen and I stand, relieved to be returning to the job of cleaning up the mess. I'm exhausted worrying about some current in the air that I can't wrap my head around.

"THERE ARE FISH TACOS," Delphina says, nodding her head at her plate. "And then, there are fish tacos." She leans back in her chair, emitting a small groan.

We're eating dinner in the kitchen, so not to be interrupted by the comings and goings of the guests. Picking up the stuffed and folded tortilla, she points it in my direction. "Rhapsody in food." Using both hands to hold it, she opens her mouth extra-wide and takes a large bite. A chunk of fish and bits of slaw fall back to her plate.

"Feel free to use a knife and fork," I say, surprised at her sloppiness. She used to be the fastidious twin. "They're a mess to pick up but magnificent to eat."

"Sorry," she says, batting her chin with a napkin. "Ever since having the baby, my manners have gone to hell. I've gotten in the habit of eating quickly. These days, I practically inhale food to make time for Coral Princess operations."

I top off Ivy and Delphina's wine glasses. "That's understandable," I say, amazed by her stamina. "I usually serve the tacos with beans and rice but thought your palate could use a break."

Delphina places the half-eaten taco on her plate. "No kidding. Every freaking day—beans and rice, rice and beans; you'd think my family would get sick of them. I sure am."

Ivy regards Delphina. Twirling her forefinger around a tendril in her lustrous curls, she speaks in a soft voice. "It must be a Cuban thing."

"I suppose." Delphina puts her face into her palms and speaks between outstretched fingers. "Don't misunderstand me. I'm so grateful for Lita's help, but honestly. Sometimes I'd like the house to ourselves—just me, Sonny and Ella. We could order pizza and microwave popcorn."

She drops her hands and looks from me to Ivy, sucking her teeth. "Yesterday, she totally lost it when I added chopped tomatoes to her sofrito. She said it made the sauce too runny. But it was delicious. Even Sonny agreed." Her features tighten. "For once."

Ivy and I look at her, startled by the sudden irritation in those last two words. "Yes, ladies, don't get me started on my husband." She takes a long, lingering sip of wine.

"Last time I was over y'all seemed to be one happy family," The unfettered gaiety that permeated the house that evening felt foreign to me. But it was as welcoming as a cashmere shawl when the air takes a chill.

"Yep. My mother-in-law's birthday." She fists her hands and pounds them on the table.

"But life is not lived in La La Land. At the rate I'm working, my baby is going to think Lita's her mother."

Her look of annoyance transitions to a soft smile. "Y'all

need to see my darling Ella. She's beginning to crawl. When she sticks that cute little butt in the air and shimmies across the floor, she reminds me of a black-eyed hermit crab."

Taking a breath, she rakes fingers through her hair. "And then, after she's asleep, there's a mountain of bookwork to mine. I need to use every ounce of energy to creatively juggle the bills. A task way more important than making sure my husband's needs are satisfied. I feel like Ella's yanking one arm, Sonny's tugging at the other, and the business is pulling at my legs, dragging me under."

The edges of her mouth tick down and her eyes blink rapidly to stymie tears. "I'm drowning, sisters, I'm drowning."

Man. I can relate. But the last thing I want to do is open up a can of worms about my recent nightmares. Tonight, we're supposed to be having fun; keeping conversation light for Ivy. Delphina must agree as, with a flurry of hands, she changes the subject.

"Oh, gosh. I didn't mean to scare y'all with the joys of matrimonial bliss. I'm sick of my life. What about you two? Come on. There's gotta be some dirt." She nudges Ivy. "Fess up, little sister. Has some man wandered into your picture—rather, painting?"

Ivy rolls her eyes. "One of the sculptors I'm working with on the city commission keeps asking me out. His name is Jonah, and I guess I might have led him on. I hung out with him once. At a gallery party. And then we..."

Her words fade mid-sentence, and she turns away from our questions. Eyes fixed on a squirrel nibbling on a frayed corner of mesh on the outside window sill, for several seconds she is silent. Then, she swivels to face us and continues.

"Now he won't stop with the texts, nosing into my business, updating me with pics showing the progression of a piece he's working on. But I'm not attracted to him. It's become awkward at meetings, so I've been finding excuses not to attend."

I wonder what she did with the guy after the event. It sounds like sex was involved, but that's her business. I reach across the table to pat her hand.

"Not going to meetings? Is that a good idea, kiddo? In your blog you wrote the effort was collaborative. Between the artists."

"Not necessarily," she replies, her gaze shooting back to the squirrel. She shivers as if an icy breeze were stirring about the kitchen. "My time is best spent painting."

Avoiding this man could, in part, explain Ivy's antisocial behavior. I finish my taco in silence, not adding a word to any conversation that circles around men. Nope. Not taking the bait. I had another date with DJ, and we had a blast.

Delphina touches Ivy's forearm and brushes away a rope of hair that's fallen into her face. "You've barely put a dent in Linnea's wizardry."

"I did have a bite––several bites––and it's delicious." Ivy turns back to her supper and stirs the prongs of her fork into the ruddy chipotle sauce. The swirling pattern she makes reminds me of a clutched chicken claw.

Looking up from her plate, her smile appears forced. "I shouldn't have been munching on cashews before dinner. I'll save it for later."

Delphina grabs her bag from under the table. "Hey. I've been dying to show you something. I found it by a reef when I was out with a tour, right before I discovered the dying coral." She removes a folded-up T-shirt and hands it to Ivy.

"This year, Christmas comes in July. I would have wrapped it, but I didn't have time."

"A present?" Ivy unfolds the T-shirt, and the musky scent of seawater emanates from the folds. She removes a hunk of red glass and holds it into the light. Gasping, she examines the piece, shaped like an arrowhead.

"Delphina," she exclaims. "You unearthed the holy grail."

Ivy turns to face me, and I'm delighted to see sparks returning to her eyes. "Red sea glass is extremely rare. Some call it the ruby of the sea."

She tips her head, staring at the glass, fingering it, seeming awestruck. "Back in the old days, folks dumped all of their trash into the ocean. Eventually, bits and pieces of glass wash up onto shore."

Ivy passes the piece to me. "Remember? Dad called them 'Mermaid Tears'. He said that every time a sailor drowned at sea, the mermaids would cry. Sea glass was their tears."

"It's nice." I run my fingertip down the smooth edge, grazing the rounded tip of the point, and then over the pocked face. "But honestly, I never understood the allure—why you and Delphina got so excited over random pieces of glass."

"For starters they're beautiful," Ivy says, staring at me in surprise, fondling the tiny silver dolphin that dangles between her collarbones. "Glass that's been tumbling through the ocean for decades develops a patina of the sea. It has a great deal of depth and often tells a story." Latched onto a topic she enjoys, Ivy jabbers, and it's fun to see her animated.

"In the eighteen-hundreds," she continues, like she's reading from a text book, "red glass was expensive to make, so they saved it for important items. Like signal lanterns, which alerted vessels of dangerous reefs and helped guide the crew to safety."

She takes the piece from my hands, studies it, and a strange look—something akin to fear—creeps across her face. Darkness returns to her eyes. "This piece was definitely from one of those old lanterns," she says in a whisper, running her finger down the indentation. "The ridge here indicates that this is a remnant from the lens."

Peering into Delphina's face, she speaks with intensity. "Once upon a time, this glass flashed a warning." Her face clouds, and she pushes the piece towards Delphina. "It called out to you."

Delphina picks up the glass, and levels it, mid-air, towards Ivy. "So, you're telling me this lovely piece of glass is trying to warn me of something?" Delphina shakes her head and laughs. Leaning across the table, she places the glass into Ivy's hand. "Oh, honey, no. I don't think so. You're the magician. Create a family heirloom, something that we'll treasure."

Ivy glances about the kitchen, seeming unsure and then slides it into her pocket. "Thank you, Delphina." She blinks rapidly and out of the corner of my eyes, I study her.

Head dipped, her mouth works as she wrings the napkin in her lap. Is she talking to herself? Why is she so skittish? Like a frightened rabbit, it's the way she acted as a teen. So unlike the commanding woman at her easel, the woman in her blog. I push away from the table. I have something that might enliven her.

"I hope you ladies saved room." I walk to the fridge, remove a pie and place it on the center of the table. Ivy squeals.

"You made my favorite, Linnea." A smile overtakes her face, and her fingers dart to her lips as if she wasn't expecting it. Dropping her hand, she angles her thumb and forefinger aside the frothy baked egg whites. "Almost two inches tall. The meringue on our pies was never this thick."

She places a tiny bit into her mouth and looks up, catching my eyes as she speaks. "Biting into this pie, I believe there is a heaven."

I smile, feeling light-headed and giddy. I *can* make her happy. I think back to the afternoons when Ivy and I would bake in this kitchen. We'd imagined ourselves scientists substituting brown sugar for white, using three eggs instead of two, selecting pecans instead of walnuts, forever trying to improve upon some former creation.

Slicing three larges wedges out of the pie, I clean my knife in the fold of a towel in between each cut. I put them on plates and pass them to my sisters.

"Let's slip into the old days, Ivy. You said you'd like to make a pie with me. Maybe sometime next week?"

"I'd like that, Linnea." She speaks in a voice as soft as brushed silk, the hunted look in her eyes fading. A shiver creeps up my spine.

I point to the clock. "Evening Hour is about to begin. Why don't we take dessert into the parlor and join the guests?"

Ivy's nostrils flare. "Think I'll pass. Y'all come up to my studio after it's over. I've got some excellent weed I'll share."

I tug at her shirt. "Come on, Ivy. Please? Liberace's making a guest appearance tonight. I promised Mama we'd all be in the audience."

She removes the piece of glass and studies it, and then leans into me, peering into my eyes. "I don't like being reminded of what happened to the Maiden or that woman who drowned."

"Seriously, Ivy?" I take the piece of glass from her hands and point the tip at her face. "You can't connect the dots. It's a legend. The lanterns were used as a safety precaution. There's no account in any legitimate record that confirms they lured ships to their destruction. There's no proof."

The side of her mouth twitches like she's holding something back. As if to scare away certain thoughts, she pulls a face before speaking.

"Fact, fiction, whatever. All I know is Daddy's tale has spoiled the poetry of the ocean forever."

"And why is that?" Delphina asks, eyebrows drawn together, a look of incredulity on her face. She stands and walks to Ivy, placing a hand on her shoulder.

Ivy looks up, her voice rising, words hurried. "Beneath the water's surface lie sunken ships and skeletons. No one will ever know their stories."

I shudder, goosebumps pricking my arms. "Thanks for that,

Ivy. Now I've further ammunition to fan the flames of my own fears."

I look up at Delphina. "You know she's right. How often do you leave the sanctity of your reefs? I can assure you that a far more formidable world lies beyond them."

Delphina rolls her eyes and squeezes Ivy's shoulder. "You ladies and your paranoia. Don't let your overactive imaginations ruin the earth's most precious terrain. A garden of paradise is what you two are missing."

Her hand travels up my little sister's neck to tousle her hair. "Please, Ivy. It's so rare the three of us spend time together. Come on. Join your big sisters for Evening Hour."

Ivy sighs, and her shoulders rise and fall, resigning herself to fate. "OK. As long as I can sit between you two. I still get spooked and besides," she says, wrinkling her nose, "I couldn't handle being stuck next to one of the guests. Small talk is impossible for me."

We giggle, smirking at our baby sister. "Tell us something we don't know." I squeeze her hand.

Wandering into the parlor, we take our seats facing the piano. As Daddy begins Evening Hour, Liberace is perched on his right shoulder, the top of the bird's head parallel with my father's. His wings are tucked into his sides, which is a good thing since the span when extended, is over three feet wide. Beak sealed shut, so far, he's on his best behavior. His only sign of movement is his long, red tail, swishing back and forth, indicating his delight at being included.

Since it's off-season, attendance is down to ten, including my sisters and me. One couple sits on an ottoman, three are situated in club chairs while the remainder of us sit in folding rattan chairs––not as uncomfortable as one would imagine. A plate of pie is perched in every lap.

The parlor lights dimmed, Mama's hands begin to ripple lightly across the keyboard, the music soft so as not to overshadow the story. She created a melodramatic medley to enhance each scene of Daddy's performance, and her fingers dance across the keyboard, striking major or minor chords as the tone of the tale suggests. Glancing at my father, she delivers a tiny nod, like a queen would give her loyal footman.

"Recapping some highlights of this morning's introduction," Daddy begins, his voice rich and commanding, "our lighthouse was built in the middle of the nineteenth century. During that time, whale lights were lit each evening and placed in the tower to guide the boats to safety. Those were the days before the great lens was installed in the belfry."

He gestures towards the Fresnel display in the reception area. With over a thousand prisms fashioned in brass trim, the showpiece was constructed in Paris and installed in 1859.

All of the guests heard the spiel this morning, so the group is more intent on eating dessert than listening to my father. I bite into the pie, and the flavor is perfection, the coconut adding a nice component to the crust, which breaks into flakes of buttery shards. Reading the rapt expressions on the guest's faces as they point to their plates and smile amongst one another, I'm sure they agree.

"Daily logs were kept for the lighthouse, which detailed such things as mechanical operations, the weather and fuel consumption. Interestingly, we discovered the original light-keeper's journal amongst the records. This was far more fascinating to us than where to purchase parts, for example, for the foghorn.

With the tips of his forefingers and thumbs, Daddy straightens his crimson bow tie. It was made with the same taffeta as Mama's skirt, which billows about her ankles, and matches his handkerchief, the triangular tip shimmering from his breast pocket like a flame.

"This much we know is accurate," he continues. "The light-house keeper had a daughter named Rossalea. The man, a widower, was deeply attached to his only child and attended to her every need. He raised her to be a fine Christian woman." He cups his hand over his mouth, clearing his throat.

"The year was 1856, and the girl had grown into a great beauty, known for her dignity and compassion. At that time, the population of our island was less than ten percent of what it is today, but the Maiden managed to catch the attention of every available suitor. Repelled by their sailorly lust and wandering eyes, she set about her daily activities, none of the men capturing her interest.

"Often, the lightkeeper recorded, his daughter was afflicted with bouts of melancholia. During those times, she lay so broken in despondency, there was nothing her father could do to help her escape her labyrinth of misery."

Daddy pauses to wink at the audience. "Who wouldn't be gloomy in a world without Smartphones?" The group titters, and he scratches his throat before continuing.

"Other mornings, however, found her tending to lighthouse chores with extraordinary vigor before taking her daily outing to the wharf. There, while procuring provisions for the evening meal, she enjoyed the sights and sounds of the dockside. The port was a place of color and lively banter; a place where she'd felt surges of abandon."

Daddy studied theatre in college, and he can project and modulate his voice on cue. His vocal ability, in fact, is that of a finely tuned instrument. The prodigious range of his voice alone can project a listener to the scene.

"One fine morning in early February," he continues, the timbre of his voice whimsical and relaxed, "when the sun was so bright as to force her to lift a gloved hand to shield her eyes... when the wind blew the strings on her bonnet so that they whipped about her face, she wandered to a one-man fishing boat. It was fitted with a wire mesh trap filled with thrashing spiny lobsters, a red and orangish color.

"Her father delighted in a Lobster Pie that was made from the common sea bug. Rossalea used the same recipe that her deceased mother had brought down from Boston, conjuring memories of her mother before yellow fever stole her away."

Daddy pauses and places his forefinger on his chin, a faraway look in his eyes. He's always been fascinated by nineteenth-century epidemics, and a detailed account of how they influenced history used to be included in Evening Hour. Mama, however, insisted that bit be eliminated as it appeared to put the audience to sleep.

"After selecting two of the largest creatures in the batch," he continues, his eyes refocussing on the audience, "the Maiden's gaze met that of the fisherman. His eyes were a thing of beauty —as dazzling and green as the sea beneath his vessel. The Maiden's composure wavered."

"Kissy, kissy, kissy," Liberace trills, and the guests break out in laughter.

Daddy smiles indulgently at Liberace and continues. "His name was Cyrus Lynch, and he was struck, as well, by the Maiden's porcelain complexion and the curve of her lip." Looking over his left shoulder, Daddy nods at her portrait displayed on the wall behind the piano.

His voice lowers to a resonating whisper. "As you see, her eyes were soft and glowing, like the light from the tower in a mist guiding the ships safely to shore."

His gaze returns to the group. "A fervent courtship began. A poor man who made his living from the spoils of the sea, Cyrus could only give her sand dollars or a pretty shell that he'd find beside the water's edge. To supplement his income, he became a wrecker, which was profitable business back then. During their long conversations, I imagine he painted a future of great wealth in the young woman's mind."

Daddy puts his hand in his pocket and Liberace, understanding the cue, squawks the words: "A wrecker, ah matey, a wrecker." The guests titter, forks poised above their pies, delighted with the show. My father retrieves a treat, gives it to the bird and continues.

"To refresh your memory, wreckers were the folks who would go out and salvage the crew and cargo of ships that had crashed into the reefs. Back in the day, wrecking provided a bountiful yield, and Key West was one of the wealthiest cities in the United States. Many wreckers were heroic, saving lives, cargo and ships. But for others"—Daddy pauses, his eyes narrowing—"for men like Cyrus Lynch, careers were born from merciless greed."

Liberace turns his head to Daddy and emits a staccato squawk that sounds like, *What?* Mama's fingers press into the keyboard delivering an ominous refrain plucked from a Rossini composition. The audience is silent, all having finished their pie, hanging on to Daddy's every word.

"Innocent Rossalea, blinded by love, accepted his proposal for marriage and the two became engaged."

As Daddy describes the romance in flowery detail, the piano music lightens as Mama transitions, with a slight of her hand, to Ravel's "Jeux d'Eau." Liberace bobs his head in time with the rhythm. I hope the old bird continues to behave; the performance is far more entertaining when he's a part of the cast.

My father continues, pointing his forefinger at the group. "The remainder of the journal was, for some reason, ripped out, never to be found. Therefore, the rest of the story is speculation, mind you, lore based on oral accounts."

Pressing his lips together, he nods with certainty, as if to suggest that he, however, believes every word he is about to speak is gospel.

"During this time, unbeknownst to Rossalea, the more wealth that Cyrus accumulated, the more insatiable he became and the more his heart began to blacken. In time, he and his cohorts devised a devious plan to use decoys to mislead mariners. They strategically placed red nautical lanterns along the shoreline that would direct them to destruction on the dangerous reefs. And they were good at their job. Shipwrecks skyrocketed, and their fortunes increased."

Daddy lowers his voice an octave, wiggling his eyebrows. "Soon enough, their acts became bolder. After pillaging the boats, they'd set them on fire. The wreckers wanted to destroy everything that could warn other ships about the dangerous reef below the water."

Mama's music assumes a sinister tone as she leans into the piano, her fingers pressing hard into the keyboard. Liberace's eyes flash, his irises enlarging and then shrinking. This is a remarkable, albeit typical, trait of parrots and is known as eye pinning. It looks bizarre to those not used to it, and I notice the couple on the ottoman flinch and grab one another's hands.

"Rossalea and her father heard the rumors," Daddy continues, "the gossip was relayed from veranda-to-veranda, across fence-to-fence. Cyrus assured them that they were lies, only the babble of idle townsfolk jealous of his newly acquired wealth."

Daddy turns his head, and his eyes meet Liberace's. "But the seed of doubt was planted. Her father insisted that, on the pretense of his declining health, the wedding be postponed." The old bird ruffles his feathers, seemingly alarmed, and Daddy's attention returns to the audience.

"The Maiden pleaded with her father insisting her fiancé's scruples were beyond reproach, and that she, herself, could dismiss the rumors with clear conscience. Rossalea yearned for the touch of the handsome Cyrus and the future he promised to deliver. She kept her ongoing romance hidden from her father."

Daddy covers his mouth, and coughs politely, preferring not to get into the nitty-gritty of their passions.

"One evening, she was awakened from a troubled slumber

by the echo of the foghorn. A ship had come aground on a reef. Grabbing the pirate scope, an anxious Rossalea climbed the tower steps to the lantern room. Opening the door to the outside, she stepped onto the catwalk, peering out into the clear inky night. What the young woman saw, as legend tells us, shocked her to the core.

"A battered ship had crashed into the reef and tipped sideways. The hull was ablaze, which illuminated the scene." Daddy's eyes widen, and his voice quickens.

"Rossalea, eye straining through the lens of the scope, watched as a woman drifted nearby in the open sea, clutching a rib of the boat. Then, she saw a man rowing towards her. She knew it was Cyrus from the flag crossed with a scarlet X." Daddy pauses, and drills a hard look into his audience before continuing.

"The desperate woman reached toward Cyrus for help. But, with the oar of his boat, he bashed her head repeatedly until she disappeared beneath the waves forever."

A woman in the audience gasps, drops her fork and it clangs onto the floor.

"Rossalea's crumpled body was found the next morning on the shoreline, close to the wreckage in the sea, her wrists slit with a kitchen knife."

This part of the tale calls for reverence and Daddy sniffs before bowing his head. The guests, predictably, follow suit, lowering their heads, eyes fixed on their empty plates. A hush descends upon the room. Breaking the silence, Liberace raises his neck and emits a low, snarling growl. For several seconds I'm fearful that he will fly away from Daddy's perch. My father rubs the bird's left foot, and his eight claws relax, remaining affixed, curling onto Daddy's shoulder.

"No one could comfort the grieving lightkeeper," Daddy continues, his voice a whisper. "He aged into a stooped and ancient man after the death of his daughter, whose passion had overwhelmed her. Maybe she didn't want to disgrace her father by having fallen for a scoundrel. Perhaps she lost her mind before ending her life. But no one truly knew what was going on inside the Maiden's head." He turns to gaze at the portrait. "And no one ever will."

The guests, too, stare in stunned silence at the beautiful woman in the painting. After a moment, Daddy turns, his attention returning to the guests.

"Cyrus paid the ultimate price for his deeds. A jury of five condemned him under the wrecking act, and he and his cohorts were found guilty of a felony, punishable by death."

Stone-faced and clutching his hands, my father's composure stiffens. "With vacant eyes, the lighthouse keeper watched as Cyrus's last breath left his lips, his body dangling from the end of a noose."

Liberace begins laughing—*ahhh ha-ha-ha, ahhh ha-ha-ha*—like a vaudeville villain. At first, it startles the guests as he sounds so human, but then they begin to snigger themselves, the somber mood of the room lifting as a dark cloud.

"You can visit that very same hanging tree if you like. It grows right through the center of a local bar—Captain Tony's on Greene Street, just off Duval."

Daddy's voice has now returned to his norm, clipped and formal, something like that of a cruise director announcing the ship's next bingo game.

"The building was built in 1851 and originally used as a morgue. Seventy-five people were hanged from that tree back in the day, and sixteen skeletons were found when they were laying a new foundation for the bar."

"These days the ceiling is hung with dusty moth-eaten bras." His nose twitches, wrinkling in disdain. "Captain Tony's raises dive bars to a wholly new level. But if you don't mind grunge, put it on your list."

He pulls the red handkerchief out from his breast pocket,

and bats it around his face. "If walls could talk."

With a flourish of the hanky, Daddy places his right forearm across his midriff, dipping into a bow. "And that, my friends," he says straightening, "concludes the legend of The Maiden Tower."

He gestures to Mama who pushes back the piano bench, stands, and curtseys. Liberace lowers his head, and the guests applaud wildly, as they do every evening. Mama takes her seat, smoothing the long, lustrous folds of her skirt around the piano bench, and resumes playing. Liberace sings a re-mix of his favorite sounds cascading from trills to whistles.

Ivy nudges my shoulder and whispers in my ear. "I'm exhausted. You and Delphina come up and visit another time."

I turn to her and weave her hand in mine. It feels cold and wet like I'm wiggling my fingers in a glass of iced ice. She squeezes my hand to the point of pain.

"I'm getting a migraine," she whispers, her face ashen, dotted with beads of sweat. Her eyes dart about the room, seeming to belong to someone else. Something inside of her seems to be shifting. Her fingernails dig deep into my flesh, and I shake my hand away. She opens her mouth, panting, and it appears she wants to tell me something, but no words emerge.

A police siren wails outside as it speeds down the street. Crimson lights circle in and out through the windows, painting the walls blood red.

I reach for Ivy, to pull her into me, but she stands abruptly, shaking me off, and rushes towards the stairwell. All color drains from Mama's face as she stares at her daughter, now scrambling up the stairs as if being chased.

I turn--heart hammering and confused--to Delphina, who is watching the scene, a muddled look of alarm and confusion pitting creases around her lips. I grasp her hands.

"We must talk to Mama about Ivy. These headaches, and whatever else it is she refuses to discuss, seem to be killing her."

16. IVY

Studying the glass crevices is like looking at my dark side, the lesions and hollows of my heart, the places where this hurt and agony are too great to bear. Caught within this ruby of the sea is more misery and pain than one could imagine.

In the frosted haze of the piece, I see the oar crashing in on her skull. Like a fishhook linked into my brain, I bear witness to her grayish-green face staring at me. I see her empty sockets—opalescent as an oyster—eyes devoured by fish. Seaweed is tangled and woven into her hair, her features forever preserved in brine.

How horrified she must have been to know she was dying. As for Rossalea, she brought death onto herself. Every fear contains a desire, and I wonder: was death the Maiden's wish all along? I place the glass on the table next to my easel, close my eyes, and wait.

Riding high on the crest of an enormous wave, I crash down, into the murky pit below sea level. The ocean surrounds me, yawning, and stretching. And in this brackish scent of time and memory, I land softly in the safe place.

Cool, deep and magical, it's the place I capture lightning bugs on a slow summer evening, where Delphina braids my hair, and Linnea and I spend hours in the kitchen. It's the place of childhood, before my brain betrayed, before the jagged angles of adolescence pierced the bubble. This place is the waiting room, where I wait for the mania to arrive.

I have a choice, you know. In my cup rests three capsules, torpedoes ready to launch me into medicated nothingness. Why can't I be good, please my mother and follow the doctor's orders? It's of no use. After taking the pills, I'm groggy, my head stuffed with cotton.

Guilt swimming in my belly, I toss them into the trash. Art needs kindling. Idea after idea for my paintings tumbles through my head scrambling for attention. Like baby chicks scuttling the ground for crumbs of bread, they scatter about my brain. I remove the canvas, kept hidden under my bed, and return it to the easel. Picking up my paintbrush, I dip it into crimson oil and fill the Maiden's lips, willing my trembling fingers to still.

17. DELPHINA

S onny and I wander hand-in-hand along the water's edge at Boca Chica Beach. To our right, little paths weave through tangles of bushes and mangroves; on our left a couple of kayakers paddle the shallow, still waters that feed into the Atlantic. For once, this late-July Sunday, The Coral Princess does not insist upon maintenance, and there are no charters to attend.

Lita took Ella to church and will watch her the remainder of the afternoon so that Sonny and I can have time to ourselves. Of late, we've been on edge with one another—quick to pull the trigger without thinking of the consequences. To us. To our relationship. We need to reclaim the couple we were before the stresses of parenthood and an overdue mortgage overwhelmed. Even if only a few hours.

This part of the waterfront is clothing optional, and a man sits on an upturned bucket, nude, facing the sea. His deeply tanned skin glistens with oil and his broad, rounded shoulders and straight back taper down to a well-honed six-pack. His image is in pleasing contrast to the creamy sand and hard blue sky. I stare at him to the point of rudeness, but his angles and curves remind me of a painting in one of Ivy's books—one of

Picasso's paintings by the sea. The man's Ray Ban-ed eyes turn to us, and I quickly look away.

"Lovely afternoon, right?"

I squeeze my husband's hand and smile. "If you don't mind the humidity, which never bothers me." I adjust my visor and lift my chin in his direction, making sure my head doesn't tip down in the direction of his crotch. I wouldn't learn anything about his manhood, even if I looked. His legs are crossed so that his penis is hidden beneath the swell of his muscular thigh.

When out of earshot, I speak to Sonny under my breath. "I can't tell if he's nude or wearing a Speedo." My eyes dart to my husband's shorts, a blue and white checked pattern that hit him above the knees.

Sonny chuckles, replying under his breath, "I figured that would be the first place you'd look."

I release his hand and snap the elastic of his waistband. I'm tempted to mention my first reaction to the man—that I found him to be a work of art, a beautiful integration into the landscape. In the past, that's exactly what I would have said, and Sonny would agree. But he's so sensitive these days. Both of us have been.

"I've only got eyes for you," I say to him instead, glancing up at his face.

He stops and swivels my body so that I'm facing him, and runs his hands across my bare skin. On a sweltering day such as today, I wear as few clothes as I can get away with.

"Sometimes, I'm not so sure."

His mouth works silently, seeming to chew on something that's bothering him. That damn ego of his. I'm tempted to fling off my bikini top to make him nuts, but I refrain. An all-too-familiar bolt of anger shivers up my spine. I take a deep breath to control my temper. I'm not going to let him bait me; today's lovely and I want nothing to spoil it.

I dribble my fingertips up his arms. "You're it for me, honey. Life is more complicated of late. But it's you who shares my dreams when I'm sleeping and awake. Only you."

He pulls me into his arms, and blanketed in humidity, his body feels damp and sticky pressed into mine. "I'm sorry, Delphy. I've been jumpy lately. Anxious. You know better than me that the money we bring in from the business is barely enough to make ends meet. It's like we can't do enough to keep up."

I push him away so that I can look into his face, my eyes stinging. "I suppose we could get service jobs at that monster of a resort they're building next to the wharf."

I kick the sand with such force that I must close my eyes, shielding them from the cloud of dust. He tucks my hair behind my ears, and slides my glasses, and then his, atop our heads so we can look each other in the eye.

Stroking the side of my face, he whispers, "At least we have each other. We can make it if we work. If we're a team."

He bends to examine the beach, which is wild, unmaintained, and the main reason why we love it. Littered with rocks and driftwood, he picks up a flat stone. Aiming it towards the water, he flings his wrist, hurling it to sea. The stone skips across the calm, glassy surface three times before sinking. He turns and places his hands on my shoulders, cupping them in his palms.

"I've missed you, Delphina. Even when we're together, when I'm speaking to you, it seems as if your thoughts are elsewhere."

I slide my sunglasses down, back over the ridge of my nose, so he can't read my eyes. This again? Always my fault. Is he trying to start a fight? I lower my head and dig a hole in the sand with the toe of my shoe. But his point is valid. At home, my thoughts are on the unpaid bills, and at work, I'm worried about the coral and missing my daughter. Ivy's off her rocker,

Mama upsets me, and Linnea is preoccupied with God only knows what. When Sonny talks to me, all I notice is his mouth moving. I don't listen to what he's saying.

His features, usually so relaxed and smiling, now look tight, sad. How long has he looked like this? How is it I haven't noticed until now?

His hands feel warm, his touch tender, and I'm glad I didn't launch a defense. Maybe he wasn't trying to bait me; perhaps I need to look at myself. My husband has his own stresses and insecurities and needs reassurance, that's all. Perhaps if I paused from the craziness of life and kissed him, made love to him instead of working and then falling asleep, this tension in our relationship would ease.

Raising on tiptoes, I lift my lips to his, opening my mouth and running my tongue against his suggesting more will follow this evening. He pulls me into him, his lips grazing my neck, and I feel him hardening against my thighs. This is no place for that, I think, stepping away and glancing up and down the beach. He crosses his hands over his crotch, attempting to hide his visible erection and I smirk, wagging my finger. It's been a while since we've been playful together and his goofy grin tells me how delighted he is to have me to himself.

My eyes drop to a small tidal pool in the sand next to our feet. I crouch to examine the life it carries, never missing an opportunity for a lesson nature may have to teach. The water pulses with hermit crabs, snails, and a Royal sea star, which is about the size of my hand. They're common in this area and make me think of a king who wears a cloak of deep purple, edged in gold. The nobility of the ocean never ceases to astound.

Sonny stoops, gazing into the puddle. "That starfish looks lonely."

"Everyone calls them starfish, but it's a misnomer. Like sand dollars, they're echinoderms and not related to fish." I turn my head sideways, to speak to him directly. "They should be called by their real name, which is sea stars."

"Should we return it in the ocean?"

"It's twitching its tentacles ever so slightly." I point at the skin, the texture resembling the stitching in a hand-knotted sweater. "It's not lonely. There's plenty of water in the pool, and it's got those lively little crabs to amuse. It's content here, so let's leave it be."

I straighten, feeling recharged and invigorated. It's the same feeling I get when snorkeling as if I can handle every stress that's thrown my way. It's only here, in the natural world, that I know I'm truly alive.

"I get why you'd want to move it back into the ocean," I flick a sand fly away from his bicep, "but it will likely wash right back onto the beach. The question should be why are starfish washing up in the first place?"

Hands on hips, Sonny regards me, tilting his head. "Ella's lucky to have a mother as smart as you."

My mouth twitches at his compliment. Patting his belly, he adds, "And I'm lucky to have a wife who put together such a yummy looking picnic. Thank you, baby. I've been smelling those paninis all day. I'm starving."

"Lemme run back to the car and get the basket. Why don't you clear away some of those branches? We can sit on the ground and use those stumps for tables." I point towards a clump of trees and then head towards the car.

An apocalyptic roar comes out of nowhere, seeming to suck up the air. I stop, dead in my tracks but unconcerned. Boca Chica Beach is in spitting distance of the Navy's runway. The Navy Base, in fact, makes this entire strip of wilderness possible. We duck, placing our hands over ears, as a low-flying jet roars overhead in an explosive crescendo seeming to break the sound barrier. In a second or two, the noise dims to a low rumble barely discernible in the distance.

Straightening, I turn to Sonny. "If I weren't so taken by the sea, I'd love to be a pilot."

"Why is that?" He wiggles his eyebrows, his expression a mixture of curiosity and amusement.

"Once you break through the clouds, into the blue beyond, there's only silence and serenity. I imagine it's like snorkeling. When I'm swimming along the ocean floor, I feel the same contentment."

As if saluting, we stretch our palms above our eyebrows and watch the plane disappear into the endless empty sky.

18. LINNEA

It's Sunday, and one of those sweltering late-July afternoons. DJ's shop is closed, and I'm giving him his first cooking lesson. He removes the spatula from my hand and kisses my fingertips.

I'm on edge. It takes great effort to remain unruffled being the sole attention of this hunk of a man in my kitchen. With effort, I unclench my jaw and flick my hair behind my neck—my feeble attempts at flirtation. I'm rewarded by his dazzling smile.

"What's the one thing that instills terror in the hearts of even my most fearless of friends?" I gaze at him coyly through my lashes.

"I'm well aware of what freaks *you* out, beautiful lady, but your friends?"

"Yep. What scares my friends?"

"Is this a riddle?"

"Certainly not." I yank the spatula away and point it at him like I'm a teacher with a ruler. "The answer is astoundingly simple."

"I got it. Snakes on a plane," he says, running his thick, square fingers along the edge of the handle.

I laugh, wishing those fingers were running through my hair, instead. "Oh, my God. Flying is bad enough but traveling on a plane full of snakes? Get a gun and shoot me." I purse my lips, placing the spatula on the table. "But no. That's not the answer."

He grabs my hands, laughing. "I give up."

Raising my brow, I answer him solemnly. "Making pie crust."

"Pie crust? For real?" Dropping my hands, he picks up the grease-spattered card off the table, the recipe I've been using since I was a kid.

"I watched you make it. It took no time at all. Seemed easy enough." He proceeds to summarize my recipe, which fills only half of the card. "Combine flour, salt and sugar. OK, then. This sentence is hard to read. Dadadadada. Cut in butter. Add water, roll out and bake."

He holds the paper into the light. "There's some high-tech equipment listed. A food processor and rolling pin." He places the card on the table and pats it with the flat of his palm. "I'm sure that anyone who can follow simple directions can make a pie crust."

Snapping the dishtowel at his chest, I stick out my chin, turning the sides of my mouth down in a flirty little pout. "And that, Mr. Know-It-All, is where you're wrong. Making crust sends most people into a tizzy. You see, there's lots of science behind it all. Great debates, in fact, are fought over the type of fat to use."

I point to a plate, where a half-rectangle of butter rests, softening in the mid-afternoon humidity. "For instance, should the cook incorporate butter, shortening or lard into the flour? Or perhaps a combination of all three?"

I gesture to a shelf mounted on the wall filled with dozens of cookbooks. "You may find this astounding, but half of those books offer recipes and techniques for mastering crust. Crusts of perfection."

Crossing his arms across his beautifully sculpted torso, he tips his chin towards me. "So, Linnea. In your world, what do you consider to be perfection?"

I consider *you* to be perfection, I think and then flinch. The thought was so loud in my head I take a moment to consider—did I say that out loud? His features are neutral, so I must have been silent. I regard this man whom I've invited into my kitchen, my safe haven, the one place where my demons have yet to haunt.

"I consider perfection to be a crust that breaks into shards of flaky, tender pastry when you bite it," I say, stacking dishes onto a tray so that my hands stay busy. I don't trust my words or the next thing I might grab.

I glance at him over my shoulder. "Creating this perfection, however, is a crapshoot for most. One day a crust comes out tender. The next day—using the same ingredients—it comes out tough. I've developed a few tricks to make sure my crusts are uniformly delicious.

Shoving his hands into the pockets of his faded madras shorts, he shakes his head. "Making pie seems on the order of performing a bone marrow transplant."

I grin, appreciating this acknowledgment of my sweat-induced efforts. "Making *perfect* pie is what I'm talking about. And don't believe what the Food Network tells you. There's nothing about cooking—at least cooking well—that's easy. And there's certainly nothing about it that's glamorous."

He takes a couple of steps towards me before speaking. "So, teach me your tricks. What, pray tell, are your secrets?"

"I demonstrated every one of them to you." My hand sweeps across the table that's littered with measuring cups, a dirty processor and a sagging, half-used bag of flour. I tilt my head sideways and regard him wearily, this silly student who told me his dog ate his homework.

"I'll show you again." I pick up the bag of flour, dump it into the measuring cup and the air clouds with powdery dust. "You, obviously, weren't paying attention."

"Let's skip class for the day," he says, lighting his fingertips on top of my hand. "I've got other things on my mind." His eyes bore into mine, and I feel the heat rising in my face. The way he strokes my hand makes me want to cry. Here, at last, is a man I can trust.

I've spoken of him to Mama—she's been curious as to the mystery person I've been seeing over the past couple of months. I'm tired of fabricating lies and pretending it's a girlfriend. After I told her of his efforts to apologize to Delphina, she, too, has forgiven him his teenage recklessness—heinous as it was. She's well aware of Delphina's deep-seated distrust of the man and has sworn not to mention his name, much less our liaison. That, she said, was my responsibility. But I haven't worked up the guts. It's been an issue easy to avoid—I haven't seen her in almost a month since the night we had dinner together with Ivy.

DJ and I've been meeting in nondescript venues where we're unlikely to run into someone we know. Our feverish kisses, wandering hands and the illicitness of it all ignite the hot aura of the chase. And then there's today. In this kitchen. Is there anything sexier than cooking with a man you're attracted to? We've yet to make love, but I can't take it much longer—it's a fire begging to be quenched.

I grab a bowl filled with sliced peeled peaches coated with a brown sugar-cornstarch mixture. The jagged creamy dough hangs an inch over the edge of the circular rim, and I dump the fruit into the pan. Then, I arrange the remaining rolled-out disk of pastry over the top and slide the pie towards DJ.

"I saved the easy part for you. Now watch my hands, you

crimp it like so." I squeeze the dough between my thumb and forefinger, making a groove surrounded by two tiny peaks. Placing my fingers over DJ's, I instruct him to follow suit. "Now, it's your turn."

Staring intently at the miraculous transformation of butter and flour, he pinches the edges of the dough around the circumference of the glass. Raising an eyebrow, he glances at me and then to the pie, proud of his efforts.

"Well, what do you think?"

My eyes travel up from his slim hips, to his broad shoulders. I brush his shaggy bangs away from his eyes. "Perfection," I say, testing the word out loud, a catch in my breath. "I think there's a baker locked up inside of you begging to be released."

His forefinger lights upon my lips. "I know of something else that's begging to be released."

Pulling me into him, I feel the warmth of his breath on my neck. I rest my head on his chest. "Rewards come to those who wait," I murmur, my neck craning back.

And wait he has. He's been so patient, so tender with me. As he bends to kiss me, he whispers my name. The feeling of his lips on mine turns me inside out, releasing something inside of me.

Mama enters the kitchen. We both jump, stepping away from each other, feeling like we've been caught stark naked. DJ runs his hand across his mouth, and his tanned cheeks now appear sun-burned.

True to form, Mama could care less, and she greets DJ with a warm smile, her hand out-stretched to meet his. She wears a long skirt, her signature, and a silky tank flutters about her hips. Both are the pale-yellow shade of lemonade, and she even smells like the drink, all citrusy sweet and inviting. I gaze at my mother, proud to be her daughter.

"DJ, welcome. I remember you as a boy." Mama removes

her hand from his and stands on tiptoe to tussle his hair. Smiling as if he were a child, for once, he's at a loss for words.

"How's your mama? Elaine, isn't it?" Like most locals, Mama knows of his mother's reputation, of her voracious appetite for a variety of men.

Eyes darting to the floor, he appears embarrassed, tongue-tied, so Mama rambles on. "Would you like a glass of sweet tea? During the summer, I like to keep a pitcher on hand 24/7 for the guests. There's nothing as refreshing as a cold jolt of caffeine and sugar on days where you can fry eggs on the pavement."

He looks up, now smiling. "I'd love that Mrs. Chandler. Thank you."

Mama's eyes widen. "Mrs. Chandler? Who's Mrs. Chandler?" In an inquisitive birdlike manner, she shifts her head from side to side, glancing about the room. "I've never heard of that woman." Then, she reaches up to place her palm on his shoulder, laughing in a tingling crescendo of notes.

"You must call me Poppy. Everyone does." She drops her arm and picks up my recipe card, fanning herself. "Whew. The air-conditioner is over-taxed as it is. And it's certainly no match for that oven. I'm marinating in this heat."

She smiles, placing the tip of a perfectly manicured forefinger on DJ's arm. "It must be ten degrees cooler in the parlor. Why don't we sit there? The handful of guests that are staying here are off on a fishing trip. We'll have the place to ourselves."

DJ glances at me.

"Why not? DJ finished his first cooking class. We made a peach pie. Witness the fallout." I gesture to the chaos spread across the table. I hate clutter, especially when baking, and have made it a habit to clean as I cook. Today's multi-tasking habits were spent, however, flirting with DJ.

"For fun, we added bourbon to the peaches." I point to a bottle of Jim Beam, the top missing in the mess. I open the door of the oven and slide the pie onto the middle rack.

Mama approaches, opens the cupboard and pulls out a tray and three tall glasses.

"How's Ivy, Mama? Has she descended from her dark horse?"

She shivers and closes her eyes like she's face-to-face with a phantom. "No, Ma'am. She 'bout bit off my head when I interrupted her work this morning."

When she opens her eyes, I glimpse a fathomless worry. Biting her bottom lip, she blinks furiously and walks towards the cabinets. Her movements are rapid as she busies herself, organizing the accoutrements for tea.

After Ivy's freakish behavior at Evening Hour, I had a heart-to-heart about my worries with Mama. She launched into the latest holistic route they're taking to muffle Ivy's migraines. The treatment, she says, shows promise. She seems adept at deflecting those baffling vibes, which, like invisible radio frequencies, beam down from Ivy's tower.

DJ remains uncomfortable, and he shifts from foot to foot, fists jammed into the pockets of his shorts. His eyes dart to the bourbon, which I grab and place on the tray.

"I love a splash of bourbon mixed with sweet tea." I force merriment into my voice, hoping an adult beverage will ease the tension.

I grab my phone and peer at the time. "Drat. It's only two-fifty-two. But our beloved Parrot Head, Jimmy Buffet, says, it's five o'clock somewhere."

This will be the first alcoholic beverage I've allowed myself with this man. At last, I feel safe enough to drop my guard. Is this happiness? It's been awhile. His eyes meet mine and, at this moment, I realize I've found at least one thing I've been searching for. I've known it since the first time we kissed.

19. DELPHINA

Side-by-side tree trunks are adorned with colorful cloth napkins and dishes. I reach into my basket and remove foil-wrapped sandwiches and arrange them on top of the plates. I made Cuban Paninis, the sandwiches that we serve to our customers on the boat, but this morning I grilled them.

The scent of pork, cheese and bread toasted in butter has lingered with us all day, encouraging our appetites. Unwrapping them, they still feel warm to the touch. Pulling plantain chips from the basket, I dig into the bag and sprinkle some on the side of each sandwich. Sonny removes a bottle of Coco Rico, a Puerto Rican coconut beverage, and my preferred bottle of guava juice from our cooler.

Bowing with a flourish, he mimes offering me a chair. I plop down on a mound of sand that he cleared of debris and covered with a beach towel. He sits at my side. When dining with Lita, we recite a traditional grace, but when it's only the two of us, it's different. Swiveling to face one another, we grasp hands and stare into each other's eyes; grateful for this life, grateful for this moment, and grateful for each other.

Sonny turns his attention to the sandwich and takes a large bite; yellow mustard dribbles from the corners of his mouth. As he chews, I gaze at my plate thoughtfully. It's a simple sandwich. But the garlicky pork—even more pungently savory after a two-day hiatus in the fridge—sings the Hallelujah Chorus in your mouth.

"Today's been nice," I say, picking up the sandwich, admiring the composition. "I'm glad we're doing this. We need to carve out more alone time. I'm feeling so much better about us. About relationships with other family members, as well." I take a large bite.

Mouth full, he nods in agreement. Beads of sweat roll down his face, which he brushes away with the napkin. The afternoon heat is getting more intense by the minute, even for me.

I retrieve my band from my pocket, re-tie my ponytail, and take a large gulp from the bottle. "I've been thinking. Perhaps I should be thankful that Mama, at least, tries to visit when she can. Actually, she did stop by a couple of times last week." I purse my lips. "Maybe this hurt I'm feeling towards her is my deal."

Sonny's eyes widen. "And when did you have this revelation?"

I shake my head. "When me, Linnea and Ivy had dinner at the inn and watched Mama and Daddy in action. I've got this notion that grandparents, especially grandmothers, should fawn, go gaga and want to be with their grandchildren every waking minute. But all grandmothers don't work as hard as Mama. It's got to be crazy running a bed and breakfast at her age."

I stick a couple of plantain chips into my sandwich and bite into it, appreciating the salty crunch it lends.

Sonny regards me, relief softening his eyes. "What you're telling me now—that your happiness does not depend on things that you can't control— is the greatest gift you can give yourself."

"And then she has Ivy to contend with," I say between bites, happy with this train of thought. "I love my little sister to pieces but..." I widen my eyes, shaking my head. "She's a piece of work. You should have seen the expression on her face when I gave her that piece of sea-glass. And the way she freaked out after Evening Hour. She claimed to be getting a migraine, but man oh man."

Sonny swallows, puts his sandwich down and tips his bottle to mine. "Remember what they say, Delphy. Drink the wine and let the world be the world."

"Maybe. But it seems to me, the world could use some help." I clap my hands together, feeling far removed from the frantic woman I was an hour ago.

"Hey. I have an idea. Let's go visit the lighthouse. After we finish lunch. Sunday afternoons are downtimes, and we don't have the baby. I haven't seen my sisters in weeks."

I pull my phone out of my back pocket. "It's after three. That's the perfect time to catch them."

"Why not call first—make sure they're not busy."

I lean towards him, peck his cheek and then wink. "Oh, no. Let's make it a surprise."

~

PULLING IN THE DRIVEWAY, Sonny guides the truck into the last available spot at the inn. Parking spaces are non-existent in tourist season, and only in off-season are we allowed to park in the tiny lot.

"You go ahead," Sonny says. "I need to return the glue gun I borrowed from your dad. I think it's buried beneath our gear."

I step out of the truck, and my eyes rest upon my family home, which is as welcoming to me as it is mysterious. Even though I have a house of my own and haven't spent a night here in years, I love The Maiden Tower with a ferocity that's usually reserved for one's offspring.

I tuck my T-shirt into my shorts and run a tube of Chapstick over my lips. It's easy to slide into memories, rekindling my youth spent within those walls. The lighthouse was always there for me, the one safe place where all mistakes were forgiven. It was my respite when I tripped, skinned my knees, and—like a wise mentor—the lighthouse always encouraged me to move forward.

Walking slowly down the path towards the front porch, I imagine that if a home had a season, summer would belong to The Maiden Tower. Her aquamarine door and the broad ribbon of teal twirling up the tower replicates the color of the ocean on a hot summer day. Her gardens host a riot of blooming exotics, and when one wilts, it's soon replaced by the next extravagant growth.

I climb the steps, lingering at the front door, tracing my fingers along the bronze plaque. And if our home truly belonged to someone, it would be Rossalea. I conjure up the beautiful maiden exiting a room and leaving behind a scent of honeysuckle, lavender and violets. My hand drops and then lingers on the doorknob. At this moment, I swear she's whispering, *Welcome back, Delphina.*

Opening the door, I hear a man's voice, sounding as if he'd just delivered a punch line. Linnea's tingling laughter is followed by Mamas. Liberace squawks as if the old bird, too, was having the time of his life.

I cross the threshold and stop dead in my tracks, stunned. DJ sits next to Linnea on the ottoman, pouring bourbon into her glass. Linnea looks at me and gasps, her hand flying to her mouth. A sudden understanding of what she's been up to flows through me like poison. Something inside of me dies.

I work my jaw from side-to-side, trying to find words, any words, that will come to my rescue.

"Hello," I mutter finally, and avert my gaze to Rossalea's portrait. After several moments, I swivel my head to look at my sister, staring at her white face in stony silence. I fold my arms across my chest. "I didn't realize I'd be interrupting a party."

Mama, not seeming to notice the ice in my voice, stands and walks over, embracing me in a tight hug.

"Delphina, my darlin'. We have company. You remember DJ. He was telling us the funniest story." Releasing me, she turns to include DJ and Linnea in the conversation. Fingers darting to her mouth, she realizes the tension, which is spreading through the room like a thick plume of smoke.

"Why," she says, confused and beginning to ramble, "he and Linnea have baked us a pie. A yummy peach pie. Your timing couldn't be more perfect."

Linnea lurches to her feet. "I've been meaning to tell you, Delphina. But you've been so busy. DJ and I've been seeing each other from time to time."

My head pounds, the blood beating so loud between my ears I can barely hear what she says. She continues to ramble, incoherently, blah, blah, blah.

"You've been seeing DJ," I say, finding my words, interrupting her babble. "How cozy. Is his old buddy from high school, Ron Patten, in on these visits too? Rumor has it threesomes are his taste." My tone may be forceful and angry, my words oozing with sarcasm, but what does she expect?

DJ's face creases with worry yet he stands, as well, giving me a little half-wave, appearing to be as miserable as the rest of us.

"Hi, Delphina."

"I...I...." I shake my head, dumbfounded. I don't know what to say. Linnea and Mama are drinking bourbon in the middle of the day with my mortal enemy. How could they betray me? Especially Linnea who knows exactly how much I despise this man.

At that moment, Sonny walks through the door, glue gun in hand. He glances from me to DJ to Linnea, and then back to me. Pressing his lips together so tightly they seem to disappear in his face, he aims the nozzle of the gun to the sky like he's begging a truce in a duel. Regaining his composure, and without comment, he lowers his arm and walks to DJ.

"Hey, man. It's been a while. How 'ya doing?"

Sonny knows what DJ did to me. And now he's shaking his hand? I try to still the tremor in my voice, my words directed to Mama. "We're here to return the glue gun. We borrowed it to make some repairs on The Coral Princess."

She places her fingertips on my arm, her green eyes searching my face. "Your daddy's running errands. He'll be back shortly, and you can give it to him yourself. Stay a bit, honey. It's been a while since you've paid us a visit."

I step away from the touch of her hand. "Speaking of visiting, why don't you stop by more often? And your visits are so prescribed––it's like they're a chore or something. I'm sure your granddaughter would like to see you more often."

"I was there twice last week." Mama frowns, a web of lines traveling across her face. "Twice, honey. I was hoping to stop by tomorrow. Why are you so angry?"

Eyes filling with tears, she tries to embrace me, but I shove her off. The smell of burning pastry wafts through the room.

Linnea checks her phone. "Oh, dear God. I forgot about the pie. It's likely burnt to bits." She makes a mad dash to the kitchen and DJ follows, anxious to exit this scene as fast as he can.

"There you go. Always running away." I cup my hands at my mouth, shouting at her back. "That's not fair, Linnea. It's not fair. All of your lies. Your little white lies. They're not so white if you ask me. In fact, they're getting dirtier by the minute."

My sister has left the room. I'm not even sure if she hears me. Nevertheless, I continue my rant, raising my voice. "The time for honesty is now, Linnea. Right now."

I turn to face Mama, my eyes cut to slits, nodding. "But that train has long since left the station, right?"

I look around the parlor. "So, where's Ivy?" I widen my eyes. "I give her credit. With a family such as ours, no wonder she's never around. Is that it? She doesn't like us? Or is the mystery surrounding *Our Girl*," I spit out the words, "yet another secret?"

Mama's head drops, seeming ashamed. It's as if she agrees with my assessment but is too afraid to admit it. Why doesn't she tell me I'm wrong? Why doesn't she defend herself? Why doesn't she defend her family?

I take the glue gun from my husband and hand it to Mama. "Please return this to Daddy."

I grab Sonny's hand, my heart racing with fury. "Let's get out of here."

20. LINNEA

"Do you still go to mass?" DJ asks.

His voice is soft beneath the whir of fans humming on either side of my bed, and his hand feels moist and weighted between my naked breasts. Even within the folds of night, Key West in August is like living in Satan's Den.

"I go from time to time," I respond. "Once or twice a year, depending on where I'm living." Languidly, I stroke his forearm. "But I'll only attend a traditional service. There's something about the rituals, the sameness of the eulogy—no matter where I'm living––that comforts me."

Since the day Delphina discovered my liaison with the man lying beside me, DJ and I have had three overnights at the Fog Horn House, eating take-out while binge-watching episodes of *Orange is the New Black*. Between sheets smelling briny, of soy sauce and sex, we talk about most everything that pops into our heads. Especially my twin sister. I haven't seen or spoken to her in over a week. I've left several messages on her voice mail, suggesting we meet for coffee, but she never responds.

How dare she? The least she could do is hear me out. Once again, I was judged and sentenced without a hearing. *Judge not, lest thee be judged*, precious twinflower. Didn't you pay attention in parochial school? I feel unjustly accused of treason, and––as nonsensical as it sounds––her nastiness was the final catalyst encouraging me to bed this man; a way to even the score.

I turn my attention to our previous conversation; to past recollections that are soothing. Gazing at the ceiling, time arches back to places my memory has bookmarked, so many of them when I was a girl singing in the choir. I hoist myself up on one elbow so that I can study him closer. "What about you? Do you attend mass?"

"I haven't been to church since I left high school. My mother left the hallelujah upbringing to the nuns. She had a plastic blow-up Santa that she'd put in the yard each December. That Santa was the extent of my religious education at home."

"I remember that Santa. It took up most of your yard."

I think of the tasteful decorations my parents use when decorating our home during the holidays. There were no bouncing plastic blow-ups the size of an elephant.

"She did mention Jesus on Christmas, told me that I should pray to him, so I could call myself a Christian. But when I found out there was no such thing as Santa, I connected the dots to mean there was no such thing as Jesus."

I look at him and laugh, incredulous. "Seriously? Don't you at least believe in the Gospel of Love?" I kiss my forefinger and touch his nose.

He rolls his eyes. "Love. Huh. What a concept. Dad walked out on us when I was four years old. I'm sure he was sick of my mother and her unexplained late-night absences. He ended up in Hanoi, of all places. He kept up with child support payments, but those stopped after I was eighteen."

"You haven't seen him since?"

"Nope."

"No letters? No phone calls? "

"Nope," he murmurs, a faraway look of pain in his eyes.

"Not even an e-mail?"

"Nada." He sits, tucking his knees into his sternum and wraps his arms around his legs.

"Linnea. The man left me." His words, even after all of these years, ring with disbelief. "I can forgive him leaving my mother, but me? I remember the last time that we were together. He was throwing a ball, which I bashed squarely with my oversized bat. I remember the sound, the solid crack of plastic against plastic. It hit him in the knees. He picked me up, held me tightly, and said, *I love you, Slugger.*"

Glancing at me through the slits in his eyes, he manages a thin smile. "For me, the words *I love you* are the prelude to goodbye."

My fingertips travel to his abs, tears misting my eyes. I wonder what he feels about me? Does a man like DJ have the capacity to love a woman? He certainly knows how to make love to a woman, and it varies according to our moods. Sometimes our sex is ferocious—both of us hungry, not thinking of anything except how good we make each other feel. Sometimes it's tender. And then, only an hour ago, we made love to each other with reverence. The one thing missing, however, is eye contact.

He knows of my intent to return to Idaho and has, at last, quit trying to convince me to stay. Now, we never speak of tomorrow and my imminent departure. But it's as much a presence in this bed as the demons who haunt my sleep. The man clearly knows about pain and suffering. But he knows nothing about fear.

"Do you still follow the doctrines of the Catholic faith?" he asks, changing topics, obviously uncomfortable speaking of his father. "What do you believe, Linnea?"

He raises his arms, stretches, and then lies back on the bed, arranging several pillows beneath his neck. Pulling the bed linens up and under his hairy armpits, he places his arm across my shoulder, pulling me into his side. Lying beside him, I hoist up my knees, tenting the sheets.

I pause, to gather and articulate my thoughts.

"This is the thing. When I look up at the sky or stoop to admire a flower, I connect to an energy, a force that transcends rational thought. Who wants clarity when you can have magic? That, to me, is a miracle. That, to me, is my faith."

Stroking the crook of my leg, beneath my knee cap, his fingers wander up, tracing the muscle under my thigh.

"What else is going on in that pretty head of yours?" he asks, his breath soft against my cheek. His forefinger travels around my neck and then rests on my mouth, tracing my lips.

I'm thinking I'm scared. I'm thinking I'm concerned about what you've said about your past and wondering if your parent's neglect ensures you'll be damaged for life. I'm thinking I'm done with this town, and I'm thinking of my sisters, who never leave my mind. But I remain silent, not giving voice to my feelings. A jumbled, ragtag collection of emotions have set up residency in my chest, guilt at being with DJ the primary tenant.

"I believe that families are hard work," I say, at last, my words an understatement, looking at him through the corners of my eyes. "Backbreaking work. Mama's running ragged. After tending to the guests and Ivy, she's doubling up her visits to see Ella."

He runs his fingers through my hair and spreads it across the pillows, which now appear to have sprouted dark glossy feathers, like some great mythical creature that fell from the sky.

"To add to the tension, as you're well aware, Delphina's stonewalling me." I twist my ring, round and round on my finger.

"No kidding." He lets out a long slow whistle. "You said

you'll figure out something to tell her. She'll come around. Let's give it time."

I pause a moment, my body basking in the tingle of his touch, my mind telling me...what? That I'm out of time? That Delphina's right, and I'm an idiot to trust this man? Now, under the spell of his fingers, I prefer languishing in the moment.

"How nice to be my father," I murmur. "Oblivious to everything."

"I see your dad around town. Usually at the hardware store. Tom's always in a hurry."

I squirm out from under his arms and straddle his torso, pressing my knees into the mattress. "That's Thomas. Don't ever call him Tom. Certainly, not Tommy. He'd be aghast. Daddy's the nuts and bolts behind lighthouse maintenance, but he's quiet, reserved, a tough nut to crack. The place would go to hell in a hand-basket without him. Mama's the charmer—all the guests love her."

"I can see why. There's a warmth about her, and she's fun. Poppy reminds me of a monarch butterfly—so graceful, colorful and..." He stalls, his eyes darting about the ceiling, searching for the right adjective to describe my mother.

"Flighty is the word you're looking for." Bending, I kiss him lightly on the mouth and then straighten, combing my hair with my fingers.

"I suppose Daddy's self-absorbed in that way so many baby boomers seem to be. He's also overly fond of rules and procedures, which makes him come across as insensitive. Particularly when he applies logic and reason to situations where people's feelings are involved." My thighs relax into the sides of DJ's chest. "Which is every day in a house full of women."

"He must have felt like the odd man out in a home exploding with estrogen. But consider yourself blessed, Linnea. It's a luxury to even contemplate what a family means. I never had much of one. I suppose that's why I don't believe in much of anything."

He directs his attention to my hips, stroking them slowly, and my focus returns to this man. I sigh, falling back into him. Turning my head towards the wall, I rest my cheek on his chest and study the nautical chart, yellowed with age. My parents discovered it in the tower after purchasing the place and had it framed.

"You can have my family. They're driving me crazy. Ivy's up in her tower painting like a madwoman. Mama's worried sick about her reclusiveness. Yet she freaks if I attempt to visit my very own sister without an official invitation. It's ridiculous."

I blink rapidly, suddenly deflated, and try swallowing the lump that forms in my throat every time I think about Ivy. Recalling her reaction after Story Hour, my eyes begin to burn.

"Your sister has quite the reputation," he comments. "I used to see her around town, at festivals and public events, but I haven't run into her in months. Last week I checked out her work at Conch House. Not that I know anything about art, but the gallery owner raved about her talent. Like she was the next Picasso or something."

A minute passes as I consider his words. Are all great artists as complicated as my sister? Does weirdness come with the territory? That would seem a dangerous road to travel.

"That Ivy is talented is a given. That she's eccentric is an absolute," I say at last when I find my words. "But she's acting like a nut case. I've tried talking to Mama about my concerns, but she attributes her strangeness to chronic migraines. I've suggested specific times that we can meet and bake together, but both Ivy and Mama shut me down. I used to get most of my information about my sister from her blog. But it's been a couple of months since her last post." Tears spring to my eyes, and I raise my voice. "Ivy frightens me, DJ. And I don't know what to do."

He remains quiet. At least he could acknowledge my anguish. Did he even listen to me, or did he stash my words into a junk drawer? I wiggle away from him and sit up in bed. Straight-backed, I extend my legs in front of me. Stretching my arms towards my toes, I bend over and grab them as the sound of the surf returns, pounding, ringing in my ears. The nightmares about me, Delphina and the sea creatures are more saturated and frightening than ever. Of late, I'm afraid to fall sleep.

Feeling a sudden urge to pee, I lie on my side and reposition my legs, crossing them, to relieve pressure off my bladder. DJ pushes into me, his semi-erection pressing into the small of my back.

I think of this man and Ron Patten as teenagers, plotting wet-dreams about my sister in some dank, moldy garage. I consider the conversation we had about our parents. His folks did a number on him, but wouldn't it seem he'd want to hunt down his father? I have a history of making terrible choices with men, and now I'm with a man who'll never have the emotional capacity to love a woman. He can't even look me in the eyes while making love. And he could have cared less about my concerns with Ivy.

My mind wakes up, snapping out of its erotic haze. Nausea settles into the pit of my stomach as a sourness travels up my throat. I let this man into my bed. What have I done?

"Oh, God, DJ. I really have to pee." Sliding out of bed, I make a mad dash for the bathroom, turn on the light, and sit on the toilet seat.

A cockroach scrambles across the floor, and I lift my feet, instantly freaked by this darting intrusion. He stops to pause and regard me. With his shiny helmeted girth and long, quivering antennae, he reminds me of an ancient warrior, something from medieval times. His beady, indignant eyes mirror my own, and we regard each other in disdain as a torrent of urine splashes noisily into the bowl.

I think of DJ grinding up roaches and then serving them to Delphina. I remember Delphina's tears when she heard the rumors, the lies he spread about their so-called threesome. What kind of perverse behavior can I expect from him down the road? My behavior's been insensitive to my sister; in fact, unforgivable. Guilt blooms in my chest. How did I not see this? How could I have been so bewitched by this man?

"Are you okay in there?" he asks, his voice muffled through the crack beneath the door.

I recall the unsettled feeling I had at his store. Who knows what he's really up to in that aquarium? There's nothing right about this scenario. This man. My family. Me being so close to the sea. Why do I linger? Scratching nervously at my belly, the pale skin is lashed with long red streaks.

I flush the commode, the gush sending the roach scuttling off into the woodwork. It's time, at last, to think about the future. It's time to say goodbye. To this town. To this man.

21. DELPHINA

L ita hands Ella to Mama. "*La pequeña princesa* had a nice nap, and now she's ready for her Noonie."

Last week, Mama gave herself a nickname for Ella to use when she's old enough to address her: Noonie. It's fitting; nonsensical and adorable. I'm glad she's finally coming around and acting like the rest of the other grandmas out there. Lately, she's made great efforts to see her grandchild more often.

Cradling Ella her in her arms, Mama nuzzles her neck. Ella laughs and makes cooing sounds, grabbing at Mama's hair, delighting her. She said she was pathetic with babies, using that as an excuse not to see her more often. Now, out of the blue, she's getting along famously with her granddaughter. At least one positive emerged from my rampage at the inn: she got the message. I should have voiced my feelings to her sooner.

She looks up and smiles at my mother-in-law, who is dressed head-to-toe in black for the loss of her friend's husband.

"I don't know what we'd do without you, Mariela, taking such loving care of our sweet little angel. I hope your afternoon won't be too depressing."

My mother-in-law smiles warmly before swishing back to

the kitchen, and Mama turns her attention back to the baby. Leaning her face into my child's, she lightly places her forefinger on the tip of Ella's button nose.

"You are the most precious little lamb in all the world, yes you are."

This is the first time Ella hasn't broken out into a fit of wails when Mama holds her. Mama nods at me, beaming victorious.

I wander around the wreckage of the living room, picking up toys and placing them into the chest. I apologized to Mama the day after that nastiness at the lighthouse. She didn't deserve what I dished out. But Linnea? That's a different story.

"Delphina. I've three hours before I've gotta get back to The Maiden Tower. Given this wretched humidity and cloud cover, we're only half booked."

She removes her earrings before Ella can grab them. "Key West in mid-August. Ugh. Is there something you need to do—errands to run for The Coral Princess? I'm happy to watch the baby."

"Not necessary. Sonny can handle today's small group. For us, business has also tanked." I shrug. "I'll never understand why. It's paradise for snorkelers. Right now, the Atlantic feels as if you're swimming between layers of fine silk."

Placing Esteban on top of the other toys, I close the chest and turn to face my mother. "So let's catch up. Business won't pick up for either of us until hurricane season has passed."

"Hurricane," Mama says, puckering her mouth around the word. "Lord. Don't say that vulgar word out loud. Remember 2005? Had to leave everything behind and stay with your grandmother."

"How could I forget? The worst year of my life. Twice we had to leave. First for Katrina and then for Wilma."

"We were blessed the lighthouse only suffered scratches and scrapes. Katrina may have trashed my garden, but the worst was the water damage from Wilma."

"I'll never forget that mess. But we couldn't complain in light of what happened to New Orleans."

Picking up a pleated down quilt crumpled in a heap on the floor, I fold it up and place it on top of the chest. "But living through those hurricanes would have been preferable to staying with Grandmother Rose. Linnea was at that college out East. It was the only time I remember ever being jealous of her."

Mama raises her eyebrows at me, adjusting Ella over her shoulder, whose tiny fingers are wreaking havoc with her hair.

"I'd close my mouth if I were you. You never know what power your Grandmother Rose can wield from up above. My mama is vindictive. No hurricane has struck the state of Florida in twelve years, but your talking about the departed like that is surely gonna jinx us."

My grandmother died a few years after we'd left home for college. Guilty as charged, her passing only brought me a flood of relief.

Carrying the baby, Mama walks to the sofa and arranges herself amongst the cushions and pillows. Disentangling Ella's fingers from her curls, she jangles a bracelet she wears on her arm, fascinating my daughter. With her little thumb and fore-finger, she tries picking off the amber beads. Mama rolls it off her wrist and hands it to Ella, who promptly gums it. Mama smiles, delighted with her antics but then straightens, startled, worried I'll disapprove.

"I'm sure the bracelet's clean," she says. "Would you prefer that I take it away?"

"No worries. She puts everything in her mouth these days. We wash her toys from time to time, but I'll never be able to protect her from every germ."

"You need to expose her to the world, so she can build up her immunities."

"As long as the elastic doesn't break." I eye the bracelet. "I worry she might choke on a bead."

"That won't happen. They're rosewood prayer beads and strung on a strong piece of twine. This darling couple who'd recently been traveling in Tibet gifted them to me after one of the Evening Hours."

She loves relating stories about guests who bring a bit of exotica to her world. She would have been a great traveler herself, but the expense of travel and demands of the bed & breakfast insist the world comes to her.

Under the weight of Ella, she shifts into the couch, smiling. "They told me Buddhists use them to count mantras—sorta like Catholics reciting prayers with a rosary."

"A bracelet with a story. How interesting. Frankly, anything that keeps the little monkey occupied is worth its weight in gold."

Ella removes the piece from her mouth, examines it, and then presses it towards Mama's mouth, encouraging her to have a nibble. Mama feigns taking a bite, delighting the baby who kicks her legs in glee.

I plop down next to them on the sofa. Placing my elbows on my knees, I rest my chin into the palms of my hands. Lita walks towards me, carrying a plastic container, which holds a coffee cake. Shaking her head, she's making those tsk-tsk sounds I find so annoying. It seems like she doesn't approve of my actions of late, and I wonder if she and Sonny have been discussing me.

"You should see your daughter at that computer, Poppy," she says, nodding at my mother. Forehead lined in worry, her eyebrows knit together in a straight bristly line. "Up long after everyone else is asleep. It's good to see her relaxing for a change."

How do I stand a chance against the Cuban militia? Placing

the cake on the table, she digs through her purse extracting car keys.

"I'll be gone through the afternoon. My friend, she's a weeper. But I don't trust her display of grief a second. She can't fool a one of us. *Ella ha estado quejándose de las malas maneras de su marido durante años.*" She tosses her keys into the air and catches them. "*Bendita Madre María.* Instead of black, we should all be wearing red and drinking rum."

We laugh as Lita bends to kiss Ella's head and then exits the front door in a bustling ebony flourish. Mama bends to pick up the bracelet that Ella dropped. Not once has Mama spoken my baby's name; voiced the word *Ella.* She can't get over our naming her after Mariela. I refrain from addressing this hurt—one issue at a time.

"Holding this precious lamb reminds me of when I had my own babies to tend," Mama says. "Over thirty years back. It's hard to believe how time has slipped through my fingers."

Here we go, I think, shifting and placing a throw pillow against my lower back. Mama's trying to pave the way for a reconciliation with Linnea. She's testing new warfare; using nostalgia as tactical ammunition, attempting to break me down as she reminisces about the two of us. But it makes my blood boil every time I think of my sister sleeping with the enemy. She has a habit of making bad choices, but this one's a doozy.

"My goodness, how the world has changed since you and Linnea were babies."

I grasp my hands together and stretch them above my head, yawning. "The world's not so different. It's the same old cycle. Diapers. Changing them. Bottles. Sterilizing them. Sleepless nights. Grouchy days. And then the process is repeated. Day after day after day."

She smiles at my words with a wistful, distant look about her face. It's as if she remembers a scene from her past when she was a young mother, a moment in time she would give anything to reclaim. She plants a kiss on the back of Ella's head and then catches my eye.

"Before your Daddy and I brought you both home from the hospital, the nurses affixed bracelets to your wrists. Your names were spelled out in tiny pink beads. You girls were identical, and they were worried we'd get you confused."

I've heard this narrative many times, but it still interests me. Doesn't everyone love hearing stories told about when they were babies before memories seeded themselves into consciousness? I don't interrupt and watch the gears shift behind the green of her eyes.

"We were certain we'd never confuse you," she continues, moving Ella to her other knee. "Why, how could a parent mix up their own flesh and blood? Two days later, I was brave enough to give you baths. Lord, I remember being scared to death. Thought you'd slip out of my hands and drown." Her fingers flutter to her throat, her eyes gauging how her words are affecting me.

"Well. Anyway. When I removed your snugglers and diapers, I also took off those bracelets. I thought surely, I'd know which one of you was which. After bathing you both, one at a time, I patted you dry and—Whoops!—I couldn't tell Delphina from Linnea. I called for your father to help me decide, but he was just as befuddled as me. We had to guess who was who."

"So, I could be Linnea. And if I'm Linnea, and she's Delphina, it could have been she who saved us in your womb." Linnea and I have posited this theory a hundred-thousand times. It never fails to intrigue.

Mama nods, her eyes dancing.

I feel a rush of warmth towards my twin. Mama's cleverness, both effective and disarming, causes me to momentarily forget my anger towards her. Since I can remember, I've imagined Linnea and myself as two half people combined to make a whole. Not a whole person but some mythological hybrid; a Minotaur, half-bull and half-human. Stolen from ancient Greece, it was an image I'd seen as a child that had captured my imagination.

Once when we were girls––thin-armed, flat-chested young things––Linnea came to my bed. We'd always spent hours together at night, whispering stories, trying to keep them *not too scary*. Snuggling into me that evening, her body curled into mine, she was shivering. I remember her asking, *What if the monster comes, Delphina?* Pulling the bedspread over our head, I whispered a little meanly under the sheets. *"We are the monster."*

My sour mood returns. She is, indeed, a beast. She betrayed me. I open my mouth to speak and Mama, reading my face, changes tack like she's adjusting the sails on a boat.

"I loved the nicknames you two had for each other," she says before I can utter a word. "I remember you called your sister Pancakes." Her eyes scrunch together, and with her forefinger, she taps her temple. "What was the name she called you?

"Nilly," I respond automatically, trying to formulate a sentence, to organize the damning words scattered about my brain.

"That's right. Nilly." Mama's smile seems to split her face. "Often she called you Silly Nilly. Many, many times, as I recall."

Before I can complain about how heartless my twin is, she switches tack, using her caginess as a weapon of surprise.

"Both of your speech was delayed, which is common with twins. But when you did begin to talk, the two of you had your own secret language. Dr. Lamar—your pediatrician—said it wasn't healthy. Antisocial is the word he used. But I refused to interfere with the private world you two created. Thought it was cute, myself."

She pauses, her irises darting about, searching for another

memory. At that moment, before she has time to further demobilize me, I double tack, turning the conversation around.

"How, Mama, how could Linnea date the man who fed me a roach when I was a child, told my high school classmates that I was into threesomes, and, most recently, sabotaged my float?"

Like trapped in a sudden squall, Mama's face clouds over. Caught off guard, she stares at me, wordless, mouth agape. Ella begins to whimper and thrusts her arms towards me, babbling "mamamamama". I reach over, peeling her gently away from my mother. I remove the bracelet from her grasp and grab one of the several pacifiers littering the sofa. I secure it into her mouth, and she begins pulling at the buttons of my shirt.

"I'm sorry, Mama. I know you mean well. But sentiment won't change the reality of what Linnea's done."

"At the very least, Delphina, hear her out, listen to what she has to say."

Ella begins to wiggle out of my arms, and I put her down on the floor. Raising her butt into the air, she crawls to a bottom shelf I've arranged with toys. She pulls them off, one by one, and drags them into a heap. She takes great happiness in this task, which can occupy her for several minutes.

Free from the baby's interruption, my head clears enough to make the final tack in the conversation. Steering all talk away from Linnea, I turn to face my mother, lace my fingers together, and rest them in my lap.

"So, what's up with Ivy? When Linnea and I had dinner with her at the lighthouse, she seemed a bit down." My lips twitch. "To put it mildly."

Her eyes dart from mine. Wringing her hands, she rocks back and forth in her seat. "She's depressed. Maybe you could bring her a little present, something to cheer her up?"

I keep my expression neutral, but inside, roll my eyes. "Depressed? Is that what it's called? So, what do you recommend? A helium balloon decorated with a monkey face? Some Ben & Jerry's Cherry Garcia?"

The sarcasm in my words slash through her eyes, and I wish I could take them back.

"*Get well soon's* won't fix what's wrong with Ivy." I continue, my voice now soft, losing its bite. "Something's always been off with that girl but whatever that something is, it's getting worse. The past few times I've seen her, I get the feeling she's—I don't know—disembodied? Not plugged into reality?"

What I'm trying to express so inadequately is a premonition, something I can't articulate. I grab my mother's hands, squeezing them hard.

"It's not healthy for her to be hanging out in her studio twenty-four-seven. She needs to get out with people that share her interests. She needs to socialize."

Mama's eyes drop to our hands, her knuckles white beneath my grip. Then, she shakes them off and leans her torso forward, her features twisting as she fights back tears. Losing the battle, she drops her face into her hands and begins to weep, her shoulders shaking with anguish.

Frightened by this sudden outburst of grief, my tummy clenches. I lay my hand, gently, on her shoulder.

"What is it Mama? Please stop being so evasive. You have to tell me what's wrong."

Her voice is muffled as she speaks into her fingers, her words broken by sobs. "She has been getting out and seeing someone, Delphina. But it's not what you're talking about. She's seeing a psychiatrist."

"What?" I exclaim. My touch on her shoulder tightens into a grip. "That's huge. A therapist is one thing, psychologist another. But a psychiatrist? He can prescribe antidepressants to her—like Prozac or Zoloft, right?"

She shakes her head and looks up, sniffling, mascara streams running down her cheeks. I reach to the side table and grab a Kleenex, handing it to her. She blows her nose and then pinches her nostrils with the tissue.

"This is not your typical depression. Therefore, putting a patient like Ivy on antidepressants is not a good strategy." She speaks slowly, her voice shaking, measuring each word with care. "They have the potential to counteract other drugs. More important drugs. Essential drugs that her brain absolutely requires."

My voice drops to a whisper, frightened to ask the question but more frightened to hear the answer.

"If it's not your run-of-the-mill depression, Mama. What the holy hell is it?"

"Her doctor's prognosis is bi-polar disorder. And not your garden variety, either, if there is such a thing." She closes her eyes and sighs deeply, shaking her head. "It's worse. Much more difficult to treat. He describes it as mixed states, ultradian-cycling bipolar."

"Ultradian-cycling? What's that supposed to mean?" My lips feel chalky, and I moisten them with the tip of my tongue.

"Mood whiplash. When cycling, it's like she's on an endless rollercoaster. No one can guess how high she'll climb or how low she'll fall. How long each episode lasts before she levels out is pure speculation. In a single day, multiple moods can hit her in rapid succession." She claps her hands. "Bam bam bam bam bam. Nonstop madness."

"You're frightening me," I say, confused, ice-cold fear hammering in my chest.

"Her hallucinations caught me by surprise," she continues, her chest heaving, as if she can't catch her breath. "Shocked your father, too. At first, we hoped that time and home remedies would alleviate her symptoms."

She frowns at the tissue, now splotched in black and then looks up to catch my eyes. "But telling her to try a different strain of pot and wait it out was our first mistake. The disease has been untreated for so long it's only gotten worse. Since December, with each passing month, she slips a bit further. She's gone from being sick to being extremely sick. Out of control sick."

She straightens on the sofa, her back stiffening. "She's been undergoing psychotherapy since January. The drugs are trial and error, and it's been an interminable process."

Tears subsided, her voice shakes as she spits on the tissue and rubs it under her eyes. She blinks rapidly, clenching the paper in her fist.

"She says she feels like a freak and requested we not tell anyone the truth about her illness. I've been honoring her wishes. Until now." Her voice catches on the words. "I'll tell Linnea, too—may as well since the cat's out of the bag. I hate that I've broken Ivy's trust, but it's impossible to keep covering for her. Only letting her come down from the tower when her moods have leveled. Making excuses for her behavior."

"So, what does the doctor say about her prognosis?" I search my mother's face, her sparkling emerald eyes now as dull and listless as swamp water.

"It's privileged information. I do know enough to tell you your little sister's ill. Extremely ill. Even if her cycling levels out with time, Ivy will need lifelong counseling and drug treatment. It will never be easy. For her. Or for any of us who love her."

She looks at me, ferociously. "She is going to be who she is—a woman managing her bipolar—for the rest of her life. And if I ever hear anyone tell me again that tortured artists produce the greatest work, I will knock out their teeth."

Shivers creep up my spine at this revelation. Head-pounding, I feel light-headed and dizzy, as if the room were sucked of oxygen. Why does society glamorize, even sensationalize artists with mental illnesses—as if the disease, itself, were the artist? And why did Mama wait so long to tell me?

She looks at her hands, chewing her lower lip. Then, she rakes her fingers through her hair, so that it's splayed and frizzed about her face. She appears to be just as crazy as the words she's been speaking, and we don't need anymore crazy in this family.

"She was drinking wine last month," I hear myself say. "The last time we were together."

"Wine?" Mama gasps, her hand flying to her mouth. "She knows she can't do that when taking antipsychotics. It neutralizes them."

"I mean, it wasn't excessive. But still. And should she continue smoking dope?"

"Honestly, Delphina. I don't know what to believe anymore. At this point, it's anyone's guess." Licking fingertips, she smooths her mane, and then ties her hair into a knot at the base of her neck, glistening with perspiration.

"The latest worry is she's been canceling appointments with her doctor. And all these drugs. It's been surreal. First, it was Lithium and Lexapro, which didn't work. Then something else, I forgot the name, but it made her fly off the walls. We think Zyprexa may be helping as long as she takes it with Wellbutrin and Atavan. God, Delphina, the list goes on and on. I only know for sure she takes the pills when I force them down her throat. Her doctor and I are considering institutionalizing her, giving her electroshock therapy--that will likely be what's next."

Her expression changes from grief to one of utter dismay. Within seconds, she appears to have aged one hundred years. At once, I feel guilty that my issues with Linnea have added to her sorrow. For every awful thing that we've said to each other, she is my twin. I need to fix things with her, with both of my sisters.

A lonely tear travels down Mama's cheek, shredding my heart into a million little pieces. My lower lip begins to tremble, out of control. The weaker she becomes, the weaker I become, which is a vicious cycle that must be broken. I take a deep breath, reclaiming what little bit of strength I can muster.

"I'm here for you Mama. And I promise to spend time with Ivy. Help support you. Help support you both. Ella will help too. At least she'll distract us." My daughter, hearing her name, looks up from her task of tearing pages out of recycled magazines, and smiles. "I'll also text Linnea after you leave."

The area beneath Mama's eyes is puffed and dusky, yet a prick of light rekindles her iris. She kisses her fingertips and places them on my forehead.

Looking me straight in the eye, she speaks softly, but with the intensity of a prisoner telling another how to escape the compound walls.

"You and your sisters can never let each other down."

22. IVY

Dipping my brush into the gloss of black—glistening and malignant—I turn to my painting. There it is. Here, on the canvas: The play of light. The tranquility of water. But underneath, there is pain, terrible pain.

The alien eyes of a Moray eel glare at me from around the edge of a seawall. Holding my breath, I dab the paint, just a pinpoint, into the green of his eyes. The darkest of the deep, that's where all the monsters hide, that's what interests me.

I was always the good girl—Our Girl—and I'm ashamed I've let my family down. I've tried to get better; God knows I've worked so hard. Mama tells me my best work was created before mania embraced me, that my disease has crippled my work instead of enhancing it. But I distrust her. These days her touch is scalding. She says it's dangerous to romanticize my demons. But, really. Who is the demon?

My shrink assures me my work will not suffer once we unearth the right combination of meds. But this delirium, this mania spawns creativity, raising the volume, brightening the colors. The drugs stifle artistry. When I take them, I feel an emotional deadness; I'm flat-lined, edgy. I lack the energy and drive to even pick up a brush. Feeling is better than not feeling.

I've complained to my doctor about this state of fog. And as he fiddles with various cocktails, I walk a tight rope, a balancing act, one foot after the other. Some days there's a net beneath. Some days not. Some days the fall is short. Some days I plummet from the canyon edge, hitting jagged rocks before tumbling into the sea, sinking down, down, down. Down to the ocean floor, down to where the ogre resides, uncoiling and re-clenching, nibbling at my brain. Delusion unlocks my imagination, so my art would rather suffer this depression with the beast.

The pain is unimaginable to those who've not experienced it, but it never lasts. And after clawing up through the ocean and making my way towards the summit, the rewards are euphoric. I'm at my most productive in this hypomanic state when the bipolar bomb explodes, and the mountain fires encircle me, unrestrained.

My moods are now cycling faster than my racing pulse, and the higher I climb, the further I plunge, my teeth rattling the whole way down. I switch brushes, dunking the sable into a pale green tint. Then, I dive from the peak, submerging into the deep, painting Rossalea by my side. Underwater, my Maiden's hair comes undone, and I paint ribbons streaming and crawling about her head as if they were snakes.

23. LINNEA

Today dawned bright and clear with a startling blue sky, unmarred by even a single cloud. Slowing my pace down to a swift stride, I hop onto the sidewalk, lean my back against a wall and text Delphina.

Still on for Coffee King? The one off Duval? I check the time on my Fit Bit: 7:15 AM. *I can be there in fifteen. Streets are empty—no parking issues.*

Within seconds she responds with a thumbs-up emo. I slide my forefinger across my SMILEYS & PEOPLE. Nope. Too lovey, friendly or silly for sisters at each other's throats. Onto ANIMALS & NATURE. Perhaps a cow? Nah. Too domesticated—looks like it belongs on a farm in Wisconsin. FOOD & DRINK, don't let me down. Here we go. I tap an image of a cup of coffee and hit the send arrow.

Squatting to tighten the laces on my shoes, I straighten and hop back onto the street. Resuming my pace, I run down the centerline, loving Duval for once, which is deserted at this hour. Since I've been down here, I time my runs to begin after the rooster's crow. The air, even oppressive at this hour, is so thick after nine, it's like dough before it rises.

Delphina's text yesterday caught me off-guard. She wrote

she was returning my call. When did texts turn into phone calls? Am I missing something? And it should have stated she was returning the many calls I've made over the past three weeks. Mama was at her house yesterday, so I've no doubt her shrewd negotiating tactics triggered Delphina's message.

I'd talked myself into not caring, but after reading her words, absolute relief blindsided me. I responded, text in kind, glad, in fact, I didn't have to have a conversation with her over the phone. This is a discussion best had eye to eye.

I suggested a public place. My hope is the faces of strangers will mollify our words, so our conversation doesn't escalate into a catfight. Both early risers, I suggested coffee, recommending we meet before our days begin. Mama, thrilled at the possibility of us *patching things up*, is preparing breakfast for the guests.

Amongst the myriad of things that slay my twin, bad coffee ranks top of the list. She's become a Cuban cup aficionado, having honed her skill at the hands of Lita, the master. The Cuban Coffee King has brews up to her standards and, fortunately, one of their two locations is not on the waterfront. I'd prefer sipping Nescafe in a mildewed closet over drinking a masterful brew next to the foaming and spewing abyss.

Heading towards a tourist shop selling T-shirts and other Made-in-China junk, a young woman stands over a large pot of flowers holding a watering can.

"Who 'ya runnin' from, honey?" she asks, waving at me with her free hand and smiling broadly.

Catching her eye, I grin. "Myself. Have I outrun her yet?"

My feet move forward, faster now, soles pounding the pavement and drowning out her reply. I'm counting down the days before I can get out of here. Boise summers, like Key West, are also big-time pressure cookers, but the humidity is far less intense, and the threat of hurricanes practically non-existent. I also miss running on hills and admiring the mountain range set against a big-city skyline. Living on a small island patch, a five-foot elevation commanding the highest point is confining. The Boise City of Trees Marathon is mid-October; I'm leaving after Labor Day and will be settled in a rental by then.

I slow my pace. The shop is tucked somewhere around here, in Key Lime Square, but is easy to miss. Stopping in my tracks, I spot the sign and hook a right. Although the town seems deserted, people are already beginning to trickle into this tiny oasis. It could be a coffee house anywhere except there are no walls, only stanchions supporting the roof. Also, chickens roam the floor. You won't find free-range birds in other coffee shops in the States. Unless, of course, they're batter fried and tucked into buns.

Walking to the counter, I place my order—four shots of espresso over ice, no cream, no sugar—and then take a seat at an empty picnic table. I grin at a speckled hen strutting across the tabletop. Only an arm's length distance from my torso, I imagine her as Gisele modeling an amber feathered sheath down a runway. Her head pops around searching for some errant morsels and then, finding nothing, she hops to the floor. A young tatted-up man wearing a bulky collection of crossbones and crucifixes brings me my beverage. I thank him.

With my forefinger, I stir the ice, hands trembling from jangled nerves. I look up and there, at the entrance, stands Delphina. She wears cut-offs and a white Coral Princess T. I note how deeply she's tanned, darker than the last time I saw her.

My skin is intentionally and perennially pale, as I never leave the house without slathering SPF 50 over my body. My sister says that whenever she uses sunblock, she feels like she's spreading mayonnaise over a piece of bread; she'd prefer not feeling like a sandwich. It will be interesting to compare how our skins fare in the next twenty years. A dermatologist should take note of us in some study. I pinch my cheeks, distress stinging my eyes. What if we're strangers a couple of decades down the line?

Tossing a half-smile and nod my way, her eyes remain hard, cold. She points to the counter, and I lift my hand in acknowledgment, my heart pounding. She turns to order, a single black braid swaying between her shoulder blades, and I dab my sweaty forehead with a napkin trying to compose myself. Maybe meeting in a public venue was not such a good idea. I undo my ponytail, rake my hands through my hair, and secure it into an unruly knot at the nape of my neck.

I watch the weave of her hips, softened by motherhood, as she makes her way to the table. A small smile crosses her lips as she threads her way around seated patrons, who can't help but glance up to admire her confident poise. She takes a seat across from me and, without a word––not even a greeting––she swivels her torso back to face the counter. As if on cue, the employee who served me brings her coffee. Glancing from me to Delphina, he smiles but doesn't make the usual comment we've heard all of our lives: *Y'all must be twins, right?* Perhaps with our stony expressions and darting eyes, the tension between us is palpable. Or maybe I appear a counterfeit, a sloppy copy of the original masterpiece.

I glance at the cup of inky black liquid dotted with cubes of ice. We ordered the same thing—the story of our lives. Threading fingers in front of her chest, elbows wide across the tabletop, her arms are angled above the coffee. Raising her brow, she glances to the right and then to the left, surveying the environment. Her look is one of disdain, and I wonder if her contempt is directed towards the venue or me. The silence is so brittle it could snap, and I remain silent, unsure as to who should make the first move.

"I've never been to this location," she begins, her eyes flickering on mine for a second. Then, with a dismissive gesture of her hands, she shoos away the chicken pecking about her feet.

"Sonny and I prefer the one by the wharf. I like to hear the commotion at the docks and watch the sunlight dance across the sea."

Romanticizing my demons, eh? Right off the bat—without even a *hello, how 'ya been?*—she throws a zinger, making a veiled reference to my fear of the ocean. Good shot, sis. Direct hit. I can't help but wince.

Glancing at me, the hard line about her mouth softens.

"But thank you, Linnea. I'm glad you suggested the King. Nice they've another location. Love their coffee—they never fail to nail it."

I cross my ankles, running my tongue across my lips. OK, OK. Maybe I'm feeling over-sensitive. I've yet to say a word, and now it's my turn. Let's get this over with. As I open my mouth, she speaks again.

"This place used to be Lobo's. They had this Greek pita thing I liked," she continues, rattling on as if small talk will clear the thickness in the air between us. She takes a sip of coffee, her eyes rising above the rim to meet mine. I remain silent. She holds the cup between her palms, lowers her gaze to the beverage, and shakes her cup rattling the ice. "Sonny liked their burgers."

I swallow, making a tiny choking sound as I clear my throat. She looks up, and we catch each other's eyes—steely blue to steely blue. Leaning into her, my right eye begins to twitch.

"DJ had nothing to do with your vanishing ribbon. I've spoken with his employees, and they are the ones who made the mistake. They rectified the problem, and you got your money back."

I don't like the sound of my voice, the way it wavers like I lack confidence. I place my fingertips on her wrist. She remains silent, her countenance as impenetrable as steel.

"I've explained this to you before." My heart rate accelerating, I refrain from tacking on the word *bitch*. Locking eyes with her, I shake my head incredulously, hoping my expression will make her see reason.

"And why do I have to explain anything? He was a stupid teenager when he said those things about you. He tried to apologize. Twice. He even wrote a letter that you tossed out before reading. He feels horrible about what he did to you, Delphina. Horrible."

Her voice level is restrained, but her words emerge in a sputter and hiss. "That's highly debatable, but what's not debatable is you lied to me. You had plenty of opportunities to tell me you were seeing Danny Jack."

Glaring at me through slitted, angry eyes, she says Danny Jack as if she were saying serial killer. Inhaling her fury, my breath catches in my throat. I retract my finger from her wrist as if she were a burning flame. At this point, I've two options: dive in or walk away. I make the plunge.

"Yes. I should have told you. But I kept stalling because I knew exactly what your reaction would be." I point my forefinger at her nose. "This. Right now. The way your face is contorted and glaring into mine. You're so angry with me, and it's so totally unfair." I lean into her so close that I see red veins emerge, like sparks igniting, in the white of her eyes. "And seriously, Delphina. Is my love life any of your business?"

She draws her face back; I may as well have slapped her. Then, she reels it in, so it is level with mine. "I suppose it isn't. I suppose the fact we share the same blood type, that we've been protecting each other ever since we shared the same womb might discount any notion we'd have a bond—that I might take an interest in your affairs."

Her voice is rising, and I note an older couple gazing our way. With their sensible thick-soled Merrells, fanny packs and map of the city spread in front of them, I'm sure they're tourists taking advantage of the cut-rate prices in off-season. Placing my forefinger to my lips, I tip my head towards the pair, suggesting my sister quieten. Glancing at the couple, her skin turns a brownish shade of crimson.

"I suppose," she continues, the volume of her words dialed down a notch, "the fact that you're sleeping with my mortal enemy shouldn't upset me in the least." She bangs her fist on the table. "Seeing my twin do something stupid is like I'm doing something stupid myself. And I resent that, Linnea. I resent it. DJ's a thug and you, dear sister, are his co-conspirator."

"How dare you," I sputter, fury boiling through my veins, not giving a damn who hears me. "Here you go, once again, sentencing me without a trial. Next to you, I'm the evil twin. So full of wickedness, in fact, I've decided to spite you by dating your nemesis." I fling my arms into the air. "Priceless, Delphina. Truly priceless. Is forgiveness a foreign concept for you? Obviously, it is. You and your unwavering set of rules—your absolute morality."

"And you with your absolute freedom," she spits back, her eyes blazing. "It's all about you. Always has been. You come and go, willy nilly, no worries, no consideration of who you hurt and who you run over."

We stand, hands on hips, facing off across the table. The other patrons are watching us with interest, some even smiling, enjoying the latest live act of Key West eccentricities. It's not even eight in the morning and two identical twins are at each other's throats, ready to duel.

"If you want to engage in a fight with something or someone," I say, shaking with rage, "fight your narrow mindset. You're stressed out about being a new mother and your relationship with your husband. And how convenient for you I've returned to town. How convenient for you I've been seeing DJ. Now you get to use both of us as your punching bags."

Delphina takes two steps back, and I continue my rant.

"I have nothing to show for the past ten years of my life. No career. No husband. No child. You're just mean, Delphina. Mean. You're like a blowfish giving the illusion you're a capable do-gooder who can handle it all. But you, in all of your self-righteous vanity, are simply puffed up with air. The only emotions you seem to understand are your own."

Her eyes widen, horrified, and her mouth gapes open.

"But no worries, sistah," I continue. "DJ's not the big bad villain you think he is. He actually has a lovely heart and wouldn't harm a flea. If only you could see the scrupulous care he takes with his tanks. And," I add, my voice dripping with anger, "not that you'd care, but he's the first man who has ever treated me with warmth, attention and respect."

With a flourish of hands, I make a sweeping gesture towards her rigid stance, which now seems carved from ice. Her silence––infuriating me more than her shouting––goads me on.

"But I've sacrificed him for you. Oh yes. Two weeks back, I broke it off and told him goodbye." I lift my chin. "DJ and I are through. I haven't seen him since."

Taking a deep breath, I step forward. "It was a mistake for me to come home. There's no place for me here. Nina's in recovery, and will soon be back at the inn, so plans are to return to Boise in a couple of weeks."

I drive the stake exactly where it might hurt her the worst. "Come September, I'll be leaving every single one of you behind."

She stares at me and then her features sag, like a fallen soufflé. Resuming her seat, she hunches over, gazing at her hands, so fisted together her knuckles are white. It feels good to see her composure collapse, to hear the catch in her ragged breath. The restaurant patrons, judging by their stares and downturned lips, appear disappointed at what seems to be an intermission following Act One.

After several moments, she looks up at me in the unforgiving morning light. A fine mesh of visible lines creeps about her eyes and along the contours of her lips. Hunh. I've never noticed those before. My complexion is smooth, fair, unweathered by the elements. The sun has begun its warfare on Delphina, and I'll wager she'll be aged beyond her years in a decade. A feeling, loathsome yet satisfying, creeps into my consciousness. I expect to see censure in her blue eyes, mirroring my own. But what I see surprises me.

A shiny pink film mists her eyes as she studies my face, searching for words. "You have it all wrong," she says, her voice breaking. "I am your twin. Your family. I want the same happiness for you that I want for myself. I've felt this way since we were little girls. I wanted us both to have the same share of cookies. The same number of Barbies..." A forlorn look engages the creases in her face compounding her wrinkles further. "The same amount of love."

Her words flow through me, touching something primal—a tender, gentle place. It's like brushing the tip of your finger over the soft spot on a newborn's head; by instinct, you would never press it hard. The same with the two of us. No matter how much we hurt each other, we will protect this one sacred place. Who else can I count on? My pulse slowed, I resume my seat, upset but not consumed with the vindictive loathing I'd felt a minute prior. Placing my palms over her fisted hands, I bite my lips, shaking my head. There's nothing left for me to say.

"You've become one thing and I the other," she continues, her voice soft, tired, lost of all its battle. Her eyes lock into mine. "It's strange that as sisters, once inseparable, we've turned out to be so different."

Now, back in our seats with our voices subdued, the other patrons—bored with Act Two—return to their coffee.

"Yep," I say, pasting on a withering smile, rubbing my jaw now aching from clenching. "I'm forever cast as the manifest failure and you the virtuous triumph. It's classic—Shake-spearean, really."

"Don't talk nonsense." She closes her eyes and shakes her head fiercely as if dismissing such a ludicrous notion. "We both need time to think this over and simmer down."

Opening her eyes, she rests her forefinger on her bottom lip and presses her ribs into the table edge to study me.

"I admire you, Linnea." Her words are spoken under her breath in a whisper, and she seems to be talking to herself. "You were the one who was brave enough to set out on your own. Whatever I feel about DJ should not come between us."

"Delphina. I told you. I broke up with the man."

She shakes her head, dismissing my words. "Maybe you're right. He did try his best to apologize. High school boys *are* idiots. Lately, I'm beginning to realize I'm pig-headed. I'm going to let it go."

She grabs and squeezes my hands so hard my fingers feel numb.

Sighing, I peer into her eyes. "That makes me happy, really it does. But it doesn't change the fact that DJ and I are finished."

Repeating the words causes sweeps of anguish to course through my body. How did it happen? Did a scurrying cock-roach answer my questions? Of course not. I've many doubts about that man. But I'll never forget the look he gave when I returned from the bathroom and asked him to leave––it was the same look of utter loss, which crossed his face moments earlier when he talked about his father.

"Why waste his time?" I continue. "Key West will never be in the cards." Shaking my hands free from her grip, I try shaking away the memory of him as well.

"Nothing feels right down here. Nothing. And those horrible nightmares. Almost every night, now. They've even begun to creep into my days."

My palms are sweating, and a sheen of moisture covers the top of my hands as well. "I'm suffocating, Delphina. Drowning."

Her face softens and the sides of her mouth twitch. "God, how I wish I could help—that I could rescue you."

Like a faucet being turned on and off, the sound of breaking waves swells through my subconscious. On and off, on and off. I turn my head to the side and watch a parade of chicks follow their mother across the floor. When the roar subsides, I return my attention to our conversation.

"I can never escape it on this island."

I turn away from her, my hands rising to my cheeks. I pinch them so hard I wince, but it still doesn't keep the tears from rolling down my face. I take another shuddering breath before turning to meet her gaze.

"But that's not the only thing frightening me. I'm afraid I'm incapable of loving a decent man. Whenever I begin to fall in love with someone nice, I sabotage myself by figuring out reasons why I should reject him. And this time, Delphina, I should thank you. You gave me the perfect excuse."

Again, my sister takes my hands, pulling them towards her, pleading for forgiveness. "I'm so sorry. I can be such a bitch. Such a mess," she muses, her gaze a bit hazy.

"We're all such a mess," I say, trying to find a smile. "I wonder. What's to become of the Chandler sisters?"

Her eyes refocus and head snaps to attention. "Did Mama tell you Ivy was bipolar—that she is seeing a shrink and taking a boatload of drugs?"

"Yep. Yesterday. After she left your house. Mixed-states, rapid cycling, ultradian bipolar, to be precise. It's quite a tongue-twister, but at least her weirdness has a name."

Unweaving my fingers from hers, I wrap my hands around the coffee cup. I take a long, slow sip to help steady my nerves and stifle the barrage of anxiety I've been feeling since my conversation with Mama.

"Our pathetic attempts at helping her, thinking we could cheer her up, was like playing with a loaded gun." My voice emerges hollow, wobbly, unsure of itself. "Her problems are so much bigger than anything we can handle. Thank God, Mama finally came clean. At least now we can all be supportive as she gets the professional help she needs."

"Amen to that. Maybe we can get a group rate." She flashes a brittle grin. "You think I'm kidding?"

Beneath the whir of coffee beans grinding, and the roasted nut smell of them perfuming the air, we sit a minute, appraising each other, taking each other in. There's something broken in our relationship, and I'm uncertain if it can ever be repaired.

Delphina breaks the silence. Rising, pressing palms into the table, she leans her face into mine so that our noses are almost touching.

"Deny it if you will, but when it's all said and done, remember this: I am your mirror. And, likewise, when I look at you, I see myself. I am the one person who has known you your entire life, who will stand by you no matter what."

Beads of moisture dot her brow, and a ruddy flush creeps up her neck as love takes shape in the air. Anger and regret have torn rips around the edges, but it remains love, nevertheless. A single tear rolls down her cheek, into the corner of her mouth, and I have never seen such an expression on her face.

24. DELPHINA

Monday, Sept. 4th Ella's mouth is pressed close, and she yanks her head from side to side, refusing the medicine Sonny offers. Legs kicking and arms flailing, she wiggles within the confines of my front pack. Attempting to keep her body from squirming out of the carrier, I feel as if I'm trying to still the shell of an upturned turtle, struggling to right itself.

Sonny, holding her head, presses the Tylenol-filled syringe through her lips, allowing the medicine to drip down her throat. Finished, he removes the plastic cylinder from her mouth. She emits a sad little wail before burying her head into my—now barren—breasts. I look helplessly at my husband and shake my head, wondering at the nightmare of the past twenty-four hours.

"At least her fever broke," he says, placing the syringe next to the bottle and securing the top. "The doc was right. There was no reason to freak out."

Last night, at 3:00 AM, after comforting her in my arms for hours, I could feel the moisture pooling from her tiny frame. I pressed my palm across her forehead, which was, at last, cool. Minutes later, I collapsed into a dreamless sleep next to Sonny.

He glances at his watch. "Give her another dose at two. One

more before her bedtime and tomorrow she should be fit to travel. We need to get out before the panic sets in. I just called Joel." Joel is a friend who runs a fishing operation in Sarasota.

"Said folks are just as antsy upstate. Lines of vehicles are wrapped around the gas stations and Walmart's out of bottled water. The evacuation routes—75 and 95 North—will be glutted within a couple of days."

He glances, once again, at his wrist. He must have checked his watch a thousand times today. "I'm thinking we get a few hours of sleep tonight and try to get out before 4 AM. Traffic's already bad, but at least we'll beat the panic."

"We can take the wheel in shifts." I cradle Ella's sobbing head into my chest. Pacing the room, I pause to kick a cardboard box sealed together with duct tape. It rests next to the outdoor furniture we've had to cram into our house.

"Please tell your mother we don't have room for this. We need every square inch in the truck for Ella's swing, her toys and her cuddle bear—things to keep her comfy."

"I can make it fit somewhere, honey. Try to be reasonable. She's been collecting those penguins ever since we moved down here."

I whip around, pinning him with my gaze. "If that's the case, I'm bringing every photograph and scrapbook we own."

He raises his arms towards me, his fingers spread wide. "Look. No weapons."

He feels more helpless in the wake of his mother and me than he does with this hurricane. "Put the family mementos in the dishwasher," he continues. "It's a vault. Even if Irma flattens the house," he looks at me, his eyes softening, "which will never happen, the dishwasher will protect our memories."

"Then I'll also save space in there for those damn penguins," I retort, the tone of my voice acrider than I had intended.

The color in his cheeks rise, and we regard each other in a

mix of anger, exhaustion and confusion. Since my reconciliation with Linnea, I've come to realize a few hard truths about myself, some of which are my knee-jerk reactions. I've worked diligently towards containing them and have done a good job. At least up until now. But damn it. I can't help myself. A freaking hurricane is breathing down our necks, and I've been up all night with a sick child. Thank you, Grandmother Rose.

Folding, my head drops and shoulders heave as I sob along with Ella. Looking up, she regards me curiously and quietens, touching my damp cheeks. My misery had at least one good outcome: she's quit crying. Bending to grab a pacifier from the coffee table, Sonny and I trade glances. With the knuckle on my pinky, I swipe away my tears and a tired smile creeps across my face.

"Sorry, babe. I'm so exhausted and stressed. All I ask is one day when I'm not trying to put out a fire. Life was enough of a hurricane before this mess."

Approaching us, he wraps his arms around the baby and me. "We'll get through this, honey. Let's stay calm, focused, and keep moving forward."

The Weather Service ranks hurricanes in categories, depending on the strength of its winds. Category 1 storms have dangerous winds up to 95 mph, which could damage homes and topple tree limbs, causing power outages. Subsequent Categories grow incrementally worse until hitting Category 5, whose winds can exceed 157 mph. Those monsters can level a city rendering it uninhabitable for weeks, even months.

Two days back, while Lita was making breakfast and Sonny and I were preparing for work, we learned of a Category 2 on The Weather Channel. It was named Irma and had developed off the West Coast of Africa. Since then, it's risen in rank to a Category 4, and they're saying if the intense low pressure over the Atlantic remains, its path could include the Keys. But that's still several days—maybe even a week—away, and they keep revising projections for the storm's direction. There's still time for it to change course. There are a lot of *what if's* in this scenario.

"I'm so sick of these damn hurricane threats," I say, looking up into his eyes. "It's like an army's on the horizon, threatening to invade the town. The Weather Channel makes such a ruckus, scares the bejesus out of everyone, and then the storm goes elsewhere. The entire time I've known you, whenever they predict a hurricane, it misses us."

"I don't know, Delphina." He raises his forearm––yet again––to check his watch. "There's no certainty about anything. It's been a long time since the Keys were this close to a major storm. Even the die-hards are leaving this time. You don't mess around with a Cat 4, and everyone's spooked after Harvey ransacked Texas."

I bite the tip of my thumb, shaking my head. "You're right. Of course, you're right. And all of those wildfires raging in California." I shift Ella to my left hip and roll my shoulders, my arms and back aching after last night's vigil.

"I'm sure the evangelists will have a field day. They'll put an apocalyptic spin on the convergence of the natural disasters— like they're some sort of end-game scenario. And with our town's crazy partying, we'd be the bull's eye." My thumb cocked, I point my forefinger at Sonny like I'm shooting a gun. "Bang bang bang bang bang. God's wrath showering revenge on the heathens."

Dropping my hand, I stroke Ella's head as she rests it against my breast, sucking her pacifier as if her little life depended on it. I lower my voice. "Whatever. But having this little one is a game-changer. We can't take chances."

"In the end, I'll bet the worst of Irma will be a power outage," Sonny says, touching my cheek, trying to comfort me. "Maybe reason enough, in and of itself, to leave. This house is a furnace without air-conditioning. After this passes, I'm getting a generator."

I raise my eyebrows. "Right. A generator. How can we afford one? This will wipe us out. Evacuations are so damn expensive."

Not only do we have to pay for lodging, but we also lose all income. Yesterday, we canceled reservations through the middle of the month. Sonny enlisted some of his friends to help haul The Coral Princess out of the water, anchor it to the ground, and they prepped the boat to reduce wind damage.

"How much is that room per night?"

"It's an Airbnb. Big enough to handle all of us and was the best deal I could find. One-hundred and eighty plus taxes a night. "

"Holy crap. That's as much as a hotel suite."

"I know. The price went up with the demand."

"How'd you pay for it? The Master Card's maxed."

"I put the deposit on a Visa—the one I save for emergencies. And we are damned lucky I grabbed the place when I did. I spoke to the neighbors. Now everything's booked, and they can't find a room. I guarantee every hotel lobby outside the state will be spread with blankets and people sleeping on couches."

He peers into my eyes while brushing my hair out of my face. A glint of amusement twitches about the sides of his lips. "We can still stay with your cousins."

"And sleep on the floor like farm animals?"

My parents and sisters are driving to Birmingham after the guests have been evacuated from the inn. They're staying with second cousins—Aunt Bet Bet and her family, whom I've only met a few times. They've one guest room where Mama and Daddy are staying, while Linnea and Ivy sleep who knows where on blow-ups. If we stayed there, we'd have to purchase additional mattresses. And sleeping on the floor next to Lita? I shiver at the thought. Our rental is only minutes outside of Nashville.

Most of our friends are driving north to Georgia, Tennessee or Kentucky. Two couples we know with kids have booked flights to New York and Michigan to stay with family. Cell phones are alight with townsfolk finding out where friends are headed.

"Look," Sonny says, massaging my temples with his fingertips. "We'll make it an adventure. Try making some fun out of the chaos. It will be Ella's first vacation."

Sniffing, I rub my nose. "I'd rather spend the money on an all-inclusive in the Caribbean."

His hands drop to my shoulders and give them a little shake. "Not in this shit, you wouldn't. Have you listened to the news? It's headed straight to the islands as we speak."

My heart skips a beat, and I bite my lower lip with such force a metallic taste swims through my mouth. What if? What if this is the *big one* and our town is flattened, every home and business destroyed?

For the first time since learning of Irma, I'm frightened, my imagination off to the races. I look anxiously at Sonny, blinking rapidly.

"Did you get enough fuel to get us through the state?"

"All taken care of yesterday. I got a couple of extra canisters filled."

My heart fills with gratitude and crazy love. When the shit hits the fan, he's here for us, keeping us out of harm's way. How can I be irritated with this guy even for a second? Pulling him into Ella and me, I rise on tiptoes to kiss him.

Entering the front door, Lita interrupts our moment, sputtering in the exertion felt by her last-minute *to-dos*. She drops the car keys and slams a box of extra-large, heavy-duty garbage bags on the table with such force I jump. Sonny releases me and walks to his mother, giving her a tight hug.

Such a Mama's boy. My mood clouds. That's why he annoys me.

"I'm telling you, they've doubled the prices on everything," she says to her son, grasping at his forearms, shaking her head furiously. "I heard about it on the news. It's price gouging, that's what it's called. Every shopkeeper in town should be arrested. *Deben ser colgados por sus pelotas*," she mutters, under her breath.

Hung by their balls? By now I speak enough Spanish to understand my mother-in-law doesn't live under a rock. I pick up the receipt, which lies on top of the bags.

"No. They're the same price as usual."

She shoots me a dismissive glance, and I smile wanly. Be nice, I tell myself. Be nice. We'll be under each other's feet for God only knows how long.

"Thanks so much, Lita," I say, with as much sincerity as I can muster. "Now I can start covering up the furniture."

She walks towards Ella, eyes leveled at her face. "Ahhh. *La pequeña princesa*. Her color's back to normal."

"You'll be happy to know our little princess is on the mend." I wiggle Ella out of the carrier and hand her to Lita, relieved to give my aching shoulders a break.

Turning my back to them, I open the box of garbage bags, removing a long sheath of shiny black plastic. I plan to double wrap furniture closest to the windows. Our home has a surprising number of them, which seem to multiply when they have to be covered by broad sheets of aluminum. Sonny did a great job––it's as dark as a cave in here now––but moisture always seems to find a way of seeping through.

He grabs the keys from the table. "I promised I'd help your dad install hurricane shutters. It will be a big job. After that, if time allows, we'll cruise the streets and see if anyone else needs help battening down the hatches."

"Ironic that today's Labor Day. Last year they closed our

street for a block party. Hey," I say, grabbing and squeezing his hand. "Take some pictures of our house and The Maiden Tower while you're out."

Our eyes latch together several seconds, reading each other's minds. We dare not say the words aloud, but the pictures might be the last images we'll ever have of our homes intact.

"Don't forget your water bottle. It's sweltering out there."

25. LINNEA

Wednesday, Sept. 6th "Safe journey," I shout, waving back to the thickset hand extended through the front door window of his Lincoln SUV. The man and his lady friend are the last of our guests driving off, escaping the possible wrath of Irma.

Vacationers in the Keys were instructed to leave today at the latest. There are always the occasional fools, however, who think riding out a Cat 5 would provide unparalleled bragging rights to their friends back home. Therefore, hotels and guest houses, such as ours, use the mandatory part to insist all of our guests depart.

Yesterday, Sonny and my father installed the shutters, so all that's left is to pack the car. We residents have been ordered to leave starting tonight. Under mandatory evacuations such as this, no one is forced by police or other government agencies to leave. But officials have issued a dire warning stating those who stay should not expect to be rescued if they are in danger.

I glance at my mother, standing by my side on the front porch, and it's not the threat of a hurricane ruffling her feathers. Through the slit of her eyes, she taps her foot—arms tightly crossed about her midriff—staring at the silver SUV crawling down the road with the speed of a caterpillar. Sandwiched in between a long snake of cars, RV's and trucks––many of them towing boats––they're all headed to Highway 1, the sole entrance to the mainland.

"I'm so relieved watching Mr. Sleaze Bucket drive away. It's a blessing his trip was cut in half. For that, I could almost forgive Irma."

The man who's earned Mama's disdain goes by the name of Phil Jones. According to my mother, she swears the name's an alias, but she has no way of knowing for sure as he pays upfront in cash. He claims he's concerned about identity theft and gives an extra two hundred for any possible damage, which Mama dutifully returns after checking his room. He's been a guest at The Maiden Tower every September for the past seven years and brings a different woman each time. Mama looks at me, her nostrils flaring.

"Since he values his privacy so much, I don't know why he can't rotate between the other hotels and B&B's. Who knows or even cares where he's from, but you can bet the creep's married with a house full of kids back home."

I put my arm around her shoulders, gazing at the stream of cars. "I'm sure he wants to impress his latest victim with the legacy of the lighthouse, Mama. There's no place like The Maiden Tower Inn, I can assure you, in the entire state of Florida."

"Hunh," she snorts, tossing her head. "If it was Season, I could claim we were booked. I don't have any excuses when half the rooms are empty. When he arrives, he acts like he's never visited the place before. Fine by your father and me. We want little to do with that skunk."

Yesterday, Irma grew to Category 5 strength, and early reports say she's wrought devastation in the Caribbean. The last I heard, it was due to hit town on Sunday in the wee hours of the morning. Delphina and her family left town 36 hours ago to beat the masses. I just received a text from her—they're six-hours away from Nashville.

I was planning to book my flight out of here after the Labor Day weekend. Now it's too late. But I'm glad to be down here helping my family. To hell with my fears. I would be out of my mind knowing they were facing this alone.

The Hurricane Center forecast said it might miss us, so now we're playing the waiting game. *Will she? Won't she?* The message from the governor is clear: Don't wait—run. As many as six million people are doing exactly that. The news said this could be the largest mass evacuation in American history. After watching the devastation wrought most recently by Harvey, we're not taking chances and are leaving for Birmingham tonight.

Even homeowners who consider riding out storms a source of pride are now packing bottled water, blankets and crated pets into their vehicles. Mama and I've been boxing up photographs, important documents and combing through an assortment of random items. Under the threat of losing every-thing, items we've taken for granted have now transformed into objects imbued with sentiment. Yesterday, Ivy and I secured her paintings into cardboard cartons. Daddy's now in the process of hauling it all to a storage facility, which specializes in keeping precious goods safeguarded in dangerous weather.

Mama and I turn, facing the front door, hesitating before opening it. I run my fingers along the plaque at the front entrance, tears welling my eyes. Our lighthouse, when newly built, survived the hurricane of 1846, which leveled two other lighthouses serving Key West. Will her luck continue? Mama rests the tip of her fingers over my hand, and I turn my head, watching sorrow travel across her face. This has been my parents' home for more than thirty-three years. I was planning to leave town anyway. But not like this.

A clamor of feet climbing the front steps jolts us out of our reverie. I turn. Oh God, it's DJ. With my tongue, I moisten my lips, combing my hair with my fingers.

His face is unshaven, smudged with dirt, and his hair hangs in limp strands about his chin. Wearing a tattered T, it's an unkempt look tallying up to...what? Heartache? Who am I kidding. It's the threat of this storm.

On automatic pilot, I reach out to him and then yank my arms behind me, backing away, my spine now pressed against the door. Stop it, I tell myself. Stop this feeling that clatters inside me every time I think of him, its commotion even louder since the night I said good-bye.

He looks at me, pain casting a web of crinkles across his eyes, and then glances at Mama.

"Are y'all OK?"

At his words, Mama puts her face into her hands and begins to weep. And I'm not talking silent tears. I'm talking wretched, ragged noisy sobs. It's like she's being forcibly dragged from her family and loaded onto a train headed off to a work camp. DJ pulls her into his arms, and I sidestep away from them, confused, not knowing how to react to my former boyfriend embracing my mother. So, I do what I usually do in awkward situations: I ramble. Make small talk. I wring my hands together, not sure where or to whom to direct my eyes or words.

"All of us are leaving tonight for Birmingham. Staying with family. We're taking Liberace, of course." I bite my lower lip, wishing my voice didn't sound so hoarse and frantic. "He's family, you know. We could never leave him behind." I will my shoulders to relax, glancing at this man so adept at consoling my mom. "What about you? Where are you heading?"

"I'm staying here," he says, patting Mama on her back,

which heaves under his touch. Daddy is all thumbs when trying to comfort my volatile mother, so she literally jumps into the arms of anyone who shows her a thread of compassion. "There, there," he says, now patting her shoulder while stealing little looks at me. "You'll see. Everything will be fine."

He swivels his head in my direction. "I'm setting up residence at the aquarium. It'll be safer staying there than at my condo. Cassie and Stanson are joining me. They can't stay on their boat—that's a no-brainer."

"But you can't remain in town. Or anywhere in the Keys. Everyone's fleeing for their lives." The tone of my voice is pleading, my eyes, begging his to escape. "Gas stations are out of gas. Everything's closed—even the bars."

I note a slight tremor in his chin, and his eyes blink rapidly. "I just walked by the Green Parrot, and they're open. People are getting wasted at the bar."

"Honestly? Are they nuts?" I grasp his forearm, my heart hammering. "Are *you* nuts? There's time enough to ship out the fish and evacuate. That's what you should do. You heard what they said. If you call 9-1-1, no one will answer."

He shakes his head. "I've wasted time going back and forth. But now I've run out of options. And you're wrong. There's no way I have time to get the fish ready for transit. Besides. My store's a fortress."

He shifts his feet under the weight of Mama's arms, still flung across his shoulders. "I'd been open for business two months when Katrina and Wilma struck. And the place only suffered a bit of water damage. I made my final decision when I heard most of the staff at Hemingway House felt obligated to stay with their cats. I figured I'd do the same with my fish."

Fifty-five cats reside at The Hemingway House; the same family of cats that have occupied the museum since the great writer lived there.

"No, DJ. You've got to leave. You're taking an unnecessary risk."

Mama pushes away from him, sniffing, swiping her forefinger beneath her nostrils. Through glistening, make-up-smudged eyes, she looks at him with respect.

"I think it's admirable. I've been concerned about the gypsies myself. One kind-hearted resident is wrapping the chickens up in newspaper, securing them with tape, and driving 'em to safety as we speak."

My head jolts back regarding her askance. "They're wrapping up live chickens as if they are burritos?"

"Yes, honey. It will keep them from panicking while they travel. I've got paper and tape in the car. If I see any on the way out, I'll capture the birds and do the same."

My mouth drops open, and I shake my head. Sharing the back seat with Ivy, Liberace and a bunch of chickens? This will be one hell of a drive. Whatever expression I'm wearing causes DJ to chuckle. Seeing the humor in the situation, I smile back and take his hand with a squeeze. Our past issues pale in comparison to whatever lies ahead.

"Let Cassie and Stanson take care of the aquarium. Why don't you come along with us?"

Mama nods, taking his other hand. "What a wonderful idea. Please consider our offer. It will be tight, but we'll make space in the van. They've got a lovely home with plenty of room in Birmingham. Delphina and her family have booked accommodations elsewhere."

She sniffs, another line creasing her forehead. She doesn't have to say it aloud, but I know she was hurt Delphina refused her cousin's generous offer.

"That's so kind of you, Poppy. And maybe I would have considered the option yesterday," he says, releasing my hand to brush his too-long mop of bangs out of his eyes. "But last night my mom called. She's too broke to evacuate, and all freaked out. So, she's joining our little camp at the aquarium."

A flock of seagulls squawking manically fly above our heads. Even the birds have sense enough to leave. Wide-eyed, I stare at DJ.

"The last report said winds might bring a monstrous sea surge flooding the town with seawater. The National Weather Center tweeted THIS IS AS REAL AS IT GETS. It was all-caps, DJ. All caps. All of you still have time to leave."

His eyes cloud over, and he bites his bottom lip, shaking his head. My eyes burn. He's a fool, but a loyal one.

"As long as you've service, would you text me? Especially after the storm. Please. I'll need..." I glance at Mama, "we'll both need to know you're OK."

Pressing his lips together, he nods. "If I can, I will. But don't worry. I'll be fine. I don't want to keep you any longer. I'm sure you've got a lot of work ahead." His eyes search mine and his words become husky. "I was worried about you. About your family. I wanted to see you and hear what your plans were."

"Right," I say, with a heavy sigh, a mix of pain, confusion and yearning welling inside my chest. I treated the man poorly, and here he is, at my doorstep, letting me know he still cares.

"You were kind to stop by." Avoiding his gaze, I grab his hand and squeeze it once more. "I'd better check on Ivy. Make sure she's moving forward."

I turn and open the door, while Mama continues to ramble on about Irma, posing hypotheticals all framed around *will she, won't she, will she, won't she.* Such a waste of words; nature will make the call.

Hustling through the lobby, I stop to gaze at the portrait of Rossalea. It's far too enormous for us to package ourselves and we don't have time to contract the job to someone else. Will this be the last time we meet? Her short life will forever remain an enigma. Secrets, lies, betrayals. Is there any truth to the legend?

Did the force of her passion really kill her in the end? Surely not. Those pages are missing from the Lightkeeper's journal. Nevertheless, it makes for a good story. Shaking my head, I climb the circular set of stairs, up to the tower.

Ivy's not at her easel, but this morning she was here. We boxed her current work in progress. I was mesmerized by her silent motions, her hair spinning about her face in a golden halo so that she seemed to be bathing in light. Her aura was in startling contrast to the piece we were packing; a dark jungly landscape, plastered with ugly globs of khaki and black, painful to gaze upon. At least now I know where it's coming from.

I walk about the studio. After we finished our task, Ivy told me she would be going to Conch House to assist with flooding precautions. She said she'd be back by 2:00. I check my phone: 3:20 PM, and there are no messages.

"Ivy," I shout. "Where are you?" My voice bounces off the walls. "Come out, come out, wherever you are."

I creep down the stairwell, into the service room, and my eyes light upon the bed where she sleeps. Atop the violet-dotted blanket, the coverlet she's used since childhood rests an envelope––*Linnea* penned across the paper in purple ink. This couldn't be good.

I rush to the note, my heart racing, and rip it open. Her feminine, slanted, Catholic-school cursive flows across the page.

Hey sis.

I know what you're thinking, so settle down. There's no cause for alarm. After seeing you this morning, I joined the exodus with one of my fellow misfits. Remember my mentioning Jonah to you? The guy who was crushing on me?

Well, I've decided to play nice. He's taking me to an artist's retreat outside of Louisville until the frenzy blows over. By the time you're reading this, we'll be halfway across the state. Forgive my deception, but I couldn't tell you. I knew you'd tell Mama and, as you're fully aware, she'd rope me up and tie me into the car. You'll hear from me soon. Be safe.

I love you. I love all of you.

Ivy

26. IVY

F riday, September 8

> Go up to the land flowing with milk and honey.
> But I will not go with you, because you are a
> stiff-necked people and I might destroy you
> on the way.
> *Exodus, 3: 8*

So, I told my sister a lie. I lied to them all. You see, they'd never understand. They'd never believe me if I told them I was saving their lives. They've pigeon-holed me as the petite, the withdrawn, all of my features turned inward. But that's a mirage.

Captured within the energy, the very nucleus of the looming storm, I've become enormous, like a giant balloon. Packed into the van like cattle, all it would take is a poke—one sharp elbow knocked between my ribs—for me to detonate, killing us all. And to pass up my first opportunity to reign over my landscape—not pestered by family, unfettered with pedestrian concerns?

Imagine this: Key West emptied of tourists. The idea of

leaving my kingdom is impossible to consider. I'm so elated, there's no room for sleep.

To say that it's a beautiful day in Old Town is selling it short. It's a giddy, neon-drenched artscape of a day, and belies the encroaching storm. Sharp, glittering sunshine penetrates a sky colored a deep shade of robin's egg blue. But silence is the true miracle; it's eerie, trippy, fantastic. The panic buying is over and —aside from a few scattered cars, and the occasional bicyclist —the city is deserted. Key West belongs to ME! And the remaining high-stepping chickens, of course. Now they can wander the streets without the fear of becoming roadkill. Head humming, I'm glorious, ecstatic, another billowy cloud hovering over the world.

Enjoying the sensation of my diaphanous dress whispering about my calves, I wander the city, incredulous at this blessing of solitude. At the corner of South Street and Whitehead, my sandal-clad feet find themselves planted at the base of the Southernmost Buoy. Painted with red, black and yellow stripes, the crest is decorated with the Conch Republic logo and is said to be one of the most popular tourist attractions in the country. Visitors stand in a line that stretches down the block for an opportunity to take selfies at this point only ninety miles shy of Cuba.

They say you can't get any further south in the continental United States than this, which is not the reality, but it's close enough. And it's not a buoy either, but a humongous gussied-up storm drain. Details, details. I run my palm over the cool concrete of the landmark, confident it would take more than a Cat 5 to dislodge the monument from its foundation.

Skipping behind the buoy, I climb up the seawall and balance on the top ledge, facing the infinite shades of the ocean's green. Shadows of clouds and patches of sunlight dance across the surface of this breathtaking living watercolor and a string of white gulls drag a line across the horizon. Lifting my face, the sun burns my cheeks as I spread my arms, waving them madly about my sides. I'm a bird about to take flight––a colorful, crazy Liberace––at last set free from the cage.

Knees buckling under the weight of absolute freedom, I stagger, almost losing my footing. Lowering my arms, I take deep breaths, steepling my fingers, trying to calm down.

I turn to face the street and hop down from my post. One report says the storm is headed for Miami, another for Key West. Plastic bags are on all of the gas pump handles, and every hospital is closed. All of the trappings of an artist have vacated my studio as well. I had to go along with the motions, evacuation protocol, so not to arouse suspicion. My canvases, my paints, most everything is gone.

All that's left to amuse are my iPhone, laptop and the sea glass Delphina gave me. Pulling it out of my pocket, I study the piece; its ruby-red color mirrors the gauze of my dress. It will be dazzling incorporated into a mosaic. I ground the rounded edge to a point and have been sanding it with a fine-grit sandpaper. Now it will fit into the triangular space reserved for its frosty sheen. The tip is almost as sharp as a blade.

Saturday, September 9

> And he said, "I am the God of your father, the
> God of Abraham, the God of Isaac, and the
> God of Jacob." And Moses hid his face, for he
> was afraid to look at God.
> *Exodus, 3: 6*

It's late afternoon, and I walk down the street passing empty parking lots baking in the sun. I'm wearing flip flops and the same dress, but today it hangs from my body––limp, bedraggled––begging to be discarded.

The clouds are strangely shaped; low, terrible and choked with brine. The humidity building, the air drips with moisture. With the edge of a handkerchief, I wipe the sweat away from the back of my neck, noting the lacy fabric now carries yellowish grime. I tilt my head and sniff the crease of my arm pit. It smells yeasty, slightly sweet. When was the last time I bathed? Was it yesterday—the day before? When was the last time I slept? Exhaustion and insomnia are co-conspirators in their merciless cruelty.

Darting my tongue over parched lips, I'm thirsty, and regret the water bottle I left on the kitchen counter. Moreover, I lament my lack of antipsychotics. In a feverish high, I rid myself of five, half-filled canisters last night.

I never responded to the phone calls from Mama, Linnea and Delphina. This morning, I quit responding to their texts. I'm tired of my fabricated lies describing the idyllic Kentucky artist's retreat that exists only in my head. Daddy hasn't tried contacting me. No surprise. But I keep checking my phone, hoping. A message would indicate that he, too, was concerned about my whereabouts. To him, I'm the weird one, the runt of the litter, the annoyance of discounted goods found damaged and unable to be returned. He's never loved me.

As for Jonah? My cover? After witnessing my train wreck at the lighthouse, he asked if I could help him understand my bipolar. There's nothing to understand, I replied. Just another flavor of crazy. It would be nonsensical to a rational mind, anyway. Like trying to explain the Holy Trinity is three persons in one God.

I told him to stay away. That it was for his own good. That I was unlovable and he'd soon be disgusted by my mess and my madness. More's the pity. Jonah's the only man I've ever dated not littering every conversation with sexual innuendo. He's an original, I'll give him that. I stub my toe against the curb and wince.

When I was away at art school, every time I said no to a man, he said yes. To them, sex was simply a difference of opinion. Before I knew better, I always relented and, with practice, learned I was good at passion. It even gave relief. Not the act itself. That wasn't the point. When disappearing into another body, I could shut down my brain. A couple of frightening experiences with men taught me casual encounters weren't worth the distraction.

I used to find solace in my faith, but of late, I've forgotten how to pray. What's the point if there's no one to listen? Do I believe in God? I want to. Desperately. My last confession was when I was thirteen, and began having impure thoughts about boys. I believed Jesus and the Virgin would save me. Back then, I was afraid of judgment from the Lord. Down the road, I was scared to be judged by men. Especially Daddy.

Water slaps against the remaining anchored boats, which clang against their moorings. Today, I find no comfort in the phenomenon of nature, either. The miracle of life requires death to maintain equilibrium, the yin and yang of population control. The weather producing our stunning sunsets and glittering stars also summons earthquakes, which suck us into an abyss, and wildfires that burn the flesh from our bones. The winds pick up further as I turn left into the marina and walk down the slippery docks. Nature conjures hurricanes that will level us in a snap. Why pretend to love a bully?

The wind shifts, carrying the anger of gulls in a feeding frenzy over the guts of a fish. I swipe a mist of sea spray away from my lips. The air, swollen with dank humidity, captures the stench of decaying sea life no amount of water could ever wash away. The threat of this storm, which has been taunting the town for over a week, is utterly exhausting. Whatever's your intention, Irma, get on with it.

I light my last joint, inhaling its vaporous nothingness. Keeling over in a spasm of coughs, an empty Budweiser can rolls towards me, tumbling down the wooden pallets like a soccer ball kicked towards a goal. Lifting my foot, I smash it down, over and over, leveling it into the docks.

Sweaty, my heart rattling and banging against my ribs, I wish I could weep, that my tears would come easy, but my eyes are dry. Why can't I, at the very least, cry? There is no release.

My faith, passion, family––all have abandoned me; even my mania, which would lift me out of this misery, has left. I feel vacated, as the eye of a hurricane might feel, slowly tunneling a path with all of that chaos circling about.

SUNDAY, **September 10**

> I have been a stranger in a strange land.
> *Exodus, 2: 22*

Squeezing my eyes shut, I shake my head furiously trying to vanquish these apparitions from my psyche. Bruised, frayed and tormented, I have never felt so close to my demons.

I untie the pages of manuscript, yellowed and speckled with age. The missing pages from the Lightkeeper's journal and the Maiden's diary are bound together by colorful ribbons. Rossalea used these satins to bind her inky black coif; they're painted in her portrait. Threads of hair from a woman so long ago dead, are tangled into the rich burgundies, verdigris and golds of the fraying silks.

I'd found the pages three years ago, up here in the Lantern Room after I'd claimed it as my studio. They, alongside a scope, were contained in a metal box under several loose floorboards. All of this time I've kept them a secret. Knowing of their existence would be quite the coup for my parents, confirming that the myth was, in fact, the reality. But in doing so I'd betray the Maiden; some secrets are best left buried.

Bringing the parchment to my face, I inhale her world, a musty fragrance with traces of vanilla and grass. She hid the pages knowing I'd find them when trying to push back terrors of my own. When reading her words——penned in a feverish, Victorian pitch——I usually feel calmed, comforted, knowing I'm not facing this maelstrom alone. But not tonight.

I rustle through the pages, finger out the bottom sheet and read, for the thousandth time, her note. What happened to her penmanship? Tonight the sentences are garbled together, difficult to read, swirling round and round on the page. I squint to make out the words. Her writing slants forward, hurried as if the words are anxious to escape the page.

An eye for an eye.
   Matthew 5:38-40

From the lantern room, I watched the mayhem. My confidence in God, heaven, in everything good is shattered. How could passion be so blind?

   All along, my father was right. I have disgraced him; let him down. Consumed with a powerful desolation and blinding heartache, there are no words to describe my affliction—a thundering chorus inside my head that refuses to quieten. Their refrain insists I make amends to the woman who my lover, like a beast, so viciously attacked.

   I will extinguish the lights. It is done.

Rossalea
   September 10, 1857

The last words she wrote, one-hundred and sixty years ago to the day.

I stare through the glass surrounding me in my studio. It's been raining nonstop for hours, and outside it's dark, menacing. Horizontal silvery ropes slash against the windows with no sign of retreat and palm fronds bend towards the ground. Trees and power lines are down and in the shrieking wind, the lighthouse trembles and moans.

Is this it, Rossalea? Is this your plan? What are you trying to tell me?

Her reply gravitates between rumbles, whistles and groans. The Lantern Room is a sweltering bubble of glass, a spaceship surrounded by hostile aliens, prying, slithery fingers trying to crawl their way in.

I pace the circumference. I need something to make the voices, now a roar, quieten. Rossalea moans, and then whispers, *Erase me. Let me go.* Terrified, I grab a box of matches and burn the pages of her diary and the Lightkeeper's journal, one by one. The satin singes at the ends, refusing to ignite.

Clutching the cylinder of empty meds, ants scuttle through my veins. Anguish, the color of a poisonous red tide, rolls and spews into the room. I drop the bottle, grasping my throat in a stranglehold and the dolphin pierces into the hollow of my neck. Wrapping my forefinger around the chain, I yank at the necklace, breaking its stronghold—exorcising all thoughts of family and any memory I hold dear. I fling it across the room.

A roar explodes, and then another, and the lighthouse sways. An enormous crash splits through the heavens and the lights in the room flicker, and then die. The Maiden Tower screams, wailing with tears. My meds, pot and art are gone. I stare at the mound of ashes and scorched ribbon. The Maiden is gone.

I stumble down the circle of stairs, into the service room. The laptop on my bedside table is the sole source of illumination. Glancing wildly about, I grab fistfuls of hair. Oh God. Mama's gone, too. I'm not worthy of her love. I need to end this before she hurts as bad as me. I scurry to the safety of my bed, to the plush warmth of my quilt. Trembling, I pull the covers up under my chin.

I reach for the piece of ruby sea glass that rests beside my computer, and with the point of it, tentatively press it into the blueish vein on the inside of my wrist: Rossalea's plan.

A searing pain causes me to gasp, and then a feeling of peace mixed into the agony washes over me, which amplifies as I press it deeper, sliding it vertically along the artery, gouging it into my flesh. Blood leaks and then squirts, smearing onto the base of my keyboard, but I feel no pain, only comfort, and the soothing warmth of blood trickling down my arm, staining my bedspread.

I have no concept of time and space, only a sense of floating amidst moonlit waves—kaleidoscopic, metallic—caressing my body. I knit my fingers together, crawl into a fetal position, and bow my head. *Now I lay me down to sleep, I pray the Lord my soul to keep.*

I am weeping, choking with sobs. As my tongue slides over my lips, my tears and sweat taste salty, like blood, like the ocean I carry inside of me. I close my eyes and drift.

Everything begins and ends in the sea, it is eternal, and the only thing big enough to contain the emotions overwhelming me. I listen to the water lap faintly, drowsily, through the universe. Through sleepy eyes, I search the shoreline for a beacon of light. And there it is, stretching far into the sea, beaming from the lighthouse, guiding me home.

27. LINNEA

Tuesday, September 12, 2017 "Linnea?"

My pulse races at the sound of his voice.

"Oh, DJ. Are you OK?"

"Totally fried. But hey, I'm hanging in there."

The lightness in his voice makes my jaws unclench, my shoulders relax.

"Your phone works. Is your power back on?"

"Not likely. Who knows when that will be. I've put my generator to good use."

I begin pacing the circumference around the kitchen island. Mama and Daddy are staring at me, their just-poured bowls of cereal and milk untouched, spoons dangling from their fingertips. Wide-eyed, they're desperate for news.

"How's your mom? Cassie? Stanson? What about your store? How are the fish? Is the lighthouse standing? Is there a town to come home to? We heard it was underwater. We've had the news on twenty-four/seven and..."

"Calm down, Linnea. No need to panic. We're safe. And I've checked out your place. At least the exterior. That big tree next to Winston Lane went down, but it landed in the street; not on top of the lighthouse. Took down a bunch of power lines. Your mom's garden is a disaster, but I'm pretty sure that's the worst of it. The inn, the Fog Horn House, and the Lightkeeper's Quarters are fine. Everything's solid. Consider yourselves blessed."

A wave of relief makes me dizzy, and I clutch the counter to keep from stumbling. Grinning broadly at my parents, I give them the thumbs up and announce, "Everything is fine."

Mama drops her spoon, which clangs noisily on the granite, and leans into my father. Gingerly, he places his spoon delicately beside the bowl and then drapes his arm around her sunken shoulder.

"Seems downed trees caused most of the major damage. You should see the house on William. The one once owned by the guy who wrote all of those children's books."

"You mean Shel Silverstein? Mama would read his stories to us when we were small. What happened?"

"That large ficus uprooted and crushed the place. Took a part of the sidewalk along with it."

Glancing at Mama, whose face is now burrowed into Daddy's chest, a tightness forms in the back of my throat. I recall evenings spent in the garden, Delphina and I curled up under her arms as she read us his stories. I can't remember our little sister being a part of those scenes. Where was Ivy?

"Stanson's boat took a serious beating," DJ continues, interrupting my thoughts. "He never got it out of the water. He's like that. Thinks his childhood was so bad, nothing else could touch it. Apparently, he's got a crappy insurance policy. It's fixable, but I'm sure it will cost him."

"Where will they stay?"

"For the time being, I told them they could sleep in the office. My condo suffered no blows, but I refuse to share my personal space with Cassie and Stanson."

"Stanson? I shudder at the thought. What about his hatchery—where he raises the fish?"

"He says all is well. Said his octopi were playing with their toys when he arrived."

"It's hard to imagine a guy like him caring so much about baby sea creatures."

"His talk's all bravado. Cassie does the nurturing."

Aunt Bet-Bet, Mama's first cousin on Grandmother Rose's side, walks into the kitchen carrying a laundry basket filled with dirty towels. I cup my hand over the phone.

"I'm talking to a friend who rode out the storm. None of our properties were damaged. I'll find out more and share details, but for now, lemme take the conversation outside."

As I head towards the entryway, Aunt Bet-Bet drops the basket and dashes to my mother, giving her a hug. Daddy, as usual, seems happy to hand off his excitable wife and stands, his expression unreadable. He stretches his arms to the ceiling.

Closing the door behind me, I sit on the top stairs of the front stoop and wave at the next-door neighbor brushing down a golden-doodle in her driveway. Then, I turn my attention to our conversation.

"You were a doll to check on things. You should have seen the expression on my mother's face when she heard the news. I wish we were speaking on FaceTime. I would have aimed my phone at her mouth—her smile split her face in half."

In truth, I wouldn't want him to see me now. I recall my reflection this morning while brushing my teeth. My hair is unwashed and lank, the violet half-moons beneath my eyes register a combination of exhaustion and worry.

"The inn was the first place I checked," he continues, "after Mama's home and my condo, of course. Right now, I'm walking the streets, surveying the damage."

His words sound breathless, hurried, mirroring the sound of my own. Anxious, I chew on a hangnail; I have so many questions.

"Have you passed by Delphina's place? She's sweating bullets in Nashville."

He delivers a sharp bark of a laugh. "Do you honestly think I'd go there? If something is amiss, if even a blade of grass is flattened, she will blame me before she'd blame the hurricane. Besides, I thought the two of you weren't speaking."

I never had a chance to tell him I met Delphina. In truth, my only plans were to disappear from the Key West landscape. Vamoose––down the runway, into the sky, headed back to Idaho.

"For the most part, we're good." I keep the tone of my voice light, casual, as I walk towards a flattened newspaper in the driveway. "We waded through our anger and patched things up before Irma hit."

"Whoa. What great news. How did that come about?"

I still haven't forgiven my sister's wrath when she learned about my relationship with DJ. How dare she? But yesterday's concerns pale against today's. Faced with the catastrophe wrought by Irma, my relationship issues and phobias seem embarrassingly banal.

I bend to grab the paper and stick it under my armpit. This week of hiatus, however, has made one thing clear: moving back to the tranquility of Idaho is a no-brainer. My departure will be delayed by Irma, of course. And I must ensure Nina's back on track. It's the least I can do. So why do I feel like I'm ripping out my heart?

I can let go of so much in this life—never seeing the parts of the world edging the sea, never finding the right man, never having a satisfying career––but it's so hard to let go of my family.

"Linnea? Are you still there?"

I was silent longer than I had intended, and he speaks with a waver in his voice, like he's concerned. Clearing my throat, I walk to the entryway and climb the stairs, placing the newspaper by the front door.

"Could we table Delphina discussions for now? Bottom line, what's the overall prognosis? Do we have a city to return to?"

"It was a hell of a storm for sure," he says quickly, obviously relieved to be off the subject of my sister. "Amazingly, I still had cell service and could track its approach. When it hit, the store was being buffeted in the gusts. It sounded like we were lying on a railroad track with a freight train barreling towards us. Freaked all of us out, even Stanson was shaking, white as a ghost. But fortunately, at least for us, Irma did her dirty work a bit north-east."

The usual jockeying cadence returned to his voice, he makes a long steady whistling sound. Is it because he's relieved to have survived the storm? Happy to hear my voice? I hop down the steps, two at a time. Best not overthinking anything these days.

Listening to DJ itemize the devastation wrought by this beast of a storm, I put my earbuds on and tuck the phone into my running bra. Grasping the railing leading up to the door, I alternate stretching my Achilles tendons. I could use a good run to clean out the cobwebs.

"The eye hit Cudjoe Key head-on," he continues. "Buddy of mine has a place there and rode it out. It tore a hole through his roof, but he claims he's lucky. Says most of the area looks like it's been hit by a nuclear bomb. Trailers ripped apart, houses flattened, boats strewn about like toys. I hear it's the same scenario at Big Pine. Maybe even worse."

I lean my forehead into the cool hardness of the wrought iron banister, my heart thudding, clutching the railing so tight my knuckles are white.

"Considering all that destruction, I feel guilty that I'm grateful we were spared. What about water damage?"

"Another reason for relief," he says. "The storm hit at low tide, so we missed the devastation of a major flood. My store, condo and Mama's house are dry. But I can't speak for every residence. Right now, I'm looking at shingles stripped from roofs, damage from trees, trashed yards, that sort of thing. Aside from a couple of bars, which wouldn't close for the second coming, Duvall's boarded up and shut down. The Southernmost Buoy took a hit. But it's fixable."

Clearing his throat, he speaks deeply, "And that's a summary of the news, three days after Hurricane Irma pummeled the Keys. Brought to you live from Key West, Florida, I'm DJ Wilson reporting for Action News."

I giggle at his silliness amid the wreckage surrounding him. It's one of the multitudes of reasons I loved our romance—brilliant while it lasted.

"You were right, after all, Mr. DJ Wilson." My heart twists, wishing more than anything that we'd met at another time, in another place. "We never should have left."

"No, Linnea. I was wrong," he says, his voice now sober. "With a storm like Irma, evacuation is always the right decision. Listening to it rage was the worst experience of my life. And now, with the power out, no water to shower and everything all hot and sticky, it's impossible to sleep."

The amusement in his voice now faded, his exhaustion is palpable. "Right now, I'm at the edge of town by the water. It smells like a decayed, overripe swamp. Debris is everywhere. If I'm overwhelmed by this mess, I can only imagine how the folks who lost their homes, boats—shit, everything—must feel."

As the reality of Irma's wake seeps into my subconscious, I'm at a loss for words.

"At least the mockingbirds are having fun," he says, after a pause. "Even the cormorants have joined in. They're making that grunting noise. Sounds like they're having an orgy. I'll aim my phone towards the sky, so you can hear them."

Straightening, standing statue-still, I wedge my buds firmly into the canals of my ears and focus on listening. It sounds like a riot of birds are conducting a playful, flirtatious serenade. Straining to hear, I can make out the cormorant's husky seal-like sounds.

I smile. "At least someone's having a party down there."

DJ begins to whistle and then makes chirping sounds in harmony with the other background critters.

"What species is that?" I ask, and then bend from the waist down, pressing my outstretched palms into the fresh-mowed lawn. He snickers as I roll up my spine, vertebrae by vertebrae.

"It was a fledgling hatched in the eye of the storm, the only place where it was calm enough to give birth." He snorts. "Sorry. Now I sound as whacked out as I feel. Operating on some crazy adrenaline high."

"You're entitled. I'm glad we left after all. At least we've got air-conditioning."

"And flushing toilets."

"Oh yeah. Yuck. I forgot about that one. Now I'm totally convinced."

"So how are y'all holding up in Alabama?"

"Ala-limbo? Given the circumstances, all's well, I suppose." I raise my right leg and swing it over the railing, stretching my torso over my thigh.

"But with reports filtering in about the devastation in the Caribbean, we've been worried sick. Liberace is feeding off of Mama's nerves. He's a mess. At first, his neurotic banter entertained my cousins, but now he won't shut up." Pressing my chest into my leg, I touch my nose to my knee, straighten, and then repeat the exercise on my left.

DJ chuckles, and I'm pleased I can distract him, at least for a few minutes. I saunter to the porch and resume my perch on the steps.

"He's a fish out of water, and we dare not let him out of his cage. Our cousins suggested we muzzle him. I'm sure they'll be thrilled when we leave. Every night I've volunteered my culinary services—they all seem happy about that—but the stress is wearing."

"Man. If I'd known you'd be cooking dinner every night I might have reconsidered your offer. Powdered milk and Cheerios are getting old. So, how's the rest of your family?"

He doesn't mention Delphina specifically, but I know to whom he's referring.

"Delphina and Sonny are fine, thank God. Living the high life in Tennessee. The baby and Sonny's mom, of course, are also with them. Delphina's uptight about how much the evacuation is costing. But she puts it in perspective."

"Yep. Perspective. Seems like everyone I've spoken to sticks that word in conversation."

"I suppose it's a catch-all to remind us we should be grateful. Even in the most heinous of situations, if we can imagine a scenario even worse than the one we're experiencing, perspective can provide comfort. Even if only for a moment."

I look down the street, at the sprawling, lush lawns, the slate-roofed Tudors with their recent cosmetic updates. I'm in an easy place to philosophize. Do the people who lost everything speak of perspective?

"How about that crazy sister of yours?" he says, a smile in his voice. "Tell her Conch House appears to be in good shape."

Sighing, I pause a moment, not appreciating the adjective he used to describe her. My sister has a complex disease. But I'm not opening that can of worms.

"No one's heard from Ivy since Friday."

"Didn't she leave with y'all?"

"It was the plan, but she pulled a fast one. Took off with some guy to an artist's retreat in Kentucky. She knew Mama'd never allow it, so she snuck off on her own. She was texting us regularly at first, but now everything goes to voice mail. Mama must have called her a hundred thousand times. She's worried sick."

"Tell her not to worry. I'll bet she forgot her charger."

As long as she didn't forget her meds, I think, not voicing the words out loud. DJ never learned the truth about Ivy.

"Most Florida residents are scattered like confetti across the States, anyway," I say, trying to sound unconcerned, trying to assure myself, as well, that Ivy is fine. "We'll all glue together soon enough."

"Like her big sister, she's a beautiful, talented artist—an original. But between you and me," he says, lowering his voice in a conspiratorial tone, "your baking is my preferred means of expression." My face grows hot at his compliment. It's hard to get a read on this man. Idaho will bring clarity.

He clears his throat. "Ivy's way too stylin' to be holed up in that tower under your mother's thumb. You know, if she's not serious about the dude she's with, I'm friends with this guy—an artsy type. I'll bet they'd hit it off."

Ivy? Stylin'? I would never use that word to describe her. Perhaps if I only knew her by her paintings. Have I ever really known her?

"We'll see, DJ. Maybe later. When the dust settles."

I sigh. Another secret to add to the list: covering up the truth about Ivy. She should have come with us to Alabama. At least Mama could monitor her meds.

I squeeze my thighs together, sit on my hands, and roll my head from side to side. The pillow they gave me is rock-hard, and my neck muscles are killing me.

He makes a drawn-out yawning sound.

"You're wiped out," I say. "Why don't you get some rest."

"I wish I could. But I've volunteered my services to help clean up streets, so they're navigable."

"Do you have any idea of when we can return? I'm sure Mama's packing our bags as we speak. Today's Tuesday. We could be back by Thursday night. With traffic stalls, Friday at the latest."

"That's not a good plan. There's a tent in the middle of Mile Marker 74 with a sign insisting everyone turn around. I seriously doubt they'll be allowing residents in on Thursday. Even Friday. Hotels are glutted, so you might end up having to sleep in your car. You should wait a few days before heading down."

"Are you kidding me? The Maiden Tower is being held hostage? My parent's livelihood, everything valuable to us, is in our home."

"Linnea. Your family is safe. Your family is your home." His words are a direct punch in my gut. I'm glad he can't see the expression on my face, the tears burning my eyes.

"It's critical emergency crews and the National Guard be able to do their job," he continues. "Power, utilities and sewage must be fixed without a stampede of returning residents. I'll let you know as soon as I hear something. They say they'll know on Friday."

"You're right. We'll stay up here for now. It's just that we're stir-crazy and anxious. Hey. Would you mind checking out the lighthouse? The inside, I mean. And only if you've time. It's not a big deal, but I wanted to put my mind at ease. I have this strange premonition that something happened to Rossalea."

"Who?"

"Not a real person. Well, she once was a real person. It's that humongous portrait of the tower's namesake in the front entry. I'm worried it was damaged in the storm."

"Oh. I remember now. No worries. Sure. How do I get in?"

"There's a spare key implanted in the bottom of a plastic

rock. It's off to the left of the front porch. It looks fake, so you can't miss it."

"I checked out the entire circumference of the exterior and would be surprised if there's any damage inside. But I'll give the inn a walkthrough. I'll ring you up on Friday. By then, I'll know when you can return."

"I'm sure you've bigger fish to fry. If you're too busy, forget it."

"I'll make time. And hey, Linnea," he says, his voice seeming to caress my name. "It's wonderful talking to you."

I stare at the empty street, transfixed by the nothingness before me, wondering if he can hear the hammering in my chest.

"And don't worry," he continues. "We're Conchs. Resilience is our middle name. Everything will be fine."

After our goodbyes, I slide my phone into my back pocket, feeling both relief and desolation.

28. DELPHINA

Saturday, **September 16** "I haven't heard from DJ. I'm still worried about The Maiden Tower."

I press the cell into my ear, eager for the latest news from Linnea. She speaks quickly, her voice breathless.

"If anything happened, water damage would be the likely culprit," she adds.

We share updates as each of our families make the two-day trek, returning to Key West. The National Guard has spent the past week clearing wreckage insuring main arteries are navigable. All forty-two of the bridges on the Overseas Highway are now safe to drive. One of Sonny's marina pals who rode out Irma, said residents of the Lower Keys were allowed to return to their homes on Sunday.

Sonny's friend walked through our house and, aside from fallen limb debris, all is well. Thankfully, The Coral Princess also steered clear of Irma's wrath. I called Linnea yesterday, and our families wasted no time packing bags.

"He said he'd call yesterday," my sister continues, "but I'm sure he's crazy busy." I can tell by her breezy tone that she's trying to be flip, to keep any doubts she may be feeling about DJ out of her voice, anchored at bay.

Of course he didn't call, I think to myself, listening to Linnea while staring out the window. I can't believe she told him where my parents hide the key. By now, I wouldn't be surprised if he's sold Grandmother Rose's sterling tea-service. Linnea said she broke up with him, so I'm surprised they're talking. Even though I told her I'd forgiven him, I still think he's a creep. But I'll keep my opinion to myself.

Billboard after billboard advertising Wendy's, Burger King and McDonald's zip by in a blur.

"Delphina," she says. "You're awfully quiet. I know what you're thinking, and it's simply not true."

"I didn't say a word."

"But you thought it. I heard you think it through the phone. He's insanely busy. Can you even imagine the clean up involved? He already took the trouble to check out the exterior, so we could put our minds at ease."

Her voice sounds like Sister Lynne, our Sacred Scriptures teacher, who whined instead of lectured. I hold the cell away from my ear.

"I asked him to check the rooms, but only if he had a minute," she continues. "I didn't make it a big deal. If I had, I'm sure DJ would have called by now."

Sick of hearing the man's name, I change the subject. "So, what time do you think you'll get to the Snow Goose?"

The Snow Goose Inn is the only hotel in the area that will accommodate Liberace; a bird the size of a bulldog. Typically roadside motels are half-vacant at this time of the year, but with the return of the natives, we were lucky to snag two of the last remaining rooms.

"Our navigator says we'll arrive around four."

"Perfect. Ours says we'll be there at five-thirty."

Passing a WELCOME TO FLORIDA/ THE SUNSHINE STATE sign, Sonny is pulling into a rest stop. Ella needs changing and Lita's craving a Nutty Buddy.

"We're traveling at a snail's pace," I continue. "We seem to be hitting every rest stop. In fact, we're at one now."

"No worries, I'll let you go. Drive safely. We'll pick up some wine to enjoy later by the pool."

"Make it two bottles, please." I tuck my phone in between my neck and shoulder and wiggle Ella out of her car seat. "Mama's thirsty. Let's drink until we drop. And make sure they're screw tops, so we don't have to hunt down a corkscrew. After dinner, Sonny and Lita can put down the baby, and then we can chill. Where shall we eat?"

"I found a cheap Mexican restaurant on Yelp that's close to the hotel."

"Sounds like a plan. I'll text you when we arrive."

⁓

"I DON'T CARE if it is gas station wine." I hold a plastic cup filled with watery amber to the early evening sky. "After last week, it tastes like the nectar of the Gods."

A couple of families were leaving as we arrived, towels wrapped around their damp torsos, and now Linnea, Mama and I have the pool to ourselves. A cleaning trolley is next to the entry of the patio, a vacuum props the gate open. The three of us—sprawled in lounging chairs, bellies stuffed with sizzling fajitas—must look like we're melting into the cushions. We'll probably have another hour or so of this apricot-tinted bliss before darkness descends. After last week, this break seems decadent.

"I've aged a hundred years," Linnea says, her eyes lit, well into her second glass. She reaches across the patio table to refill my cup. "So, how was Nashville? Did y'all ever leave your rental?"

I think of the piles of laundry. How Sonny had to repair the washing machine before it would work. I recall the air-conditioning unit, so filled with cottonwood fluff, we had to clean it before it came to life. And don't get me started on the refrigerator. I had to bundle Ella's formula on ice to keep it cold. But in light of what others had to deal with? I decide not to bitch.

"Lita watched Ella one night so Sonny and I could cruise honky-tonks. The music was great."

Mama turns her head lazily to me, swatting a mosquito on her leg. "Your father and I went to Nashville before we bought the lighthouse. That was back in the early eighties, right before I was pregnant with you two. Oh, memories. That week was such fun."

Her voice has a dreamy quality to it, the light silvery notes sounding as if she's no more than sixteen. She bites her lower lip, gazing into the still waters of the pool.

It's difficult imagining the people your parents were before they were parents. In a flash, I understand their attraction to one another. Mama—nutty, warm, whimsical and emotional—is nothing like my father. Perhaps, one of the reasons why he loves her. Mama loves my father, in part, because his steady, dependable nature balances her eccentricities. Yin-yang-whatever, it seems to work. At least well enough.

"We haven't gotten away since then," she continues. "I mean, just the two of us."

My jaw drops. "That's been over thirty-five years, Mama. It's criminal. How do you keep your relationship alive?"

Taking another sip of wine, my eyes slide up Mama's lean, toned body. She's forgone her usual floral sheaf for a T-shirt and jeans. Oversized shades cover half her face. With those glasses, she could pass for my age. Or, at least, a woman in her forties.

I wonder why I never paid more attention to my parent's life as a couple. Do children ever? I suppose they do if their parents are always at each other's throats. My sisters and I are lucky to have been raised in an environment filled with laughter, not rage.

"If you allowed kids at the B&B—even if just to visit—I'd come over with Ella." My voice is soft, reflecting on how lucky I am that she's my mother, for a change. "We could give the two of you a break, so y'all could have some date nights. They show great films at the Tropic Cinema."

A smile plays about her mouth. "Hell. That train left the station light years ago. I want more date nights with my grand-daughter." She shifts to face me, removing her glasses. "You know, I've been thinking. That no-kids rule is ridiculous. It's certain adults who should be banned from the inn."

She snaps her fingers. "As of now, right this minute, I'm abolishing that silly regulation." She looks at me, tenderness softening her features. "I'll change the language on the web site to say the inn is family-friendly. You and Ella can come and go every minute of every day, as far as I'm concerned."

Pleasure swells through me, and I decide to test my luck. I lean into her, not letting my eyes waver from her face.

"Mama. Something has been bothering me. Maybe it's the wine talking, but what's going on between you and Lita? I know she can be overbearing—it's who she is—but is there some-thing else upsetting you?"

Linnea straightens, all ears at this intimate turn of conversa-tion. Turning away from my gaze, Mama finishes her wine in a gulp and then directs her words to the bottom of the cup.

"I'm embarrassed to talk about it. Makes me seem shallow."

I press on, my head inches from her face. "What is it, Mama. Please. Tell me."

She levels me with her eyes, and I can see the ache in her gaze. "The truth is, was…I don't know…I guess it still is…"

"What still is?"

"I'm just…" her voice wavers, "I suppose I'm jealous of her."

I laugh, incredulous. "You? Jealous of Lita? Heck. You run circles around the woman."

Mama leans into me, speaking rapidly. "She lives under the same roof with your family. You even gave the child her name —Mariela."

Bingo. I knew that was the reason, I just knew it. Mama flushes, shaking her head. "Oh, my goodness. I absolutely loathe how I sound right now—so hideously petty. You know, I've been doing my best to get over it."

I remove the empty cup from her hand and refill her glass. "We should have had this talk months ago. All Lita has in this entire world are me, the baby and Sonny. Your life is so rich. So full. I didn't think you'd mind."

Mama's face twitches, and her eyes become watery. She swipes her forefinger under her nose.

"I know, I keep telling that to myself." She looks at me, unblinking. "I've been trying my hardest to get over this doggone ego of mine. Bottom line is I need to see my grand-child more often. But it's so hard escaping the demands of the inn. Your father and I, or at least one of us, needs to be there all the time."

"Have you and Daddy considered selling it?" Linnea asks, leaning into her legs, so she can see past me to Mama. "That property is a gold mine. Y'all could invest the proceeds and buy a condo. Something manageable."

"Ha. Me without a garden? Heaven forbid." She takes a sip of wine, and is quiet a moment seeming to contemplate our words.

"But you're right. As much as I love The Maiden Tower, the house and business exhaust me. I'd consider selling in a year or two." Clasping her hands together, her eyes dance. "I fantasize about living in one of those cute little Bahamian clapboards right outside of town."

She leans into the table, grabs the wine and tops off her

glass, finishing the bottle. I glance at the other, chilling in a bucket of ice. A good thing we bought two.

"But it's hopeless trying to convince your father," she continues. "His plan is to die there with a hammer in his hand. He told me as much. The lighthouse is his life." She lowers her voice to a breathy whisper. "His other woman." She giggles to herself.

"But don't you girls worry about us," she continues after a pause, her voice rising along with her glass to make a toast. "We consider ourselves fortunate. We live every single day in one of the premier vacation spots in the world, an area where folks come to retire. If I had to choose one place on this planet to live, knowing I could never leave, it would be Key West. Hurricanes be damned. Here's to our fair city."

I touch my cup to Mama's, and then Delphina follows suit. After taking a sip, she shifts the lever on the lounge chair upward, straightens and then pulls her legs into her midriff.

"I can't wait to get home, although I'm sure we'll have a mess on our hands. But if we had to spend one more day in Alabama, I'd go running for the hills. Not that I didn't appreciate your cousin's generosity. They did backflips, making sure we were comfortable."

"So how are the kinfolk?" I ask, shifting onto my side and sinking my elbow into the cushion's scratchy fibers to face them. "I can't remember the last time I saw them."

"You'll see 'em soon enough," Mama replies. "I invited them to stay at the lighthouse this winter. It's the least we can do. We tried to make the best of things catchin' up and all."

She smiles at Linnea. "And your sister made some marvelous meals. If it had been a normal visit, I'm sure we would have had a grand time."

"We were so uptight about the storm, it was hard to relax," Linnea adds. "But dinner table conversations were interesting. I learned some new tidbits about Grandmother Rose that blew everything else out of the water."

Linnea cocks an eyebrow at Mama. "How come you never told us the extent of her craziness?"

She shakes her head, a smirk playing about her peach-tinted lips as if our grandmother's lunacy was no big deal.

"Why bother? Whatever deranged beast possessed her finally took his leave after I left for college. Except for an episode once in a blue moon, she wasn't so bad by the time you two came along. So, why rehash the drama? It'd be like beating a dead mule. Everyone knows it's best to let sleeping dogs lie."

This verbal tack allows platitudes and Southernisms to explain away her most nonsensical reasoning. Mama's such a crafty little strategist, she should have been a politician's spokesperson.

"Anyway," she continues, "y'all already knew Grandmother Rose was peculiar."

"Peculiar? That's putting it mildly. Aunt Bet-Bet made it sound like she was as crazy as a Betsy bug."

"It was a bit chaotic living under her roof, especially after Daddy left."

Linnea leans forward, clasping her hands, widening her eyes at me. "Aunt Bet-Bet said when she was ten years old, she was sleeping over and remembers Grandmother Rose barreling into their room in the middle of the night. Like a madwoman, she was screaming the Yankees had freed the slaves and set fire to their home. Made the girls run out of the house in skimpy nightgowns during the dead of winter."

I cup my hand over my mouth, trying to suppress a giggle. "Seriously?"

"I was used to her behavior. In her mind, the South won the war. It embarrassed me more than anything." Mama shakes her head while examining her toes, the polish on her nails chipped.

"But the experience scared my cousin witless. That was the last time your Aunt Bet-Bet was allowed to visit."

She looks up, eyeing me through her lashes. "You know in Alabama we're proud of our crazy relatives." Wiggling her toes, her eyes begin to glow as a smile plays about her lips. It's as if she's stumbled upon a pleasing notion.

"At first we try to hide them. But when the storm passes, and their cockeyed look begins to fade, we invite them to parties. They can be so entertaining."

Linnea and I trade glances, wondering how she could be glib about mental illness, especially since it has wreaked such chaos in her life. All of our lives.

She sighs. "Like a fine wine, my mother mellowed out with age. Your Grandmother Rose was eccentric. That's the word. Eccentric."

Again, she looks down at her feet. "I could really use a pedicure."

Our mother could well be described as eccentric. But our grandmother? Nevertheless, we understand that she's reassuring herself. Mama said that age settled down our grandmother. If Ivy has Grandmother Rose's genetic issues, maybe our little sister will also level out with time.

Linnea stands, iPhone in hand, and walks to the pool, a teeter to her step. Sitting on the navy-tiled edge, she drops her feet, splashing her toes into the water. She's been pounding the wine even harder than me, upset, I'm sure, DJ never called. I wonder what's up with those two? But if they reconcile, and he can keep her down in Key West, Danny Jack Wilson will be my new best friend.

I watch my mother rise, amble to the pool, and sit next to Linnea. She places her arm, bedecked with copper bangles, around my sister's shoulders. Linnea pushes Mama's fiery mane away from her forearm and leans her head into the crook of her neck. In the purplish cast of twilight, I will see this moment stamped forever in my brain—one of life's gallery of portraits. All of my worries evaporate, and I'm consumed with a breathless mix of gratitude. Everything would be complete if Ivy were with us now.

I place my wine on the table, walk towards them, and sit on the other side of Mama. She puts her cup on the lip of the pool and drapes her other arm over my shoulder. For a minute we're quiet, at peace, listening to the music of the crickets and katydids.

"This evening is a miracle," I comment, content for the first time in recent memory. "Except for Ivy, every member of our family will be snuggled safe and sound under the roof of the Snow Goose Inn. I guess it will take more than a Cat 5 to wash us away."

"If only I weren't so worried about Our Girl," Mama says, her voice breaking, cracking on each word.

"You know Ivy." I untangle a hoop earring that is caught in one of her curls. "The little brat stinks at communication."

Mama looks at me, shaking her head, a vertical line cutting a groove between her eyebrows. "The least she could do is let me know she's OK. Don't you think she'd be curious to know if The Maiden Tower is still standing? It's been a week since her last text. An entire week."

"And in that week a hurricane touched down, laying waste to everything in its path. The entire state of Florida is helter-skelter, and communication channels have been thrown for a loop."

"But only in Florida," she says, a whimper hovering about her words. "She was well aware we were leaving the state. She could have called one of us."

"Mama," Linnea says, stroking her hand, also trying to calm her. "You and I have gone for weeks at a time without talking. Not even a text. Did you freak out about me?"

"No. But a hurricane just ripped through the Keys. And you and Delphina are different than Our Girl."

I pause, glancing at my sister. "Since we were kids, Linnea and I wondered why you and Daddy started calling Ivy––*Our Girl.*" There's a hitch in my voice when I say the words.

Mama's eyes mist. She gazes at the pool as if needing a minute to consider the question and then shakes herself out of her reverie.

"Your daddy started calling her that. From the moment she took her first step, we knew she was different than the two of you. So delicate, insecure. We felt she was far too sensitive for such a relentlessly hard world. We needed to protect her fragility, have our love bolster her, make sure she knew that–– no matter what hurdle life shoved in her path––she would always be Our Girl."

Lowering her head, she winces, obviously distraught. "Ivy is broken. She can't be away from her doctor, and it's critical she takes her meds." Pain cuts through her face and her fingers dig into my shoulder.

Dropping her arms, she puts her face into her hands, which muffles her words. "The drugs stabilize her. At least when she takes them. What if she's run out of pills? I don't know what to think."

Recalling the expression on Ivy's face after Evening Hour, a sense of dread overwhelms me. How would she cope amongst strangers in one of those states? I dare not voice my concerns, adding kindling to the flame.

I take a deep breath, forcing a lightness into my words. "I'm sure she has them. And if she runs out, there are drug stores in Kentucky. She's more than an illness, Mama. You told me that yourself. She's a grown woman."

I roll my ankles in the water, relaxing my feet, and feel a pang of sadness for Mama. Who listens to her, nurturing her when life overwhelms? My father is incapable. Certainly not

Ivy, and Linnea and I've never thought about it. Having been raised by Grandmother Rose, was she even nurtured as a child?

Turning, I hug her with every ounce of strength I can muster. "I love you, Mama. And right now, you have other things to worry about. You've got a bed & breakfast to run when you return."

She sniffs into my shoulder and then presses her palms into me, pushing away so she can meet my eyes. "Ha. Every reservation we have through October was canceled last week. Maybe your father will be forced into retirement, whether he likes it or not."

Linnea's phone rings. As she grabs it, I glance DJ's name on the screen.

"I'm so glad you called. We're holed up in Gainesville for the evening. Even Delphina's family's here. We'll leave at the crack of dawn tomorrow and should be home by dusk." Her words rushed, she speaks rapidly without a pause. "Is everything OK? Did you have a minute to check inside the lighthouse?"

She presses the phone into her ear and, forefinger raised like a sentry to her mouth, motions us to silence. Tipping her head to the side, her eyebrows knit together hanging on to his every word. Her smile fades, and worry lines fret across her forehead. After a minute, she speaks.

"I don't understand. It doesn't make sense. You'll meet us at The Maiden Tower?"

As she listens to whatever it is he's saying, the slits in her eyes register concern.

"What's up, DJ? What's wrong?"

The evening air grows cool, the insect serenade turning sinister.

"OK. Whatever. But you've upset me now." She pauses, listening, her forefinger tapping the phone.

"Oh well. All right then. I'll try not to worry. Bye, now."

She slides her phone into her running bra and, grasping her hand on the edge of the pool to support herself, ambles clumsily to her feet. She looks down at us and presses her lips together before she speaks.

"That was odd."

"What did he say? Are the roads still blocked?"

"No. He said we won't have problems getting home. The barrier's removed. But other than that, he was vague. Right after the hurricane, he sounded tired but fine. He even amused me. Now he sounds awful––like he hasn't slept in weeks. He certainly wasn't up for small talk."

She bites the side of her mouth. "But he did ask, practically insisted, that we all show up at the lighthouse at the same time. You, too, Delphina. All of us. Tomorrow evening. The minute we get to Key West." She rubs her left eye, now twitching madly. "He wants me to call him when we're an hour away."

So now we're following DJ's directives. My family must prolong an excruciating trip with an irritable baby when we're all so anxious to see our own home. Whatever for? My sister makes questionable allies. We've been watching the news twenty-four-seven and know pretty damn well what to expect.

Mama wrings her hands, sighing quietly. "I knew it was too good to be true. I'll bet something smashed into the house, and it's flooded." Her head jerks up towards Linnea. "He had to say more to you than that, didn't he?"

"Yeah. He tried to calm my worries. Said we needed to be briefed about the hurricane aftermath as a group. I've been concerned about the portrait of the Maiden, myself. The top of the frame is directly beneath a seam in the crown molding, right below that warped section of roof. But he would have told me about that. Like I said, he was vague."

Circling a group of patio chairs, Linnea begins to pace, her hands opening and closing, grasping at straws. Then, she stops, staring at us, a question in her eyes. "Maybe something happened to Bill."

Mama's eyes widen, stunned alarm registering across her face, and she lifts her arms up towards my sister. Linnea pulls her onto her feet.

"I'll bet that's it," she says. "Bill. The ole' coot refused to leave his home. And his walls are so rickety."

I stand, joining them, gazing at Linnea, incredulous I have to be a part of whatever it is this Danny Jack Wilson has to tell us.

"But if something bad happened to Bill," I say, my voice blooming with irritation, "why would I have to be there? None of this makes sense. Why would he want me, and my family involved in whatever it is he has to say?"

Mama touches my forearm, a slight tremble in her fingers. Red veins begin tracking across the whites of her eye.

"Delphina. Listen to Linnea. For some reason, the man wants to brief us." Her words are hoarse, emerging from her mouth in a stutter. "Nothing about the past couple of weeks has made one iota of sense. All that matters is we're safe and sound. We'll hear from Our Girl," she continues. "Soon." She tacks on the word quickly.

Goosebumps prickle the back of my neck. When she said soon, it felt like forever.

We form a huddle and embrace, our arms wrapped around each other's shoulders. Then, we touch our foreheads together, trying to quieten a new worry—itching, festering and unspoken—between us.

A young man in a pale green uniform breaks our silence as he rolls the cleaning trolley towards the pool. We disband and grab the empty bottles and glasses. Bobbing our heads in his direction, we scuttle back to the sanctity of our four wall enclosures.

29. LINNEA

Sunday, Sept. 17 Daddy pulls into the driveway of The Maiden Tower and parks in the empty lot usually reserved for our guests. We sit in the van, silent, as Sonny maneuvers his truck into the space on our right. Liberace, recognizing he's returned to his element, turns his head from side to side, squawking in riotous glee. In the confines of his cage, he tries flapping his wings, but he's the only one happy to be home.

Through the car windows, it's impossible to ignore the wreckage of the garden. Mama's face is white and expressionless, and she sits as straight as a statue cast in marble. After undoing my seatbelt, I place my hands beneath my thighs to wipe away their sweat and silence their shake. Daddy, as usual, is difficult to read, but the flicker in his eye is the same as mine. It's not the devastation of the garden, however, which has us so agitated. It's wondering what awaits us, and why we must be briefed. Last night, none of us got much sleep.

The trip from Gainesville to Key West, which generally takes eight and one-half hours to drive, took almost thirteen in the congested snake of returning residents. After exiting the mainland, traffic especially crawled. We spoke little on the drive, a mixture of fear, nervousness and uncertainty permeating our vehicle like a poisonous cloud.

Crossing the bridges, I wore a sleeping mask so I wouldn't have to look at the water fanning out beneath both sides of the thoroughfare. Truth told, I wore it most of the trip down. Phobia aside, the shield also prevented me from having to bear witness to the stark reality of the devastation wrought by Irma. Pictures in the media are easier to digest.

I've been googling site after site, poring over photographs, reading story after story. Islands in the Caribbean and a bulk of the Keys were devastated. Houses were pancaked, businesses flattened, and walls, windows and doors were blown away—one-hundred and twenty-nine people died in this storm. How is it that Key West, for the most part, was spared?

I called DJ after we passed Big Pine. His words were softly spoken, kind and reassuring but shrouded in mystery. Something is wrong, big-time wrong. We're home now and will find out soon enough. Mama turns towards the back seat and catches my eye. I nod. With a heavy sigh, I open the car door. She and Daddy open their doors as well.

Standing by the side of the car, my stomach coiled into a knot, we wait for Delphina's family. Placing her into Delphina's front pack, the sleeping baby nestles into her like a baby kangaroo. Mama carries Liberace's cage and Daddy holds her other hand. We walk towards the front porch, Sonny and Lita trudging silently behind.

The windows of the lighthouse, bare of curtains, seem like dim and distant eyes, daring us to enter. DJ and some guy I vaguely remember are standing on the front porch, alongside another woman I don't recognize. They walk down the stairs when they see our wary little group approach.

Three people? No, no, no, no, no. Something horrible has happened. I pinch my cheeks so hard they're sure to bruise. Mama and I exchange glances, dread in our eyes, not wanting to take another step, not wanting an answer to the question we haven't dared voice: Is this about Ivy? I avert my eyes from hers. Yes. It has to be.

"Andy?" Delphina asks, breaking the silence, the first to approach the steps. "I haven't seen you since I was almost trampled in that mob."

I gaze at the man feeling drugged. Andy Nevins. I didn't recognize him without his uniform. He went to school with us and carried Delphina to Sonny after her incident at the parade.

He takes her hand. "Delphina. Let's get your family into the house."

In an instant, she jerks her hand away from his, as if it were ablaze. "What's wrong? Why are you here?" She points at the woman who wears khaki pants and a navy blazer, even in this heat. "And who are you?"

Feeling faint, I stumble. DJ looks at me, his face ashen, and takes my arm. The woman introduces herself.

"I'm Renée Hollister. Officer Nevins asked that I be here." She has a gentle countenance and looks to be around Mama's age. Soft, steel gray curls are pulled away from her face with a white headband, and she gestures to the front door. "Please. Let's go inside so we can find a place to sit. I'm a social worker with the city."

A social worker? Oh, God. The truth seeps in. Ivy never left. She stayed, and something terrible happened to her in the storm. Trudging up the stairs, I feel like I might get sick. Right now. I might vomit all over the front porch. Hunched forward at the door well, choking back bile, I glance at my parents. They stand motionless yet clutch each other's hands so tightly their knuckles are a mottled white mass of bones. DJ hands the key to Andy, who fumbles with the lock.

"Here," DJ says, moving to Andy's side and taking the key. "Allow me. I had a hard time with this door myself." Opening the door, he glances at me over his shoulder as if apologizing.

We walk through the entry. When we left, storm shutters boarded every window. Now, light streams through our home, lending a sense of normalcy, a sense that everything has remained the way we left it. I glance around the lobby and parlor. But there's nothing normal about this scenario.

"Andy and I took the liberty of taking the shutters down," DJ says, gesturing towards the windows. He appears miserable, a shadow of the boyish man I'd once found so adorable. The aftermath of a hurricane and God only knows what else—the truth, I suppose—rests on his shoulders.

I nod at him, and then my eyes dart to the portrait of Rossalea. There's something new, something I've never noticed before, some wretched haze around the darkness in her eyes. She's trying to tell me something. Is there an epilogue to her story? Is this the *unfinished business* of which DJ was referring? I wrap my arms around my gut as bile washes up my throat.

Mama and Daddy sit on the ottoman, Liberace in his cage at their side. The others drag chairs towards them, while I pull out the piano bench and sit, quivering, away from the group.

Ms. Hollister walks to my parents and then kneels on the floor in front of them. Taking their limp hands in hers, she looks directly into their eyes and proceeds to confirm the worst possible thing.

"I am so sorry, Mr. and Mrs. Chandler. Your daughter Ivy has died."

Mama jumps to her feet. "It's impossible. She can't be dead. She wasn't here. She left. We have a letter she wrote to us from Kentucky."

"Oh Mama," I cry out, shaking my head, disbelieving the unfolding nightmare. "Your thoughts are scrambled. I never told you she mailed that note from Kentucky. Ivy wrote the letter when she was in the tower. I showed it to you before we evacuated. She must have faked her departure."

Daddy slumps forward, putting his face into his hands as

my heart shatters into bits. Mama makes a high-pitched keening sound; a noise I've never heard and not entirely human. Then, she slides onto the floor. Ms. Hollister pulls her into her lap, stroking her cheek. Mama begins to cry, and then she howls, causing me to gasp and then break into a feverish pitch of sweat and tears.

Liberace, sensing calamity, shrieks in his cage and Ella begins to wail. Delphina stands, aghast, as Lita and Sonny spring to action. Lita slides the wailing baby from my sister's pack and walks towards the kitchen. Sonny stands, framing my sister with his body, and places his hands on her shoulders to steady her.

"We'll take Ella and the parrot to the garden," he says. "Lita will give her a bottle. I'll settle the bird in his aviary and then return."

Delphina nods as her husband rushes towards Liberace and grabs the cage. My sister isn't crying. Her features appear set in stone, and she stands, motionless.

"She can't be dead," she says, her words directed to the social worker, anger in her voice. "She can't be. Was she in a building that collapsed? Did a tree fall on her? What the holy hell happened down here? Please tell us the truth right this minute."

Now, the tears well up in her eyes and then begin streaming down her rigid cheeks. Andy walks to her, takes her hand, and this time she doesn't pull it away. I sit alone, bent and sobbing into outstretched palms. And then I feel a hand on my shoulder. I look up. DJ.

"Did you find her? Was she here?"

He glances first at Delphina and then to me. "I was doing what you asked—checking out the place late Friday for water damage. I found her up there." With a trembling hand, he gestures towards the stairwell. "In the tower."

"I was beside myself," he continues, his jaw working as he

chews the inside of his mouth. "I didn't know what to do. At least by then, the power was back. So, I called Andy, and he took over from there."

His fingertips dig into my shoulder. "I'm sorry I didn't call you after I found her, Linnea. But I couldn't. You and your family had to be told in person. By a professional. By someone who knows what the hell they're doing. I knew enough to hire a hazmat team to clean up. I met them here this morning." The blood drains from his face.

"What the hell," screams Delphina. Her eyes, cold and blue, blaze at DJ. "A hazmat team? It was that big of a mess? Now, I'm not asking. I'm demanding. What the hell happened to my little sister?"

DJ looks imploringly at Ms. Hollister, who remains on the floor, consoling Mama in her lap. Tears, as well, are running down the social worker's face. She pulls a pack of Kleenex from her shirt pocket and dots it around her eyes. Then, she slides the package across the floor in my direction. I ignore the gesture, wiping my nose with a corner of my T, my eyes begging hers for answers.

Biting her lower lip, her eyes lock into each of ours, one by one. She clears her throat before speaking. "Although the cause of death hasn't officially been confirmed by the coroner's office, the medical examiner believes Ivy took her own life." She nods at DJ. "Mr. Wilson found her. We believe the autopsy will confirm this."

I jerk my head towards DJ in horror. "How? How did she do it?" Shaking his head, he holds my gaze, not uttering a word. He shoves his hands deep into his pockets.

My lips move, but no sound emerges. When I finally find my voice, it is barely there. "Why, why, why? Why did she do this to herself?" I look at Mama, pointing at her fiercely. "Mama. Mama. Look at me. Look at me."

Mama returns my gaze and takes a shuddering breath,

making no effort to wipe her wet face and streaming nose. Her swollen eyelids resemble petals of decaying violets, and her nose is crimson. She stares at me, sobbing softly now, her mouth open and hollow, her eyes empty.

"Has Ivy ever attempted suicide in the past?" My words are now loud, frantic, needing to make sense of what is happening.

She shakes her head. "Never. No no no. She's never attempted something so crazy, so dramatic."

She staggers to her feet, swooning, and then collapses onto the ottoman next to Daddy. Straightening, he flings his arm over Mama's shoulder, drawing her into his side, trying to protect her. When he speaks, his voice is thick with pain.

"There were no suicide attempts. There were no suicidal inclinations." He looks down at Ms. Hollister, who is nodding at him, encouraging him to continue. "And that's because she never wanted to kill herself." His voice breaks. "I know my daughter. She would never bring this desecration onto herself. She would never do this to our family."

Mama grabs the sides of his head, her hands forcing his face around to meet hers.

"We need to see Our Girl right now. She's alone. Scared. She needs me. Not another minute can go by. I will never leave her side again."

She releases Daddy's crumbling face and clasps her hands together in a fist, pleading with Ms. Hollister. "I must see her."

The social worker stands, blows her nose, and leans into my parents. She rests her palms on each of their shoulders. Tilting her head sideways, her face inches from my mothers, she speaks to her gently.

"Of course. You and your husband should see your daughter, Mrs. Chandler."

She nods at my father and then straightens, her eyes touching everyone's in the room. "All of you may visit her, as often as you like until arrangements are made. That is if you feel comfortable doing so."

Mama lurches up and rushes to the tower stairwell. Ms. Hollister follows and touches her hand, which grips the banister. "She's not up there, Mrs. Chandler. Her body isn't here."

Mama grabs her shoulders, shaking her. "If she's not in her studio or in the service room, where is she? Where did y'all take Our Girl?"

Ms. Hollister responds, speaking slowly so that her words might find a crack to slip through the thick, suffering air.

"The medical examiner and members of the police department were here on Friday. They took her to the coroners to perform the autopsy."

Her voice is several octaves lower than that of the crazed feverish pitch of my family. "She was released this afternoon. Now she's at the morgue. The one here in Old Town." She takes Mama's hand and leads her back to Daddy.

Andy clears his throat and then addresses our weeping family. "Given the chaos that ensued in the aftermath of the hurricane, we followed Florida law," he lowers his voice, and looks at the floor, "and suicide protocol to the best of our abilities."

Suicide. I place my hands over my ears. Everyone stop saying that word.

Sonny rushes back into the room and wraps his arms around Delphina's shaking body. She buries her face into the crook of his armpit, sobbing quietly. For a minute, no one says a word. All I hear are the sounds of grief.

Delphina––her eyes bloodshot, face glistening with tears––turns her head towards Andy. She takes a small shallow breath that ends in a hiccup. "Did she leave a note? Everyone leaves a note. Where's the note?" Anger subsided, her voice is now ragged.

"There was that one note," Andy nods towards Mama,

"indicating she'd left town before the storm. There appears to have been others—but it looks like she burned them. Of course, we don't know that for sure."

"I need to see my baby," Mama cries. "Can y'all please understand me? There must be something I can do for her. To make it all better. I need to see her now."

"You can, indeed," the social worker replies, her voice level, checking her watch. "It's after hours, but I can make that happen. I must warn you, however. Her body's gone through serious trauma. Not so much by her actions, but by the fact she wasn't found for several days. You may want to wait until later after the funeral directors have seen to your daughter first."

"She's Our Girl," says Mama, sobbing uncontrollably and choking between words. "A part of this family. She doesn't have to look pretty. We just need to hold her."

30. DELPHINA

Sunday, September 24 I lament the practice of wearing veils at funerals has fallen by the wayside. A welcome cover and escape from the world, they served their purpose.

Head half-bowed, my hair falling towards my nose, I glance around the cathedral, furtively, so I don't catch the eyes of any one of these people who pack the church. I suspect they're curious as to how the Chandler family's holding up, considering the circumstances surrounding this death are far from run-of-the-mill. At least within the gossip mill, funerals for suicides aren't the same as regular ones.

Lita's at home with the baby. Sonny and I sit up front in a linear rectangular row of sameness, a threadbare cushion protecting our butts from the wooden bench. Mama's grown-old features are laced with edgings of late-morning light. Her eyes are red-rimmed and hazy from Valium.

Daddy's demeanor, usually immaculate, has not been given so much as an afterthought this week. Beneath his arm pits, yellow sweat rings stain a wrinkled white shirt. He mops his brow and Linnea, who sits at his side, takes his hand. The three of them look empty, like myself, I'm sure. Shells of our former selves, we're like the skins of cicadas, a brittle reference to what was once within.

Those of us Catholics who've received communion have returned to our seats. The service is interminable and judging from the program pages we've yet to cover, there's no end in sight. The congregation repeatedly stands and sits, stands and sits. Like a creamy flood of tears, towering tapers––now half spent––are dripping wax profusely. A friend of my mother's with hair the color of gunmetal and soft, doughy cheeks rises from a pew two rows back. She clears her throat.

"We pray for Ivy Elizabeth Chandler, who has died. May God now welcome her into his heavenly home of eternal happiness and peace."

Most of our friends aren't Catholic. And they peer at the program before thumbing through prayer books with the solemnity of students studying for finals.

"Lord, hear our prayer," everyone responds, our voices as one.

Now, silence descends upon the church as we compose our prayers for Ivy. Or not, depending on the intimacy felt with the Almighty. I try my best to pray, but it's no use. The pungent sweet fragrance of lilies grouped beneath the alter assaults my senses; I stifle a sneeze. Our family requested that instead of flowers, donations be sent in Ivy's name to The Brain and Behavior Research Foundation. But Mama's pals, knowing of her love of this trumpet-shaped plant, couldn't be held back.

No allusion has been made about the cause of Ivy's death, and I am grateful to the church and community for that. No note of the S word in the local paper, no mention in the words of the priest or friends who've stood up to speak of my sister. All avoid the Chandler No-Fly Zone. Behind closed doors, I'm sure it's the discussion of the hour. But maybe not.

The town is reeling from another type of hurricane, the sort of which tropical environs are accustomed. The sort The

Weather Channel can cover in five-minute bites. The sort whose funneling energy can flatten a town in minutes. But, given time and resources, that devastation can be rebuilt. My family will never recover from our storm. But at least in the eyes of our community, The Chandler story—suicide now a part of the script—might, too, be swept away in Irma's aftermath. Which is OK.

The S word, as well, has been muzzled amongst our family since the night we learned of the *accident*. It's like a landmine will detonate if one of us dare make a verbal misstep. This is not OK. Avoidance of the topic charges our every move with toxic portent. Something is about to explode.

A middle-aged woman is now standing, speaking at the pulpit. As if in defiance to the tradition of funeral black, she wears a splashy dress of classic Florida Keys oranges and teals. The owner of Conch House Art, her name is Lucy, and she speaks of Ivy's brilliance as a painter. The cover of the program she's now describing is a copy of one of Ivy's earlier works.

She picks up the pamphlet and points to the bold strokes of golds and bronzes. "This," she explains in a laconic Southern drawl, "was created in Ivy's 'light' period."

She smiles brightly, not following her observation with, *the period before darkness descended into her work.* But the words hang unspoken, like a heavy cloud. Mama muffles a sob, and I dare not look at her because I will cry, and I have cried enough. I bite my lips, trying not to lose it, and Sonny takes my hand and squeezes. Dry-eyed, I lean my head onto his shoulder.

We were married in this church, and I haven't been back since. We decided Ella was to be baptized at Lita's place of worship. I sometimes join them there on holidays, or when I'm down. The cleansing rituals give me a leg up.

I wonder how Ivy would feel about this ceremony? She was miserable in Catholic School because she didn't fit in, which had nothing to do with her faith. As adults, we never spoke about religion. Like my own musings, perhaps she was tangled up in the mystery of it all. My little sister, even in death, will remain a mystery to me, as well.

Anyway, whatever her beliefs, it's said funerals are to comfort those of us left behind. This, at least for my parents, is true. They lean forward, their mouths agape, hanging on to every word that is spoken by this woman who once knew their daughter.

To the backdrop of hushed whispers and the rustle of papers, the woman returns to her seat. A tall, lean white-haired man wearing a goatee stands and pushes his glasses into the bridge of his nose. He looks like a cross between Jimmy Carter and Colonel Sanders. A friend of my parents, he sits on the board of the Key West Arts and Historical Society and was responsible for ensuring our lighthouse was designated a historical landmark. Obviously comfortable in addressing crowds, he speaks with authority and solemnity.

"The family and friends of Ivy Elizabeth Chandler seek consolation and comfort. Heal their pain and dispel the darkness and doubt that comes from grief."

"Lord, hear our prayer," responds the congregants, each word pronounced deliberately.

I glance at the program as a young man seated at the organ begins playing Chopin's Nocturne in E flat major. He was Ivy's favorite composer, but I doubt she'd care for his compositions on the organ. Mama insisted Chopin's Funeral March be omitted. We find the melody kitsch; something befitting a dirge for a deposed Queen.

The funeral was pulled together in a week. There were so many things to be done: Meeting with the priest. Deciding Ivy's resting place. The notice in the paper. Organizing the memorial service. Picking out the urn—I couldn't help with that part, it made me sick to my stomach. Selecting prayers. Asking friends to stand up during the service. Arranging flowers. Planning the get-together for after the service. How did we manage?

Aunt Bet-Bet. That's how. She, too, is seated in the front pew but on the other side of the aisle. Head-to-toe in black, her mouth is quietly working as she bookmarks the hymns we'll be singing next. Linnea—apparently the only one of us thinking clearly—called her last Sunday after receiving the news. Our aunt flew down on Monday. And so, the procession began, following the rules of funeral protocol, ticking off the checklist, the business of death keeping us arm's length from our shattering grief.

Yesterday, Linnea's list in hand, I went to the grocery store to gather provisions to supplement the food brought to our door from well-wishers. We're hosting a *Celebration of Life* to honor our little sister. Basically, it's a party for our friends. More aptly a parody given Ivy is dead, and she was miserable at social gatherings.

The event will follow the service and be held at the inn. Shopping was the first normal thing I've done in weeks, and while searching for a box of gluten-free crackers, I started to cry. I was overwhelmed by all of the people going about their everyday lives and could barely make out the rest of the list through my kaleidoscope of tears. It was unbearable.

The last time I saw Ivy was late June, the evening we'd had dinner together at The Maiden Tower. If only I'd known that night would be the last chance I'd have to reconcile our distance, the last time I'd ever see her alive. If only I'd known she would use my gift, the sea glass, as a loaded gun. If I had advance notice on every *last time*, the present would be unbearable. It is unbearable. When I think of her slashing her wrists, emptying her veins...I can't un-think it.

Clenching my jaw, I glance at Mama, who is fumbling with a prayer book, clutching a balled-up handkerchief in her hand. What role did she play in this tragedy?

I didn't go with the others to see Ivy the night we learned of her death. I needed alone time with my little sister. I went to the mortuary to see her the day after, on Monday, after the morticians did their job.

The years had fallen away from her in death. She wore a long, creamy gown. Her face was smooth, untroubled, and her lips were partially open like she was expecting a gift, a child waiting for Santa. I touched her slack jaw, the right side of her mouth, the place where it dimpled when she smiled. I held her hand. It was cold in mine. I stroked her hair, shimmering with golden glints. I apologized for not probing deeper, trying to understand the pain she expressed in her art. I apologized for not taking her seriously when she tried refusing the glass. I kissed her forehead, thinking of all the things I need to tell the people I love. Before it's too late.

How am I to move forward after this? Will I ever feel normal again? I feel only anger, sadness, regret, and that loaded word: guilt. It's ironic and yet so perfect we're Catholics. My family may not be in the card-carrying community, but guilt is sanctioned in our blood and will now be the brick and mortar of our lives. Guilt is the one sure thing we can worship, the one thing we know to be true.

Surrounding me are the guttural recitations from the prayer book. The priest, in the embroidered vestments of his sanctity, carries Ivy's ashes to the columbarium, which is a recessed vault in the wall with niches for urns. It reminds me of the back of a DSW outlet, with compartmentalized shoeboxes waiting to be filled with overstock.

I turn my head sharply to the left, so I don't have to bear witness to what's left of my sister being placed inside that wall, consigned to darkness forever. Grief this deep is a silent, lonely thing.

Sunlight illuminates the maroons and violets of a stained-glass window facing east. Like an illustration in a children's bible, it's a depiction of St. Francis feeding a deer, a dove perched on his shoulder. I study the innocence of this scene, how the bird is gazing into the saint's tender face, how baby lambs rest as wooly blankets folded about his feet, and as my eyes rest upon this sanctity of goodness, as I listen to the soft sound of Mama's sobs muffled into her handkerchief, I lose it.

❧

THERE'S A SCRAPING sound behind me as Linnea drags a heavy wooden chair next to mine.

"Pity our guests," she says, under her breath leaning her face into mine. "It's hard making small talk with the bereft."

"I know. Right?" I sigh, wishing for the life of me I could fast forward this afternoon. "They can't wait to escape this hall of gloom. Tennis rackets, snorkeling gear and a bag of charcoal are waiting for them in the trunk of their cars."

Taking her seat, Linnea glances about the parlor, her face pale, mouth twitching. "I wish Daddy didn't banish Liberace to the Lightkeeper's Quarters. He could have at least livened up the place."

She takes a sip from a glass that could be water or vodka, a slice of lime floating on the top. "Once they get past—*She was so beautiful. She was so talented. Please accept our condolences,* they don't know what to say. It's as if normal conversation were off-limits."

"They must be especially tongue-tied after a..." I pause, piercing her with my gaze, "suicide." I savor the sound of the word, its finality as it rolls around my lips.

Linnea straightens, startled, dangerously close to tears. In her darting eyes, I read everything her ears refuse to hear.

I lean towards her. "Yes. I said the S word out loud. Maybe no one's responsible. But maybe someone is. Who or what can be held accountable, Linnea? Until recently, there was no mention of the b, as in bipolar word, either." My breath catches. "And witness the fallout. We need to talk about what happened."

Her face contorts, her expression begging me not to say the things that will push her over the edge.

"Now is not the time," she whispers, hissing her words. Tears trickle down her cheeks, which she swipes away with her wrist.

I rest my fingertips on her forearm, overcome with remorse. "You're right. Oh, God, you're right. I'm sorry."

She speaks slowly, her words resigned. "No worries, Delphina."

My face falls into my hands. "This life. It's all so hard. One day we're sure of ourselves, going through the motions––rather, the illusion––that everything is permanent. And then 'poof,' a hurricane ravages your town."

"Poof," Linnea adds, flattening her palm and blowing at her fingertips. "Our little sister vanishes from the face of the earth forever."

I straighten, moving my chair closer to hers so that the rims of our seats are touching, relieved to steal some privacy.

"Strange, agreed? This—celebration." I make air quotes around the word. "Quite the eclectic mix we have here today. Let's see. Over to our right, we're hosting a high school reunion."

I point my elbow towards a circle of women passing their phones around, screens filled with perfect children and perfect lives. Conversation halted when I joined them a few minutes ago. They fumbled for words of condolence, not one of them inquiring about my Ella.

A group of men standing next to the ladies create another knot. A guy I recognize from high school chorus apparently makes an off-color joke and, leaning their heads back, the group bursts into laughter. Just as quickly, they glance at us and quieten. Linnea gives them a small, weak smile, a thumbs up, but then looks down to her sandal-clad feet, a single tear rolling down her cheek.

Trying to lift her spirits, I continue my spiel, my voice that of a guide giving a Hemingway House tour. "You'll note to our left, we're hosting a meeting of Mama's gardening club, which appears to be in full swing. Judging from today's turnout, their e-mail distribution chain is as prolific as their orchid germinations."

"Where's Mama anyway?" Linnea asks, clutching her glass in both hands, anxiously looking around the room. She's not impressed with my performance, my attempt to add levity to an atmosphere that is anything but.

"It's been a good hour since I've seen her," she continues, eyes darting, pinching her lower lip with her forefinger and thumb.

"Daddy took her to the Lightkeeper's Quarters," I reply. "She did her best to keep it together. That is until Bill spoke of a memory he had of Ivy when she was a child. How she'd rescued a baby bird that had fallen from a tree. When he spoke of her digging up worms to feed the fledgling, Mama's floodgates released."

"Hunh. Maybe funeral platitudes serve their purpose after all."

"No doubt. Her tears sure upset Bill. For all his gruffness, he's a fragile ole' dude. It hasn't been long since his wife died. Daddy had to escort both of them back to their respective chambers."

I take a sip of wine, while Linnea has a three-swallow chug of whatever it is she's drinking. I've never known my sister to be a tippler but since that night in Gainesville, when dusk makes its appearance so, too, does the bottle. She may be excused. I take a large swill from my glass. We both may be excused.

She stirs an ice cube in her drink with her forefinger, her

eyes swollen and red-rimmed. Then, she looks up, pointing her pinky finger at a group huddled around the piano.

"How do I know those people?"

I follow the trail of her eyes. "Oh. Those are some of my friends. You remember them. They were dancers on my float. They look different out of costume."

Linnea's chin trembles. "That was only four months ago."

"The Before," I say, raising my brow.

"And this is *The After*," she replies, before pressing her knuckles into her mouth.

Our eyes lock, aware that last week a line of demarcation was drawn, defining the before and after of our existences forever.

"Life can turn on a dime." I shake my head, grinding my molars together.

Linnea sighs and turns away. In the whisper of her shaky breath, I understand she's faced her own demons this week. She nods towards a woman wearing a black camisole with spaghetti straps, a minuscule leather skirt and stilettos. Her outfit looks odd at a funeral gathering.

"Isn't that Ivy's friend from Brooklyn? Over there. By the bar."

"It is, indeed. She was on my list of people to call."

The woman wobbles a bit, maybe because of the shoes or perhaps it's because of the brandy she's clutching at the bottle-neck. Sonny tries to stabilize her, and she smiles into his eyes, digging blood red nails into his biceps. My husband glances at me with a sheepish grin. I'm used to women ogling him, and it doesn't bother me. From what I hear from girlfriends, however, trusting my hubby is a feeling not common to many in this town.

Walking to a table laden with food, Sonny scoops a mound of pasta salad onto a plate and stabs a fork into a piece of rigatoni. He returns to the woman and hands it to her, encouraging her to eat. That's my man. Forever trying to fix things.

Linnea regards this scenario curiously, and, for a moment, is distracted from her grief.

"She's the one who paints boobs at the Festa-Palooza, right?"

"Yep. She's also a conceptual artist. Ivy admired her work."

"She sure has her hooks in your husband. What a get-up for a funeral."

I give a hollow laugh. "I suppose Brooklyn has a different dress code for events such as this. And Sonny?" I shrug. "It's OK. I guess she didn't see his ring." I uncross my legs, kicking off my heels and push them under the chair with my feet. "She and Ivy were close. She fell apart on the phone when I gave her the news, which made me feel good. Like Ivy had friends who loved her."

"I suppose. But I don't think I could be that magnanimous towards a woman who had eyes on my man." Linnea continues studying the group while sipping her drink.

"At least she's found her people. Those are artists, some of the folks who show at Conch House." I tilt my head towards the portrait of Rossalea. "Ivy's beard is over there. The one with the haggard face. His hands are shoved in his pockets, and he's standing under the portrait, staring at the floor. I recognize him from a photo in the paper."

"Her beard?"

"You know. Jonah, her cover. He was the guy she was supposedly leaving with for Kentucky."

Linnea's eyes fix on the man for a moment. And then she swivels to face me, her eyes wide and glassy.

"Why, Delphina? Why did she do this to herself? Why did she do this to *us*?"

I know that voice—shrill, fragmented and broken. She's

thirty seconds away from a meltdown. She shakes her head, furiously. "I need to understand."

Leaning over and placing my wine on the floor, I regroup, trying to find calming words. Straightening, I put my arm around my sister's shoulder, pulling her into me.

"If I understood anything about this life, Linnea, you'd be the first to know. She had scary bipolar juju going on. She was on heavy drugs." I try sounding matter of fact, but the tremor in my voice betrays me.

She pushes away, staring into my face. When she opens her mouth to speak, I shake my head.

"I'll say the words." I look down into my lap, and toy with my wedding ring. "Mama could have stopped this. Ivy should have been in a psych ward. Mama knew the extent of her illness, but she didn't sound the alarms until it was too late. She lied to us."

Several moments pass before I look up. Linnea's hair hangs limp around her shoulders, unwashed and uncombed. Two red splotches mark her pale complexion, like cherries branded onto her cheeks. She's been pinching them relentlessly a week now. She reminds me of a rag doll once fiercely loved, and now a forgotten heap in a toy chest.

"It's time," she says, in an *I've finished a glass of vodka* voice. She squints at me as if peering through fog.

"Time? What do you mean?"

"It's time to return to Idaho." Words slurred, her head wobbles on her neck.

I remove the empty glass from her hands and place it on the floor next to mine. My hands begin to tremble, out of control, so I clench them together in a fist. I take several deep breaths to control my anger before speaking. The last thing this shindig needs is a scene. Leaning my mouth towards her ear, I talk to her in a whisper.

"So, you're going to leave us now? When the shit has truly

hit the fan. I must say your timing is brilliant. Is it because of your thasa...thasa..whatever it's called?"

Lowering her head, her words fall into her lap. "Thalasso-phobia. And no. That's not the only reason. I'm also leaving because of me."

Elbows on knees, I lean into her, torquing my head to the side to peer into her face. "But what about me? What about our twinship? I need you, Linnea. Don't you need me? Don't *we* matter enough for you to stay?"

The scraping of another chair pulls up, this one sliding over to Linnea's side. Are you kidding me? DJ? Gotta' hand it to the man. Like my sister, he has his timing down to a science.

I stand, smoothing my navy linen skirt and then bend over to retrieve my shoes. "I've been negligent of my duties as a host." My words drip with formality. "I'd better get back to our guests."

Linnea looks up at me as I slide into my heels. Her face is a muddled shade of white and red, and it screws up like she's about to cry. She's wasted. DJ looks down into the vanishing foam of his beer, and I make my escape.

I join the group of fellow Catholic school alums now deep in the throes of a discussion about hurricane clean-up. They look at me, startled.

"Oh, no, please. I'm interested in hearing this." I do my best to crank a smile and seem alert.

The president of my high school class has the floor of this conversation. Her kinky red curls are held off her face with brown barrettes, and she wears funky cat-eye frames, which convey a sly intelligence. She places her hand on my forearm, pats me like I was her lap dog, and continues.

"As I was saying," she says, her hand not leaving my arm, "if we ever want the tourists back, they should do a better job of cleaning the debris off the streets." Which leads another woman to say, "But first they should repair the Southernmost

Buoy. It's our main attraction, and it's not recognizable." Which leads to, "Did you hear what happened to Tina's bedroom? That tree she was so fond of? She was lucky the roof didn't crash over her head while she was sleeping." Which leads to, "Insurance rates are gonna' go sky high after this mess."

All are nodding their heads in agreement, but no one seems to be listening to anyone, only eager for the person who's speaking to finish so they can get their two-cents in. And ole' cat eyes is still petting my arm.

Aunt Bet Bet (who is explaining to the Garden Club how she removes the fungus on her rose bushes) and I are the only members in our family left standing. And I'm the only fucking member of my immediate family trying to keep up appearances when all I want to do is go to the beach, run into the ocean and scream. Words swim about me in all directions, fighting for my attention. I excuse myself from the conversation, walk to the front door, and release a trickle of guests.

"Y'all were so sweet to stop by. It means the world to my family."

They give me a tight hug. "We're here if you need us, honey."

They practically run to their cars. My head pounds and I want to vomit. I reenter the house and Linnea's sobbing into her hands. DJ's palm rests on her heaving back, and he's leaning into her, whispering words of comfort, I'm sure.

The remaining guests welcome this spectacle of raw grief, finally giving them an excuse to leave. *It's time to leave the family to themselves*, they say, ushering themselves out the door. *We don't want to be a further burden in this sensitive time.* Sonny and I grab trays and join Aunt Bet-Bet, clearing the tables of glasses, dirty plates and half-eaten platters of food. No one says a word.

When a semblance of order has returned to the inn, we leave Aunt Bet Bet prone on the sofa, a glass of wine in her hand. Linnea and DJ have vanished. Sonny and I climb into our

THE RUBY OF THE SEA

truck and drive. We simply drive and drive—silent, numb—at last, finding ourselves at Boca Chica beach. Removing our shoes, we exit the car and walk around the tangled paths of shattered palms, mangroves and mounds of debris. We have the beach to ourselves. No one wants to hang out in this post-Irma mess.

Standing at the shoreline, we made it in time to see the sunset. The sun, hung low in the water, colors it blood red and orange. It's like a fertilized egg was cracked over the horizon, the yolk bleeding across the endless aquamarine of the Atlantic. The end of the day in Key West is so beautiful it will break your heart. For a few seconds, my spirits lift.

A gull swoops down nosing into the glass of the sea, and immediately shoots up, beak empty, catching a breeze that will take her to a better feeding ground. My misery returns. How nice to be Linnea. To simply pick up from wherever you are that displeases you and ride the wind to another locale.

I grab a rock the size of an ostrich egg and hurl it into the water with such force, I fall forward. Sonny kneels down and strokes my face as I lie here, covered in damp, dirty sand, aching from loss, tears streaming down my cheeks.

31. LINNEA

Today, four days after Ivy was buried, we're...

Rewind.

That's not the right word. Burying implies the priest lowered the urn into the ground and each of our family members took a turn shoveling dirt over her ceramic-corseted ashes.

Ahem. Today, four days after we lay Ivy to rest in the columbarium, we're...

Rewind.

This suggests that after having a nice long nap, she wakes up, has a cup of coffee, and makes a dinner date with a friend who died of bone cancer last year. There's no need for fear in this scenario, no need for anxiety about what lies at the end of that lonesome highway.

Let's get real.

Today, eighteen days after Ivy committed suicide, we're...

Ahhh. Much better. Delphina's right, after all. We need to say the word out loud as we attempt to right ourselves while going through the motions of the living. What choice do we have but to move forward?

So, let's take this from the top, a bit of authenticity this time around:

Today, eighteen days since Ivy committed suicide, we're limping about The Maiden Tower—Mama, Daddy and me. All of us have adopted facial expressions, expressions we've never before worn. As wounded lions, we're too exhausted to roar, and left only with energy enough to lick the crusted blood from our paws.

Do these words resonate? I hope so. I don't know what else to say, how else to express the sadness that has hijacked our souls. I ask God for help, to instill a compass in my heart, to help me guide this family through unimaginable loss. It's been a long time since I've prayed.

Having drunk myself silly at Ivy's farewell party, DJ carried me out of the inn before the vodka came out as quickly as it went down. Delphina and I've spoken several times on the phone since. At first, our conversations were apologetic and stilted. Me, embarrassed; Delphina, distant.

Our relationship had been gasping since I've been home anyway. How can it survive suicide? But in the past few days, our words have loosened up. She seems happy to talk to me, eager to better understand Ivy's disease. She's been spending time kayaking, letting her family tend to her and her to them. Sonny, Lita and Ella have enveloped her in their cocoon, protecting her in her grief.

In fits and starts, I've been helping Mama with various chores around the house and garden. Nina returned the day after the funeral, and she and Mama cried themselves silly in each other's arms. Her sister told us the tragedy did a better job sobering her up than rehab.

Aunt Bet Bet, relieved Mama has someone other than Daddy and me for comfort, flew back to Alabama yesterday. She's called to check on Mama several times since. My parents have plans to reopen The Maiden Tower for business in mid-

October. Daddy's way of coping with this magnitude of loss is by plunging into the business of running the inn. He's already begun accepting bookings.

And me? I bought a one-way ticket and am leaving for Boise at the end of next week.

This afternoon I'm helping Mama remove all of Ivy's paintings, which decorate the lighthouse. She says she can't live with the daily reminders. The daily reprimands, I think, correcting her, not daring to say the words out loud. Mourning has extracted all of her giddy chatter and passion, and she walks about The Maiden Tower as a shadow of her former self.

Delphina and I believe she could have done something to prevent this tragedy. She should have taken her to a doctor much sooner. She should have been honest with us, helped us to understand the extent of Ivy's condition before it was too late. Working together as a family unit, a united front, we could have done something to help our sister. But we would never be so cruel as to infer such to her, or to anyone. The blank spaces left from the art—rectangles of wallpaper several shades darker than the rest—are as chilling as a scream.

"This is one of my favorites," Mama says, as we gaze at a painting hanging on the wall above the guest register table. "It's one of her earlier works. She was delighted when I told her it reminded me of the interior of a circus tent." She points to an elongated face of a woman whose open mouth takes over most of her countenance.

"Look at her expression. Isn't it perfect? If Ivy couldn't capture a painting the way it was in her imagination, it wasn't acceptable. Our Girl was a stickler for perfection."

"The most talented artists are perfectionists." This is the first time our conversation has tread on solid terrain since that evening in Gainesville.

Tucking my hair behind my ears, I drop my head to the side and smile. "The composition is brilliant. And I love this color." I point to a bold splash of a greenish-blue color Ivy was fond of using before she got into the muddier shades. "I forget the name."

"Cadmium."

"That's right. I remember her telling me that. Cadmium."

I'll ask Mama if I can take it back to Idaho with me. But now is certainly not the time. I don't want to remind her I'm leaving.

"No one was harder on Our Girl than she was on herself," Mama says, tracing her finger around an image of a fish. "When she was fifteen, she pulled away from me. At the time I was certain it was typical teenage behavior––I'd already been through that with you and Delphina. So, it didn't occur to me, she needed professional help. I knew she was sometimes depressed, but I had no idea it went so deep."

She peers into the painting, perhaps looking for clues as to the tipping point, what made my sister take her life.

"Oh. Here it is. See the play of light, the silvers, greens, blues, the tranquility of water?" She holds the piece towards me and then brings the work closer to her face, wincing.

"There. It's hard to detect. I've never seen it before. But deep beneath the water lies dark strokes of pain. Terrible pain."

She swipes away tears and carries it to a corner of the parlor. Bending, she rests it on the floor, leaning it against the wall, along with the other paintings we've removed. She stoops to regard an unfinished piece. One of Ivy's recent works, it's a disturbing interpretation of Rossalea. Lips swollen and painted blood red, pain is etched across the Maiden's face, tears swelling her eyes.

"Your sister had a chemical imbalance. A disease." Her back to me as she speaks, she glances at me from time to time as she organizes the art according to when they were painted. But she never meets my eye.

"She'd swing from the highs of mania to the lows of depres-sion––you never knew how long an episode would last. You know, mental health experts connect manic depressive syndrome to the creative side of the brain. That's why so many actors and performers are bipolar. Women are also more likely to suffer from it."

Mama wants to talk. After years of silence, excuses, and only recently uttering the word bipolar, now she wants to talk. She wants to have a conversation about her illness. After Ivy's dead. I walk to her side, kneel on the floor and place my arm around her shoulder.

She picks up the painting of Rossalea, studies it, and yanks her head towards me. "You don't think the Maiden...you don't think Rossalea was like Ivy. That she..."

I shake my head briskly. "It's over, Mama. We'll never know. Let this be done." Biting my lower lip, I take the drawing from her hand and turn the image around to face the wall.

Since Ivy's death, I've had troubling feelings and intuitions myself. Can one soul reach through time to capture another's? Perhaps these ephemeral sensitive women burned too brightly and weren't meant to wade through the vulgarities of life. Maybe Ivy and the Maiden were heavenly beings that God yanked back after realizing he'd made a mistake.

A trembling sensation grips me as I grasp for an answer that I'll never have. My theories—visions, if you will—shouldn't be overthought. Best to leave them behind, hovering in the gray.

"Let's have a cup of chamomile tea. Maybe some pie, if you're up for it." I pat down her wispy hair and it feels soft and light, like goose down between my fingertips. "You've shrunk down to feathers and bones. A baby chick. That's what you are."

Like a child anticipating a treat, she smiles shyly as we stand, and follows me into the kitchen. This tragedy has beat her into submission. I pull out a chair for her, put the teapot on to boil and then walk to the fridge, pulling out a box that contains a pie. It's not fresh-baked but store-bought, something a friend dropped by. The thought of baking these days seems ludicrous. I would be squandering energy that could be used to fix something. Something that will forever be broken.

Slicing a piece for her, I place it in between her forearms, Then, I bring the kettle to the table, placing it on a trivet.

"Here you are," I say, handing her the fork and taking a seat beside her. She looks at me in gratitude and then thrusts the prongs, so that the stem is upright, into the pie. Removing her hand, she directs her words to the utensil.

"When she'd tumble into her dark place, I'd rally, try to cheer her up. We used herbal vapors and experimented with medical marijuana." Her voice is hollow, desperate; the voice of a woman fallen down a well. "I was the one who drove to Miami to buy it. On-line, we'd read it reduces psychotic symptoms."

She chews her bottom lip, drumming her fingertips on the tabletop. "The internet can be a dangerous place to diagnose a life-threatening disease. But I had no clue her symptoms were potentially fatal."

She looks at me, her eyes expressing a yearning that she could go back in time and handle things differently.

"Thomas knew of her illness," she continues, "but he didn't understand the disease, either. I mean, who does? Ivy was ashamed. She believed mental illness was a character flaw and would imply she was incompetent, not to be trusted. And what normal person would want to be her friend? Mental illness would also imply that it was somehow her own fault, something she could mitigate if only she were stronger, more self-aware."

She chokes back a sob. "On some level, although I never said the words out loud, I believed this too. She swore your father and me to secrecy. It was easier than the truth. So, we lied. Chronic migraines are easier to digest than mixed states, ultradian-cycling bipolar." After saying the words, her hand flies to her mouth and she gags.

I slide the prongs of the fork through the tip of the slice and try handing it to her. She shakes her head, so I put it in my mouth, instead. The crust tastes of musty cardboard, the filling like a gelatinous glob of goo. I spit it into my napkin and push the plate away. It's the same reaction I've had to everything I've eaten of late.

"After Ivy was diagnosed, after she was prescribed her meds," she continues, "it dawned on me that my mother must have been manic depressive, too. But it wasn't spoken of back in her day. Apparently, her brain, like her grandchild's, was starved for the chemicals it needed to regulate moods."

Mama shakes out her napkin and folds it. "The seeds of my mother's madness took root in my child," she continues. "But your grandmother's storm seemed to pass; she mellowed out with age. After Ivy's diagnosis, her doctor insisted there was no time to waste. So we worked our way through drug changes and adjustments. Lexapro for severe depression. Wellbutrin for daytime sedation. Ativan for episodic anxiety––that one turned out to be a disaster." Mama crosses her arms around her torso and shudders.

"I was praying for some elixir to snap her back in place, meanwhile, covering for her the best I could."

Her voice is deadpan. Her expression is that of a woman pitching a tent in a camp of refugees, who've crossed the border of pain into the lower banks of suffering.

Over and over, she shakes and folds the napkin, shakes and folds, smoothing out the wrinkles. I remove the cloth from her hand and weave my fingers into hers.

"You were a kid when Grandmother Rose was at her worst. And your father divorced her. You had to fend for yourself."

She nods and looks out the window. "I was in my early teens when he left. But I got by. I spent most of my free time at my friends' houses. You know, after school and weekend sleep-overs. It was the mid-seventies. I listened to Elton John and fantasized about becoming a famous pianist."

Turning her head, she meets my gaze. "But my driving desire was to one day have my own children and provide the sort of childhood I was denied."

My hand squeezes hers. "And you did, Mama. You did."

She shakes her head as if to refute my words.

"I thought I was doing my best, but with Ivy? My mistakes were fatal. Mental illness was something I had been raised to shy away from, so I tried to erase her disease." She squeezes my hand so hard it throbs.

"It was hard for me, but it was harder for her. Every day, she had to fight her brain. Now I understand that our home reme-dies and the passage of time only worsened her illness. Made it more difficult to treat. You missed the holidays this year. That was when Our Girl's mania—her biology—took a turn for the worst. Scared your father and me to death." I lean into her, straining to hear her words.

"Delphina's family invited us over for family festivities, but I lied, made excuses, told them we were too busy to attend. I knew it upset Delphina, especially since the baby was only two weeks old. But we were batting off demons that were control-ling Ivy, demons we didn't understand. After the New Year, Thomas and I took her kicking and screaming to see the psychiatrist. At that point, she was too ill to understand how sick she was. We—your father and I—never sounded the alarms in time."

Never sounded the alarms; Delphina's exact words after the funeral. Misery wells around my temples, but my eyes remain dry. Unweaving her hand from mine, she looks beyond me, out the kitchen window, seeming to speak to the clouds.

"That was when the rapid-cycling began; when her mania spiraled out of control, again and again. We never knew when it would hit. At that point, there was nothing I could do but try my best to get her to take the pills—the antipsychotics." Her eyes flit briefly to mine and then dart away.

"Hiding her disease from the world gave us license to believe that just like Grandmother Rose's, it would go away. Her doctor told me that rapid-cycling increases the risk of suicide and she should be hospitalized. Immediately. But we felt," she pounds her chest with her fist, "we truly believed in our hearts, that Our Girl would never harm herself. Harm every one of us in such a hideous and permanent way. But we were wrong. Dead wrong."

I pour the tea into two delicate china cups, both so thin and fragile, one slip of the fingers and the porcelain will shatter. Mama reaches for the cup and brings it to her mouth. Without taking a sip, she returns the cup to the saucer. Her jaw falls open, vacant and remote as a bottomless pit, as tears trail down her cheeks. I stare at her, speechless, unable to come up with any soothing words or sentiments.

She picks up the napkin and rubs it under her eyes. Then, she bats it about her face.

"This morning," she continues, her voice rising, "when I walked into your sister's room, I looked into the mirror and saw myself." Mama rakes at her face and shakes her hair, her wild mane flying. "My eyes, my face, my hair. All of this I gave to Our Girl. All of this I took from her."

Mama is acting certifiable and, frightened, I grab her hands. "Stop, Mama. You can't blame yourself. You didn't know. Who would? You did everything you could to help her. She wasn't in her right mind when the hurricane hit. DJ told me it was a horrific experience. I'm certain she was terrified. Equally certain, she was not taking her drugs. The disease is what killed her. Not you."

"It's not natural to outlive your child," she says, her voice broken, cracking on every word. "That's not God's plan. What kind of mother am I? My own mother was toxic and so am I. Even worse! My baby committed suicide. And the buck doesn't stop there. I've alienated Delphina and her family."

Mama seems transparent in her skin. Crushed by the air alone, it's as if she's nothing more than a cloud of dust. All it would take is for me to give her a tiny nod, agreeing with her self-assessment, and she'd vanish.

"And now I'm chasing you away, too," she continues, her palm on my shoulder. "I'm sorry, Linnea. Whatever I've done to make you run away, to give you your own set of demons, I am so so sorry."

Suicide is so horrible, strange, miserable and sad. Delphina and I had to blame someone for this nightmare. At the end of my rope, something inside of me breaks. Folding my arms on the tabletop, I drop my head, resting it on my forearms. She strokes my hair, running her hand down my back.

My body is wracked with sobs, and she slumps down to embrace me. A clump of her hair becomes caught in my mouth, and I taste the salt of my tears. Or maybe they're hers. How are we to live with this intensity of grief and raw emotion? If I tell her the truth about myself, about what happened the night that keeps me away from this town, at least she won't have to blame herself for my departure. Here I am. Trapped by the woman who has taught me to hate lies and yet also use them as cover.

Gasping, I try to catch my breath, and, with shaking hands, she hands me a napkin. I blow my nose and then rub fists into my eyes like a child. Our eyes, swollen from crying, lock together. It's time to revise my narrative.

"There is one thing, Mama, you can cross off your list of guilts."

Her eyes thin, chin trembling.

"I didn't leave this town because of you."

I swipe my forefinger beneath my nostrils and sniff. "The

nightmare began the evening y'all gave Delphina and me our Sweet Sixteen birthday party. We pretended to go to bed after the celebration, but we donned babydoll dresses, made up our faces to look older and snuck out after you and Daddy went to sleep. We both had fake IDs."

Sitting rigid, she nods her head for me to continue.

"We went to Salamander's. You remember. The dive that was raided and closed down for serving underage kids? Anyway, we got drunk—I mean, plastered. We'd experimented with the occasional beer before, but this was the first time we were ever seriously wasted. Delphina and I got into some sort of argument at the bar. I can't remember what it was about. Something stupid, and she left.

"Then, I met a man who bought me another drink. I think it was my third. Maybe fourth. Anyway, it was one of those rum drinks that goes down easy and messes you up fast. The guy was dressed nice, and he was well-built and handsome. He was an older man. I mean, for me when I was sixteen, thirty-four seemed old at the time. Not a local. I forgot where he said he was from—Georgia? I remember he was down here with some other guys on a fishing trip."

Mama's lips purse and then she brings her thumb to her mouth, biting a hangnail.

"He was funny at first. Complained there were no good beaches in Key West. And so, I argued with him. Told him there were a couple of good beaches—you know, we were flirting, playing around. I mentioned Higgs Beach. The next thing I remember I'm in his car and I'm showing him how to get there."

My body is overtaken by the shakes. Mama's shoulders heave as if she's crying, but no tears fall from her eyes. She puts her arm around my shoulder, drawing me into her.

For seventeen years, I've guarded my secret. If I say the words out loud, if I speak of my shame, it will be real, out there, a part of my story. Then, crushed with the knowledge of everything I've lost, I will lose the battle. Why did anyone need to know?

Shutting out the truth and ignoring the symptoms has only made it fester. Now, it's controlling my life. So, what if the opposite is true? What if vulnerability is power? Lies and secrets have ripped this family apart at the seams. People speak of their *Aha Moments*, and this is one I own.

My head tucked into her neck, I continue, not leaving the cradle of her arm.

"He got a beach towel out of the trunk of his car and said something about taking a walk. I don't know what happened next. It's all jumbled up in my brain. All I remember is us kissing on top of the towel. It was so dark; the moon was covered by clouds. Then, he rolled on me, pinned me down, and pulled up my dress. I cried *stop, stop it*, and then, and then he…"

She pushes her face into mine so that our noses are an inch apart. Her eyes flash a wildness I've never before seen.

"I know what he did to you." Her words sound gritty, venomous with rage. "You don't have to go further. I will find that animal and bring him down. I'll skin him alive and then stage a public execution. That's what I'll do. I don't know what the statute of limitations is, I don't even care, 'cause believe me, after I hunt him down…I'll…I'll…" Her voice breaks into a sob as she pulls me into her.

"I was a virgin, Mama. A virgin. I should have screamed. I should have kicked him." My words are muffled into her chest. Pushing away, I see her face––like mine––is wet with tears.

"The face on his digital watch was neon, and it had a creepy orange glow. It was midnight. After he finished, he left me there. All by myself. Lying in the sand. He even took his towel. I ran into the ocean, to wash off his nastiness, and then I was stung by a swarm of jellyfish."

"Wild beasts should not be allowed to roam in a civilized society," she says, her voice a growl. "They should be shot down or locked behind bars."

"I didn't know what to do. My only option was to walk home. I was wet, and my legs were covered in red, itchy, burning welts. Delphina was asleep, passed out in her bed, and I took a shower. I was so ashamed. I didn't want to admit I'd been raped. I didn't even know if you could call it that. I only wanted to erase the night."

I rest my head on her shoulder, words tumbling from my lips. "I was so relieved when my period came and never told a soul. But then nightmares about sea creatures began plaguing my sleep."

I raise my head to catch her eye. "You remember. It's when I asked for my own bedroom." She nods, biting her lower lip.

"To this day," I continue, fighting back tears, "whenever I glimpse the ocean, I feel shame, embarrassment and fear. The only way I feel better is by getting as far away as possible. It was like God sent the jellyfish to punish me for what I'd done."

"There, there, baby girl," Mama says, rocking me in her arms, cooing into my ear. "There is no need for guilt, Linnea. You are a victim. You were *raped*," she says, spitting out the word. "Not only did that man have sex with you––dear God, take your virginity without your consent––he's been distorting your reality ever since. You're letting a rapist define *you* to yourself. The bastard's still filled with power. You can't let what happened to you after so many years paralyze your life."

Pushing away, words explode from my mouth, indignant, with the rapidity of a series of gunshots. "My rapist, mom? Are you sure that's what he's called? He didn't gag me and force me into his car. I was drunk, dressed provocatively, and went with him quite willingly. I even showed him how to get to the beach. I was kissing him at the bar and on that towel. I was leading him on. Wasn't that a green light? These days, I don't even know what rape is."

Rage in her voice, her eyes draw to slits. "You were raped, Linnea. Raped. No ifs, ands or buts. You were underage, and he was a grown man. You must erase the lies you've been telling yourself—that it was your fault. Separate yourself from your anxiety and look at the real culprit. Adults are supposed to know better. He was a predator. Worse than some flea-bitten alley cat in heat. He should have been thrown in prison. That's the reality."

We tell ourselves these stories, living within the nucleus of concentric bubbles, contorting reality so we can make it through the day. My fading tears turn into a hot knot inside my throat, as the bubbles begin to pop.

"I only wish I had known, honey. I wish you'd felt comfortable enough to tell me." She continues to hold me, stroking my hair, rocking me in her arms. "But it's not too late to find help. To help you get better. You are not alone, Linnea. There are many, many women out there who understand your suffering. No one can take away the pain, but at least you can find people who can hold your hand and say, *It also happened to me. I know what you mean when you speak your truth.*"

My heart thuds, rattling the ribs inside of my chest. It feels like I've stopped to catch my breath after crossing the finish line of a 10K.

I peer into her face. "I don't need a support group. At least not yet. I need my mother. So, does Delphina. We need you to show us how to swim back up after you've hit rock bottom."

Her eyes pooling, she nods furiously and clutches me in her arms as if she wants to take on my grief. We rock in the bosom of our buried memories, swaying in what feels like a lifetime of lies, secrets, suffering and fear.

At last, I smile, but push away, rubbing my neck.

"What's wrong honey?"

"It's nothing. Just a crick."

Her face falls, and it seems she never wants to let me go.

"Why did you have to grow up so fast?" she says, softly, smoothing my hair, tucking it back behind my ears.

"We both grew up too fast." Leaning into her, I kiss her cheek.

THE DOORBELL RINGS. The Fed Ex guy is at the front porch, delivering a package for my family. We only know him of late because he's been showing up every day with a bereavement gift.

He hands the package, which looks to be another food basket, to Mama.

"I'm sorry for your loss, Mrs. Chandler," he says, grabbing his belt and hiking up his navy shorts.

This delivery man, this man to whom we've never been introduced, knows of Ivy's death.

"What?" Mama exclaims, annoyance illuminating her face. "You're sorry for our loss? It's more than a loss. It's a catastrophe. It's as if a bomb was tossed into the heart of this community. It is a loss to our city, a loss to our world. Do you know of my daughter's brilliance?" Her hands fly to Ivy's paintings, leaning against the wall. "Have you ever heard the name Ivy Elizabeth Chandler? Well, if you haven't, you will soon enough."

Daddy rushes towards the door and signs paperwork attached to a clipboard, a look of apology on his face. He's getting used to playing goalie, defending her from do-gooders. Of late, visits from the assistant priest who believes his words will lift her spirits. She turns, irritation deepening the creases in her face, and walks towards the stairwell leading up to the tower.

Daddy glances at me. I give him a weak but sympathetic smile as the delivery man makes haste to leave. All the poor guy did was say he was sorry. But in my heart, a sliver of me smiles. A glimpse of what makes my mother who she is has returned.

I walk to Daddy's side. His eyelid twitches madly as he leans into the doorframe. Chest heaving, he reaches into his pocket to pull out a handkerchief and places it over his misbehaving eye.

"When Our Girl started having her episodes, it scared me half to death." His words are directed towards the doorjamb, his voice crippled in a supreme shuddering effort to keep his emotional state at bay. "I backed away from her. I withdrew. I never told her the truth. How much I loved her. And now it's too late."

I speak to him under my breath, placing my palm on his forearm. "Ivy knew you loved her Daddy. After all, you were the one who began calling her Our Girl. But now you have to do something for Mama."

We turn to regard my mother, his wife. Her hand on the banister, she remains still, looking up into the darkness of the stairs. "You have to figure out what you can give her that Delphina and I can't."

Daddy closes the door and walks to Mama. Pulling her away from the stairwell, he presses his hand into her cheek and stares into her face. He opens his mouth, tries to speak but his voice breaks, and no words follow. But nothing needs to be said. His eyes speak his emotions. Taking her hand, he leads her to the piano. The two of them sit in front of the keyboard.

Mama plays the D Minor chord over and over, and it echoes through the empty parlor, the saddest note of all.

32. DELPHINA

"Thank God you're home. Now it's my turn to escape."

Sonny stands in front of the dresser in our bedroom. Removing his iPhone from the back pocket of his jeans, he then runs a comb through his hair. I slide out of my shift and step into a swimsuit.

I move to him and with the side of my hip, push him away, so I've space to open up a drawer.

"Babe," he says, stepping out of my way. "What's the hurry. Don't I even get a kiss?"

Leaning my face into his, I peck his cheek. "It's almost 5:00. I've only got a couple of hours before the sun begins to set." Opening the drawer, I dig out a pair of cut-offs. "Wifey needs her downtime."

It's only been three weeks since Irma, but on Sunday, the Keys officially reopened for tourists. They're not busting down walls to vacation here, however, and our snorkeling business has taken a hit.

Although it's early October and the waters are warm and pristine, we've decided to close shop and not take any bookings until January 2nd. Sonny took a temporary job with the city as a Cleanup Coordinator, and I'm using the opportunity to spend more time with Ella. This gives Lita her own freedom, and she spends three days a week volunteering with Disaster Relief efforts. She's been gone all day.

The alone time with my daughter has been a sweet consolation. After last month, all I want to do is nurture her and cook healing foods for my family. Today while Ella napped, I made Rotini with Basil Pesto and Broccoli, using whole grain pasta. In this hiatus, I want to ensure she develops a palate inclusive of cultures besides Cuba's.

I glance about our bedroom, at the sheets balled up at the foot of the bed and the overflowing trash can. We're one diaper change away from chaos. Perhaps while the baby sleeps, I should focus more on housework. Then again, why can't Sonny do more to help around the place? Glancing at a pile of his dirty clothes heaped into the corner, a wave of slow anger travels up my spine. He's making things worse. I turn to face him, flinging my arms about the room. I hear Lita entering the house, so I lower my voice to a hissing whisper.

"Are you blind to this mess? Would it deflate your masculinity to put your filthy clothes in a hamper instead of dumping them on the floor? Couldn't you, at the very least, empty the trash?"

He looks temporarily stunned, but then recovers, placing his hands on my forearms. "Where the hell did that come from? Hey. I'm sorry. I'll take care of it. You make it sound like I sit around on my ass all day. I didn't so much as take a five-minute break at work and I just finished strapping your kayak onto the truck."

He walks towards the corner and picks up his clothes and moves toward the bathroom where we keep the hamper. He stops, arms filled with crumpled t's, jeans and dirty socks, and looks at me over his shoulder.

"There's a gulf between us," he says, concern deepening the

crease between his brow. "Things were bad enough, but now you don't even look at me."

The distance I've enforced between us since Ivy's death is not worth the pain I hear in his voice. As if I were Ella, deflated after throwing a tantrum, I walk to him, painting a shaky smile across my face. He turns to face me. Like an unlucky angel, a pair of white underwear falls from his arms and his eyes cloud with worry. I'll bet he's concerned his wayward boxers will push me over the edge.

I bend to pick them up and place them on his pile. "I'm sorry, honey. I didn't mean to bark at you like that. I've been difficult lately." Peering into his face, I'm hoping my expression conveys one of a person suffering more than can be expressed in words; a person who should be excused.

"You're in so much pain, baby. I get that. But you need to think about what you say to me before lashing out. Hey. I'm a sensitive guy. I'm here for you no matter how bad it gets, but let's discuss things peacefully. I love you. I want to know what's going on in that head of yours."

I walk to the bed, sit at the edge, and put my face into my hands.

"I'm grieving, Sonny. That's what's going on. I'll never cease to wonder how Ivy found this life so agonizing to endure." I drop my hands into my lap and look up at him across the room, his body now a silhouette in the grainy bedroom light.

"Her eyes haunt me every time I close my own."

"You can't keep beating yourself up, Delphy. No one can take the rap for what happened. Her brain was a tempest. All biophysical, bad wiring in her genetics and bipolar robbed her of who she was. She was handed a bad deal, and her struggles overwhelmed."

Regarding me, his features soften. I know the look. He wants to rush to my side and wrap his arms around me. We're two pieces in a complex puzzle, trying to find their fit in the larger picture. For the first time in months, hope for us simmers inside of me bursting into a smile. The reflex feels foreign, and I touch my lips in surprise.

He looks at me, and then his armful of clothes, and returns a sweet, shy smile, before walking into the bathroom.

In the ten days since the funeral, I've stayed away from The Maiden Tower, taking full advantage of the fact that Linnea's still around to take care of Mama and Daddy. When she's gone, it will all be on me. We've struck some sort of unspoken truce—twins are telepathic about these things—realizing each of us must move forward the best way we can. Maybe Idaho, after all, is a healthier place for her. But the thought of her leaving breaks my heart.

We've spoken several times on the phone. The honesty pervading our conversations, especially about Ivy's condition, has provided me insight into the heinous nature of bipolar. We've planned to have dinner Friday, the night before she leaves. There are other things she says she needs to tell me. Things she wants me to know about herself. Have the seeds of the family curse taken root in her? Is she, too, plagued by depression? That would explain those fears. I await the conversation, dread twisting hard in my gut.

I glance at the clock. 5:10. I'd better get hustling if I want my precious hour on the reefs. But the least I can do is tackle the mess in the sink before leaving.

Entering the kitchen, I see Lita at work. Not even five minutes in the house and she has an apron tied around her waist, her sleeves rolled up and attacking the dishes. Ella is nearby, still happy in her playpen.

"No no, Lita. It's my mess." I rush to her side and remove a crusty plate from her hands. "Let me. I don't know where the day went."

She smiles and puts an arm around my shoulder. "Now it's your turn to take a break. Have a seat at the table, and we'll trade notes about our days." She removes the dish from my hands.

"Mine is of no interest. You know the routine." I smile at Ella who, with her tiny fist, takes a whack at a ball on her mobile. "I don't know how you do it, Lita. Take care of her plus get everything else done."

I think of the times when Lita's made me crazy, when I felt she was taking over my house or controlling my husband. After Ivy, those sentiments seem petty. I'm glad I held my tongue. She is as much my family as anyone.

"I'd have to be loca not to count my blessings," Lita says, her hands busy in the froth of suds. "To see my son and *su bella esposa* every day. To witness my beautiful granddaughter, grow up to..." she shakes her head at the ceiling. "Who knows? Maybe I live to see her be president of the United States? *Podríamos emplear a una mujer inteligente en la tienda.* Who could want more from this life?"

I smile. "If you don't mind my leaving, I'd love to get out into the coral before the sun sets. I made a pasta salad. It's in the fridge. Y'all go ahead and eat. I'll have leftovers when I return."

"Enjoy yourself," she says, smiling, and then turns back to the dishes. She's been solicitous to me since Ivy, and it's much appreciated. If we ever catch up with our bills, perhaps we should take that trip to Antarctica. I wonder how old Ella would have to be to appreciate it?

I dart into the bedroom and give Sonny—who is making the bed—the sort of kiss he deserves, injected with the promise of more to follow. Scuttling into the living room, I search for my iPhone and find it sandwiched between sofa cushions. I nuzzle Ella's neck, taking several seconds to inhale the redolence of sweet baby nectar.

Lita wipes down counters while singing the "Rhythm is Gonna Get You", a Gloria Estefan favorite. Her hips sway with every swipe. I blow her a kiss, leave the house and climb into the truck.

Pressing earbuds in place, I harness myself into my seatbelt, flip the ignition, and ring up Linnea. I look forward to sharing a few minutes in Sisterville. Pulling out of the driveway, I hear the smile in her voice when she answers her phone.

"Is this Silly-Nilly?"

I clear my throat, tears stinging my eyes.

"Hey, Pancakes. What's flappin'?"

UNCLAMPING MY KAYAK, I slide it off the rack and then balance it onto my shoulder. Gripping the edges, I walk towards the water, feeling annoyed Linnea was at DJ's shop when I called. I have many things to say about that man, and they all have four letters. But at least I've reconciled myself with the fact she's seeing him. When Linnea returns to Idaho, it will be a moot issue anyway.

At the shoreline, I rest the kayak in the sand and run back to the truck for my paddle, snorkeling mask and drinking water. I hide my iPhone under the driver's seat—a couple of years back, I sacrificed my phone to the bottom of the ocean.

After securing the bottle and mask into my bungee, I slide the vessel into the Atlantic and climb into the seat well. Digging the oar into the ocean floor, I use the leverage to push out into the water. The air smells of baking seaweed in the late afternoon sun. There seems to be no horizon, only a hazy orange splotch in the sky. I've got over an hour before darkness falls, and it takes just fifteen minutes to get to the reef if I paddle quickly. I adopt a leisurely pace, stopping for a couple of minutes here and there to drift, floating on an ocean of infinity.

Even if I never know the feeling of elation again, at least— at this moment—I feel at peace. Why did it take such a horrible event to make me realize how happy I used to be? These days I feel an urgent need for solitude, and in certain parts of the ocean, I can be all alone like I were on a desert.

I paddle forward, picking up my pace. The air feels rich, heavy; the sound of gulls and water slapping against my boat is speaking my language. Glancing over my shoulder, the gap between the stern of my kayak and the island has grown into a gulf; soon, Key West will vanish.

What could be more poetic than this? Perhaps the shore is like Ivy. Not visible, yet a manifestation of her exists somewhere, on a different plane. There are so many minuscule things about her that I will never forget. The dimple on the side of her mouth, that freckle on the inside of her thumb. I could smell the sun in her hair when I hugged her. I mourn all the conversations we could have had but didn't.

I'm heading to the same inland reef where I found the sea glass. Thinking of what she did with it feels like a burn crossing my body. I dip my hand into the water and drizzle it over my skin. As twilight descends, the ocean is still, clear and feels as tepid as bathwater.

A motorboat comes into view at the edge of the mangroves, and I paddle closer. No one's in it. It's an older boat, royal blue, and is moored a few feet away from the reef. It appears to be Randy's, a friend of mine, one of the dozens of professionals and volunteers, who are inspecting the coral after the storm. I glance at my diving watch. It's after six. There's time to lend a hand and still get back by sunset.

Making a slip knot in my rope, I secure our boats together at their cleats and climb aboard the motorboat. I look about the cockpit, aghast, as a sour taste travels up my throat. I'm in the company of five containers, each one filled with a rainbow of motionless fish. This boat does not belong to Randy.

Horrified, I bend and tap my nails against the plastic, which contains blue tangs and parrotfish. I detect tiny movements.

They're alive. Alive but paralyzed. In an instant, the clumps of dying coral makes sense.

The owner of this boat is cyanide fishing—spraying the fish with sodium cyanide. This method temporarily stuns the prized specimens, so they can be captured with ease. Once revived, they're sold at a premium to retail stores, like DJ's, and hobbyists. Even restaurants, in certain parts of the world, consider them a status symbol and pay top dollar to feature exotic species on their menus.

This type of preying causes staggering ecological damage; the highly toxic substance bleaches the surrounding coral. The practice wreaks havoc on the planets most beautiful ecosystems and is illegal in our country. But it's obviously happening, in our backyard, under my nose.

I've got to get out of here. I leap into my kayak. I fumble with the knot, trying to control the shake in my hand. The moment our boats separate, I see the cylindrical tip of a breathing tube gliding towards me. Horrified by its proximity, I watch, stunned, as a head emerges half-covered with a scuba mask. Black hair is plastered to a man's head, which is attached to a monstrous neck.

As if it were a rubber toy, he tosses a clownfish, a canister and then a net into his boat. Wheezing from exertion, he turns his attention back to me. Red pus-filled zits dot his shoulders, and he wears a wife-beater that appears glued to his massive chest. He pushes his mask atop his head. Dog-paddling, he stares at me, confused, like I'm an apparition.

His heavy-lidded eyes are those of a dolphin. My heart is loud, pounding between my ears. With both hands, he grasps the edge of my kayak and flips it. I swim out from under the boat, in the opposite direction of him. My arms, like blades, cut through the water. Underneath my forearm, the sun rests above the black stitched line of the horizon. I turn to the left, towards the shoreline, swimming frantically.

He grabs my ankles. Trying to kick him away, he reels me in like a fish caught on line. His grip forms a vise around my torso. I am filled, not only with the terror of dying but with the irony of it all.

I will die in the seagrass, next to the coral, in the place where I found the glass. Ivy was right; it was trying to warn me. Warn us both. Unimaginably sad, I think of my family. They will believe that I, like Ivy, had enough of this world and followed her lead.

I suck greedily at the air, gasping, gulping, trying to fill my lungs. The heaving pressure surrounding my belly is fading, the splashing water now muffled and distant. Please. God. Don't let me die. Taking my last ragged breath, Ella's face looms in my brain as his arms twist around me like serpents, pushing my head into the sea.

33. LINNEA

I glance at my ringing phone.

"Oops, sorry," I say to DJ, who sits facing me from behind his desk. "I know I just got here, but can you give me a couple of minutes? It's Delphina."

"No worries," he replies. His face tightened when I said her name, but he recovered quickly. Delivering a wobbly smile, he picks up a folder.

I stand, turn away from him to exit the office, and swipe the screen to answer. "Is this Silly-Nilly?"

"Hey, Pancakes. What's flappin'?" I hear a catch in her voice when she says my old childhood name.

Of late, our tone has struck a safe and familiar chord reminiscent of the old days. DJ's store closed at five, fifteen minutes ago, so I wander out of the office and into the showroom. Here, I can chat with her and visit the fish in their bubbling aquariums.

She asks if I'm at The Maiden Tower. I pause a moment, deciding whether or not to tell her where I am, concerned it might taint our conversation. I decide against it. Lies have not served me well in my life. As they say, the truth will set you free.

"Nope. I'm at DJ's aquarium."

"I've got a pocket of freedom. I'm going to that reef with the new growth of Elkhart coral." Although she skips the niceties of inquiring about me and DJ, the tone of her voice doesn't sound annoyed.

"I need to clear my head," she adds.

"Is that the place you take your customers?" I ask.

"Yep. It's my favorite of the inland reefs. It's only a mile or so into the Atlantic. A straight shot west from the Ellis construction site. It's the place where I found the sea glass."

She inhales sharply, and I remain quiet. For several seconds neither of us speak because when it comes right down to it, there are no words.

"Are we still on for Friday?" she asks suddenly, steering the subject away from the glass.

"Wouldn't miss it for the world."

"Super. I'm gonna hang up now. I need to call Sonny and tell him where Ella's blankie is. It calms her down when she's fussy. Chat with you soon."

"Ta-ta for now." I turn off the phone. For the first time since the suicide, there was no mention of Ivy in our conversation. We could use a breather.

Watching the fish frolic in my favorite tank, I spy Angelina, the disagreeable angelfish. I suppose her fierce personality ensures no one wants to purchase her. Perhaps that's the intention. Aiming my phone screen towards my face, I take a selfie next to the tank. This will be as close as I ever get to a tropical fish. Then, I return to DJ's office.

Cassie is now seated in the chair that I'd vacated. Today she wears several rubber bracelets on each of her forearms, the same midnight shade as her eyeliner. Her T, like her jeans, is symmetrically ripped. DJ sits on the edge of his desk, two containers at his side. Forearms on thighs, he leans into Cassie, concern mapping a web across his face.

I stand in the doorway. He looks at me, shaking his head,

his features drawn and stricken. Cassie swivels to face me. Her hand darts to her mouth, and she looks startled, her face scarlet.

"Cass," he says, sliding his eyes back to her. "She can hear this, too. I'm not keeping it under wraps. No way. This isn't my deal. Well, at the moment it is. Whatever. My entire operation will come toppling down if we don't take this to the cops."

"Take what to the cops?" Perhaps my visit will be shorter than I had intended. I've had enough drama to last well into my next life.

DJ picks up one of the containers, a white rectangular canister. Ignore the orange skull and crossbones imprint, and it could be a container of laundry detergent.

"Every reef fish that Stanson claimed was legally caught was captured using this." He unscrews the lid. "This here's sodium cyanide. Says so on the label."

He aims the opening at me, and I note the contents are half-filled with a white crystalline substance. He shakes it, brings it an inch or so under his nostrils and sniffs.

"Smells like almonds." He places it on his desk and picks up the other container, which looks to be a translucent water bottle with a hose-like nozzle attached. "This delivers the cyanide-laced cocktail, which paralyzes the fish."

"I emptied it before putting it in my pack," Cassie explains, touching the place on her lip hosting the pierced ring.

"Cyanide fishing. There's no other reason Stanson would have this," DJ says, slamming the container into his desk, fury in his eyes. "It's been used for decades as an anesthetic. Knocks out fish to facilitate their capture. It doesn't kill them, but it does destroy their habitat. The practice is illegal in the States."

Cassie turns to me, her voice quavering. "A couple of days back, I was cleaning out the guts of the boat and found it. I'd been suspicious. I mean, Stanson could catch dozens of the most gorgeous reef fish in the span of a couple of hours. No one can do that."

Chin trembling, her eyes dart from mine as if she were about to cry. "He also took your sister's ribbon when we were decorating our float. When he was opening the box, I pointed out Delphina's name, which was on the label. He laughed and told me she could afford it."

Blood feels like it's draining from my face. I stare at DJ. Now it's my turn to judge: guilty by association. His wide eyes search my face as he shakes his head. Beneath the fluorescent light, his hair takes on a yellowy-orange glow, the color of ocean floor anemones. Delphina was right about this man. I should have trusted my own suspicions, as well; these people are horrid. Cassie looks up to me, pleadingly, and touches my hand, her shark-like features pinched.

"I'm so sorry, Linnea. Back in the spring, when DJ asked me if I knew about the decorations, I lied for my boyfriend. After all, it was only ribbon. And I made sure your sister was reimbursed," she adds quickly, inferring the money excused the cover-up.

"But this is so much worse," she continues, beads of sweat popping out on her forehead. "I'm not stupid. I read. We all know how important the reefs are to our community. To the world. So, I had to do something. Confronting Stanson was not an option. And if he finds out I told you, he'll kill me. This is his favorite time of day to fish. When everyone's gone. I'll bet he's out there now."

Momentarily frozen, instinct kicks in, panic pummeling me. My sister's in danger. My words are explosive, tumbling, tripping and spitting over each other as I pace the office, looking at DJ through slitted eyes.

"Delphina's on her way to one of the reefs. Right now. A mile off the coast, from where the Ellis Construction site's located. Drive me there. Now. And get a boat to find her."

Heart clattering, I dial her number, and it goes into voice mail. My voice becomes shrill. "Oh, God. She's not answering. I'll call the coast guard. And then, Sonny."

DJ hops off his desk. "So we're clear. You want me to take you out into the ocean."

"Yes," I scream, rushing towards him, grabbing and digging my nails into his forearms. "Right now. Right this minute. Delphina's in trouble. I know it. I can feel it."

"I'll have a boat ready. The marina's close to the construction site. It will only take a minute or so to get to the reef."

Without a word, he pulls his phone and keys from the pocket of his shorts. He nods at Cassie, now shaking like a leaf, her mouth open in silent sobs. DJ and I press buttons on our phones as we dash from the store.

A male voice speaks with authority into my ear. "This is Watchstanders at sector Key West command central."

Trying to control the panic in my voice, I gather my wits and explain exactly where they can find her.

ARRIVING AT THE MARINA, DJ peels off his shirt, bolts from the car and I follow on his heels, racing to the dock. Cigarette dangling from his mouth, his friend wears cut-offs and is beckoning to us from the pit of a motorboat. We jump in and the ignition's flipped.

With a nauseating jolt, we exit the marina hurtling into the ocean. The sun sits on top of the horizon, an orange ball ready to be slam-dunked into the Atlantic. DJ takes the seat next to his buddy and points to an area in the distance. Then, he grabs a life jacket from under the seat and brings it to me. I shake my head. Dripping with sweat, if I make one unnecessary move, I'll get sick.

As the boat careens forward into the greens and blues, a

deck of frightening sea creatures' shuffles through my brain. Streaking through the water, I feel like I'm being sucked into a vortex. I bend over the side of the vessel and vomit. The wind smears it over the side of my face and into my hair. Suddenly, the boat stops, and the suddenness of the motion causes me to fall forward.

As I'm righting myself, DJ dives into the ocean. With the speed of light, he cuts his hands through the water towards a sea creature, tentacles dangling down his chest, who is pushing someone's head under the water. Nearby, an upturned kayak is drifting in the sea. Jumping up, I balance on the edge of the boat. DJ's friend hands me a float, and I jump into the water.

The ocean roars about me, screaming in my ears. Buoy tucked under my arm, I side-crawl towards a cyclone of swirling water. I stop, catch my breath and watch as DJ slams his fist, over and over, into the creature's face. Wild hands and arms emerge from the water, flying helter-skelter every which way, with everything happening at once.

Delphina, now released from his grasp, bobs up and down, arms thrashing, her gasping mouth parallel to the surface of the sea. I swim to her, all of my fears evaporated, and push the buoy into her chest. Panic darting about her face, she wraps her arms around it. I hook the crook of one arm under her armpits. Clutching my sister's back into my chest, I swim backward, my legs crawling through the sea like a frog towards the boat.

Nearby, the sound of engine revs. Two rubber dinghies race towards us and the ensuing waves pitch us up and down. One stops a couple of feet away. A guy wearing a helmet, neoprene orange shirt and life vest reaches into the water and hoists Delphina, gasping, into the pit.

"I'm OK," I shout, clutching the buoy. "Take care of my sister." Crouching beside her, he swipes his forefinger through her mouth. Then, he presses his ear on top of her chest. Positioning her onto her side, he rights himself, giving me a thumbs up.

"Breathing's steady."

Shock and relief make my body go limp. In the other dinghy, the amphibian resident of the black lagoon sits next to DJ in the pit. I paddle towards them. God. The monster is Stanson. What appeared to be tentacles in the distance, was a snorkeling hose, dangling from his mask. His arms are pinned behind him, handcuffed.

DJ is hunched over, his head tucked in between his knees. The rescue operator cranks the engine. The dinghy sputters forward towards the Coast Guard's response boat, which is next to The Coral Princess.

With one hand, Sonny grips the mast of his boat, with the other, he waves at me frantically. I can't read the expression on his face. I wrap my arms around the buoy and flutter-kick towards him, my tears mingling with the salt of the sea.

34. DELPHINA

I should have drowned, but I didn't. The world should have stopped, but it didn't. Twenty million people are starving in Sudan right this minute, desperate to live. Twenty million people across the world will attempt to take their lives this year, desperate to die. Planets orbit the sun at their usual pace, and the world keeps spinning, it just keeps on spinning.

I push my oar deep into the volume of sea, the vastness of the Atlantic reminding me how tiny I am, and how much there is in this life I'll never understand. But this much I know is true: I should have drowned last week, but I didn't. Linnea should have left for Boise, but she didn't. A life's direction can be changed in a minute when you're lugging a suitcase full of grief and figure where to put it.

Dropping anchor off the bow, I slide on my mask. This area is one of the nesting grounds of the loggerhead turtles, and it's been over a year since I've visited them. Sliding out of the boat, I crawl through the ocean, relieved to be back in my element.

Three of the turtles encircle me, their nimbleness and grace belying their girth. Accustomed to divers giving them treats, they paddle in closer. Gazing into their ancient eyes, my mind slips into the fissures of a timeless place before civilization, before language, before our bodies were beings with a name. In this unknown land, I make a promise to myself: everything I do will be informed by my knowledge that my existence on this beguiling planet is temporary. So, what gift to this earth will I leave behind?

One of the turtles doesn't notice me above it. Before I've time to swim out of the way, it rises up, its shell meeting my torso as it surfaces for air. Thrust out of the water on the back of this magnificent giant, my flesh is now one with the slick, barnacle-studded armor. For several glorious moments, I glide through the sea on a turtle back-ride, victorious, gazing at the sky, laughing at the wonder of it all.

You've got this, Delphina. You're going to be OK.

~

MY ELATION CARRIED into the evening, into the smells of Lita's sofrito—the onions, peppers and garlic simmering on the stove; into the comfort of Ella tucked into my arms—the peal of her cherished laughter as I made silly faces at the picture in her storybook; into the bed with Sonny—who, since the incident on the water, seems to be having worse separation issues with me than my baby had when I was weaning her.

"My brain can't silence it," he says, pulling me into him. "When you were out there today, I was worried about you every single second. The thought of you not being in my life..." His words trail into the night, and he shakes his head, his eyes misting with tears.

I kiss the tip of his nose. "Nothing will ever happen to me again. I promise. Even when I infuriate you to the point where you wish I did disappear, I will remain by your side."

Like a cloud crossing the sun, the concern mapping his face shifts to relief. I run my fingertips down the contours of his biceps. "You know, I've been thinking."

"Oh no, here it comes. I smell trouble." He shifts to rest his weight on an elbow. Wrapping his hand around my neck, he brings my lips into his, in a slow, lingering kiss.

With the flat of my palm, I push his chest away. "That's nice. But I'm serious. Hear me out. This is important stuff." He winks, nodding.

"You, dear husband, see a part of me I've never seen myself: my second nature. This particular behavior is so obvious to me, I follow its cues without thinking. Ironically, I'm not aware of it, so you know more about this part of me than I do, myself."

Sonny chuckles. "You got that right. But I try to hold my tongue." I bat him with my fist.

"OK. Agreed. Perhaps that side of me isn't pretty. But I know a part of you you're blind to see, as well. And it's not your most flattering angle, I might add. My point is, marriage is about creating a truce. A contract to take the bad with the good. Am I right?"

"Delphina's never wrong," he says, chuckling, stroking my forearm. "But, hey. I hear you. And the past few days I've been reflecting on our marriage, too."

I giggle. "Reflecting? Has someone stolen my hot-blooded Cuban and replaced him with a philosopher?"

"What idiot wouldn't be reflecting after what happened? Watching you lie in that dinghy wrenched out my guts." Beads of sweat pepper his forehead as he speaks. "They told me not to swim to you. That it would interfere with the Coast Guard doing their job. I felt so helpless."

"Thank God you missed Stanson in action." Under the sheets, I find his hand and lace my fingers into his.

"That's what upsets me," he says, squeezing my hand. "I want to kill him, and I can't. If I'd been the one out there rescuing you, that dude would never have ever seen the light of day." His jaws work and the gold in his eyes dim. Rage and hatred cross his face every time Stanson's name is mentioned.

"He'll get his dues, Sonny. I'm sure of it. Let's get back to what you were talking about. Your *reflections*." I grin and untangle my hand from his, saying the word with air quotes.

"OK. I'm trying to be serious, here." He clears his throat. "Marriage is like sailing to a destination—a place that's familiar to both of us. And then a storm catches us unawares, causing our sails to luff, forcing us to change tack. So, we set a new course, search out a new port, one to which neither of us has ever been.

"And it's the strangest thing," he continues, a dreamy look smoothing the lines above his brow. "When the boat's keeled sharply into the sea, water splashed over the decks, and we're slipping and sliding, losing our balance, that's the place where we discover we're tougher than we think." He kisses the tip of his forefinger and presses it between my eyebrows. "And, oddly, it's also the place where I've discovered what's truly precious in my life."

I regard him in admiration, this man who never ceases to amaze, tracing my finger along the edge of his ear. "Wow, babe. Intense. We need to write that down."

"Did it carry enough wisdom to satisfy my beautiful maiden? Are we done with this conversation?" He pulls me back into his arms. "Can we get on to more important things now?"

His eager eyes hold so much more than lust, something humble, something I will forever trust.

"Yes," I whisper, loving this man, my husband, with every bit of my being. "But you can't keep me up all night. Linnea invited us over for Sunday brunch tomorrow."

Untangling myself from his embrace, I fold the sheets at the bottom of the bed, remove the throw pillows and dim the lights. Ella will grow up and find her own way in life. My parents and Lita will die. And if fate will have it, Sonny and I will walk together, hand in hand, into old age. I slide into bed, lying prone, staring at the ceiling.

"So, tomorrow at the lighthouse?" he says, rolling on top of me, pinning me down and nibbling at my earlobe.

I nod. "That's right, big guy."

"Ummm. Brunch. You're making me hungry." He gathers my hair into his fist and then licks my throat and breast.

Our lives are impossibly fragile. If you're fortunate enough to have a loving family, you have to hold onto them with infinite care. Yet it will be Linnea, my twinflower, who will be the one to share a certain set of memories—painful, poignant and precious—captured within the walls of The Maiden Tower. Like old war veterans, one day she will be the only one left who knew me as I used to be and as I truly am today.

As he curls his hands around my hipbones, I place my heels atop his buttocks, sliding them down, so they rest in the bend of his knees. We're trying to make another baby.

What a wonderful way of saying yes to being alive.

35. LINNEA

Liberace, perched on my shoulder, nibbles at the beads on my necklace. It's his way of expressing affection, and even though it causes a ticklish irritation at my neck, I let him be. The old bird has suffered along with the rest of us these past few weeks, and until we re-open the inn, he has free rein in the lighthouse.

I press the crust into the edges of the pan, my fingertips coated with graham cracker, sugar, coconut and melted butter. Overcome with love for the people who'll be eating it at the brunch I've planned, I'm calling this meal *A Celebration of Life*. My family prefers today be the day we honor Ivy, which will help carry us and her memory forward.

The last time I made dinner for her, I also served Key Lime Pie, giving her the biggest piece. The memory of one specific moment pierces my heart so suddenly I flinch:

She looks up, catching my eyes as she eats. "Biting into this pie, I believe there is a heaven."

Looked, not looks. Ate, not eats. My little sister is past tense. But pies have power—no one can tell you otherwise.

Licking my fingers, I walk to the sink to let soap and water finish the job. Liberace jumps from my shoulder, landing on the dish counter at the side of the sink. With relish and messy abandon, he pecks at a chunk of mango leftover from the smoothie I made this morning.

Returning to my work station, I whisk together my assembly of egg yolks, condensed milk, lime zest, juice and cream. Pouring the filling into the crust, I then place it on the middle rack of my preheated oven.

Picking up the index card, my eyes mist at the earnest angular penmanship of the twelve-year-old girl who wrote the recipe. The girl instructing her little sister on how to crack an egg without getting so much as a tiny piece of shell into the bowl. Ivy and I had planned to make this pie again. It never happened.

On impulse, I triple the ingredients for the meringue topping. Now, there's only one thing left to do: I scrub the counters with such muscle they gleam.

"I DON'T KNOW what to say. I was thinking about writing you." Delphina nods at DJ, who is seated at her side. She tilts her head, her eyes misty, momentarily at a loss. "But how do I find words to let you know how grateful I am? Words are awkward. I keep stumbling over their arrangement. Besides. A letter seems ludicrous considering the gravity of what you did."

"Never forget to send a thank-you note, Delphina," Mama says, straightening her back and lifting her chin, "however insignificant or majestic the deed."

Delphina's jaw drops as she leans forward, eyes widening toward our mother. "A thank you note for saving my life? On monogrammed stationary, no doubt. You can't be serious?"

She balls up her napkin and throws it across the table.

Mama catches it mid-air and then bursts into a glorious, ringing peal of laughter, the sort of laugh I haven't heard in this house for weeks. Everyone at the table smiles, our countenances visibly relaxing. Then, her hand darts to cover her mouth, and she quietens. Her mirth seems to have taken her aback; surprised her. Everyone's smile fades.

"You and your 'Bama bullshit," Delphina exclaims, blowing her a kiss. She smiles broadly, her eyes touching everyone's face around the table, daring us to be somber.

She returns her focus to DJ, placing her hand over his. "Perhaps there aren't words. But I'll say it anyway: Thank you. You risked your life to save mine."

"What about me?" I exclaim, feigning indignation, trapped in the web of her gaiety. "Who brought you the buoy?"

"That's what sisters are for."

Locking eyes with her, I make a sound someplace between a laugh and a sob. It is indeed. She saved my life before we were even born. Or was it me who saved hers? No matter; our souls are one and as immutable as the sea.

I look about the table, at the half-emptied champagne glasses, the plates wiped clean of the Lobster Hash topped with Poached Eggs and Caviar I'd made. This occasion called for splurging.

I smile at Liberace, so well-behaved through the meal. Long black talons wrapped around his perch, his feathered red head moves from side-to-side as a well-seasoned sentry protecting his clan. A three-toothed, gummy-grinned Ella—her baby seat hooked onto the table—has also been on her best behavior. At ten months old, she looks like a miniature version of her father.

"So, what's next for the predator," Daddy asks, his head turned to DJ, left eye twitching furiously. "This Stanson? Can you give us an update?"

"He couldn't make bail, so he's in jail. It will likely go to trial," DJ replies. Tapping the tip of his forefinger on the table, the muscles along his jawline tighten.

Sonny places an arm around Delphina's shoulder. Pulling her into him, he looks down at her, wrapped into the wing of his arm.

"We can't wait until Season," he says, dotting a kiss atop her head, "when we can get back to our own business with The Coral Princess and put this nightmare behind us."

Lita turns to Ella and wipes a bit of egg away from her face. Mama raises her hand, which pauses mid-air, momentarily hovering over Lita's back. Then, biting her lower lip, she places her palm on Lita's shoulder.

"While they're at work, would you mind if I stopped by to help out with Ella? I'd love to see more of her."

Lita turns from the baby and wraps her arm around Mama's shoulder, drawing her in and kissing her cheek. "Poppy. You never need an invitation to visit."

With an imperceptible nod, Mama looks into her face. "Thank you, Lita."

Sonny pulls my sister in closer to his chest. She appears uncomfortable scrunched up beneath his armpit but makes no move to push away. Throughout the meal, he's been using any excuse to reel her closer and closer into his side.

My eyes dart from Sonny to his mother, noting the similarities in their countenances; their generosity of gesture, their natural instinct to protect manifested by physical displays of affection. I glance at my father with his arms wrapped tightly across his midriff. I've never questioned his love, but there are lessons the Pagano family can teach him, teach all of the Chandler family if we're willing to learn.

Delphina sighs, wiggling away from her husband's grasp. On the other hand, that steady stream of touchy-feelies would drive me nuts.

"Can you imagine what would have happened to the coral if

that beast continued poisoning them?" Delphina asks, shaking her head. "We caught him in the nick of time."

"Jail time for cyanide fishing will be detention hall compared with what he'll be facing for attempted murder," DJ remarks, nodding at my sister, trying to suppress a smile tugging at the sides of his mouth.

"If he's put away for good, his sentence will be doing the world a favor," she replies, brushing crumbs from the tabletop into the palm of her hand. "Now he can't wreak havoc on the reefs."

He did me a favor, too, I think to myself. After I'd confessed my secret to Mama, my nightmares about the ocean began to fade. And then, as I watched the creature trying to drown Delphina, my phobia washed away in the currents of the sea. Since the incident, I've been on an endorphin high, relishing this unfamiliar freedom from anguish and fear.

Dusted and done? For the moment, yes. For the long run? Unlikely. I'm sure the demons of my past will return to rev up their torment. But, with Mama's help, I've found a therapist I trust. At last, I'm turning inward, doing the work, and this journey, surprisingly, is pointing the way to my future.

"What happens to Cassie?" I ask, turning to DJ.

"She's moving back to Indiana," he replies, knowing my desire to better understand this peculiar woman. "Her grandmother is not expected to live much longer. She wants to spend that last bit of time by her side. She's also guaranteed a job at an aquarium in Fort Wayne. She never wants to return to Key West." He looks at me, his gaze unfocused. "Who can blame her? She had as much to do with saving Delphina as anyone."

My hand lights upon his. "I'd like to see her before she leaves." He nods.

As if it were yesterday, I remember the first time I laid eyes on Cassie, studying her on the plane. She seemed so rude, and I recall my disdain. What fate wove her into our lives? In the end, she saved my sister and, by doing so, saved us all. Without a word, Delphina and I clear the plates. Both of us, I'm sure, are humbled by this woman's strength. Betraying a brute like Stanson, took a great deal of courage. I bring out the pie, placing it on the center of the table.

Everyone whistles admiringly at the concoction of egg whites, vanilla and sugar magically transformed to this crowning glory of crests, valleys and swirls.

I fling my hand towards the billowing froth. "I piled the meringue so high, I imagined its peaks touching Ivy's fingertips above the clouds."

For a minute, silence falls upon the room, and everyone's eyes drop to their laps. Delphina breaks our sober mood as she carries a pan filled with hot water, a chef's knife, and places them beside the pie. The meringue's quite fragile, and unless cut with a hot, wet knife, it will collapse.

Resting fists on hips, her lower lip protrudes. "Y'all were laughing a few minutes ago. Why so glum now? You know she'd want us to be happy. She's in our lives as long as we talk about her. Remember her." Looking up, we glance hesitantly at one another, shaky smiles returning to our faces.

Daddy stands. "Before you slice into that miraculous creation, Poppy and I have been talking about the future of the lighthouse." His eyes fix on her profile. "The future of us. We'd like to share our thoughts with you."

Mama angles around to look up at him. Delphina and I stand, frozen in place.

"After Ivy's death, I was approached by the historical society. They asked if we'd consider selling the lighthouse to them. For a handsome sum, I might add. They'd open it to the public as a living museum. The Lightkeeper's Quarters and the Fog Horn House would serve as additional museums housing the works of contemporary Florida painters."

He pauses, his lips quivering, and casts his gaze above our

heads. "It's simply an idea, and we have plenty of time to mull it over."

"They promised the parlor would be reserved to house Ivy's works exclusively," Mama adds, pride in her voice. "Our Girl's tragedy, at least in part, will be vanquished by her paintings."

A single tear rolls down Daddy's cheek, which he brushes away with his handkerchief. He bites his bottom lip.

"Poppy and I aren't getting any younger. And this place"— his eyes travel to the stairs leading up to the Lantern Room —"holds so many..."

His words break so Delphina and I come to his rescue. "That's a great idea," we say, speaking brightly at the same time. Everyone looks at us, relieved Daddy didn't dissolve into a pool of tears. We've never witnessed that before and, frankly, wouldn't know how to cope. Delphina and I return to our seats.

We watch as my father rights himself, pulling his features inward. He takes a deep breath, bends to retrieve his champagne glass and raises it above his head in a toast.

"Time won't heal this family's wounds, but at least it will give us the tools to endure them. Here's to our beloved Ivy."

Everyone raises their glasses to his. "To Ivy," we repeat.

After placing my stem on the table, I pinch my cheeks and then immediately drop my hands. I must break this habit; a couple of broken blood vessels have emerged recently. Delphina bites the bottom of her lip and Sonny looks straight ahead, blinking rapidly, each of us fighting back tides of tears.

Mama stands and walks to a corner of the room where Ivy's paintings are stacked, leaning against the wall. She removes one of them entitled, *Self-Portrait*. On the canvas, Ivy's glorious mane glows as if on fire. Her arms reach out to some vast unattainable landscape, represented by streaked, vertical strokes of rust, the color of old coins. It looks like she wants to fly away.

Mama begins hypothesizing her interpretation of the work, and her words serve as an incantation bringing Ivy back to our table. Daddy joins in, disputing her theories, and Delphina espouses her own explanation for the piece. For the next several minutes, all we do is talk about Ivy. My little sister is more alive in death than she was in life.

I push back my chair, stand, and slide the pie towards me. With careful deliberation, I slice seven pieces and pass them around the table, serving everyone except myself. I smirk as Ella pushes her face into the meringue, surfacing with a dollop of white froth at the tip of her nose.

"You're not having dessert?" Mama asks, looking at me in concern. "That's not like you."

She fiddles with Ivy's dolphin necklace, which dangles around her neck. Purplish shadows crouch beneath her eyes and the silhouette of her departed daughter is burnished deep into the green of her irises.

I stare at her for several seconds, spellbound by my beautiful, wounded mother. Clearing my throat, I find my voice.

"I'm going for a run." I bop my head with the heel of my hand. "Need to clear the cobwebs. I'll be back in an hour or so and will enjoy it then."

Her smile lingers on mine and then she leans across the table, to share a funny memory with Delphina. Although I don't so much as glance at her portrait, I feel Rossalea's watchful eyes upon me.

DJ stands and walks me towards the door, opening it. At the entryway, we step over the threshold and pause. He searches my face for an answer I can't give him, and I'm reminded of the waves returning to lap the shoreline, no matter how often they're pushed away. Never inquire about the future, my eyes try to say. And the past is simply that: the past. I want my life, this life right now, to have meaning.

I'm overwhelmed with a feeling that I matter, that I can speak to a greater change by helping victims of bi-polar and sexual abuse. I have so many questions about mental health, none of which my most recent readings––or even my thera-pist––can answer. No more am I the victim on the beach. No more will I hide behind my lies. No more will I be defined by my environment, a man, or even my family. Now, I know better.

I plan to apply to Boise State, finish my undergraduate work and enter medical school, followed with a residency in psychia-try. A current resident of Idaho, my in-state tuition will be manageable, and the college has a program that will support my ambitions. I'm consumed with a passion for studying this science of mental disorder and brain chemistry, and then to lend my perspective to a field that has no easy answers.

I will work to find relief for people like Ivy, staying strong in my conviction that I can make a difference. I'm loving the person I'm becoming, because of my fight to become her.

The people closest to my heart––DJ, my family––won't be pleased with my decision. But what matters is that I know why I am leaving. This time, I'm not making a move out of fear, anger or small-mindedness. My choices will come from a place of honesty, strength and self-awareness. I am following my heart. Soon enough, everyone will understand.

Reaching into his pocket, DJ pulls out a plastic bag and hands it to me. Curious, I remove what appears to be long strands of old wrinkled satin. Singed at the edges, several black threads of hair are twisted about them.

"I found them in the Lantern Room. After your sister––after Ivy..." I touch his arm, shaking my head to stop his words.

"They were under the ashes," he continues. "There was also an old spyglass inside a rusty metal box. I saved that for you, too. They're safe at my condo. I shouldn't have tampered with the evidence, but I suspected they might be important. Impor-tant," he repeats, his words coming out haltingly, "for you."

Fingering the gold, maroon and blue-green silks faded with age, the back of my neck tingles as realization dawns. These appear to be the ribbons in Rossalea's portrait; the ones she wove through her hair. And the scope? Where did Ivy find them?

According to legend, through a pirate scope, Rosslea watched as Cyrus murdered a woman at sea. Rossalea bore witness to a tragedy, just as I watched Stanson try to drown Delphina. Like the sea glass, were my nightmares also a premonition––some sort of warning––connected to the Maiden? That's ridiculous. Good sense rejects such nonsense.

There is this one thing, however, pushing back reason as I grapple with the truth: The legend is a factual account; now there's proof. The Maiden had issues of her own, the story being she'd been disposed to *melancholia* back in the days when mental health disorders were a nameless, invisible plague. There are so many odd coincidences linking the past to the present––mania, suicide, mayhem at sea––all of them circling back to this woman. I run my fingers through the fragile silks, imagining the care Rosselea took in arranging her hair to perfection.

But interpretation is elusive, perspective impossible, and I dismiss any notion of some sort of supernatural connection she had with my sister. Mental illness is the only connective, unsolved mystery in this story. As the legend has it: *No one truly knew what was going on inside the Maiden's head. And no one ever will.*

No one ever will?

All of us have tragedies in our lives, many of which are unavoidable. But Ivy's misfortune, perhaps the Maiden's, as well, could have been averted. I've learned so much from what I've experienced in the past six months. And I will use this knowledge as a springboard when working with others to unlock the chains of mental illness. Breaking the curse of ignorance. Breaking the curse of the Maiden Tower.

DJ's mouth twitches as he shuffles his feet, obviously curious as to my explanation of his findings. How could he guess their significance? I never did invite him to Evening Hour. Sighing, shaking my head to clear these thoughts, I breathe deeply, shakily.

"Thank you, DJ. That was incredibly kind of you to save them for me. They are important. But I don't know what to think. I need all of this to settle. Let's talk about it later."

When I say the word *later*, his face cracks into a grin.

"Sure, Linnea. Later. More mystery surrounding ribbon."

An overwhelming sense of gratitude and longing makes me catch my breath. I owe so much to this man who expects so little and gives so much. Standing on tip-toe, I fling my arms around him, hugging him tightly for what seems to be an eternity. Then, I let him go.

Turning, eyes fixed steadily ahead, I walk across the porch, down the steps and hear the door shut softly behind me. Tenting my palm across my forehead, I look up to the lantern room, my eyes stinging with tears. I swipe my forefinger under my nostrils and then move forward, one foot in front of the other, not knowing the length of the path, but certain of its destination.

At the Fog Horn House, I place the ribbons in a mariner's manual, kept in a drawer on the bedside table. What should I do with them and the scope? How much, in fact, should I keep of the past and how much do I let go?

Will I return to Key West and establish a local practice after I finish my studies? Will DJ and I have a future together? I can't wait to show him my mountains.

I kick off my flip flops, change into shorts, a T-shirt and running shoes. Pausing, I pick up the booklet and clutch it to my chest, closing my eyes. They belong with Ivy's paintings, protected, in the newly proposed museum.

Then, I bolt from my room, break into a run, cross Simonton, swing a right on White Street and sprint towards the Atlantic.

Running won't bring her back. Everyone says it's family, friends, and time, which will heal. But I'm finding my peace in the gray––in the irrationality, the paradox and the humility of faith. Faith that Ivy and I will find each other in another place. A place where she will be running beside me. I'm chasing faith, if only I could catch up.

A squall comes from out of nowhere, as they often do at this time of the year. A deluge pounds the streets washing all light from the sky. Suddenly, it lessens to a soft patter of raindrops, and in the haze, there's a vast space around me where nothing else exists. And then she appears, crossing an invisible threshold. It's just my little sister and me, running through the misty clouds, giddy as schoolgirls, sharing secrets which we should have shared but never did.

As fast as the downpour descended, it clears, and everything sparkles with new energy under the sun. As if I've emerged from a black and white photograph, I'm surrounded by brightness, by lush vegetation and colorful gingerbread homes. But Ivy is gone.

I will never get over her death, and I'm not supposed to. Yet, for the first time since learning she died, I'm able to breathe without sorrow.

What a wonderful way of saying yes to being alive.

THE END

AFTERWORD

I was a child in the sixties, raised in the Woodstock era of *open-mindedness* and *enlightenment*. Except, oddly, when it came to discussions about mental health and sexual abuse. These conversations were closeted, tight-lipped, issues of which to be ashamed.

As a teen, my family quietly dismissed the bizarre, undiagnosed behavior of an extended family member. Shocked, we suffered the fallout in the gut-wrenching aftermath of their suicide. Only as an adult, have I learned the sexual abuses inflicted upon my dearest childhood friends; molestations that have plagued them through their lives. I never knew my pals as well as I thought I did.

Platitudes abounded then, and—in the guise of social media memes—still do.

As if *choosing happiness* and *thinking happy thoughts* were a choice for those suffering from chemical brain imbalances. As if telling a desperate friend that *this too shall pass* will prevent their next panic attack, or advising a colleague that practicing yoga and soaking in lavender-infused baths will wash away a history of abuse.

The #metoo parlance of our times has been a tremendous boon for women. And we need to keep the conversation flowing, moving the needle forward.

There's another conversation to have: the romanticizing of mental health disorders and artists plagued with the disease. Hashtag bipolar art, bipolar memes, depression, dark poetry, Kurt Cobain and you'll see what I mean.

I wanted to write things differently for Ivy. I wanted her to find strength to fight the hardest battle she would ever fight, and believe––finally––that truth and beauty can only be found in clarity, never within the chaos of psychosis. I wanted to armor her with the understanding that controlling her illness would never have made her any less of an artist, but it could have saved her life. I wanted to write things differently for Ivy. Our Girl, however, insisted I not soften the consequence of the mismanagement of her disease.

Delphina and Linnea, too, whispered in my ear, directing the book's conclusion. Charging themselves to move forward and make the world a better place would be their realized truth; their way of saying yes to being alive.

Please be aware that this is a work of fiction. Despite my familiarity and intimacy with the subject matter, the material found within these pages should never be used as a reference guide.

If you or someone you know has a mental health problem, there are ways to find help. Talk to your primary care doctor or another health professional. Ask them to connect you with the right mental health services. Lady Gaga's Born This Way Foundation launches youth-focused programs facilitating mental wellness. The Brain and Research Institute, a global non-profit, funds cutting-edge research to alleviate suffering caused by mental illness. In Canada, Bell Let's Talk promotes open discussion surrounding mental health, attempting to lift stigmatization. The National Suicide Prevention Lifeline number, available 24/7, is 1-800-273-TALK (8255).

ACKNOWLEDGMENTS

The most difficult part of writing this message of gratitude is where to begin. It took an army of professionals and friends to lend perspective and authenticity to Linnea, Delphina and Ivy's story. I looked more to the council of others than I had done in my previous novels.

First things first. If it weren't for my husband, Richard, who insisted we explore Key West's kitschy, tourist side, I would have remained ignorant about the town's fascinating history. Certainly, my imagination would never have been sparked to envision The Maiden Tower, Rossalea, and her history. A former Director of Research at St. Joseph's Mercy Hospital in Ann Arbor, Michigan, his contacts also provided valuable insight into mental illness. Because of Richard, the seeds of a plot began to germinate, culminating in this story.

Navigating the waters of the book industry without my dear friend and fellow author, Alison Ragsdale, to hold my hand would be unthinkable. Friendship aside, she and her husband, Bob, have graciously given their time and support to help this neophyte negotiate some of the trickier terrain in this industry.

Guillermo Flores and his sister, Mayra Flores Márquez, provided valuable insight into the Cuban culture and insured

Mariella's Spanglish was authentic. Muchos besos for your patience with my fumbling Spanish, and I look forward to sharing a bottle of rum—sooner, rather than later. And then there is Linda Lighthall, a friend who spent hours recounting her feelings of what it is like to have an identical twin. In fact, she lent me her story of the mix-up with her twin sister at bath time. I am also indebted to the colorful, gracious townsfolk we met on numerous visits down to the southernmost city. I couldn't have drawn Linnea, Delphina, Poppy, Ivy, and Mariella without their stories.

In the publishing world, a heartfelt thank you to my agent Wendy Sherman, and to Kelli Martin and Krista Stroever in the developmental stage of the editorial process. This book is richer because of you. I'm also indebted to the eagle eyes of David Young, Judy Harvey and Carol Peters, all beta-reading pals with professional expertise and backgrounds in the craft of the King's English. Each one of you lent perspective and caught missteps that would have had the Maiden haunting me into the afterlife.

I'm grateful to my fellow authors and the supportive group of readers in Facebook's Blue Sky Book Chat, who share my journey with the written word.

When all is said and done, where would authors be without their readers and book bloggers who ask, When will your next book be released? I may not have met you face-to-face, but each and every one of you are kindred spirits.

And finally, gratitude to my precious children, Greta and Zan, my home soil.

ABOUT THE AUTHOR

Peggy Lampman is the award-winning, best-selling author of THE PROMISE KITCHEN and THE WELCOME HOME DINER, both published by Lake Union Publishing. She was born and raised in Birmingham, Alabama. She holds a Bachelor's Degree in Communications, summa cum laude, from the University of Michigan. After graduating, she moved to New York City, where she worked as a copywriter and photographer for Hill and Knowlton, a public relations firm. She moved back to Ann Arbor, her college town, and opened up a specialty foods store, The Back Alley Gourmet. After selling the store, she wrote under a weekly food byline in The Ann Arbor News and MLive. This is her third novel.

ALSO BY PEGGY LAMPMAN

THE PROMISE KITCHEN

THE WELCOME HOME DINER

Made in the USA
Columbia, SC
03 August 2020